# ROSEHAVEN

## Catherine Coulter

She whipped about so quickly, she fell on her bottom. "You," she said. And if that was too much, she quickly added, "Watch where you step. That is rosemary beside your foot. Don't crush it."

He moved away from the rosemary. "I care not about this rosemary. It is a silly name, a female's name. Why is the rosemary so valuable?"

"It makes your marten's pork very tasty. If you have a cramping belly, it will ease you. A man should drink it for nine days if he has debilitated himself with venery. Perhaps you would care for some right now?"

"Do not mock me again." He came down on his haunches beside her. "The other women were days ago. I took you only once. I doubt I'm debilitated. I told you to remain within."

"I am within. Look about you. There are scores of my people."

"My people. I am lord here now."

"Very well. There are scores of people who would yell down the heavens if someone came too close to me."

She should be safe enough here, he thought, yielding the point since there was a much meatier bone to pick.

# ROSEHAVEN

## Catherine Coulter

JOVE BOOKS, NEW YORK

This Jove Book contains the complete text of the hardcover edition. It has been completely reset in a typeface designed for easy reading and was printed from new film.

ROSEHAVEN

A Jove Book / published by arrangement with the author

PRINTING HISTORY
G. P. Putnam's Sons edition published July 1996
Jove edition / June 1997

The Putnam Berkley World Wide Web site address is http://www.berkley.com

ISBN: 0-515-12088-X

A JOVE BOOK®
Jove Books are published by The Berkley Publishing Group, 200 Madison Avenue, New York, New York 10016.
JOVE and the "J" design are trademarks belonging to Jove Publications, Inc.

PRINTED IN THE UNITED STATES OF AMERICA

10  9  8  7  6  5  4  3  2  1

*To my husband,*
*who's a hell of a guy*

# 1

*Early Summer, 1277, East Anglia, England*
*Oxborough Castle, Home of Fawke of Trent,*
*Earl of Oxborough*

HER FATHER DIDN'T LIKE HER, BUT HE WOULD NEVER DO THIS to her, never.

Even as she swore over and over to herself that it couldn't be true, she couldn't stop staring at the man. The air seemed to stir in seamless folds about him as he stood utterly still and silent. She knew somehow that he wouldn't move, not until he had judged all the occupants of the great hall of Oxborough Castle. Only then would he act.

His face was dark, his expression calm and untroubled. Sharp sunlight poured in through the open doors of the great hall, framing him there as he stood motionless. She stared at him from the shadows of the winding stone stairs. She didn't want to look at him, didn't want to accept that he was here at Oxborough. But he was here, and he didn't look like he had any intention at all of leaving.

His eyes were as blue as the sea beneath the bright morning sun, yet they seemed somehow old and filled with knowledge and experience a man his age shouldn't possess, and distant, as if part of himself was locked away. She could feel the strength of him from where she stood, feel the determination in him, the utter control, the deliberate arrogance. He looked to her like the Devil's dearest friend.

His finely made gray cloak moved and swelled about him even though there was no wind. The black whip coiled about his wrist seemed to whisper in that thick, contained air. But he made no movement. He was still and calm, waiting, watching.

He wasn't wearing armor, the whip around his wrist and the huge sword that was sheathed to his wide leather belt were his only weapons. He was dressed entirely in gray, even his boots were a soft, supple gray leather. His tunic was pewter gray, a rich wool, his undertunic a lighter gray, fitting him closely. His cross garters were gray leather strips, binding his leggings close.

No, her father couldn't mean this. Surely this wasn't the man her father had brought to Oxborough to marry her. Hastings wasn't afraid. She was terrified. Marry this man? He would be her husband, her lord? No, surely this couldn't be the man, more like he was an emissary from Hades or a messenger from the mystical shades of Avalon.

Her father wanted to make this man of his line? Leave him all his possessions and land? Bestow upon him his titles since all her father had produced was her, a single female, of little account in the long scheme of things. Except for this marriage. Except to bind her to a man who scared her to her very toes.

This was the man her father's longtime friend Graelam de Moreton wanted her to marry? Lord Graelam was her friend, too. She remembered him throwing her squealing into the air when she was naught but seven years old. Graelam was as good as family, and he wanted this unearthly creature to be her husband, too? Indeed it had been Graelam, now striding into the castle's great hall, who said this man was a warrior to be trusted, to be held in respect and awe, and who held honor more dear than his own soul. Hastings didn't know what it meant. Of course she shouldn't have heard his views, but she'd been eavesdropping two months before, bent low in the shadows behind her father's chair. Now her father no longer sat in his chair. He no longer ate his dinner in the great hall, in his finely carved chair, served by his page and squire, both vying to give him the tastiest cut of beef. Now he sipped broth in his bed, praying it would stay calm in his belly.

The man's cloak seemed to move again and she thought she'd scream. All the Oxborough people in the great hall were huddled together, staring at the man, wondering what would happen if he became their master. Was he violent and cruel? Would he raise his hand when it amused him to do so? Would he brandish that whip as her father had done when he had found that her mother had bedded the falconer? Hastings hated whips.

The man's cloak rippled yet again. There was an unearthly shriek. She stuffed her fist into her mouth and sucked herself farther back into the shadows.

The man slipped his gloved hand beneath his cloak and pulled out a thickly furred animal with a bushy tail. There was a low hiss of fear from all the Oxborough people in the great hall. Was it a devil's familiar? No, no, not that, not a cat.

It was a marten. Sleek, thick-furred, deep brown in color save for the snow white beneath its chin and on its belly. She had a beautiful sable cloak made from this animal's fur. She'd wager this animal would never have to worry about being a covering for someone's back. Not held so securely by this man. What was this warrior doing with a marten?

The man brought the marten to his face, looked directly into its eyes, nodded, then very gently slipped it once again beneath his cloak inside his tunic.

She smiled, she couldn't help it. The man couldn't be all that terrifying if he carried a pet marten next to his heart.

Graelam de Moreton stepped up behind him and slapped the man on his back—as if he were just a man, nothing more than a simple man. The man turned and smiled. That smile transformed him. In that moment when he smiled, he looked human and very real, but then he wasn't smiling, and he was as he had been, a stranger, a dark stranger, with a marten in his tunic.

The two of them were of a size, both taller than the oak sapling she'd planted three summers past, big men, too big, taking too much space, crowding everyone around them. She'd never feared Graelam, though. She knew from stories her father had told her since she'd been small that he was a warrior whom other soldiers backed away from if they could, that her father had once seen Graelam sever a man in half with one swing of his sword and kill another three men with the same grace and power. She had never before considered that a man could be graceful while he butchered other men.

"Graelam," the man said, his voice as deep and rough as a ship pulling at its moorings in a storm. "It has been too long since I have tapped my fist into your ugly face and watched you sprawl to the ground. All goes well with you?"

"Aye, too well. I don't deserve what I have, the luck God has bestowed upon me, but I give thanks daily for my life. I caution you never to call my face ugly in front of my wife. She has a fondness for it. She may be small but she is ferocious in her defense of me."

The man said, "She is a special lady, unlike any other. You know why I am here."

"Naturally," Graelam de Moreton said. "I regret that Fawke of Trent is very ill and cannot be in the great hall to welcome you. Hastings should be here to greet you but I do not see her. We will sup, then I will take you to him."

"I wish to see him now. I wish to have this over with as quickly as possible."

"Very well." Graelam nodded to her father's steward, Torric, so thin Hastings had once told him that she feared he would blow away whenever there was a sharp wind off the sea. Graelam then motioned for the man to precede him up the winding stone stairs that led to the upper chambers. "Then," he said to the man's gray-cloaked back, "you will want to meet his daughter."

"I suppose that I must."

When they were out of sight, Hastings drew a deep breath. Her future would be sealed at her father's bedside. Her future and the future of Oxborough. Perhaps the man would refuse. She walked into the great hall. She called out to the thirty-some people, "This man is here to see Lord Fawke. We will prepare to dine."

*But who is he?* she heard over and over.

People were whispering behind their hands, as if he could hear them and would come back to punish them. Their faces were bright with curiosity and a tinge of fear. This was the sort of man who would wage a siege and show no mercy.

She said aloud, "He is Severin of Langthorne, Baron Louges. He, Lord Graelam, and their men will dine here. MacDear, please return to the kitchen and keep basting the pork with the mint sauce. Alice, see that the bread remains warm and crisp. Allen, fetch the sweet wine Lord Graelam prefers." She shut up. They were all staring at her, all filled with questions. She raised her hands, splaying her fingers in front of her. "I believe," she said finally, "that Lord Severin is here to wed with me."

She didn't listen to the babble. She was frankly surprised that everyone, all the way to the scullery maids in the kitchen, hadn't known who he was or why he was here. A well-kept secret. She knew he had just returned from France to find his older brother murdered, his estate beggared, his peasants starving, nothing there but devastated fields destroyed by marauding outlaws.

Aye, he was here to wed her, the heiress of Oxborough. She'd heard this when her father had asked Graelam what he knew of the man, what he thought of him and his honor and his strength. And Graelam had praised Severin, told him how King Edward had requested Severin ride at his right hand when they had been in the Holy Land during those final battles with the Saracens. He had stood beside Edward on the ramparts at Acre.

He was called Severin, she'd heard Graelam say, then he would add as he rubbed his callused hands together, "Aye, Severin, the Gray Warrior."

• • •

"Severin is here, Fawke."

Fawke of Trent, Earl of Oxborough, wished he could see the young man more clearly, but the film that had grown over his eyes was thicker than it had been just this morning, blurring everything, even his daughter's face, which was good since she looked so much like her mother, and it pained him to his guts to look at her. Too much pain, and now death was coming to him. He hated it, yet he accepted it. At moments like this, he welcomed it, but first he had to see this through.

"Severin," he said, knowing he sounded weak and despising himself for it.

The young man gripped his wrist, his hold firm and strong, but it didn't hurt Fawke. It felt warm and powerful, a link to both his past and the future, a future of many generations, and his blood would continue to flow through those warriors who would come after him.

"You will wed my daughter?"

"Aye, I will wed her," Severin said. "I thank you for selecting me."

Graelam said, "I have told you she is comely, Severin. She will please you just as you will please her."

Fawke of Trent sensed the young man freeze into stone when he said in that damnably weak voice of his, "All I ask is that you take my name. I have no son. I do not want my line to die out. You will own all my lands, all my possessions, collect all my rents, become sovereign to all my men. You will protect three towns, own most of the land in the towns, accept fealty from three additional keeps. I have nearly as much coin as King Edward, but I have told him I am barely rich, for I don't wish him to tax me out of my armor. Aye, you will wed my daughter."

"I cannot take your name, Fawke of Trent."

Graelam said, "Severin, you need not efface your own name. It is long known and you will continue to wear it proudly. Nay, what is to be done is that you simply add the family name of Trent to yours and the earl's title to your current one. You will then become Severin of Langthorne-

Trent, Baron Louges, Earl of Oxborough. King Edward agrees and has given his blessing to this union.''

It would serve, Fawke thought, wishing again that he could see the young man clearly. His voice was deep and strong. Graelam had assured him that he was of healthy stock. He said, ''My daughter will be a good breeder. She is built like her mother. She is young enough, just eighteen. You must have sons, Severin, many sons. They will save both our lines and continue into the future.''

Oddly, Severin thought of Marjorie. He remembered clearly the glory of her silvery hair, her vivid blue eyes that glistened when she laughed and darkened to a near black when she reached her release. Then her image dimmed. He had not thought of her in a very long time. She had long since been married off to another man. She was buried in a past that he would no longer allow to haunt him.

He said to Fawke, ''Graelam has told me her name is Hastings. Surely a strange name for either a male or a female.''

Fawke tried to smile, but the muscles in his face wouldn't move upward. He felt the deep weakness drawing on him, pulling him toward bottomless sleep, but he managed to say low, ''All firstborn daughters in my line since the long-ago battle have been named Hastings in honor of our Norman victory and our ancestor, Damon of Trent, who was given these lands by William in reward for his loyalty and valor, and, of course, the hundred men he added to William's force.''

His eyelids closed. He looked waxen. He looked already dead. He said, voice blurred with pain and weariness, ''Come to me when you are ready. Wait not too long.''

''Two hours.''

Graelam motioned for Severin to follow him from the chamber. He nodded to a woman who went in and sat beside Fawke of Trent, to watch over him whilst he slept.

''Aye, if we can find Hastings, it will be done in two hours,'' Graelam said. ''She is usually working in her herb garden. Aye, it must be tonight. I am afraid that Fawke won't survive until the morrow.''

"As you will. Trist is hungry. I would feed him before giving my name to this girl Hastings." Severin reached his hand into his cloak and pulled out the marten. He raised the animal to his cheek and rubbed his flesh against the soft fur. "No, don't try to eat my glove, Trist. I will give you pork." He raised his eyes to Graelam's face. "No other of his species eats much other than rats and mice and chicken, but when I was captured near Rouen last year and thrown into Louis of Mellifont's dungeon, he had more rats on his dinner plate than a village of martens could eat. He didn't have to hunt them down. All he had to do was wait until one came close, kill it, and eat. After I escaped, he wouldn't hunt another rat. I believed he would starve until he decided that he would eat eggs and pork. It is strange, but he survives and grows fat."

Graelam said, "He poked his head out a few moments ago. It seemed to me he didn't like being in Fawke of Trent's bedchamber. He quickly withdrew again."

"He remembers the smell of sickness and death from the dungeon. Not many of us survived."

"Aye, well, now he will eat all the pork he wishes." Graelam paused a moment on the winding stone stairs. "Severin, I have known Fawke and Hastings for a goodly number of years. Hastings was a clever little girl and she has grown up well. She knows herbs, and over the years she has become a healer. She is bright and gentle. She is not like her mother. As the heiress of Oxborough, she will fulfill her role suitably. I will have your word that you will treat her well."

Severin said in an emotionless, cold voice, "It is enough that I will wed her. I will protect her from the scavengers who are already on their way here, just waiting for the old man to die so they can come and steal her. That is all I promise—that, and to breed sons off her."

"If she were not here to be wed, then you would have to become another man's vassal. You would still be Baron Louges but you would watch your lands turn hard and cold with no men to work them."

"They are already hard and cold. There is naught left there."

"You will have the money to make things right. You will have Hastings as your wife. She will oversee the management of Oxborough when you are visiting your other estates."

"My mother wasn't able to oversee anything. When I arrived at Langthorne, she was huddled in filth, starving, afraid to come into the sunlight. I doubt she even recognized me. She is a woman with a woman's mind and now that mind is mired in demons. She is quite mad, Graelam. She could not hold Langthorne together. She could not do anything save whine and huddle in her own excrement. Why would I expect anything different from this Hastings? From any woman? What do you mean she isn't like her mother?"

"Her mother was faithless. Fawke found she had bedded the falconer. He had her beaten to death. Hastings isn't like her mother." He thought of the girl Severin had wanted to wed, this Marjorie. He had spoken of her long ago, with a dimmed longing. Did he think little of her also?

"We will see."

Severin was a hard man but he was fair, at least he was fair to other men. Graelam knew there was nothing more he could do. He missed his wife and sons. He wanted to leave as soon as these two were married. He rather hoped Hastings would approve her father's choice, though that didn't particularly matter.

## 2

*Sedgewick Castle*

RICHARD DE LUCI STARED DOWN AT HIS WIFE'S VOMIT-
stained night shift. He wished it was a shroud. When would
she die, damn her? She moaned, her back bowing upward.
Pain rippled the slack flesh of her face. Her mouth twisted
and opened.

He wished he could just throttle her right here and now,
but the priest was standing at his elbow, four of her women
hovered next to her bed, and his steward hadn't left the
odorous chamber for three hours.

He knew that Severin of Langthorne must be drawing
near Oxborough. He knew of the negotiations and that King
Edward had given his permission. But once he had Hastings
of Trent it wouldn't matter if the Pope himself had given
his blessing. The man who took her first and wed her would
be the victor.

He flexed his fingers. Why hadn't he just poured all that
white powder into her wine? Surely that would have felled
her immediately, not brought her puking to this bedchamber, lying in her own vomit and filth for the past day and
a half.

If she had complained that she didn't like the taste of the

wine, he could have simply ordered her to drink it, pouring
it down her throat if necessary. She'd been reciting one of
her interminable prayers as she sipped at the wine into
which he'd stirred that wondrous white powder the gypsy
had slipped to him. In return Richard had parted with the
red silk scarf he had given his bride when they'd married
seven years before.

What if she didn't die? He twisted his hands together so
hard the knuckles were white. Damn the bitch, he would
hunt down that gypsy and gullet her.

She moaned again, lurching upward.

"Lie still, my child. Lady Joan, lie still." The priest
pressed her back. She was heaving now, sucking hard for
breath. Richard hoped she couldn't find any. He hoped she
would choke to death on her own vomit. *Hurry it up, damn
you,* he wanted to scream at her.

Then, suddenly, with no warning, with no more retching
and gagging, she was dead. The last gasp for air caught in
her throat, leaving her mouth gaping open, her eyes wide,
staring up into his face.

"It is over, my lord," the priest said. He closed Lady
Joan's eyes and tried to press her mouth shut, but her lips
parted again. He stood and pulled the cover over her head.
"It is done," he said. "The poor lady suffered so with the
grippe of her belly, but now she is with our Lord, her im-
mortal soul free of its fleshly agonies. I am sorry, my lord."

Richard de Luci realized the man wanted him to do
something, to say something. What? Fall over her meager
body and moan his grief? He said to his wife's women,
"Prepare her for burial and clean away the filth in this
chamber." Then he forced himself to bow his head a moment at his wife's bedside. But a moment later, he strode
from the bedchamber, nearly crashing into his small daughter, Eloise, who was crouched beside a chair near the doorway. She shrank back beneath the chair. For once he did
not notice her.

At last the bitch was dead. Joan of Rotham was gone.
He was free. He shouted for his men as he walked quickly
through the hall of his castle. Such a small number of

soldiers in his employ. But soon he would have more than he could count. He had to hurry. That damned Severin of Langthorne had to be close now, very close to Oxborough.

He was away from Sedgewick Castle within the hour, his warhorse fresh, ready to gallop the seventeen miles to Oxborough Castle on the coast of the North Sea.

She was to marry the devil who wore that gray cloak. In two hours. Soon she had to return to the castle, bathe, and let her women dress her in the lovely saffron silk gown with its beautiful embroidery that Dame Agnes had been sewing since Hastings had reached her twelfth birthday.

No, not just yet. She was riding Marella, her palfrey with the white star on her forehead. Her mare was gray. She wondered if he would take her horse, this man who seemed to wear no other color. She wasn't using a saddle, only the bridle she'd slipped over Marella's bobbing head before she led her from the stables that were built against the thick curtain wall of the outer bailey. Once mounted, she passed by Beamis, her father's master-at-arms. Three knights and their squires were all responsible to him, and fifty soldiers. They lived in barracks that lined the outer bailey. It was immense, the only grass and trees in the huge open space in the east corner where an apple orchard stood.

Beamis raised his hand to her. He was going to call her back. Then Squibes the armorer caught his attention. Hastings let her mare pick her way through the crowd of men, women, and children as well as animals in the outer bailey. She lightly kicked her sides as they went through the portcullis of the eight-foot-thick curtain walls onto the drawbridge that spanned a chasm dug by her great-grandfather in the last century. There was another wall beyond, this one not as thick as the curtain walls of the outer bailey.

Two miles beyond lay the village of Oxborough, nestled about the mouth of the narrow River Marksby that flowed into the North Sea. It was a small trading town, walled, protected by Oxborough for well over two hundred years, most of it owned by her father. In less than two hours it would become the property of Severin of Langthorne.

The walls weren't as thick here, but they surrounded the entire enclosure and the village of Oxborough below. Just beyond was a small line of trees, then the decline worn smooth over the years that led down into the village. Here the air was fresh and sweet. She didn't want to greet any of her friends in the village, but she didn't see a way out of it when Ellen, Thomas the baker's daughter, waved madly at her from near the archery range.

"It is chilly today," Ellen said, patting Marella's nose. "My pa says there will be a storm off the sea this evening."

"I didn't know your father ever brought his nose out of his ovens to see if there would be a storm outside," Hastings said, and Ellen obligingly laughed.

She was a comely girl, sixteen, with nice teeth and a pale complexion. "He comes out when he's swept all the ashes from inside the ovens so he can sneeze. You will marry this day, Hastings?"

"Aye," Hastings said, and that was all. Not an hour before no one had known. But now Ellen knew and that meant that all the village of Oxborough knew as well.

"I heard he was impressive, this man who wears naught but gray. Mayhap handsome and well fashioned in the way of strong men who are warriors."

Hastings just smiled, watched the wife of the goldsmith throw a pail of slops out of an upper window, heard a man curse, then said, "I must go back. There is no more time."

"God speed, Hastings," Ellen said, and backed away from the mare.

Hastings rode beside the long curtain wall, waving to her father's men on the ramparts above, and let Marella make her way down to the beach. The water was turbulent and dark; waves hurled against the mass of black rocks at the base of Oxborough Castle.

The air was so sharp it nearly hurt to breathe it. The tinge of salt burned her skin. The wind whipped her hair and slapped against her cheeks. There were many waders, rushing forward when the waves receded, only to race back to the dry sand when the waves crashed in again. Oystercatchers, curlews, and redshanks shrieked and wheeled about above her head. She'd forgotten to bring them scraps.

She had to return. There was no more time. She breathed in deeply, wondering when she would next be able to come here to feel the freedom of the sea, to draw the salty air into her lungs, to hear the wind whistling strangely through some of the hollowed rocks strewn haphazardly below on the beach.

Tuggle took Marella's reins as Hastings slipped off her mare's back. He said in his soft, deep voice, "The lord is ready. You weren't here. He did not yell or curse, just spoke low, yet all knew he was not pleased. He asked Lord Graelam if you had run away rather than wed with him. Lord Graelam assured him that you were not such a block-head."

"Why would anyone believe I would run away from my home? I'll go in now. Thank you, Tuggle. Please rub Marella well. She's run hard."

He had missed her? But she had time, nearly an hour. She picked up her skirts and ran toward the wide wooden doors that gave into the great hall. They were thrown open, warming the hall, and she slipped inside, pausing a moment so her eyes could adjust to the dimmer light.

He was standing directly in front of her as if he had known that she would be coming in at that moment. His gloved hands on his hips. "You are Hastings of Trent? You are the girl I am to wed?"

She thought she would swallow her tongue. Her head felt blank with fear at the harshness of that dark, cold voice. Then, suddenly, the marten peeped out from beneath his tunic. She couldn't help herself, she smiled, reaching out her hand.

"Nay, he isn't always friendly. He could bite you."

But Trist didn't bite the girl who would soon be Severin's wife. He lifted his head higher when she rubbed the soft, thick fur, all white, beneath his chin. Then, just as suddenly, he pulled back and slipped beneath his master's tunic.

"I'm Hastings," she said, her fear now gone. If the marten didn't fear him, then why should she? "You are Severin of Langthorne. You are the man my father has selected for me to wed."

"Aye. You smell of horse, your gown is dirty, your hair looks like it's been pulled from your head and thrown back on by a careless hand. Go to your chamber and ready yourself. We will wed by your father's bedside as soon as you are prepared." With those tender words, he turned on his heel to stride away.

"It is my greatest pleasure to meet you," she called after him. "Perhaps Lord Graelam could tutor you in manners to be accorded a lady."

He paused, his body still, so very still, then slowly he turned to look back at her. "You will prove to me that you are not your mother's daughter. Then I will treat you like a lady. Go. The sight of you doesn't please me." He turned away again.

Her heart pounded with the words that had come out of her mouth. Then the marten's head appeared behind Severin's head. He stared at her, his head bobbing up and down. It looked so funny that she laughed. Severin whirled around and stared at her.

"You don't please me either," she said, flipped her long ratty braid over her shoulder, and walked up the solar stairs. "I don't like gray," she called back, but only when she was out of sight and, she hoped, out of his hearing.

She heard laughter. From Severin of Langthorne? No, it was Graelam de Moreton.

She stood beside her father's bed. His eyes were closed, his breath shallow and quick. "Father. I'm here. It is time."

He opened his eyes and looked at her. He drew away, crying out, "You're here, ah, Janet, you're here. How do you come here? How?"

"I'm Hastings, Father, not Janet. I'm not my mother. I'm her daughter. Your daughter."

He was sweating, his gray flesh greasy and slick. He was breathing hard now, still not believing, for she knew he couldn't really see her with the white film over his eyes.

She'd ground up cornflower blossoms, called hurt sickle by the Healer, boiled them in water, and used it as an eyewash. It gave temporary relief, but it hadn't improved his vision. His sight remained blocked by a slick veil of milky white and it worsened by the day.

He turned away from her, saying not another word. She stared down at him. Graelam de Moreton said at her elbow, "Father Carreg is here."

"Did my groom come as well?"

"Aye, I am here if you would but turn to see me."

She turned to see that he was garbed exactly as he had been earlier in the great hall, all in gray. But he'd removed his sword and the whip. The marten was wrapped around his neck like a thick, soft collar.

"You look better," he said, his eyes on her face, then moving down to her breasts and lower to her belly.

"I do not want this," she said to Graelam, her fingers clutching at the rich velvet of his sleeve. "Truly, I don't want this. I don't know him. What is he? Who is he? Is there not another way?"

"You will speak to me, madam, since in a very few minutes I will own you as I will own everything, even to the gown on your back and the slippers on your feet."

"Very well, I do not know you. I would prefer to wait."

"You know that isn't possible." He paused, then shrugged. "We must be wed before your father dies. There are greedy men who would do anything to capture you and force you to wed with them. Your only protection is to be my wife."

She'd heard this argument spewed several times from other mouths. Her father had spoken of Richard de Luci, a man she truly feared when she had met him accidentally at a tourney two years before.

She said, "But Richard de Luci is married. He is no threat to me."

"A wife would not slow him," Severin said, his voice uncaring, curt. "I imagine that his wife is now dead."

"I'll whip you as I whipped your mother if you do not do as you're bid. Do it. Now."

They all stared at Fawke of Trent. He had managed to pull himself up on his elbows. He was looking from his daughter to Severin of Langthorne. "Do it now. My end is near. You must wed each other to save my lands and to give my name permanence."

And I am little of nothing, Hastings thought. Her father had ignored her since he'd had her mother whipped to death, a deed that her nurse had prevented her from witnessing. But she'd heard her mother's screams. Her mouth felt dry. She licked her tongue over her lips. "I am ready," she said. She thrust out her hand and Severin took it.

Father Carreg was quick. As he spoke the words from the Latin parchment that he himself had penned, his eyes darted from Severin back to Fawke of Trent. He quickened and Hastings knew that he had skipped parts of the ceremony. Her father breathed his last just as Father Carreg gave them his blessing. Father Carreg gave a sigh of relief and mopped the sweat from his forehead. "I have given him last rites," he said to Hastings. "I will pray over him now. Make your good byes."

"It is done," Severin said. He leaned over and gently closed Fawke's staring eyes that hadn't seen much of anything in weeks. Hastings watched him, feeling numb. Her father lay dead and she was married. What good-byes should she say? Thank you, Father, for wedding me to a man who could be as violent as you were? She lightly touched her fingertips to her father's cheek, then drew back.

The marten stirred for the first time, stretching, his thick tail brushing Severin's face. Then the marten froze, making soft mewling sounds deep in his throat.

"It is death," Graelam said. "The marten hates the smell of death."

"See to your father's laying out," Severin said to her. "Then come to the great hall and we will sup. I would have more pork for Trist. He appears to like the way the cook prepares it."

Father Carreg said, "My lord, I have instructed everyone that your name is now Severin of Langthorne-Trent, Baron Louges and Earl of Oxborough."

"The name matters little. I am now their lord. That will suffice." He turned and left the bedchamber, the marten wheezing until it was beyond the door.

"I trust him," Graelam said, and drew Hastings into his arms. "He is a good man."

"My father is dead."

"Aye, but he had a good life, Hastings, a full life. He was a good friend to me. We will mourn him."

"Must I bed this man on the same night my father has died?"

"Nay. I will speak to Severin. He will leave you alone tonight. But attend me, Hastings. He is a man, a warrior, he is now the lord of Oxborough. He must spill his seed in you not only to protect you but also to seal the union. It is the way things are done. You know that."

"I like the marten."

"Aye, Trist is a wily fellow, smarter than many men I've known. He travels everywhere with Severin. Severin told me that you touched Trist and he didn't bite you. It took me months before the marten would allow my hand near his head. Now, your women will lay out Fawke. You will come with me to the great hall. This is your wedding feast. We will do it properly."

"How old is Severin?"

Graelam cocked his head to one side even as he was warming her hands between his. "Young, but twenty-five summers, I believe, not an old man of thirty-one as I am."

She paused, looking back at her father. Two women were already preparing to bathe him. "Good-bye, Father," she whispered, and turned to Graelam. "I remember when I was very young. My mother told me that my father was pleased when I was born because I was the firstborn girl, and thus the name of Hastings was carried on. But then there were no boys. I think he came to hate me for that."

"Come," Graelam said, having no answer, and led her away.

# 3

THE MARTEN LOOKED AT HER SEVERAL TIMES DURING THE long evening but made no move toward her. He remained very close to Severin, never more than a paw length beyond his right hand.

Hastings, well aware of the cautious conversation coming toward her from all the Oxborough people, was sipping on her wine, staring at the peas on her trencher, when Severin suddenly leaned toward her. "Graelam tells me you don't wish me near you tonight." They were the first words he'd spoken to her since Father Carreg had finished their marriage lines and Severin had left the bedchamber.

Her fingers tightened about the goblet. It was pewter, as cold a gray as the thick band he wore on his left arm. She wondered what the band was for.

She simply couldn't imagine this man, this stranger, touching her, taking her as men did women who were their wives because it was their right to do so. She supposed it was his right to do anything he wished to. He was a man. He was born with the right to own his wife. Hadn't her father killed her mother? She doubted even Father Carreg had uttered a single rebuke.

"No," she said at last, "I wish to remain as I am for as long as I can."

"Tonight, then. I give you tonight."

"My father will be buried tomorrow. Tomorrow night seems too soon as well."

"Tomorrow night it must be done."

"You do not sound like an enthusiastic bridegroom."

"I'm not," he said, and stretched, rubbing his neck. "I am weary. I pushed my men and myself to arrive at Oxborough before your father died. So that I would be controlled with you, I even bedded several wenches on our way here. But now, seeing you, I do not believe you even know how to assist me to enthusiasm. So, it is likely that I will have you lying blank-eyed and cold beneath me and that will bring me no pleasure. Sleep in your bed, Hastings. But tomorrow, whether I wish to take you or not, it must be done. Nothing is safe until I have breached your maidenhead and spilled my seed in your womb."

She looked at the marten. He was lying along the length of Severin's arm now, looking sleek, his belly stretched with all the food he'd eaten.

"He is fat."

"Aye, he doesn't hunt much. Not enough time has passed since he suffered so in Rouen. He will improve."

"Lord Graelam told me of your captivity and why Trist eats pork."

"He shouldn't have. It is not your affair."

"Evidently he didn't agree with you. Since we are married, isn't it right that we know something of each other?"

He stared down at his pewter plate that still held its slice of thick bread with meat chunks on top of it. The thick gravy had congealed. He saw that she hadn't eaten much either. Not that he cared. He said aloud, "It isn't important to me. You are my wife. You belong to me. You are an obligation. I will protect you as I will protect all else that is mine."

She'd been an obligation to her father, keeping her distance, treading quietly around him, seeing to his comfort, but still she was her mother's daughter, and thus to be despised. She remembered hearing one of the other women say to Dame Agnes that Hastings's mother had cursed when she'd borne a girl rather than an heir, even though the girl child would be named Hastings and thus carry on the tradition. No, Janet had wanted an heir because she knew Fawke would make her go through pregnancy again until she bore him one. But Janet had come to love her daughter, Hastings was more certain of that than she was certain of anything else in her life. Aye, her mother had loved her dearly until she had died, beaten to death by order of her husband. Hastings shook away the memories. She looked at her husband, another who saw her as naught but an obligation. "You said you had bedded women before you arrived here. I do not understand that."

A black brow went upward. "What is there to understand? I am a man. I told you, I wanted to have control with you."

Because the marten was lying fat and replete along his arm, because she couldn't fear a man with an animal lying on his arm, she said, "When I was fifteen the jeweler's son kissed me. I liked it. I suppose I should have enjoyed him more before I wedded you."

His arm must have locked because the marten raised his head, readying himself to move quickly. Severin drew a deep breath, then rubbed the animal's head with his finger. Both his arm and the marten eased.

He speared a chunk of beef with his knife, looked at it a moment as if it would perhaps poison him, then ate it. He chewed slowly. Finally, he said, "You are not meek. That is a requirement in a wife. You will hold yourself silent. You will obey me. You will not mock me with an eye to angering me."

"I am not mocking you, merely jesting with you. Well, mayhap there is irony to be gleaned from my words. Do not misunderstand me, my lord. I see that you are a man. I am assured that you are a strong and an able protector, a warrior. I accept that. I will even accept you as my husband, since I have no choice, but I will not become one of the rushes for you to tread upon. Even my father, who had no affection for me, did not expect that of me."

"A husband is not a father."

She felt as if she were battering herself against the curtain wall of the outer bailey. "No," she said quietly, "I believe you are right."

"You are not grieving for your father."

"I have grieved for the past two months. I could ease his pain, but nothing more. I couldn't cure him. Not that he wanted to accept anything from my hand that would ease him."

"You are truly a healer?"

"I try. Sometimes I succeed. Sometimes the illness overwhelms the victim and all my efforts to heal."

Lord Graelam cleared his throat as he rose. "Listen, all. Let us all drink to the new lord and lady of Oxborough."

Everyone did drink and cheer, but it was an effort. No one knew this man who was their new master. All were wary. Most, she knew, were worried for her. Even Beamis and her father's men-at-arms had kept their distance, but she saw they now seemed more at ease with Severin's men.

She left the great hall as soon as she could. Tonight would be her last night of freedom. Tonight would be her last night to be herself. Dame Agnes, who had sewn her gown and had been her mother's nurse and hers as well, accompanied her to her small bedchamber. "It is kindness on the lord's part," the old woman said, "that he not come to you tonight. But tomorrow night, my little pet, you must allow him to take you. I will pray that he won't hurt you, but know that it will hurt a bit the first time. But it isn't important. You lie still and let him do what he must. Later, we can speak of other things."

What other things? Hastings wondered. She said, "I know what he will do, Agnes. I've heard that some women even enjoy the act. My mother must have enjoyed Ralph the falconer since she willingly went to his bed."

"You are not your poor mother. She was unhappy for a while, but then Lord Fawke gave her no chance to change. It is a tragedy."

"What do you mean? She wanted to return to my father?"

Dame Agnes tightly seamed her thin lips.

"Come, my mother has been dead many years now. My father is dead. There is no one here to feel their pain anymore. Tell me, Agnes. Don't you believe I deserve to know?"

"Hold still," the old woman said.

Hastings said nothing more, just raised her arms and moved this way and that until Agnes had removed the precious saffron silk gown. "You will keep it safe for your own daughter," she said. "I doubt I will be here to sew her wedding gown for her."

"Of course you will. I grow more efficient with my herbs every day. You will see, by next month I will be able to cure the plague. Mayhap even old age."

Dame Agnes smiled. It was a nice smile to Hastings, even though the old woman was missing most of her teeth. "You keep your head about you, Hastings. You hold firm. A woman bends, that you must remember, but she can still keep her place unto herself. Our new lord, he is a mystery, but he is still just a man, and no man I've ever heard of can hide himself for very long."

"I dare say his marten won't let him."

"Ah, the marten. A strange companion for a warrior. Now, little pet, let me assist you in your night shift. It belonged to your mother. I have been keeping it safe for you."

"Why should I wear it tonight? He will not come. He swore to me that he would not."

"Ah, I had forgotten that. Aye, just wear your shift. There's my little pet. You will sleep now. Hear the storm. You have always loved the storm blowing in from the sea. Let it give you sweet dreams."

Dame Agnes leaned down, pulled the soft wool blanket to Hastings's throat, and kissed her cheek. She pulled her fingers through her thick hair. "How beautiful you are, Hastings, with your lovely chestnut hair, just like your mother's. And those green eyes of yours, aye, they're more vivid than the moss in the Pevensey Swamp. And now, you are my lady. I will inform the servants that they are now to curtsy when they see you and not just sing out your name as all of them have done since you were a tiny little mite.''

Hastings just smiled. It was difficult to believe all these changes could occur overnight.

The bedchamber was dark. The rain pounded against the closed wooden shutters that covered the only window in her room. She listened to the roiling waves crash against the ancient rocks some sixty feet below. She was lucky, all in all. She wouldn't have to leave her home as did most girls when they wedded. So she was beautiful, was she? She wondered if her new husband believed her beautiful. He probably didn't care.

The last thought in her mind as she fell asleep was of the marten, lightly snoring, his face cupped in Severin's hand. A large hand, callused and strong, the nails clean. She shivered.

The dream wasn't sweet and vague as her dreams usually were during a storm. She felt someone pull down the blanket. She heard someone breathing close to her face. She was cold. She shivered. Hands were touching her, untying the ribbons of her shift.

Her eyes flew open. There was a single candle burning next to her narrow bed. She looked up into the eyes of her husband.

"You're awake. Good. Hold still so I can take off your shift."

He was no dream. He was here in her bedchamber. "What are you doing? You said you would leave me alone tonight." He said nothing and she began to struggle, hard, and soon she was panting. "What are you doing here? Damn you, you lied." She jerked away from him, but only for an instant. He grabbed her arm and pulled her back.

She yelled again, "You lied! You aren't to be here. You swore you wouldn't bother me this night."

He was pulling on the ties of her shift. But he was clumsy. With a growl, he grabbed the soft cotton in his hands and yanked it apart, the ripping sound obscene in the small bedchamber.

He grunted as he stared down at her breasts.

He whipped away the blanket and looked down the length of her. He leaned down to pull off her torn shift. "Nay," she shouted, and jerked up her legs. She struck him squarely in the chest. It knocked him off balance and he careened backward, flailing the air with his arms until he regained his balance.

She saw his anger, indeed, she felt it, and knew she wouldn't like what he would do. She knew she should lie upon her back and just let him have his way. But she couldn't. She struggled up onto her knees. She flung out her hands to ward him off. "Why did you lie to me?"

"I didn't lie. I meant what I said to you, but now everything is different. I now have no choice. Hold still. Stop fighting me." He was on her, pulling her onto her back, lying by her side, holding her still with an arm over her chest and one of his legs covering hers.

He jerked up the shift, baring her to her waist. He stilled, but just a moment.

Then his hand was prying open her legs. She felt his fingers touching her, pushing into her, and she cried out.

He cursed, low and long. He probed more with his fingers. She flinched and struggled. Suddenly he left her. He walked to the small table with its narrow mirror. He was looking at the jars on top of the table. He opened one, smelled it, then nodded. She watched him smear a goodly amount of the cream on his fingers. Then he turned back to her. God, what was he going to do with that cream? Stuff it down her throat? He would poison her now that he had what he wanted? Since she was fighting him, he no longer cared if she lived or died?

She leapt from the bed and ran to the door. She heard him curse her, but she was fast. She got the door open and was into the corridor, the hard stone cold and sharp beneath her bare feet. In the next instant she ran into someone. Strong hands went around her upper arms.

"Hastings, stop it."

It was Lord Graelam. He shook her, then pulled her

against him. She realized dimly that she was wearing only a shift that was nearly ripped from neck to hem. She jerked back to see him in the dim light. She was shaking violently, all rational thought fled from her brain. "Graelam, please listen to me. He lied. He is here to hurt me. You must not let him, Graelam. He promised to wait. Please."

"Hold still," Graelam said. He looked to see Severin standing in the open doorway. "You plan to hurt her?"

Severin raised his hand. "Look you, Graelam. My fingers are covered with cream to ease my member into her. She's drier than the Saracen desert."

He took a step toward her.

"No!" She managed to jerk away from Graelam, but he caught her quickly enough.

"You are nearly naked, Hastings. Now, listen to me. Go with Severin. He must take you tonight. We have word that men—probably de Luci's soldiers—are very close to Oxborough. There is no choice. Just allow him to get it done. It won't be bad."

She felt Severin's arm come around her waist. He lifted her and carried her beneath his arm back into her bedchamber. He said over his shoulder, "I won't hurt her overly," then kicked the door closed with the heel of his boot. He turned the key in the lock, carried her to the bed, and threw her down onto her back.

"Don't move. We will get it done if you will but stay there. If you struggle, it will just hurt you more."

She looked at him, at his two fingers covered with her special cream. "What will you do with that cream?"

"You heard me tell Graelam that you are dry. This will ease my way. Damn you, don't you know what I must do?"

"You will leave my bedchamber. You have not my leave to be here. I will hold you to your promise. Those men, they cannot enter Oxborough. Oxborough is a fortress. If you have any honor, you will hold yourself to it."

He sat down beside her. "Listen to me, my lady. I'm certain that it is Richard de Luci who is outside the walls, hiding in the forest. His wife is dead, doubtless murdered

by him. He is here to take you. I must get this union sealed.
I must rend your maidenhead and spill my seed in your
body. I have tonight. Tomorrow I might be in battle. Do
you understand?''

That drew her back into her mind. She calmed. ''Why
didn't you tell me that instead of just silently forcing yourself upon me?''

''I told you I had no choice.'' He shrugged. ''Besides,
you are my wife. What need was there to say more?''

He made no move, just stared down at her.

Her father lay in his shroud in the chamber below. Richard de Luci was close. There was no hope for it. She said,
''Very well. I won't fight you anymore. I would ask that
you not tear any more of my clothes.''

He grunted, then pulled the shift off her and tossed it
aside. ''Now you're naked. There are no more clothes to
tear. Part your legs.''

This was more difficult than she'd thought it would be.
She parted her legs. She also closed her eyes.

''Bend your knees.''

She bent her knees.

She knew he was looking at her, looking at her where
no one had ever looked. She swallowed. She felt his fingers
touching her. She felt his fingers parting her. She felt his
fingers, coated with the thick cream, shove into her. She
felt his fingers rubbing the cream into her cold flesh, pushing deeper.

She tried not to move, but her body recoiled and tried to
jerk away from him. ''It hurts.''

''You are doing well. You will bear it. Soon it will be
over.''

He left her.

''No, leave your legs open for me.''

She opened her eyes to see him opening his trousers. His
man's sex was there, surely too big, surely, but then he
rubbed the rest of the cream on his member.

''Lie still and it will be over quickly.''

He came over her, the wool of his tunic rubbing against
her breasts, and it hurt. He pushed her legs wider and she

watched him hold himself as he pushed into her.

She tried not to move, but suddenly she couldn't help herself. It was too much. She cried out and jerked away from him. His palm flattened against her stomach. He drove into her and the scream swallowed itself in her throat.

She lay there, as motionless as a dead woman while he heaved over her. It was over soon, he hadn't lied about that. He made some strange sounds in his throat, flung his head back, jerked into her, then he stilled.

In the next moment, he was gone, standing over her, panting, his breath jerking and deep. She didn't look at him. She stared toward the tapestry on the wall opposite her narrow bed. It was lifting lightly as the storm winds buffeted against the keep walls.

He said, his breath still fast and harsh, "It is done. Now you are safe."

"Safe? You just treat me like I am worth nothing at all and you bray that you have made me safe?" She turned to face him as she spoke. He was still standing there, breathing hard, his member now lying flaccid against his body. It looked shiny and wet, wet with his seed and her blood.

"I hate you," she said with great precision. "You're naught more than a rutting animal. I will never forgive you this. Never."

He began to straighten his clothes. "An animal doesn't use cream to ease his way. I spared you what pain I could. A virgin has a maidenhead. I had to force my way through it. The next time it will not hurt you."

He had used the cream. She'd give him that. "You are still wearing your boots. You tear off my clothes yet you keep yourself clothed."

He was done. He looked down at her and shrugged. "I just wanted to get it over with. Now, draw the cover over yourself. Your legs are sprawled apart like a trollop's. Don't bathe my seed from your body. The sooner you are with child the more secure will be my possessions." With those words he leaned down, picked up the key, and opened the door. He turned in the doorway. "You will remain within the keep tomorrow. I will find Richard de Luci. If he is a reasonable man, I won't kill him, though I fear he is just the first of many. Until you are with child, you are at risk.''

Aye, she thought. Severin was sorely tried. The poor man—marrying an heiress was the very devil.

He was gone, his boots sounding loud on the stone floor. He had still been garbed in his gray clothes.

She lay there, her legs still sprawled wide, feeling as though she'd been ripped inside, which, she thought, she had, since he'd torn through her maidenhead. She hurt. She lay her hand on her belly. She was no longer herself, no longer just Hastings.

No gentleness from him, no soft wooing, just the cream, which cost him no kind words. She had been married for six hours and she had no kind thoughts for the man who was her husband.

4

"SHE IS GONE."

Severin blinked down at the old woman. "What did you say? Who is gone?"

"Hastings. My lady, your wife, is gone. What did you do to her? Hastings is never imprudent, yet I cannot find her. She is not within the keep."

"What the devil is this?" Graelam demanded as he strode to Severin. "Hastings is gone?"

"Aye, my lord Graelam. There was blood on her bed and bloody water in the basin. The lord broke his word to her. Her father is to be buried today, surely he should have left her whole last night."

Severin said, "It was not possible. Richard de Luci nears. He will try to take her. Now you say she is gone." He cursed. "I should have locked her in her bedchamber. You say she is never imprudent. If she has tried to leave the castle, he will take her. That is stupidity beyond anything I can fathom." He hit the heel of his hand against his forehead. "I expect wisdom from a woman? I am a fool. I believed she understood. I believed her cowed. Well, Graelam, all is changed now. I must find her before Richard de Luci does. Damnation. I will punish her for this. Never again will she go against me."

Graelam turned to Dame Agnes. "It is only seven o'clock. Did you only go to her bedchamber?"

"I have looked everywhere. If anyone has seen her, then they are lying fluently."

"Did you go to her herb garden?"

"Nay, I have looked just within the keep. I will go there now."

"I will go," Severin said. "I told her she was to remain within the keep. She must be taught obedience."

He felt more relief than he was willing to admit when he saw her on her knees, garbed in an old woolen green gown, sweat between her shoulder blades, working the soil in her herb garden that stood fenced in beside a small pear orchard. All around the fence were blossoming flowers. He recognized the blood-red roses, tall, the blooms incredibly large. And the daisies, with their bright yellow centers and stark white ray flowers. And so many more he couldn't begin to put a name to. As for her herb garden, it was neatly plotted, the different plants carefully set inside a rectangle, all of them looked healthy, many ready to harvest.

He shook his head. Who cared about her herb garden? The storm had blown itself out. The morning sun was brilliant, the sky clear. She hadn't heard him. He supposed with all the noise surrounding her nearly every hour of the day, it wasn't surprising. Ah, but she would learn to hear him. Soon, when he came to her, she would be on her feet, her eyes lowered, ready to curtsy when he drew near enough. Her hair was braided into a thick single rope that hung down her back. He stepped over the protective wooden fence and stood over her, his shadow cast long and dark. She looked to be working furiously.

Hastings loved the damp earth on her hands, the feel of it, knowing her precious herbs would thrive. She sat back on her heels for a moment, looking at her patch of thriving rosemary. The pleasure she felt working in her garden helped just a bit to ease her soul-deep anger at the blow he'd dealt her. It was absurd, this excuse of his that Richard de Luci could somehow sneak into Oxborough and take her.

She heard movement behind her and said without turning from what she was doing, "Is that you, Tuggle? Please bring me Marella. I would ride out in an hour or so."

"I think not."

She whipped about so quickly, she fell on her bottom. "You," she said. And if that was too much, she quickly added, "Watch where you step. That is rosemary beside your foot. Don't crush it."

He moved away from the rosemary. "I care not about this rosemary. It is a silly name, a female's name. Why is the rosemary so valuable?"

"It makes your marten's pork very tasty. If you have a cramping belly, it will ease you. A man should drink it for nine days if he has debilitated himself with venery. Perhaps you would care for some right now?"

"Do not mock me again." He came down on his haunches beside her. "The other women were days ago. I took you only once. I doubt I'm debilitated. I told you to remain within."

"I am within. Look about you. There are scores of my people."

"*My* people. I am lord here now."

"Very well. There are scores of people who would yell down the heavens if someone came too close to me."

She should be safe enough here, he thought, yielding the point since there was a much meatier bone to pick. "You thought I was Tuggle. You told me to ready your mare. You were going to leave, weren't you?"

"Aye, but just for a short time and I would have asked Beamis to send several of his men with me. I must go to see the Healer, a knowledgeable woman who lives deep in the Pevensey Forest. I have learned nearly everything I know from her. Even she could not save my father."

He threw up his hands. "Then send a man to bring her to the castle. Have you no ability to think?"

"She won't come here. She never leaves the forest. I have asked her many times."

"Then you won't see her for a while." He reached out his hand and cupped her chin. She stilled instantly. "You will listen to me now, lady. You will remain here, in this garden, or within the keep. You will go no place else until I have taken care of Richard de Luci. Do you understand me?''

''Since you are near to yelling, it would be difficult not to.''

''Nay, that simply means that you hear me, but not necessarily that you understand me. I will have no more disobedience from you. Why did you wash my seed from your body? I told you not to.''

She reached for the trowel. She wanted to strike him as hard as she could. She wanted to smash his head. His gloved hand hit the trowel hard, her fingers just inches from the handle. ''How do you know what I did?'' she said, staring at that handle, at his fist covering the trowel.

''Your old nurse told Graelam and me. There was blood in your water basin.''

She watched him rise. Her fingers closed over the trowel handle. ''Aye, I scrubbed myself clean of you.''

He said even as she raised the trowel, ''You dare to raise a weapon to me?'' He made no move toward her. He remained utterly still. It was that same stillness that had made her want to cross herself when she'd first seen him standing in the great hall, the sun framing him through the wide doorway. He was again garbed all in gray. She felt the rage pouring from him.

It happened so quickly neither had a chance to react. A shadow fell, then there was a blur of movement. It was Hastings who saw the dagger in the man's hand and it was but moments from Severin's back. She yelled, and threw herself against Severin, knocking him off his feet and onto her patch of thyme. He fell onto his side. The man's hand flashed down and the knife sank into Severin's shoulder.

She didn't think, just jumped to her feet, flinging herself at the man even as he raised the dagger again to strike. She knew he wouldn't dare hurt her else his master wouldn't gain her in marriage and would thus lose all. She struck his head as hard as she could with the trowel, but it just seemed to bounce off his skull. Her fingers went to his eyes.

He managed to jerk back, but not in time. He screamed in pain. She felt ribbons of his flesh wet beneath her fingernails.

He covered his face with his hands, groaning. She threw the trowel at him and kicked him in his groin, sending him to his knees. Two men were running toward them, but they weren't Oxborough men or Langthorne men. She grabbed the dagger from the man's lax hand and rose to meet them even as she yelled as loud as she could, "Graelam! *A moi! A moi!* Beamis!"

They were on her in a flash, but she kept slashing that dagger in front of her. "Filthy cowards, are you afraid of one woman? Come on, my fine warriors. Come."

"Aye," a voice came from behind her. "Come and let me cut your gullets."

It was Severin. She almost whirled about to see him, but knew she couldn't. If he wasn't wounded badly enough to stand, then he could save both of them. She saw the flash of his sword, heard the scream of one of the men, saw the blood spurt from his chest even as he lurched forward to fall not an inch from her feet. The other man wasn't a fool. Oxborough men were coming, and soon he wouldn't have a chance. He turned on his heel and ran.

She turned to Severin, who stood there, sword dripping the man's blood onto his hand. He was holding his other hand against his shoulder, blood seeping through his fingers.

"I had believed you safe here," he said. "I do wonder how they managed to get within the keep. Are your men so slack?"

She had no time to answer. There was yelling, a man's scream. Then Graelam and Beamis were there, men piling behind them. Beamis was pale, his eyes on his new master. "I don't know how they got in. I don't know, but it won't happen again, my lord."

"If it does, I'll flail the flesh from your back," Severin said. "I want the other man alive."

"He's alive."

"Good," Severin said. "I will question him." He looked

at Graelam, then down at the blood oozing between his fingers, opened his mouth, looked astonished, and fell right on top of her rosemary and horehound. His right boot landed on the small patch of mugwort.

Severin felt the deep twisting pain before he opened his eyes. But it was pain, nothing more, and he knew from long practice that he could control most pain. He'd fainted. Like a damned female, he'd fainted. He'd had to be carried and laid on his bed. He felt shame curdle in his belly. He couldn't help it. Then it wasn't shame curdling in his belly. He lurched up and vomited in the basin she held for him. He drew a deep, steadying breath and said, "You will go away. I don't wish you near me."

"Why not? Had I not been here, had I not known that your belly would probably rebel, you would have puked on yourself."

He wanted to kill her.

"Do you still have that trowel?"

"Nay, I threw it at the man I felled."

She had saved herself, damn her. And she'd saved him as well, curse her to hell and beyond. A girl who was half his size and she'd hurled herself at him, knocking him to the ground. If she hadn't knocked him off balance, perhaps he would have seen the man in time. Perhaps. He'd seen her rip the man's face with her fingernails, kick him in his groin. Who had taught her that? A lady would have swooned, surely, not knocked him out of danger and flung herself upon the attacker. His voice was sour as he said, "What are you doing to me?"

"Ah, a reasonable question. It's about time. But your mood is foul as your breath."

"Don't mock me, lady." He felt the bed give when she sat down beside him. She wasn't looking at his face, but at his shoulder.

He reached up and grabbed her wrist. "What are you doing?" He sucked in his breath at the pain. He closed his eyes a moment, gaining control. He had to, she was watching him.

"Drink this."

She held a goblet to his lips. He tasted the sweet, crisp liquid, felt the foulness ease in his mouth and through his body.

"Good. Now hold still." She added in a matter-of-fact voice, "I'm cleansing the wound with a paste I make of eryngo root, and bandaging it. You will survive, my lord."

"What is this eryngo root?"

"Many call it sea holly. It grows just above the tide line. I mix it with pearl barley and water boiled with just three leaves from the gentian plant. Don't fret, my lord, it won't kill you."

"Finish your bandaging and leave me be. I must question that other man."

"Keep on your back for a bit longer, Severin," Graelam said from just beyond Hastings. "She has got the bleeding stopped. I have spoken to the man."

Severin felt a movement on his belly. Trist poked his head from beneath the covers that were pulled to Severin's waist. He realized he was still wearing his breeches, but not his boots. He said gently, as he brought his hand to lightly touch the marten's head, "I am all right, Trist. Don't fret."

The marten made a strange, soft purring sound, then flattened his chin on Severin's belly, staring up at his master's face.

"He wouldn't leave you," Hastings said. "He did leap away when you vomited, but you felt too wretched to notice. Then he crept back. He wasn't with you this morning when you came to my herb garden. When Graelam and Beamis and your man, Bonluc, carried you in, he leapt onto you, yowling, sort of. I could not make him leave and I did ask him very politely."

This damned wit of hers. Where had it come from? Why had she hidden it from him? It annoyed him. He looked at her then and said, "This would not have happened had you obeyed me."

"No," she said, surprising him, "it would not have."

"The man," Graelam said, looking from one to the

other, "won't speak of anything to the point. He won't even admit to being Richard de Luci's man. He just keeps whining that he's from the village, here to trade furs. Indeed, he did have four or five pelts fastened to his belt."

"I will rise soon. I will make him speak. I learned much in the Holy Land."

"As all of us did, Severin."

"You needn't torture him," Hastings said. "I will have him willing to tell you his deepest secrets within minutes."

Severin grunted, making Trist raise his head and stare at Hastings. She reached down without thinking and lightly stroked the marten's head. To Severin's shock, the marten closed his eyes and lowered his head again to Severin's belly, stretched out his short legs to Severin's navel.

"Just how will you do this?"

"I will give him some sweet ale to drink that will cover the bitter taste of the mandrake and the yarrow root. Within a few minutes he will begin puking up his innards. No man can withstand it. I will offer to give him the cure for it if he will speak the truth."

"I don't believe you," Severin said. "What would you give him to cease the vomiting?"

"Columbine and just a bit of gentian. I grind up the flowers and mix the powder into sour beer. The gentian seems to add calm to the mind and thus to the belly. Aye, you just had a bit of gentian to calm your belly."

"Ah," Graelam said, "you mean bitterwort. My Kassia uses that. She was complaining when Harry had a bellyache that her recipe wasn't effective enough."

She smiled at him. "I will send her mine. I learned it from the Healer last year."

Severin cursed. Both turned to him, Graelam's eyebrow arched. "Calm yourself, Severin. Because Hastings is seeing to you, you will be well much sooner than you deserve to be. Now, Hastings, would you like to mix up your belly poison for our prisoner?"

"Gladly. I must do some grinding and boiling. It will take me a while."

"No! I forbid that you do this. I wish to see him and—"

"And what? Pull out his fingernails? Lash him until he bleeds? Mayhap kill him without finding out anything?"

"It is none of your affair, damn you. I am lord here. I will do just as I deem right. I will have nothing more out of your mouth and—"

Suddenly, Trist inched up Severin's chest, rubbed his chin on Severin's chin, then laid himself over Severin's mouth, his long tail curling around Severin's ear.

"Drink this," Hastings said to him. "It is more gentian to calm you." But it was Graelam who gently moved Trist and held the goblet to his mouth, not moving it until Severin had drunk it all down. "The witch will poison me," he said, then closed his eyes.

"No, I shan't poison you. I would rather hit your head with the trowel."

His eyes closed. His breathing deepened.

Hastings said, as she stared down at him, "He's a very big man, Graelam. That first bit of gentian I gave him wasn't enough."

"Aye," Graelam said slowly.

The man retched violently for five minutes before he begged for her to cure him. He lay on his side in pools of his own vomit, clutching his belly, whimpering. "Please, lady, please save me. I will tell you what you wish. Please."

Hastings smiled at Graelam and Severin. She motioned to the pathetic man and rose.

She prepared the gentian flowers, smashing them into a fine powder, then mixing them slowly with warm ale that had sat in the sun. She swished it about in the goblet as she watched Severin stand over the man, careful not to step in his vomit. There were at least another dozen men forming a circle around them. The sun shone hot overhead. The stench was bad.

It had been Graelam's suggestion that they haul the man outside. Why befoul the dungeon?

"You are no villager as you've claimed. Tell me where your master is and what his intentions are."

The man paled. His eyes flew around the circle of men. He started to shake his head. His belly cramped viciously and he vomited, dry heaves for there was nothing left to come up. When he caught his breath, he whispered, "My lord Richard is just beyond with two dozen men in the Pevensey Forest. The three of us disguised ourselves as villagers. Since it is market day, it wasn't difficult to come into the castle gates. We saw her and took our chance." He turned miserable eyes toward Hastings. "Give me the cure, my lady, I beg of you."

Hastings looked to Severin. He looked thoughtful. If she didn't know of the deep wound in his shoulder she wouldn't guess there was anything wrong with him at all. She waited, swirling the liquid about in the goblet. It smelled foul but tasted sweet, the flower mixed with the ale. The man was staring at that goblet. She didn't blame him. Still, she just waited. It was Severin's decision. She wondered if he would simply slip his dagger into the man's chest.

Severin said, "Give him the potion, Hastings."

She came down on her knees and gently tilted the goblet into the man's mouth. "Drink slowly," she said. "Very slowly. Then the men will carry you into the shade and you will sleep for a while. When you awake, your belly will be calm."

When the man slept propped up against the side of a pigsty, Severin said to all the men, "I am releasing him. He will take a message to Richard de Luci. Graelam, come with me whilst I write the message."

He knew how to write. She wasn't really surprised. She supposed nothing he did could surprise her. Actually, she was relieved. It meant that she wouldn't have to keep a close eye on her father's steward, Torric. Her father had also known how to write and he'd been proud of that fact, telling her that a man shouldn't be at the mercy of another man, particularly when it came to goods and money.

She trailed after the men into the great hall. She wondered if she would have released the man or stuck a dagger in his gullet. Her father would have killed him with great relish, denying him the curing potion, very probably taunting him with it until he stuck his sword in his chest.

It was late that day when they released the man. He looked toward Hastings, his eyes bright with gratitude. Had he already forgotten that it had been she who'd brought on his vomiting in the first place?

"I expect an answer from your master on the morrow," Severin said. "If he refuses to exercise his reason, I will kill him and then I will raze his castle."

Graelam said, "Before Severin dispatches Richard de Luci to hell, our lady here will force a potion down his throat that will make him vomit until his head bursts open."

The man paled and nodded. After he rode from Oxborough, they buried Lord Fawke of Trent, Earl of Oxborough, in the plot beside the wife he'd had killed eight years before. Father Carreg spoke the words. The men were silent. Chickens squawked in the background, pigs rutted in the midden, cows mooed from beyond the wall.

Then Father Carreg raised his voice. "I hereby give Lord Fawke's sword to his heir and successor, Lord Severin of Langthorne-Trent, Baron Louges and third Earl of Oxborough."

Severin drew the sword from its sheath. He raised it high over his head as he spoke in a loud, clear voice, "I accept my responsibilities and hold them as dear as I will hold my possessions. I will accept fealty from all my men before the end of summer."

There was loud cheering, not just from the men but from the women as well. She could even hear shrieks from the children. Several dogs barked loudly. The entire inner bailey pulsed with sound and life. And acceptance. Of him.

For the first time, Hastings realized to the very depths of her that her life would never be the same again. Everything had changed. There was no going back. There was a new master. He was her master.

All owed fealty to him now and to him alone. She knew he would travel to her father's three other castles—now his possessions—accepting oaths of fealty, determining which men would act in his stead during his absences. She wondered if any of her father's vassals would object to Severin's rule.

5

SEVERIN PAUSED A MOMENT OUTSIDE THE BEDCHAMBER door. He'd had her father's large bedchamber thoroughly cleaned, surprised even as he'd given the order to Dame Agnes that Hastings hadn't already seen to it. Regardless, he did not doubt that her women had told her about the cleaning. But still she hadn't been there awaiting him when he'd left Graelam.

No, she wasn't there and it enraged him.

His shoulder hurt, but not so much that he wasn't going to take her again, as he knew he must. Mayhap this time she wouldn't call him an animal. Or mayhap she would. He didn't care. He was a man set on his course.

He opened the door and strode into the small chamber, silent, his boots clipping lightly on the bare stone. She was standing in front of the small window, the shutters open, a crisp night breeze blowing in, ruffling her hair. She still wore her gown, a soft green wool with long fitted sleeves, but her hair was free down her back. She had lovely hair, filled with colors, from the palest blond to a dark brown. Rich-looking hair, and soft. Perhaps he would touch her hair tonight, feel its texture in his hands and against his face. He liked a woman's hair, if it was clean and sweet-smelling. He reached out his hand, then dropped it at the stab of pain in his shoulder. He clenched his teeth, focused hard on her, and controlled the damnable pain the way Gwent had taught him when he'd been knifed in the leg by a street bandit in Jerusalem.

She didn't turn though she sensed a presence. "Agnes? I'm glad you have come. I have no wish to go to bed yet. Stay a moment with me and let us share a goblet of the sweet Aquitaine wine Lord Graelam brought."

"I am not Agnes. I passed her on the solar stairs and dismissed her." He was still displeased that the proud old woman had not immediately obeyed him, but had looked at him with doubt and opened her mouth to object. But she'd kept still, wisely, unlike her mistress.

She turned slowly to face him. "Why are you here? What do you want?"

He took another step toward her and smelled the heady scent of some herb he couldn't identify. He said slowly, very precisely, as one would speak to an idiot, "I am your lord. I am your husband. Why are you still here in this maiden's bedchamber? It smells of strange things, all these herbs you collect and grind. You will come to the master's bedchamber. If you please me, if you obey me, I will consider letting you use this room for your herbs."

"Ah," she said, and then she had the gall to shrug. "You forget so quickly that it was my skill with herbs that took care of your wound? I doubt you would be so stupid as to do away with them."

He wanted to strangle her. His hands fisted at his sides. She saw it and he knew that she paled. Good, she should fear him. He wouldn't accept anything from her except gentleness and submissiveness. He'd expected it from the moment he'd wedded her, but it hadn't happened yet. Very well, she would be submissive as of now. Then Trist peered out from his open tunic and reached a paw toward her.

She laughed, waggling her fingers at him. "I have wine. Does Trist like wine?"

His damned marten. He'd forgotten he was sleeping in his tunic. Why must Trist poke his head out of his tunic and make her laugh just when Severin had his boot nearly settled on her neck? He would deal with Trist later. Just how he would deal with him, Severin wasn't certain. He wanted to shove the marten back inside his tunic, but his hand stilled. Trist was making a soft purring sound deep in his throat. It had been nearly three months since they'd been rotting in that dungeon in Rouen. The marten had made no pleasurable sounds since then, until now.

"My marten has never tasted wine." What was happening here? "No, he drinks only ale." Why were they speaking of Trist and wine? He shook his head. "I asked you why you are here. You will answer me and you will do it immediately. You will not try to distract me again."

"I gave it no thought," she said, her eyes still on the marten. The animal, all stretched out, at least ten inches of him hanging down the front of Severin's tunic, gave her courage. "Why would I wish to share a bedchamber with you?"

"I do not care what you wish," he said. "Come with me now, it is time."

Slowly, she shook her head. "Nay. You took me last night. There is no more need, surely. I have no wish to be hurt again."

He cursed and plowed his fingers through his hair. It sent a sharp pain through his shoulder. He ignored it. He would not back down now. "Damn you, I did not want to hurt you! I used the cream. I eased you."

"Your yelling has disturbed Trist." The marten had twisted onto his back and was now looking up at his master's face. He looked ready to fall out of Severin's tunic. "If you do not wish to have wine, I bid you good night, my lord. I have some drying chamomile to see to."

So that was the scent he smelled so strongly. "What do you use chamomile for?"

"For many things, but most desire it when their head aches after they've drunk too much ale." She started to take a step toward him, then stopped. "Also, you should be in your bed. Are you not weak? You must give your shoulder time to heal. It is not too late for a fever to come upon you."

She turned away from him, back to the open window. Very gently, while her back was turned to him, he lifted Trist from his tunic and laid him on her bed. Ah, it freed him.

He strode to her and grabbed her shoulders. He jerked her around to face him, ignoring the pain in his shoulder. He was pleased to see her pallor. She was wary of him, at least part of the time. It was a good beginning. It probably meant also that her father had punished her when she had deserved it. He was twice the size of her father. She should tread warily around him.

Her courage came from seeing Trist hanging off his neck, and he knew his marten had charmed her, and because of his charm had bestowed upon his master an easiness that didn't fit him at all, at least with regard to her, his damned wife. But this misapprehension on her part would pass, he would see to it.

He shook her for good measure. "Listen to me, wife. You will come with me now. I will take you again and again until you are with child. It must be done. Understand, it gives me no pleasure, save a man's quick release for his lust. I must do it. It is my duty to my line."

He raised his hand to the neck of her gown.

"Don't rip my clothes."

"Then do as I tell you now."

Her pallor changed to a dull red. That dull red seemed to climb to her hairline. What was going on here? "You are no longer a maiden. Why are you flushing? I have already seen you naked, Hastings. I've seen you with your legs sprawled wide apart, my seed and your blood on your white flesh. It makes no matter to me. All women are the same. All have breasts and a belly and a passage for a man's sex. You are nothing out of the ordinary. You have no reason to be embarrassed, if that is what you are."

Her eyes fell. She hated him, hated him desperately. She said very quietly, "Let me go. Stop shaking me. Stop yelling at me."

He drew a deep breath and said in a low voice, "Then

obey me or I will tear your gown off you and take you here against this tapestry.''

"You cannot," she said, her eyes on his boots. "You cannot," she repeated when his hands tightened on her upper arms.

"I can do anything to you that I wish to. That you are an heiress makes no difference. You are nothing more than what I choose to make you. Very well, I won't rip your gown. I have no wish to listen to your woman's plaints." He reached down and gripped the hem of her gown and pulled it up.

She shrieked.

He was so surprised he let her gown drop. "Saint Andrew's teeth, what is the matter with you?''

She tried to back away from him but couldn't move. He had her pressed against the tapestry her grandmother had woven more than thirty years before, a grand hunt with beautifully gowned ladies looking on. She flattened her palms against his chest. "You cannot, Severin, you cannot. Oh, I wish you would leave or fall in a heap with a fever. You have the feelings of a damned toad."

What was this? She was railing at him? Where was that lovely pallor of hers that showed him clearly that she was afraid of him? What was this nonsense about feelings?

"Of course I have feelings and not those of a toad. When that knife drove into my shoulder, think you not that I felt it?''

"I don't mean those kinds of feelings. I mean that you don't care what I feel. You don't care if I'm upset or frightened or angry."

"I do care, sometimes. It's just that a man doesn't have time to dwell upon such things. Believe me, I've remarked upon it every time you look at me pale with fright. It shows proper respect, aye, a good thing for a wife to feel for her lord and husband."

She had never doubted his feelings on that, yet she couldn't prevent her incredulous stare or the shock in her voice. "Are you a brute? Do you like to hurt those with less strength than you have? You like it that I fear you?''

She had said quite a lot, and all of it annoyed him. How dare she question him? Make him sound like a mindless brutal savage? On the other hand, a woman who feared a man perhaps could do him in. That woman could put one of her noxious herbs in his ale and make him retch up his guts. He had seen her do it. "Sometimes it is right for you to stand in awe of me."

"Leave me, Severin. You anger me now. Go away."

"You will never give me orders. Now, you will cease your insults." He reached down to grab the hem of her gown.

She yelled, "It is my monthly flux."

He straightened stiff as a bow. Her monthly flux? "What lie is this?"

She shook her head, her forehead touching his chest because she still wouldn't look at him. "I don't lie. You cannot touch me."

"The good Lord give me patience. It matters not to me if you bleed. You will bathe me after I take you."

She looked up at him now, her face pale and set. "If you force me, if you humiliate me, I will never forgive you."

"You already swore that you wouldn't forgive me. Do you forget your promises of last night?"

"This is more. This is humiliation and I will not bear it Leave me be, Severin."

"Does your belly cramp?"

"What do you know of that?"

"Damn you, do you think me ignorant?"

"I did not believe men knew of such things and if they did, they didn't admit to it because they find it distasteful. Men do not want that sort of knowledge about women. They do not care in any case. I have no belly cramps this time."

"I do not find you distasteful. Come with me. I would bed you. Whenever I wish to bed you, you will come willingly and arrange yourself the way I wish it." He was ready to sling her over his shoulder when he felt Trist's claws dig into his leg. He looked down to see the marten climb up his leg, skim as light as a feather over his wounded shoulder, and settle himself near his neck. He was mewling loudly. He was rubbing his whiskers against Severin's cheek.

Severin cursed. "This goes beyond what I will stand," he said, but he made no move to pull the marten from his shoulder. He looked down at her. Slowly, he released her arms. "Your arms will be bruised. Do you have a potion for that?"

She nodded.

"Good. This is why you believe I have the feelings of a toad? I didn't comprehend quickly enough that you bled? I didn't care if you bled while I took you?" He shrugged. "You're right. A man doesn't care about that. Why should he? A woman's blood comes naturally from her body, it makes no difference. I told you before, it isn't distasteful. If that is what worries you, it shouldn't."

"Worry has nothing to do with it. It would just be horrible."

"You have no knowledge of that." He turned on his heel and strode away from her, adding over his shoulder, "You were a virgin until last night. You are the ignorant one here."

"You mean you have been with a woman who was having her monthly flux?"

"Certainly. There is sometimes no choice." He shrugged, sending a remarkable shaft of pain through his shoulder. He felt a groan deep in his throat and managed to swallow it. Pain was lancing through his shoulder, trying to twist him in upon himself, but he wouldn't let it. He wondered if he would even be able to take her now. Aye, better to wait. Tomorrow night, when he had more energy, when his shoulder wasn't hurting like the Devil's own tail, when he had enough lust to stiffen his rod, then he'd take her. He couldn't imagine trying and failing in such an effort. He would give himself tonight; he was not giving her a reprieve. He turned on his heel and left without another word.

She stood there, staring at the closed door, wondering at

this man. She knew, deep down, that he would not have hestiated to humiliate her had the marten not climbed his leg to stare him down. She would prepare a special pork dish for Trist on the morrow. She knew that martens never ate all their food, but stored some away for lean times. She prayed she would never find a mess of rotted pork in some corner of the keep.

She wondered how badly his shoulder hurt him. She hoped it would hurt him a good deal during the night.

It was Graelam who awoke her when the sun was breaking over the horizon.

"Hastings, you must hurry. Severin has the fever."

She merely nodded and rose. She had wished it on him but now, with the reality of it, she was afraid. She walked quickly to the wooden chest with its myriad drawers, each exquisitely sketched with the herb that was within. She said over her shoulder, "I will make an infusion of gentian." She picked up a handful of a dark brown herb from one of the drawers and rose. "Go downstairs and have Margaret— she assists MacDear as much as he allows anyone to—boil some water. I'll be along quickly enough."

He nodded and left her bedchamber.

When Hastings came into the large bedchamber some minutes later, her old bedrobe wrapped around her shift, she paused, unable not to smile. The marten was seated on the pillow next to Severin's head, his paw outstretched as if he would stroke his master's face. He looked profoundly worried. He looked over at her and mewled softly in his throat.

"Don't worry, Trist, your master will be all right. I truly believe he is too spiteful to sicken more." At least she hoped he wouldn't. If he died, she couldn't begin to imagine what Graelam and the king would do. They'd probably deliver her up to a man more offensive than Severin. At least Severin was young and comely. "I've brewed it to the count of two hundred. Now I will strain it and he will drink it whilst it is hot."

Graelam held Severin's head as she slowly poured the

liquid into his mouth. He was raging with fever, so hot that he'd flung the covers away from him, and the single blanket came only to his belly. He was quite naked.

She sat down beside him and continued the slow business of getting the potion down his throat.

When at least he'd drunk all of it, she said, "Now we must wipe him down with cold water. The Healer taught me that last year when one of the men-at-arms was ill."

"Did he survive?"

She shook her head. "No, he was too ill of other things as well as the fever."

Hastings wrung out the cold cloths and handed them to Graelam. When Graelam started to push the blanket to his feet, she said, "No, it is not necessary."

"He's big," Graelam said after nearly an hour, standing up to stretch his back.

"Aye, nearly as big as you are. I hope for the sake of your wife that you never become fevered. Now, let me look at his wound." She unwound the bandage. "This man is amazing. Look at the pink flesh. I have never seen such speed of healing." She took dried bramble blossoms and laid them on the wound, then wrapped it again.

"Then why did he get the fever?"

"I don't know. I don't think anyone knows why it strikes some and not others. Mayhap it is his foul humor. He was very angry with me last night. He came to my chamber and made threats. Mayhap he'll believe I cursed him and the result is the fever. Aye, I like the sound of that."

"What do you mean he came to your chamber? He said naught to me of going to you again and we played chess in here until well after midnight."

"Ah," she said, and nothing more.

"You're turning red, Hastings. What happened? What were his threats? Was he rough with you? Did he hurt you?"

"I think he wanted to but he didn't. He left me alone after he raged at me. Aye, his own nastiness brought on the fever."

The marten mewled, lifting its paw toward them.

Severin was shivering now, the burning heat turning into a wasteland of cold, freezing him from the inside. He felt the weight of blankets, so many of them, and they were but pressing him deeper into himself, into that frigid wasteland. He hated the weight of them but he didn't have the strength to throw them off. He heard a strange noise, it was close, too close. He realized then that it was his own teeth chattering. He hated this, the helplessness, this endless Devil's cold, but there was naught he could do because his mind spun away, leaving him awash in the misery and with no ability to control it.

Suddenly, he felt a spurt of warmth and turned his face into it. Trist was curled next to his head, his fur thick and soft, but he didn't feel heavy, not like all those deadening blankets. His thoughts returned as the cold slowly lessened. He heard her voice and knew she was close. He felt her hands on him, easing the weight of the blankets off his shoulder. He didn't want her hands on him. He didn't want her to know that the blankets were grinding him into frozen pulp, making the pain in his shoulder unendurable. He didn't want her to see him helpless.

"He's quiet at last," he heard Hastings say as she and Graelam stood over him. "That's a good sign."

"If he gets the fever again, I just might let him drown in his own sweat. I would rather fight the infidel than wipe down his big body again."

She laughed. "Do you know," she said after a moment, "it is said that when a mandrake is uprooted it shrieks and will bring death to the one who has destroyed it. The Healer told me always to have a dog do the uprooting."

Graelam smiled. "I will tell Kassia the tale. Mayhap she will believe it. She has a streak of witchiness in her. Aye, she just might believe it. You have put me off long enough. Did Severin hurt you last night?"

Severin wished he had the strength to snort. Hurt her? Of course he hadn't hurt her. He'd shaken her, naturally, she'd deserved that. St. Peter's thumbs, he was the one who was hurt, couldn't Graelam see that?

"Nay, Graelam, he didn't hurt me, not really, but know

that he doesn't like me, truly. He believes me an encum-
brance, nothing more. I am part of this prize of his, very
likely the only part he doesn't want. He is a warrior, ruthless and hard. He wants to treat me like a possession—he
probably sees me as less desirable than his bathtub over
there. That bathtub does what it is supposed to do. That is
what he expects of me. I'm to be humble as that damned
bathtub, do his bidding without question or argument, and
do it without thought. He is very angry with me. Do you
think he will kill me once he has secured my father's possessions?''

So she believed him a murderer of women as well as an
animal? He cherished evil thoughts before the pain in his
shoulder made his mind go blank.

"Don't be foolish, Hastings. You are tired. You are not
thinking correctly. Severin won't kill you, but I fear that
you will not mind your tongue when he angers you with
his orders and commands. And you are right, of course.
Severin hasn't known much easiness or softness in his short
life. But he is a man to trust."

"Trust, you say? Well, we will see about that. At least
he won't be giving any orders today."

His mind came back into his body when she spoke those
words. As soon as he had the strength he would give her
more orders than her feeble brain could take in. And it
would be today. If it killed him he would give her all those
orders today. Was it still today?

"Now, I need to give him more gentian mixed with a
bit of poppy, then he will sleep for many hours."

He didn't want to sleep through the day. He wanted to
think about what he'd heard. Graelam had said he was a
man to be trusted. Naturally he was. He was a man of
honor. She doubted even that. Perhaps he wasn't a model
of the minstrel's songs of the chivalrous knight. He was a
man and a warrior and he would rule his possessions. She
was one of them. But, damn her, she could trust him. Kill
her? Mayhap he would want to thrash her, but not kill her.

He wanted to tell her so, he wanted to give her at least
one order, but he simply had not the will to open his eyes

and tell her that he resented her speaking so plainly to Graelam. Graelam wasn't her husband. He wished Graelam
would tell her that he, Severin, didn't have the feelings of
a toad.

There was something else. Aye, he wanted to tell her
that he could mend himself without her damned potions.
He did not want to have to show her gratitude, not that he
had any intention of doing so in any case. But the goblet
was at his lips and he felt her fingers prying open his
mouth. He had not the strength to fight her.

When it was done, when Hastings was satisfied that he
would rest easily, Graelam called for Severin's man Gwent
to stay close to him. Gwent was a giant of a man, larger
even than Lord Graelam. There was a wide space between
his front teeth and a very deep dimple on his chin. He had
large hands, a rough tongue, and, she saw, a gentle manner
with both Severin and Trist. But what relieved her mind
was that the marten liked him. That satisfied her.

"I will bring you some ale and bread, Gwent, and Trist,
well, I will find something to interest him."

"The little lordling likes eggs that are lightly boiled, not
firm on the inside, just very hot, the yellow and the white
a bit clingy. Once the yolk was too hard and Trist spit on
the back of my hand. I thought I should warn you. But the
marten is not spoiled, not really, and it amuses Severin to
please him."

Little lordling indeed, she thought. "You've been with
Lord Severin long, Gwent?"

"Since he was a lad of seventeen, just arrived in the Holy
Land. He saved my life in a Saracen ambush. My master
had been killed. I swore fealty to him on that day. Aye, I
have never known boredom with Severin."

Of course Gwent hadn't ever known boredom, Severin
thought, feeling as though his brains were as sand trickling
through a sieve, except for those hideous weeks in the dungeon in Rouen. Why was she asking Gwent all these questions? When he was himself again, he would see that she
kept her woman's curiosity to herself. He wanted to tell her
that Gwent would protect her while he was still lying flat

on his back, but why should he bother to tell her anything? No, he thought, he would remain as silent as the night. He breathed deeply, feeling the inexorable blankness seep into his brain.

Hastings wished she could stay and ask him to tell her of every happening in his master's life since his seventeenth year, but she couldn't. It was late. The servants needed instruction. She needed to speak with MacDear the cook, a brawny Scotsman who had a special way with roasted capon and honeyed almonds. His use of spices rivaled her own knowledge of them.

She leaned down and lightly touched her fingers to Severin's cheek, felt the coolness, and left him with Gwent. He was sleeping deeply now. He would live.

# 6

"I KNOW," SEVERIN SAID TO GRAELAM. "YOU MUST LEAVE. You and your men grow restless."

"I will leave on the morrow when I am convinced you will have the fever no more. Hastings has told me you won't, but she isn't always right. I must visit Edward in London to tell him that all has gone well."

"I hope that whoreson Richard de Luci rides away from Oxborough."

Graelam said as he smoothed on his gauntlets, "The man you spared will tell him the Oxborough heiress is both wedded and bedded, that is certain. There is nothing for him here. I worry only that he might try to assassinate you, for he is a mangy coward, so greedy it is said he dug the gems from his father's sword handle before he allowed him to be buried. Northbert told me he'd heard it said that de Luci poisoned his wife but that she didn't die speedily enough, thus he was late getting to Oxborough before your wedding to Hastings. It was also said that de Luci would have gladly assisted his wife to a quicker end but the priest stood by her bedside throughout her ordeal."

"He should be dispatched to hell, Graelam. When I am back to my full strength, I will do it. Do you know that

Hastings made Trist an egg that was boiled just until it was congealed on the inside?''

"How do you know that?''

"He brought it to show me. She had cracked the top of the egg so he could easily shuck it aside. He ate it on my chest. He even let it cool a bit so it wouldn't burn me.''

Graelam was still laughing when Hastings came into the bedchamber, carrying a tray on her arms. Severin saw her smile at Graelam, a full, easy smile, a lovely smile that showed straight white teeth. Then she looked at him. Her smile fell away as she neared the bed. He didn't care if she ever smiled at him, damn her. She would fulfill her role— the one he would assign her as soon as he was on his feet again—and that was all he wanted from her.

She said nothing, merely set the tray down on the bed beside him, then leaned down and gently laid her palm on his forehead. He brought up his hand and wrapped his fingers around her wrist.

"I am not fevered.''

"No,'' she said, withdrawing from him even though she did not move a finger, "I can see that you are not.''

"Damn you, do not treat me like a puking old man who has not the wit to gainsay you.''

She straightened. He released her hand. "I have brought you food. MacDear is the Oxborough cook. He is excellent. He has prepared you barley broth. You will eat the broth, if it pleases you to do so. If you do not wish to eat it, why then, throw it into the rushes. My lord Graelam, Northbert wishes to speak to you.''

Graelam stared at the two of them. Hastings, that confiding girl he'd known for years, warm and laughing, always humming and singing, rarely showing fear because her father usually ignored her. He'd struck her only in moments he lacked control. Perhaps it would have been better had Fawke thrashed her more often, even threatened to beat her as he had his wife. Then she would treat Severin with more deference. She would tread more warily around him. Now she was dignified as a matron and stiff as Severin's onyx-handled sword. She didn't look like she'd even bend in a strong wind, much less bend to a man's will, much less a husband's will.

But no, Graelam thought, he didn't want her to be any different. He prayed that Severin would not hurt her. Perhaps he would mention it to him, tell him privately that to strike his wife just might kill her and then who would see to his comfort and to his meals? Who then would bear his children?

Graelam wondered, as he met Northbert, his master-at-arms, in the inner bailey below, what Severin had done to her the previous evening. The tension coming from her was like the swirling cold winter winds coming off the North Sea. Yet she had not hesitated to save Severin's life when de Luci's man had tried to stab him in the back, nor had she hesitated to attend him, not leaving him until he slept.

He doubted he would ever understand the workings of a woman's mind. Not that it mattered, not since his own wife adored him, not minding his bad habits, not berating him when he was testy or sore from bruises he'd gained on the practice field. Ah, but she would leap upon a stool so she could yell in his face when he was an oaf. He realized he was grinning fatuously, seeing her as she kissed his mouth whilst he held their babe, stroking the soft black hair—his black hair—whilst Kassia cooed at both of them.

He listened, at first unable to believe what Northbert told him. He rubbed his hands together. He thought of Severin, then shook his head. No, he would deal with this. It would be his last act here at Oxborough. He felt his blood stir. Aye, he wanted to do this. It wasn't a duty, it was a pleasure, making his blood stir.

Hastings watched Graelam ride out with Northbert and his dozen men not long thereafter. He had not come back into the keep. That meant Severin had no idea that he had left.

She ate some soft goat cheese and some warm bread fresh from MacDear's oven. She sipped at her milk, watching two of her women clean down the trestle tables. She knew she would have to return to Severin to see if he was continuing to mend, if the fever stayed away from him. He had to be still asleep. She would work first in her herb garden.

She knelt first to weed the Canterbury bells and the lupines, both blooming wildly. One tall pink lupine was leaning over the hyssop planted at the far edge of her herb garden. She sat back on her heels, wondering what to do. No need to think about it really. She pinched off the tall spike and tossed it over her shoulder. She needed the hyssop and the savory that grew beside it. Both needed sun and a lot of air.

She hummed as she worked, as she always did. She felt calm flowing into her. She plucked off a good dozen ripe strawberries to grind up. They were excellent for whitening teeth.

It was midafternoon before Graelam rode back through the giant gates of Oxborough, past the thick curtain outer walls to the heavy iron portcullis of the inner wall that the porter had to raise since it had been locked down from the moment of the attack on Severin. He and his men rode into the inner bailey, chickens, goats, pigs, dogs scurrying from the path of the destriers' hooves. Children of all ages grouped together watching the twelve warriors.

It was Severin who met Graelam on the deeply hollowed stone steps leading into the great hall. Graelam saw him immediately, standing on those steps garbed all in gray as was his habit, looking strong and fit and very angry. He couldn't yet be all that fit. Graelam had left him sleeping. Hastings could not have agreed to allow him to leave his bed, not that Severin would listen to anyone when he had made up his mind about something.

Graelam wasn't fooled by his stillness, that was just a part of him that baffled his enemies. No, Severin was going to want to bring his mace down on his head, particularly once he heard what Graelam had done.

His hands were on his hips. He didn't realize that Hastings was standing behind him. Graelam met her eyes and smiled.

"You left without telling me anything," Severin said, that deep voice of his soft and low. "You left me filled with the drug she poured down my throat. I do not know what you have done, but I know it is something I won't like. I am not pleased, Graelam.''

Graelam grinned and slapped him on his unwounded shoulder. ''Come inside and I will fill your ears to over-flowing. Hastings, can my men have ale? Also there are some wounds for you to see to, if you do not mind.''

Severin turned to see her standing there, the early summer breeze ruffling the hair around her face. ''See to Lord Graelam's men. Fetch them ale. Graelam and I will have the Aquitaine wine if you and Dame Agnes have not drunk it all. Ah, yes, I will see to Graelam.''

''You will not hurt Graelam,'' she said.

Severin looked as if he'd spit at her. But Graelam laughed. ''See you, Severin, I have a protectress. Harm me not.''

''Go, mistress,'' Severin said to his wife, and turned on his heel. She hoped his shoulder hurt.

She called out to Northbert.

''Keep your sword sheathed, Severin,'' Graelam said easily as he wiped his hand across his mouth. ''Else I might call upon your wife to protect me. Nay, don't growl. This is excellent wine I brought you. Kassia's father lives in Brittany, you know. He has vineyards in Aquitaine.''

''Graelam, whatever you did I know I will not like it. But I am ready. Tell me, what did you do?''

''The man you sent back to Richard de Luci, well, he was grateful to you for not torturing him—''

''Not torturing him? Christ's bones, Hastings made him puke up his toes. He wanted to die. He was a pathetic scrap. All he did when he wasn't puking was lie there on his side, his knees drawn up to his chin, moaning.''

''Aye, but then he was well again and his body was intact. No broken bones, no bashed head, no cracked ribs. As I say, he was grateful to you. He believed you would slay him after he told you what you wanted to know, but you didn't. You sent him back to his master.

''It was Richard de Luci who nearly killed him since he had failed to dispatch you. But the man—Osbert is his name—he survived. When he had the strength, he came here, asking for you. When he heard that you were still abed, he asked for me. In short, Severin, I have done my best by you. You have one less enemy now.''

Severin felt the blood pound in his temples. "No, you would not do this to me, would you, Graelam? Tell me you did not kill that damned whoreson. You did, didn't you? You dared to kill my enemy. He wasn't your enemy, Graelam, he was mine, and yet you had the gall to kill him. And you said nothing to me about it. Nothing, Graelam, you bastard.''

Hastings heard Graelam laugh. She saw the fury on Severin's face. She knew he was enraged even though his voice was low and steady and he did not move. Her father had always yelled his head off when he was angry, always. It gave everyone time to run because right after he yelled, he struck. But not Severin. Would he strike?

Northbert had told her what had happened. Men, she thought, were they born wanting to hack and maim and destroy? Well, mayhap it was wise to destroy Richard de Luci. She eased closer. Severin was red in the face, the pulse in his throat pounding so furiously she could see it, but that was all.

"He is dead, his holding is without a master, and he has a daughter, I am told, who is now his heir. There are no sons.''

Severin said, as he clutched the wine goblet so hard his fingers showed white, "You were wounded. There is a binding around your arm.''

"Aye, but 'tis nothing. I imagine Hastings has already seen to my men. I lost no men, but four were wounded.'' Graelam leaned back in Hastings's chair, drank down the rest of his wine, wiped his mouth, and grinned hugely. "Ah, it was good. We ambushed the whoreson with the information Osbert gave us. They were eating their dinner. There were naught but twenty of them. We took the guards, then the rest was easy.'' Graelam rubbed his hands together. "Aye, it was good to exercise my arm. Bloodletting always clears a man's brain and makes him forget any pains he has.''

Severin rose, calmly and slowly, took the end of the trestle table in his large hands, and upended it, sending it crashing into the silver laver that stood close by. The laver sent scented water flying on the sleeping wolfhound, Edgar, whose eyes flew open. He leapt up, growling, ready to tear out an enemy's throat.

"Enough, Severin, enough! Hold your temper. I do not want you to destroy the keep.''

Severin turned to see his wife of two days on her knees, picking up the laver, that thick hair of hers cascading over her shoulder nearly to the rushes. She looked up at him even as she cradled the damned laver against her chest. "You have dented the silver. It belonged to my grandmother. I prized it. I polished it, I—''

He cursed long and loud, then shouted, something Graelam had never heard him do, "Shut your mouth, Hastings! This has nothing to do with you. Fetch my sword. I will gullet this mangy villain, this villain I believed my friend.'' The wolfhound growled. Servants and men-at-arms were standing silent along the walls, wondering what would happen, wondering if they should do anything.

"Why?'' she said, rising to her feet, righting the laver. "Because he acted without your lofty permission? Because he knew you would demand to fight and he feared you would become fevered again? Tell me, my lord, why are you angry? Are you not an intelligent man, a reasonable man?''

He was on her in an instant, his hands under her armpits, lifting her and shaking her. "You will hold your tongue else I will take you right here on this trestle table and that damned wolfhound can smell your blood and howl.''

She turned whiter than the soft bread she had eaten to break her fast. He shook her yet again.

"Let her down, Severin.'' Graelam's hand came down on his shoulder, his wounded shoulder, and squeezed. "Let her down. What mean you? Would you shame her here in the great hall amidst her people? Would you wound her so that she bled? Is that what is in your mind?''

Hastings couldn't bear it. She would kill him. She went completely limp. The wound in Severin's shoulder ripped pain through him at shaking her, that and the weight of Graelam's hand on his shoulder. He lowered her slowly to the rush-covered stone floor.

She looked up at him, her eyes nearly black with rage. She kicked him as hard as she could in the shin. He sucked in his breath, jerking back, leaning down to scrub his hand over his shin. "You will pay for that, madam," he said between teeth gritted so tightly she barely understood him.

She knew she probably would pay, she just didn't know him well enough to judge the manner of payment. She turned on her heel and ran from the great hall.

"Severin, you will sit down now and you will close your eyes and think about your shoulder and your shin. She could have kicked you in your groin but she didn't. She spared you."

"She didn't kick me in the groin because she knew I'd kill her if she had. Besides, I move quickly, I would have turned away from her knees in time."

"Possibly, but Hastings is fast." Graelam sighed. "You know you wouldn't have killed her. I doubt you would have raised your fist to her, would you?"

Severin brushed his palm over his hair. He was tired. His shoulder hurt. Damn her, he had feelings. He was not a toad. "I would have made her believe that I would have crushed her beneath her herb garden. Sometimes she does believe that. However, as each day passes, she grows more brazen, more bold. And it has only been two days. What will she do when a fortnight has passed? I will not tolerate it, Graelam."

"You are weaving where you stand. Sit you down, aye, that's it. Now drink the wine. It will calm your ire. I wonder if I fell into rages as do you when I had six fewer years to my life?" Graelam paused a moment, then nodded. "Aye, I believe that I did act the outraged fool. And that was only three years ago. My dear wife left me, I was such a bastard to her."

"Kassia left you?"

He had gained Severin's full attention. Now was the time to deliver his small moral. The younger man was staring at him as if he'd found a snail in his broth. "Kassia? She truly left you? I do not believe that."

"Aye. I had to go to her father's keep, Belleterre, in Brittany, to fetch her home."

"Did you thrash her?"

Graelam smiled and shook his head. "Nay, I begged her to forgive me. If I had ever struck her, why, it would have killed her. Certainly you know that you cannot strike a woman, Severin. A woman is slight, weak, helpless. Nay, Severin, tell me you have never struck a woman."

"Damnation, Graelam, this is all nonsense. You are weaving a fine tale. I believe you not. No, I have never struck a woman. All I have known have obeyed me without hesitation, without question. But now I am married and what I fully expected I did not get. My wife is ordered by God to obey me. She ignored God's will. Will I discipline her? Aye, I doubt that not. The how of it, however, I have not yet decided on that as yet."

That was something, Graelam thought.

"What am I to do now that you have taken my manhood and hunted down de Luci yourself?"

"You will take your men to Sedgewick Castle and put Sir Alan in charge. He is a good knight, a fair man, and more than that, you can trust him. He can be your castellan until the king decides what is to be done with de Luci's daughter and his property. I would also suggest that you remove the girl child and bring her here. Hastings can look after her. I think that King Edward might make you her guardian, to protect her from greedy men, just as you married Hastings to protect her. On the other hand, the king might well appoint himself as her guardian and send his own man to control Sedgewick."

"Aye, it depends on the wealth of the property. The king is no fool. Did you kill Richard de Luci yourself?"

"Actually, he slipped on a pile of rabbit bones and fell, striking his head against the rock upon which he'd been resting. He died right there. We left some of his men alive to see to him and the others that we killed.''

"I would not have let him slip on a rabbit bone. I would have fought him, knife to knife, and I would have slid it into his belly.''

Graelam just smiled. "I suppose these things happen and we must swallow our wounded vanity and be relieved that we are alive to tell the tale of our dead enemy. Think you, Severin, do you believe this Richard de Luci is pleased to be in hell, dispatched by a rabbit bone and a rock rather than fighting to the death with an equal?''

There was no hope for it. Severin grinned. Then he laughed. He righted the fallen trestle table. He looked up to see the servants talking again, not in whispers now, not since they heard his laugh. Edgar snored again on the hearth, his huge head resting on his folded paws, paws the size of bowls. The silver laver was dented. He frowned at it. She said it had belonged to her grandmother. It was old and now it was dented. He would ask the armorer if he could pound out the dents.

His shin hurt.

Yet he laughed until Graelam said, all sober and cold behind him, "You lied to me, didn't you? You wouldn't have really forced her here in the great hall? You wouldn't have really hurt her so that she bled?''

"No," Severin said, and turned on his heel. He said over his shoulder, "It was the only threat I could think of that would bring her to heel. I would not have wounded her. The blood is hers. It is her monthly flux.''

"Ah. Your threat to bring her to heel. It worked. I had wondered why she fled. How is your shin?''

HASTINGS DIDN'T TOUCH THE LITTLE GIRL, JUST CROUCHED down in front of her. "What is your name?"

The child just stared up at her, pale as a bolt of undyed cotton, her blue eyes wide and unblinking.

"My name is Hastings. Come, what is yours?"

The child's lashes fluttered. "My name is Eloise," she whispered, her eyes on Hastings's neck, no higher.

"A lovely name, much nicer than mine, but Hastings is a good name, the name of the firstborn girl in my family since Lord William's famous battle."

"I know about that," Eloise said. "Mama said that Lord William was sent by God to redeem the savage Saxons."

Hastings had never before heard that particular opinion on God's use of William. Her knees hurt. She rose and held out her hand to the little girl. "Would you like a cup of milk? Gilbert the goat has blessed us today. And you can taste some of MacDear's almond buns. They're quite delicious, you know."

The thin little girl with large blue eyes just stared up at Hastings and slowly shook her head. Her skinny brown braids didn't move. "My mama said gluttony was a special sin."

St. Osbert's elbows, what was this? "I won't let you eat

more than just one of MacDear's almond buns. No, just a small bite of one, all right?''

The child looked very worried. She tugged on her ugly, faded green wool gown that was several inches too short on her, showing small scuffed slippers and baggy woolen stockings that had been mended many times. ''I can't ask my mama if it is all right. She went to Heaven.''

''Aye, I know, and I am sorry, Eloise. I don't think she would think just one almond bun would be gluttony.''

''Aye, your mama would quickly pronounce it gluttony, and you know it, Eloise. I'll thank you, my lady, not to tempt the child.''

Hastings turned to the older woman who wore a very ugly black gown, her black hair pulled back in a severe knot at the back of her head. Her face was severe, a black mustache on her upper lip, her expression cold. She gave the woman a look she would give to a servant who had spoken out of turn. ''You are?'' One of her eyebrows arched up. That was always a good effect, one her mother had taught her so many years before.

The woman fidgeted. That was a good sign. She fidgeted some more, saying finally, ''My name is Beale, my lady. I am Eloise's nurse and was Lady Joan's nurse as well.''

''Then you will go with Dame Agnes. She will show you Eloise's chamber. It is small, but no matter, so is Eloise. As for you, Beale, you will sleep with the other female servants.'' She nodded and turned back to the child. ''Come, Eloise, let us look at MacDear's almond buns.''

She heard the woman Beale suck in her breath. She waited, but the woman held her tongue.

Severin came into the great hall some minutes later to see Hastings seated at a trestle table, the girl child seated beside her, staring at an untouched bun. Her fingers seemed to crawl toward the tray then stop and back up. The child was pale and skinny. Severin frowned. She was a child, she should be stuffing those buns into her mouth.

He'd left Sir Alan, his own man, and a good dozen of Trent's men-at-arms at Sedgewick Castle. No. He had to remind himself that they were his men now, every last one of them. They'd all sworn fealty to him the day he'd wedded Hastings. Three days ago.

He'd had his men bring the child and her nurse back here to Oxborough.

"Let her eat, Hastings," he said, striding up. The little girl's fingers fell away and she seemed to shrink in on herself. Very slowly, as if hoping Severin wouldn't notice her, she slid off the bench and crawled under the trestle table.

"Eloise, what are you doing?"

There was no sound from Eloise.

Hastings frowned at Severin. "How very odd. At first she was frightened of me but at least she didn't crawl under the table. Did you perhaps yell and rant when you were at Sedgewick?"

"Of course not. There was no need. Everyone was glad to see me after they realized I wasn't going to butcher all of them. Besides, I don't frighten women and children."

"Ha. Nay, don't yell at me, you'll just scare her more." Hastings got off the bench and went down on her hands and knees. The child had wrapped herself in a tight ball, pressed against the far leg of the table.

"It's all right, Eloise. Come, Severin is very big but he is also very nice. He won't hurt you."

The child seemed to tuck herself into an even smaller ball.

Hastings looked up over her shoulder to see Severin, standing there, looking baffled and impatient. Then Trist slithered out of his tunic and jumped onto the table. He smelled the buns, then backed away.

"He doesn't like sweet buns like that," Severin said.

"Eloise, would you like to meet Trist? He isn't a man, he's a marten."

The child lifted her head. "What is a marten?"

"He is an animal, long and furry and very soft. He likes to eat eggs that are boiled just enough so that the insides are clingy."

Slowly, the child inched out from under the trestle table. Severin had sat himself down so as not to frighten her. He was eating an almond bun. Trist was sprawled out next to his hand, his head on his front paws.

"That is Trist. He belongs to Severin. Isn't he beautiful?"

The child stared at the marten. As if he knew he was being watched, Trist cocked an eye open and looked at the child.

"Does he eat almond buns?"

"Nay, he does not," Severin said, as he reached for another one. "But he would like to see you eat one. He just said that you didn't eat your breakfast."

The little girl blinked and took a step back, bumping into Hastings's knees. Hastings lightly laid her hand on the little girl's shoulder. "Eloise, this is Lord Severin. He is my husband and the master of Oxborough. He will protect you. You are not to be afraid of him."

"My father hit me."

"Severin isn't your father. He will see that no one will ever hit you again, I swear it to you. Severin will swear it as well as soon as he has swallowed the last of his bun."

"I swear it, Eloise. You will remain here at Oxborough until King Edward decides where you will live. My lady will look after you."

"She is very young," Eloise said, staring hard at Trist. "Beale said she was too young to know anything at all about children." Trist stretched out his full length, which was nearly a foot and a half. Then he stretched out his paws. He looked at the little girl. She said in a whisper, "Beale won't like it. She won't like any of it."

"Beale has no say in it," Hastings said. "I was a little girl like you not at all long ago. I'll wager that Beale can't even remember when she was a little girl."

"Is she that sour-faced old woman dressed in black with the black hair on her lip?" Severin asked.

"Aye," Hastings said shortly. "Here, Eloise, try a bit of the bun."

But the child backed away. Even Trist at his most charming didn't move her now. Hastings could feel her retreating even though she was standing very still now.

"I cannot. Beale is right. Mama will look down from Heaven and curse me."

So be it, Hastings thought. She said matter-of-factly, "Then what would you like to eat? Surely your mama would not want you to starve."

"Bread and water. That's what Beale said I should eat."

"Why?"

The child hung her head. She twisted her foot about in the rushes. "Because I am not good."

Hastings looked at Severin. He was staring hard at the little girl. She saw he would speak and shook her head. She smiled at Eloise. "Very well, I shall have Alice fetch you some bread. But the milk is better than water, particularly Gilbert the goat's milk. After you drink the milk you will feel very virtuous. I remember Father Carreg told me that."

Eloise blinked up at her.

Trist mewled. He stretched out a paw toward the child.

But Eloise didn't move. She swallowed. "You are right. Trist is very beautiful. My mama said that beauty was sinful."

"Trist is not beautiful," Severin said. "He's an ugly varmint." He rose. The marten looked up at him, stretched again, and leapt gracefully onto his arm, scurried up to his shoulder, and wrapped his thick tail around Severin's neck.

Severin said to Hastings, "I know not what has been done to the child but I do know that Richard de Luci was an animal. You will fix it, Hastings."

He nodded to the little girl and strode from the great hall, Trist's tail swinging around his neck.

"Ah, here is your bread." Hastings added, "Eloise, this is Alice. She is very virtuous. You will like her."

Alice enjoyed the men-at-arms, and surely that must hold virtue for she made them smile and sigh.

Hastings waited with Eloise until she had eaten a thick slice of MacDear's bread smeared with butter and thick honey. She thought to leave her and work in her herb garden, but she chanced to see the woman Beale standing in the shadow of the solar stairs. No, she wouldn't leave the child to that horrible creature.

She held out her hand. "Come, Eloise, Lord Graelam is going to leave. I wish to say good-bye to him."

Very slowly, faltering, Eloise finally put her small hand into Hastings's.

Graelam looked down at the little girl, drew off his gauntlet, and laid his huge hand beside her cheek. "You will be a good girl. Hastings will take care of you. When you are older, perhaps you can come to visit me in Cornwall."

Hastings watched this with a smile.

She also noticed that Eloise was too terrified to move. She stood there, her eyes wide with ill-disguised fright on the warrior who was leaning over her. It was as if Graelam noticed it as well. He sighed, smiled, patted Eloise, and straightened.

He said quietly to Hastings, "Her father brutalized her. Her mother evidently treated her like she was the spawn of the Devil, which she is, I suppose, but it isn't her fault. Several of the servants told me Lady Joan had the child on her knees for hours every day before her prie-dieu. The Sedgewick people are glad their master is dead. I could see very little mourning for Lady Joan either. Did her husband poison her so he could kidnap and wed you? There is no doubt. But that is all in the past now. I don't think Sir Alan will have any difficulty with any of the servants or the men-at-arms. Severin probably told you that there were several cheers when the people realized he was to be in charge. Even some of the farmers were cheering. Richard de Luci was a despicable man."

Severin said as he strode up to them, "I have tried to find where they buried Richard de Luci. No one could or would tell me."

"That seems odd," Hastings said. "Since the Sedgewick people had no love for him, why would they not tell you? Why would they care?"

Severin shrugged. He looked down at the little girl who was, in truth, a scraggly little crumb. When she grew up he imagined she would be the kind of heiress a man would have to take to wife to gain her holdings. Unlike Hastings.

He frowned at that. "You will send me a message when the king decides what to do with the child?"

Graelam nodded. He hugged Hastings, saying against her temple, "Be patient, Hastings. He is young. You will help him become as he should be."

"And what would that be, my lord?"

"A man who cherishes his wife, a man who looks upon her and sees peace and love and lust."

She tried to laugh, but it caught in her throat. "You speak of yourself, Graelam. This is very different. I am not Kassia, and Severin is nothing like you."

"I see similarities. At least between Severin and me. As I said, be patient. You might consider holding your tongue on occasion, just to surprise him and throw him off guard. For the most part, a man needs a woman's sharp tongue. It keeps him in good form."

This time she did laugh. She hugged him. She didn't want him to leave. Graelam was known to her, loved by her, and now he would leave and it could be years before she saw him again. She felt tears swim in her eyes. "God go with you, Graelam."

"Aye, God and my man Northbert."

Hastings, holding Eloise's hand, watched Graelam and his men ride out of the inner bailey, Severin and several of his men riding with them.

"It is time for her prayers."

Hastings turned slowly to face the woman Beale. "What did you say?"

"It is time for Eloise's prayers. She must pray for three hours before she can eat her evening bread. It is what her mother wanted. Come, Eloise."

The child was leaning one way and then the other. It took Hastings but a moment to figure out what was wrong. "First, Beale, Eloise must visit the jakes."

It was in the jakes that Hastings saw the raw sores on the child's knees.

"Hold still, Eloise. This won't hurt. Indeed, it will make your knees feel cool." Very carefully, Hastings laid the soaked bramble blossoms on Eloise's raw knees. She hadn't felt such anger in a very long time. Well, she had, but this was a very different anger from the sort she felt at Severin. She wanted to hurt someone. She wanted to hurt the child's dead mother. How could a mother do such a thing to her child? Severin had said it—Lady Joan believed her own daughter to be the Devil's spawn.

Eloise didn't make a sound. Hastings wrapped her knees with strips of soft white wool. "There, you will be doing no praying on your knees for a good long time. Try not to bend your knees so that the bandages will stay tight."

"But I must pray. My mama said I would go to hell if I didn't purify myself each day."

"What did your mama say when she saw your knees?"

The child hung her head. "She didn't know. I never told her. She wanted me to pray, she wanted it so much."

"Beale must have seen them when she helped you to dress and bathe."

Eloise just nodded, her face still down. "Beale told me it was God's punishment because my heart had black spots on it, black spots from my wicked father."

Hastings turned at the sound of her chamber door opening. Beale was standing there, peering into the room. "The child must be at her prayers, my lady. I have come to get her. We will be in the chapel."

Hastings slowly rose. "I don't think so, Beale. I have seen Eloise's knees. I have treated them. They will heal but she will do no kneeling for a very long time."

"You have no say in this, my lady." Beale came closer. The black mustache on her upper lip quivered. "I am the child's nurse. It is I who must see to her soul now that her mama is dead, poisoned by that devil. Eloise carries his blood and his foulness. She will be cleansed. It matters not if her knees are a bit scraped."

Hastings turned to see Eloise standing tall and straight beside her. "I will come with you, Beale. I don't want Mama to suffer if I am wicked."

"Your mama is in Heaven," Hastings said. "She suffers no more." She turned again to Beale, who was looking at the child as if she would beat her. "No, Eloise, you will stay with me. I will teach you about herbs. You will learn how to use them to help people. Beale, have you ever considered that Eloise is Lady Joan's child, that she has the goodness of her mother and not her father, that she has no need for all this purification?"

"She looks like him, just like him, with those sly blue eyes and a tongue that twists with lies. She must be purified or she will become like him, evil and remorseless. She will die and none will mourn her."

That did it. Hastings said even as her hands fisted in the folds of her gown, "I have decided that you will no longer tend to Eloise. I will see that you are returned to Sedgewick."

"You cannot do that, lady! Your lord said I would see to her as I always have. He will see that you do not go against me. All know that he had to marry you, that he had no choice in the matter. He will protect me."

Would Severin turn Eloise back to this wretched woman? If he even considered it, she would simply have to talk him out of it. "You will leave tomorrow morning, Beale. Your very presence offends me. You will have no more sway over Eloise. God doesn't wish for children to be tortured."

"God allowed my sweet lady to die in agony God allowed her swine of a husband to murder her."

"That is quite enough." Hastings turned to Eloise. "Listen to me, here is Dame Agnes. I wish you to go with her. She will show you my flowers and my herb garden. You can meet Gilbert the goat. You can help feed the chickens. She will show you the armory and you will meet Giles. He will make you a bow and arrows. I will teach you to shoot."

Dame Agnes didn't wait. She strode like a conquering warrior into Hastings's chamber, took Eloise's hand, and led her out. The child was clearly uncertain. She looked up at Beale. The woman said, "If you do any of these godless things, you will burn in hell, Eloise. Your mama will see to it. God will show you no mercy, for He will listen to your mama. God will listen to me. God always listens to me.''

Hastings waited until she heard Dame Agnes' and Eloise's footfalls on the solar stairs. She then walked to the woman and slapped her hard, making her head snap to the side. She grabbed her skinny neck between her hands. ''Listen to me, Beale. You are the wicked one here. You will never speak to Eloise again. Go now to your chamber and ready your clothes. You will leave early on the morrow.''

''Your lord will not allow this,'' Beale said, Hastings's handprint stark on her cheek. She was panting, not from the blow, Hastings was certain, but from rage. ''You will pay dearly for this, lady. All men are the same. When he hears ill of you, he will believe it, and he will strike you down. I could see it in his face. Even though he is young, he is debauched and hard. He will grow harder and more brutal as he gains years. You will learn that you have no power. You will learn that you cannot treat me as you have. You are young and foolish. You will die young and foolish.''

''I suppose you will see that I die?''

''God gives us tools to help ourselves. I will see that you pay.''

Hastings wanted to strike her again but she didn't. Beale was the first person she'd ever hit in her life. No, she remembered poking Tim the blacksmith's son in the arm when she'd been all of ten years old and grown so quickly. He'd called her a maypole.

''Get away from me, Beale, before I vomit. Stay out of my sight until you leave in the morning. Aye, I will watch you leave to make certain it is done.''

After Beale had finally left the bedchamber, her venom still hanging in the still air, Hastings replaced the bramble blossoms in their marked drawer. She ground hyssop and savory. She worked slowly, careful not to spill any of the precious herbs. She began humming. Time seemed to slow and the very air around her seemed to become softer and warmer. She calmed.

She worked until the door opened and Severin looked in. He looked healthy, strong, his face and arms darkened by the bright sun. He was dressed all in gray, as was his habit. For the first time she saw him as a man, a young man in his prime, his body as solid as the keep walls. He was not at all displeasing to look at. She remembered that first time she saw him, the utter fear she'd felt when he'd stood in that bright shaft of light, large and mysterious, hidden, really, perhaps not really a man, but the Devil's messenger.

She smiled at him.

He stopped short, staring at her as if she were a stranger. He looked down at her neat piles of ground herbs and frowned.

Her smile fell away. No, he wasn't like Graelam and she wasn't a bit like his Kassia. She was herself and it was obvious she didn't please her husband. "How is your shoulder?"

As he walked toward her she noticed a tear in the sleeve of his gray tunic. He merely shrugged, saying, "It is sore but healing well. You saw it yourself this morning. What is happening, Hastings? That sour woman Beale with her black mustache accosted me and accused you of interfering in the child's religious lessons. She said she was the only one to take care of Eloise, that Eloise's mother had placed the child in her hands."

"I wish you could have seen the child's knees, Severin. They were raw from all the hours she'd been forced to kneel on the stone floor to pray. You're right. I interfered. I gave Eloise over to Dame Agnes, who will begin to teach her about how to run a household. She will also teach her to play, perhaps even to smile eventually. I told Beale that she was leaving on the morrow."

"She said you struck her."

"Aye, I did. I slapped her as hard as I could and I did take her scrawny neck between my hands. I wanted to strangle her and I wanted to hit her again, I really did, but I managed to gain control. She is a frightening woman, Severin. I cannot trust her around Eloise."

To her immense relief, Severin nodded. "I have two men going to Sedgewick on the morrow. They will escort her back."

"Thank you."

He paused a moment, looking down at the row of wooden drawers. "I remember my mother picked daisies at the full moon, crushed them, mixed them in some kind of oil, and laid them on her face. I remember that my father just laughed and told her that her freckles wouldn't fade. But you know, I remember that they did."

"Were the daisies white?"

"I do not remember the color. How much longer do you bleed, Hastings?"

How quickly she had become used to his frank speech. "Four more days." A day longer than she'd known him. A day longer than she'd been wedded to him.

"My shoulder is nearly healed now. I do not like waiting. It isn't wise."

"Richard de Luci is dead. Who else is there to fear? I am your wife and no one can possibly know that you aren't with me ten times a day."

He laughed at that. "Your ignorance is piteous. You claim to be a healer, yet you know nothing about men. A man can't take a woman that many times in a single day. Four times, perhaps five, if the woman is sufficiently skilled and enthusiastic. Beauty helps as well to stir a man's passions."

She was shaking her head. "Nay," she said. "Nay, it would be too great a punishment. Five times?" She actually shuddered. "Even you would not force me that many times." She saw him over her, felt him shoving into her, felt the grinding pain. No, it wasn't possible.

"If five times is too many in your ignorant mind, then why were you braying about ten times?"

Her hands fluttered and fell to her sides. It was difficult to face him. "I don't know. It was just a number I lifted from the air. I meant nothing by it, not really. I just said it. Besides, even five times would not be possible for you."

"Now you insult my manhood." He took a step toward her.

She said quickly, taking a step back, "Nay, I mean no insult to you. The insult is to myself. I have no skill, no enthusiasm, and I am not beautiful. You said that I was very ordinary."

He did not like this quickness in her. This logic. He said with natural perversity, "I will teach you to be skilled. You are not ordinary. I said that simply because I did not want you to believe that since you are an heiress what beauty you possess places you above me."

She'd never believed there was a vain bone in her body. She said, "You think I am beautiful?"

# 8

SEVERIN STARED AT HER A MOMENT. "NAY," HE SAID slowly, wondering what was in her mind, "I would not extend myself that far, but you are comely for a wife. All know that wives are not meant to be anything above the ordinary. If they happen to be heiresses, as you are, then it is a joyous thing if they don't have rabbit teeth, no more than one chin, and no hair sprouting off their lips like the woman Beale. In this, you have pleased me. It is not painful to look upon you. But still it doesn't matter. Wives are not made for a man's pleasure. They are made to bear a man's children."

"Lord Graelam loves his wife. He believes her beautiful. I believe he feels a great deal of lust for her. He told me that he missed her and their sons."

"I do not understand why Graelam has fallen into this snare. I have met his wife. She is small, her smile is sweet, yet she jests with him and he smiles. She adores him. Perhaps it is this worship she has for him that has softened him toward her. Aye, that must be it."

"That is ridiculous. You are ridiculous."

He stared at her mouth. She knew he must be wondering how this mouth of hers could say such things to him. She wondered as well. She didn't know him, she wasn't stupid, and thus she took a quick step back.

"Aye, you'd best keep your distance, Hastings. I dare say that Kassia never spoke thusly to Graelam. None of this matters. I have told you how things will be between us. I will not tell you again. I will give you your four days, Hastings, then you will not leave my bed until I tell you that you may. You will bear a child in nine months. You will do it. I will not hear you say nay."

"But becoming with child isn't at all certain, Severin. Even I know that. There are women who never bear a child. Something is either lacking in them or in their husbands. No one knows what makes this happen, but you cannot be certain that we will be lucky."

"You will become quickly with child. I know it."

"How can you know that? Have you sired many bastards? Nay, that isn't possible. You are too young."

He laughed. "A man can impregnate a woman each time he spills his seed in her. Years have naught to do with anything. But no, I haven't sired many bastards. None here in England, but in the Holy Land, aye. All the women who came to me were skilled in preventing conception. Regardless, three of them became with child."

There was stark pride in his voice. It amazed her. "What did you do about your children?"

"None of them survived. I was sorry for it. Two were sons. But there is all the proof I need. My seed is potent. Your belly will swell by the fall. Don't argue further with me. You will have your four days." He paused a moment, staring toward her herb drawers. "You will use nothing to prevent conceiving my child, Hastings."

She could but stare at him. "I would have no idea how to even if I wished it. Do you think I have no honor, Severin?"

"You are a woman. Naturally you have no honor. Such a notion is beyond you."

"Then why did I save your life? Why did I shove you out of the way of the assassin's knife?"

He knew he was being unfair, but he didn't care. He'd

had to wed with her to gain enough wealth to bring Lang-thorne back. He had sworn to protect her from vermin like de Luci. What else could she expect from him? He said sharply, "You didn't shove hard enough, did you?"

"Next time I will not shove at all."

"There will not be a next time. Very well, you showed bravery, I will grant you that. And you healed me, but in all other things you haven't pleased me. I ask not that much of you. See to the keep. See to the child. See to my shoulder. Obey me. There is nothing else for you to do."

She actually smiled up at him. "And what will you do, Severin?"

"I? Whenever your woman's perversity keeps you from me, I will take Alice to relieve my lust. She is comely and enjoys men. I have remarked several comely women here in the keep. They will see to me."

Without thought, with all her strength, Hastings threw the three-legged stool at him. It struck his belly, hard. He winced. She saw it and it pleased her until he was striding toward her and then she ducked around him. But she wasn't fast enough. He grabbed her arm and jerked her back to him. He grabbed her other arm and shook her hard. He lifted her off her feet and brought her nose to nose. "You dare?" His breath was of the sweet ale MacDear made for the men.

She prayed that Trist would poke his head out of Sev-erin's tunic. That was why she'd thrown the stool low. She'd been afraid she would hit the marten.

Trist wasn't with his master.

He shook her again.

"You struck me. You struck your husband, your master. You threw that stool at me. I would kill a man for a lesser assault."

Even though she was afraid, she heard the outrage in his voice. He simply could not believe what she had done. He shook her again.

"You will not shame me," she said, knowing well that he could kill her with but a single blow from his fist. In the next instant it would matter, but in this instant it didn't.

"I am your wife, that is true, thus you will not take any of my servants to your bed. That is your responsibility to me. Just ask Father Carreg."

"You think I cannot do precisely as I wish? You believe I am somehow bound to you and only you? That is lunacy. If you do not become properly submissive, then after you bear me my son and heir, I will have you confined as a madwoman should be." He released her and pushed her back. He streaked his large hand through his dark hair. He cursed. "I did not come here to argue with you, yet within a very few moments, you throw a stool at me and I am shaking you as I would the branch of an apple tree. Perhaps I will let the Beale woman remain at Oxborough. Perhaps I will let her guard you. What say you to that?"

Hastings was rubbing her arms. They were bruised from the previous night. They ached. She looked at him, seeing the anger in him, but more than that, she saw confusion writ on his face. "What do I say to that," she repeated slowly. "If you do what you threaten, then I will mix allium with felwort. I believe that the two together, slipped into your wine, will make your bowels so watery you will have to sleep in the bailey."

He turned on his heel and left her, slamming the door behind him.

Actually, she had no idea what to mix with what to make a man's bowels watery. She knew how to stop it though—ground borage mixed with rose petals, violets, and anchusa.

She wondered as she returned to her herbs how Severin would look in a tunic that wasn't gray. Perhaps a light blue. She would gather some purple stock. Aye, it made a wonderful pale blue dye.

MacDear cooked an egg and pork stew for Trist that evening. Hastings saw many of her people looking at that stew, wanting it at least as much as they wanted the chunks of beef that floated in a rich brown gravy. There were peas fresh from the Oxborough garden, onions that were fat and sweet, and a brace of partridges for the lord.

Eloise sat beside Hastings, looking at the food but making no move toward it. Hastings served small portions of everything on the brightly shined pewter plate. She smiled at the child. "I have prayed, Eloise, with Father Carreg. He told me that God wants to see His children well fed and thus you must eat to please God."

As a lie it would serve, but not for all that long. Hastings had already spoken to Father Carreg, a man who surely loved God and loved a well-baked pheasant as well. It would take time. She looked down to a trestle table where Beale sat, her head bent. Suddenly, the woman raised her head and stared at Hastings. Hastings drew back, her back pressed against her chair. The look of pure malice made her tighten all over.

"What is wrong?"

Hastings just shook her head. The woman would be gone early the next morning. She would forget Beale's venom in time. She said, "MacDear bakes the pheasant in special herbs. He will not tell me the recipe. I always try to guess and he will tell me mayhap if I am right, but he will just shake his big head when I am wrong. He tells me I am ignorant and must keep studying before I learn what he knows. I have known him all my life. I remember how he would let me help him knead bread in the bread trough. I sunk nearly to the top of my arms in that dough."

This, Severin thought, as he cut off a chunk of the partridge with his knife and slipped it into his mouth, must be how a husband came to know about his wife. He didn't mind her speaking of things of this nature to him. He found himself picturing her as a small child but only for a moment. He said, "It is very good. I taste basil, do I not?"

"Aye, and fennel. There is also a goodly amount of salt, and that is what makes it so tasty. We have always been lucky at Oxborough. My father loved salt and thus was willing to buy it even when it was in short supply and the price very high. I once went without hair ribbons so he could buy salt."

Aye, he thought, as he ate the peas, he would have no difficulty with this husband business. He turned to watch Hastings as she coaxed another bite of peas into Eloise's mouth. The child was fidgeting. She kept looking down the trestle tables. He followed her vision and saw the woman Beale. He tore away a chunk of bread and chewed on it as he watched her. She looked up then and he was smitten by the longing in the woman's eyes. At that moment, Severin could not imagine Hastings striking her. Surely she had been overly harsh. The woman looked very alone and sad. Perhaps he should allow her to remain at Oxborough. Perhaps Hastings would come to deal well with her.

He would speak to Hastings about it. No, he would tell her what would happen once he had made the decision. He said to Hastings, "We will continue to buy salt, no matter how high the price."

"Very good, my lord."

He wondered briefly if she laughed at him, but no, that wasn't possible. He nodded and turned to Gwent, who sat on his right. He'd taken the steward's place, and the man, Torric by name, looked as sour as the woman Beale. He wasn't old enough to look so pinched, his mouth so seamless and tight. Even his shoulders were stooped forward. As for the rest of the Oxborough people, they were less wary of him now. They behaved as people did in most large keeps. There was laughter, arguing, shouting, children leaning against their parents' sides, already asleep, dogs chasing bones tossed to them, fighting with each other, growling and leaping about.

He felt good. He was the master here. He finally belonged. His line would follow, even though he had to share her name. Langthorne-Trent, Baron Louges, Earl of Oxborough. Ah, that was his and his alone. He leaned back in the former earl's elegantly carved chair with the Oxborough crest beautifully etched into its back. A lion stood tall on its back legs, its claws sunk deep into a griffin. Behind was a bower of roses, blossoming wildly, and he could tell that the lion would return to that bower once he'd killed his prey. The motto carved beneath the crest was *EN AVANT.* Forward.

He turned as Gwent said, "The steward was not pleased when I told him that you were learned, that you read and ciphered. His eyes shifted to and fro when I told him. I fancy he mayhap has lined his pockets with pilfered gains.''

"I will see to it on the morrow. If the man has cheated, I will find it out and kill him. I will let you punish him first, Gwent. I know well your hatred of thieves. Keep him under your eyes tonight so that he has not the chance to change his records.''

"Aye, I will keep close to the mangy little squirrel.''

Severin didn't long remain in the great hall after Hastings had taken Eloise's hand and led her up the solar stairs, just long enough to drink another goblet of Graelam's Aquitaine wine, just enough time so she could see to the child's needs and put her to bed.

He yawned hugely, aware that his men were looking at him, grins on their ugly faces, knowing that he would bed his new bride. They would be drunk on laughter were they to know that he wasn't bedding her because of her monthly flux. Let them believe that he was plowing her belly. He'd been soft with her. He should not have allowed her to dictate what he did. She might be an heiress but she still belonged to him. Aye, he'd been as weak as a puking timid lad.

She wasn't in his bedchamber, not that he'd expected her to be there. No, she would be in her own chamber and he would have to order her to come to his.

When he came into her bedchamber, holding a lighted candle high so he could see her, Hastings was pressed hard against the mattress of her narrow bed, the covers drawn to her chin, staring at him.

"No, give me no arguments. You will accustom yourself to being with me, to lying next to me in bed, to hearing me breathe in sleep. When I take you, it will be as nothing. You will not even care that I look at you. Aye, Hastings, you will accustom yourself.'' He strode to the bed, picked up her bedrobe, and said, "Stand up.''

She didn't want to but she knew she had no choice. She pushed back the covers and swung her legs over the side of the bed. Her shift slid up her thighs. She grabbed the bedrobe from him and wrapped it tightly around her. She'd known he would come. Aye, she'd known.

"Come," he said, and held out his hand. It was a large hand, long blunt fingers, darkened from the sun, the backs covered with black hairs.

She pictured Eloise finally slipping her small hand into her own and smiled. She thrust out her hand, felt his enclose hers, and walked beside him to the large bedchamber. He did not ask her to remove her shift, just the bedrobe. She had never before slept with another person, not even her mother when she'd been a little girl. It felt strange. At least the bed was large, the covers sweet-smelling since Dame Agnes had had the servants wash them in lavender water after her father's death.

He did not touch her. She lay stiffly on her back. Suddenly she felt soft fur against her check and she smiled.

"Good night, Trist," she said. The marten rubbed his whiskers against her chin. She laughed.

Severin cursed. "I am surprised that Trist is here. He was missing for two hours today. I believe he prepares to return to the woods to mate."

"He did not eat much for dinner. Perhaps he hunted in the forest and fed himself."

"I have told him that he may stay within the keep walls. I have told him that I mind not feeding him, but he does not attend me. He is like you. I don't like it."

Trist mewled louder.

"When you spoke to him, Severin, did he answer you back?"

"Don't mock me, woman. Trist understands me well enough. Just listen to him. His sounds are louder than a soldier's snoring. His—"

Suddenly the door was thrown and Gwent burst into the chamber. "My lord! The woman Beale, she has the child. She is at the gates, swearing she will kill her if Alart doesn't allow her to leave."

"Saint Peter's teeth," Severin said. "This is idiocy. I will be there in a moment. Distract her, Gwent. Don't let her harm the child. Go!"

He was naked, prowling the chamber, gathering his clothes, but Hastings didn't notice. She grabbed her bed-robe, flinging it on even as she dashed past Gwent.

"Hastings, damn you, come back here."

She paid him no heed, just sped down the solar stairs, the indented stone hard and cold beneath her bare feet. Servants and men-at-arms were milling about in the great hall. She ran through the great doors to the keep and into the inner bailey. Gilbert the goat looked up, an ancient discarded gauntlet in his mouth. A chicken, disturbed from its sleep, raised its head and squawked. A horse snorted. The moon was high.

She stopped short, breathing hard, about twenty feet from the portcullis. She saw Alart gesticulating wildly at the woman Beale. She heard him saying, "I cannot, woman. I cannot let you leave without the lord's permission. He would kill me if I did. Where is the master?"

Hastings heard Severin close behind her. She didn't know how she knew it was him, but she was certain. She turned. His feet were bare, as were hers.

"Saint Egbert's elbows, I don't believe this. Look, she has a knife at the child's throat. Don't move, Hastings, you'll just make things worse."

"How could I make things worse? What can you do that I cannot?" She turned as she spoke, but he had already eased past her and appeared as only a dark shadow against the bright moonlight. Then Gwent appeared beside her and he called out, "Beale, I have spoken to the master. He will be here soon. He will allow you to leave. Do nothing that would displease him else you will regret it."

"What am I to do?" Alart shouted.

"Hold to your place," Gwent said. "The master will be here soon. He is clothing himself. The rest of you men, stay back. Make no move toward the woman."

It was as if they had planned this, but Hastings knew they hadn't had the time. No, they had done this before. Severin was now within twenty feet of Beale. He was as soundless as the night itself, blending into the shadows as would a specter made of spun darkness. Gwent turned to her and said low, "Speak to her, distract her." Hastings called out, "Beale, listen to me. I was wrong. It is true that you belong with Eloise. Listen to me. Bring the child back into the keep and you and I will speak of this."

"Stay away, you lying bitch!"

Hastings lurched back at the venom in the woman's voice. "Don't hurt Eloise, Beale. Hurt me instead. You want to, do you not? What if I come to you? What if I agree to do whatever you wish?"

"You lie! I will kill you later. I will make you suffer just as Richard de Luci made his poor wife suffer. Aye, for two days she was in agony, and he watched, furious because we wouldn't leave her alone and let him finish killing her. Aye, I will make you regret that you tried to take my place, that you corrupted the child—"

Severin's left arm went around Beale's neck, his right hand squeezed the knife from her fingers. His grip tightened. She didn't make a sound. She went limp. Eloise flew toward Hastings, great sobs tearing from her throat.

Severin eased his hold. To his astonishment, the woman's bony elbow shot back into his belly. He didn't release her, but it hurt. Had she hit him lower, he would be rolling on the ground, holding his groin.

He tightened his hold and heard her gurgle deep in her throat. If he kept the pressure for just a few more moments, she would be dead. He cursed, released her, and shoved her away from him hard. She went sprawling to her knees on the cobblestones. Her dark hair hung loose on either side of her head to the ground.

"Gwent, come take the woman to the barracks. Lock her away until she returns in the morning to Sedgewick. Sir Alan can be responsible for her then."

Gwent picked up Beale beneath her arms. She shrieked at Hastings as Gwent hauled her toward the barracks, "You'll go to hell just as Eloise will, my proud lady. Aye, both of you will die. Both of you will return to the Devil."

Gwent slapped his hand over the woman's mouth. She kicked him, but his hold didn't loosen. He just dragged her faster.

Hastings was holding Eloise against her side watching Severin stride toward her. His legs were bare. He was wearing only his tunic.

"Is the child all right?"

"Aye, but she's frightened. As am I."

To Hastings's surprise, Severin went down onto his knees. He lightly touched Eloise's shoulder. The child slowly turned to face him. "I am sorry, Eloise. Had I believed she was as mad as my own mother surely is, I would not have left you alone. I promised you that no one would ever hurt you again. Because I was careless, someone did. Forgive me."

The child just stared at him, frozen in fear. Then, slowly, she stretched out her arm and lightly touched her fingertips to Severin's cheek.

"You saved me," she whispered, choking down tears as she spoke. "I forgive you."

Severin said nothing, just smiled at her. He didn't move until finally she dropped her arm. "Will you let me carry you back to your bedchamber? Nay, I have a better idea. You will sleep with me and Hastings. I have found that it is not good to be alone after a nightmare, and this was surely a nightmare."

And thus it was that Hastings spent her third married night in her husband's bed, Eloise, daughter of Richard de Luci, between them, Trist on Severin's pillow, his tail fluffing against Eloise's cheek.

# 9

"NOW, ELOISE, ALLIUM IS ALSO CALLED LILY LEEK. IT'S said that it kept Ulysses from being turned into a pig during his travels."

"Who is Ulysses?"

"He was a man who took many years to return to his home. He lived many hundreds of years ago and had more adventures than many men ever have in three lifetimes."

"Was he a sinner?"

Had this been the only point in the child's life? "Well, actually, he lived long before people worshipped our God."

Eloise didn't understand that at all. Hastings was smart enough to keep her mouth shut. She gently clipped off columbine, saying, "If you ever have a sore throat, I will grind this up and mix it with just a bit of hot water. You will be shouting about within a day."

"You know so much," Eloise said. "I do not know anything. I'm glad Beale is gone. But I'm afraid too, Hastings."

"She will not be allowed into the bailey if she returns. Alart knows her and he will keep her out. Besides, how could she return here?"

"God would fly her here on clouds."

"I don't believe God thinks too highly of Beale, Eloise.

Now, here's Dame Agnes. She told me that today you would learn about making bread from MacDear. What do you think of that?"

"MacDear is very big."

"Aye, but you are not to fear him. He likes children. You will see. Go now and I will see you later."

Hastings watched the child walk away with Dame Agnes. She'd been here four days now, and it seemed to Hastings that her step lagged a bit less, that she took a person's hand more quickly than before. She still did not eat enough, but she was improving, so Hastings held her peace.

Tonight, she thought. All thoughts of Eloise fell from her mind. Tonight Severin would come to her. She wasn't afraid, but she did wonder what would happen, if it would hurt as badly as it had the first time. Severin had looked at her some hours before as she sat at the trestle table breaking her fast. He'd said, "I have not forgotten, Hastings, and neither have you. I can see it in your eyes."

"Do you believe my eyes are as ordinary as the rest of me?"

"Do not test my temper. I have told you that you are less ordinary than many ladies, particularly heiresses. Nay, your eyes are a nice green, at least when you are smiling. When you are mocking me, they turn quite dark and ugly."

Could that possibly be true?

"Your eyes, Severin, they become darker than the inside of one of MacDear's cooking pots, as dark as a moonless night, regardless of your temper or mood."

"That is enough, Hastings. My eyes are a simple blue, not a Moorish black. I wish a good meal to sustain me. Then I will see to my duty."

A duty. She was naught but a duty. It was disheartening. She had watched him stride from the great hall, drawing on his gauntlets as he walked. Trist was nowhere to be seen.

Well, he would get an excellent meal. Hastings rose and wiped the dirt off her hands. She went to the kitchen to see MacDear. It was a large chamber attached to the keep. It was always hot, what with the fireplace and the three ovens billowing out their heat into the room. Allen, one of

MacDear's helpers, was taking fruit pies out of the oven. Nan was chopping herbs from the garden to make sauces for the beef and pheasant. A joint of beef was on a spit, turned by Hugh to cook evenly. MacDear was bellowing and sweating, as always, no matter the season, no matter how hot or cold it was outside.

She heard MacDear suddenly laugh his big, booming laugh and saw that Eloise was smiling. Excellent.

"Is this saffron I taste, MacDear?"

She lifted a spoon again to taste the stock from a roasted capon. It was thickening nicely.

"You think it is, Hastings?"

"Aye. I know, next you will say that mayhap I am right. You vex me, MacDear. Ah, Eloise, you are learning to separate the egg yolks and whites. You are doing it well."

"Allen, you miserable whelp, you nearly dropped that peach pie. By Saint Thomas's nose, I'll clout you, boy!"

Eloise turned as colorless as the egg whites she had separated into a wooden bowl. Allen just tossed MacDear a cocky grin, but he was watching more closely now. He was shoveling ashes out of the open oven so he could put in more pies.

"Ah, little one," MacDear said before Hastings could open her mouth, "don't fear that I'll clout you. It is just the spittle cock boys who need threats and roaring, never lovely little peahens like you."

"Aye," Hastings said, coming to stand beside Eloise. "MacDear never even yelled at me when I was young. He waited until I gained my adult years. Don't fear him, ever. I see you are making barley bread. I spent hours mixing the dough, Eloise. MacDear is a stern taskmaster. I will leave you now. The smells make me so hungry I would eat my dinner now were I to remain."

She met Severin when she went into the great hall. It was already filled with men-at-arms, squires, servants, children, and four wolfhounds, Edgar, the leader of the four, chasing a stick a little boy threw for him. The noise was deafening. Everything was normal. She smiled. It was difficult to believe her father had died but a week ago.

She tried to mourn him, she truly did, and she did say prayers for him, but in her heart there was little regret, for in his life he'd never paid her any heed, never showed her any particular fondness, clouted her when the mood struck him or, more likely, when the ale wasn't to his liking.

She said to Severin even as she grabbed up her skirts when Edgar the wolfhound bolted toward her intent on the stick that had landed just beside her, "Eloise is with MacDear in the kitchen. He is showing her how to make barley bread. Are you hungry, my lord?"

He looked down at her. "Aye, mayhap I am. You have not yet attended me in my bath. Will you do so?"

She'd seen him naked for the past three nights. "Aye, if that is your wish."

"Go to our bedchamber and await me." He turned away from her then to speak to Gwent. Hastings went to her bedchamber. No, now it was their bedchamber. She called Alice to fetch her bathwater. She waited, and waited more. She turned to the bed and saw a lump beneath the covers near Severin's pillow. She lifted the covers and pulled out the jar of cream he'd used that first night. He'd remembered. He had thought about it and decided not to take any chances that he would hurt her again. Perhaps, she thought, as she replaced the cream, he did care, a bit. Mayhap it would be nice, this mating.

She waited some more, but still he didn't come. She shrugged and climbed into the wooden tub herself. She was lathering herself with sweet lavender when he strode into the room. She stopped in mid-lather and stared at him.

He walked to stand over her. "When you are finished, I will bathe. You will wash my back."

"I waited for you but you did not come."

"Do you wish me to wash you?"

"Oh no, I can manage it well enough."

"What is that smell? It is nice."

"Lavender. The Romans brought lavender with them when they invaded Britain many hundred years ago. I believe it comes from the Latin *lavare* that means to wash."

"Where did you learn that?"

"I am not ignorant, Severin. It is from *Leech Book of Bald*, written some two hundred years ago. I have also read *The Physicians of Myddfai*. If you will leave me now, I will finish and then fetch you."

He just shook his head, walked to the bed, and sat down. He began unwrapping his cross garters. She washed her hair and rinsed herself as best she could. The drying cloths were on a stool three feet from the tub. She looked at him, now pulling his tunic over his head, at the cloths, and quickly climbed out of the tub. She had just wrapped the cloth around her when she heard a low laugh.

"You move quickly, Hastings. I like your legs. They are long and smooth. They will go nicely around my flanks."

"Why would you want my legs there?"

"You will see. I—"

There was a knock on the door.

"Enter."

He frowned at her for speaking so quickly, but said nothing. It was Alice carrying a bucket of hot water, two lads behind her carrying more buckets. Hastings gripped her bedrobe and held it in front of her. The lads, however, just hefted the tub and carried it out to empty it.

"Thank you, Alice," Hastings said, then saw that Alice was looking at Severin, a very soft smile on her face. A smile? Then she remembered. He'd said he would take Alice if Hastings continued to vex him with her monthly flux. She just stood there, watching Alice, a girl but three years older than she, sweet-natured, a good worker, a girl who loved to laugh and jest, a girl who'd explained to Hastings why she was bleeding that first time when Hastings was thirteen years old. Had Alice been with Severin, her husband?

"Alice, come here and help me with my boots. My squire is still on the archery field. I doubt your mistress could make a good job of it."

Hastings didn't say a word, merely watched as Alice walked quickly to Severin, bent over, and grabbed his boot, laughing, even as she backed closer toward Severin, who was looking at her bottom. He reached out his hand, then frowned down at that hand and pulled it back.

But Alice didn't have any reticence. She wiggled, actually wiggled her bottom in his face. She saw Severin staring intently at Alice's bottom. Would he take her right here in front of his wife? His wife whom he was going to bed this very evening? He had never looked at her so intently. He appeared utterly absorbed, the knave.

"You lecherous bastard," she yelled at him. Hastings didn't think, she grabbed up a bucket of hot water and threw it on him. He yelped. Alice jumped away, one of Severin's boots in her hands.

"Hastings, I did not know you were still here. I thought you had gone behind the screen to dress. Why, I—"

"Get out, Alice. I thought you were my friend, yet here you are, wiggling your bottom in Severin's face. He is my husband, Alice. I will not allow that."

Alice looked perplexed. "Aye, Hastings, I know that he is your husband, but he is just a man. What does that have to say to our friendship?"

Severin had his tunic over his head and was wiping himself off with it. His hair was plastered to his head, the bed cover was wet, and there was Trist, his beautiful coat sticking up in wet clumps.

There was murder in Severin's eyes. He rose, tossing his tunic to the floor. He was quite naked.

"Leave us, Alice."

Alice frowned from one to the other. "My lord," she said very softly, her voice gentle as summer raindrops, "my lady does not understand the ways of men. She is possessive. She does not realize that play is nothing more than that—just play. I've seen you smiling at me, looking at me the way a man looks at a woman he wishes to bed. Your man Gwent told me you found me comely and wished to dally. As for my mistress, she—"

"None of that matters. Get out, Alice, else I'll thrash her in front of you."

Alice looked at Hastings, saw her pallor, saw that she had only a drying cloth wrapped around her. Alice had meant no harm, she'd not lied about that. Had Severin asked her, she would have willingly run her hands over his body, enjoying his strength and hardness, probably sat on his lap, easing his sex up into her. Why, they would have laughed and groaned and had a fine time. But now, Hastings had displeased him. By Saint Peter's knees, she'd thrown hot water on him. She had shown jealousy. Alice nearly shuddered. She couldn't imagine such a thing.

Hastings jealous?

Alice knew her duty to her friend. She drew herself up. "I think I had best remain, my lord. If there is punishment to be meted out, then I should receive it, not my lady."

Severin looked at the sweet-faced Alice, whom he'd planned to take during the past four days but had never seemed to find just the right moment, what with Hastings and Eloise and Trist in his bed with him and so much to be done during the days, what with new men-at-arms whose skills he had to measure. She had backed up to stand next to Hastings, her hands on her hips. "Aye, my lord, I cannot allow you to hurt my mistress."

Hastings was staring at her naked husband. She'd seen him naked, but just parts of him, and for brief moments. But here he was, furious at her, standing there, his legs parted, not moving, his hands fisted at his sides. His sex was flaccid in the nest of thick dark hair at his groin. She wished at that moment that time could reverse itself. Just twenty minutes. Of course time remained moving as it always did.

She found her mouth was very dry, still she said, "Alice, you will not try to protect me. This is ridiculous. I did not realize that men and women took each other whenever either wished it. You are right. He is just a man and we have been friends for years. Please leave us now. If he wishes to strike me because I threw water on him, then he will, whether you are here or not. Go, Alice."

Trist shook himself hard, then leapt gracefully off the bed and ran to Hastings. He grabbed the drying cloth and climbed up until he sat upon her bare shoulder. He rubbed his whiskers against her cheek.

"The little lordling will not allow the master to strike

you, Hastings,'' Alice said very quietly. ''All know that the master would do anything for the marten.''

Severin was just standing there, ready to shake Hastings, aye, at least he could shake her, and Alice was trying to protect her, and now his damned marten was trying to protect her. Again. His damned marten whom he'd raised from a scraggly little lump when he'd found him freezing and nearly dead next to the stump of a tree some two years before. It wasn't to be borne.

He strode to Hastings, grabbed her arms, and lifted her to eye level with him. He found himself looking into Trist's eyes as well as Hastings's.

He shook her. Her drying cloth fell off. She squeaked, trying to grab it, but failed.

He shook her again. ''Get out of here, Alice. I think I'll take your sweet mistress right here, right now.''

Alice didn't move.

''Get out!''

Alice knew when a man was serious. The master was very serious. She looked at Hastings, at that marten, whose face was between the master's and Hastings's, and fled.

''Now, let me look at what I have purchased with my honor.''

''Honor? You purchased something? Not here at Oxborough. Your honor didn't purchase you a single chicken. All you did was ride in with your men, marry me, and become the lord.''

''You have angered me beyond my limits, and my limits have stretched more and more with you with each passing day. I will take no more of this from you. No, I will not hurt you, but I will use you so that finally you will come to understand that it is I—not you—who allows you to be what you are. You have no say in anything. No, hold still.''

He dropped her to her feet, then hauled her by the arm to the bed. Both Hastings and Trist went flying back onto their backs. Severin stood at the bedside staring at her. She was sprawled, her legs apart, and he knew immediately that he needed no sermons about his duty to mount her. She was white and very nicely shaped. Her skin glowed with health and youth. He wanted her badly, very badly. She'd thrown water on him. She didn't deserve that he treat her other than as a disobedient wife.

"It is you who have pressed me, Severin." She rolled to her side, bringing the covers over her. "Nay, I do not want you to touch me now. You are angry. You will hurt me."

"Hurt you? Nay, Hastings, I won't hurt you, though you well deserve it." He leaned down and pulled the jar of cream from beneath the covers. "Now, turn on your back and show yourself to me."

She didn't move.

He roared at her, "Pull off those covers."

Instead, she flung the covers at him and rolled to the far side of the bed. He grabbed her ankle and pulled her back. Damn her, she deserved that he hurt her. But he couldn't. He grabbed the jar, dipped his fingers into it, and came down beside her. "If you move, if you fight me now, you will regret it." He shoved his finger into her. She quivered but didn't make a sound. When he came out of her, he found that he had some control. He needed control with her. He looked up and down her body.

"Your breasts are adequate," he said. She didn't move. Neither did Trist. He just mewled loudly, staring at Severin. "Adequate, no more."

Severin touched his hand to her breast. "You adequately fill my hand. You will adequately suckle our sons."

She tried to pull away from him, but he held her down, his leg over her belly. "I do not like this. You do this to punish me. Let me up, Severin. I must go downstairs to see to your evening meal."

"Shut up, Hastings. The cream is inside you. When I come into you, it won't hurt."

His hand moved to her other breast, cupping it, lifting it, squeezing gently. "Aye, adequate." Then he looked down her body. He splayed his hand wide over her belly. "I can barely reach your pelvic bones. Aye, you're made to bear children. At least you have some worth." Without another word, he grabbed her arms, lifted her, and shoved her down onto her stomach. She reared up, but he just pressed his hand against her waist. "Don't move." She felt his hands stroking over her hips. She wasn't afraid of him, hadn't been afraid even when he'd lifted her up and shaken her. When he touched her breasts, she still didn't fear him. His callused fingers scratched at her smooth flesh. It felt odd. But now, he was staring down at her bottom, feeling her. She realized that he was measuring her again to see if she would carry his children. It was too much.

Far too much.

# 10

SHE COULDN'T BEAR IT. SUDDENLY, HIS FINGERS EASED BE-
tween her thighs. He touched her woman's flesh. She reared
up, sending Trist to scurry down her back and up Severin's
arm.

"Don't fight me, Hastings."

He pulled her onto her back again, bent her knees, and
opened them. "Now," he said, staring down at her.
"Now." Without another word he came into her fast and
deep.

She felt the fullness of him, felt herself stretching, but
the cream made her slick and it didn't hurt. She felt him
deep and hard inside her. She closed her eyes, seeing him.
She wondered what he felt when he pushed into her, when
he moved inward, then pulled out again.

She said, "What are you feeling when you do this to
me?"

Severin's eyes opened. He stared down at her even as he
moved, for he couldn't stop himself, couldn't bear the
thought of stopping. "It is beyond words," he said, his
voice hoarse and raw, deep in his throat.

Trist mewled loudly. But Severin didn't stop. His eyes
closed again. He felt her womb. He shuddered. But he
rested there only for a moment. She wasn't moving. He

wished she would. He wished in those moments that she would wrap her legs around his flanks. But of course she wouldn't. She was just lying there whilst he heaved and jerked over her. She didn't care. She hated him. The only reason she wasn't fighting him was because she knew she couldn't win, not with him inside her holding her down.

He stiffened above her. He could feel her squeezing him, and he knew he couldn't keep control much longer.

She froze, watching his face, watching his intent expression when he looked down at her, looked down at where his body joined hers. Then he threw back his head and yelled. He was jerking over her like a palsied man. She didn't move.

She said very clearly when he finally stilled above her, "You are an animal. I hate you. If another assassin comes after you again, I will smile and invite him to come closer. If you become ill, I will leave you to yourself. Leave me, Severin. Surely I am not skilled enough, nor enthusiastic enough, nor beautiful enough for you to want to do this to me even one more time. Leave me. I pray you'll leave Alice alone. She doesn't deserve this. No woman deserves this."

He came out of her quickly, coming to his feet beside the bed. He was still breathing hard. His marten was staring up at him, motionless beside Hastings's shoulder. She was very pale, her eyes dilated. But her hands were fists. He turned from her at the knock on the door.

He shouted out, "Who goes?"

"My lord, we have brought back the bathing tub."

Severin grunted, went to the door, and opened it. He didn't allow the servant into the chamber. He lugged the tub into the bedchamber himself, slammed the door, and dumped in the other buckets of water. He looked over at Hastings, who hadn't moved, then climbed into the tub. His sex was covered with the white cream and with his seed. He hadn't hurt her. He said over his shoulder as he lathered the lavender soap on the bathing cloth, "Dress yourself and see to my evening meal."

She said very clearly, "No."

He twisted around, astonishment writ clear on his face. "What did you say?"

"I said no. I will have nothing further to do with you. You do not deserve me nor do you deserve Oxborough. My lord Graelam and King Edward made a grave mistake. My father probably saw right through you, saw the kind of man you really are, and recognized a kindred evil. I will have nothing more to do with you, Severin. Nothing."

"You will come here and wash my back."

"I will put a knife in your back."

At that, he rose, water pouring over the sides of the tub. "You threaten me? You, a woman, dare to threaten me?" He struck his palm against his forehead. "I just took you. I probably should not have used the cream. I went easy with you. Do you never learn restraint, woman?"

She simply shook her head, rose from the bed, and walked slowly, bent like an old woman, to where the drying cloth and her bedrobe lay on the floor. She looked weary. He watched her pull on the bedrobe.

"You are very white. If you would but moderate your speech, if you would but tend me when I tell you to, there would be no need for cream, no need for me to have to force my way into your belly. You are supposed to enjoy me, yet you refuse to."

She looked up at him with blank surprise. "Enjoy you? That is a cruel jest no woman would believe after the first time. Aye, you're right, Severin. It is all my fault. I think you should have hurt me because what you did was your punishment. Aye, you showed your weakness by using the cream. You should have showed me how very merciless you are, what a powerful warrior you are, how I am nothing compared to you. Am I truly supposed to enjoy you? Am I truly supposed to scream with delight when you drag me to the bed, insult me, and stuff yourself into me?" She turned on her bare heel and left the bedchamber.

He yelled, "Don't you dare leave. I did not give you permission."

But she didn't turn. She closed the door very quietly. Slowly, Severin sank back down into the water. He finished bathing himself. There was only the drying cloth she had used. It was damp. He dried himself as well as he could, then slowly he began to dress. Trist made no sound. He just looked at his master, his eyes dark and clear.

"She continues to fight me, Trist. I did not hurt her. You saw that I did not hurt her. She just lay beneath me like a sacrifice. Aye, she was soft and warm, but she wasn't there, Trist. She cared not.

"I did not wish to marry, Trist. We made our way quite well until we returned to Langthorne, and there was naught but devastation, and you know I had to have an heiress then. Ah, and now I have everything a man could wish. I am a man of substance, a man of worth. What is a wife? An annoyance, nothing more. I will take her, be she an unmoving log."

The marten kept staring, making no sound.

"She is but a woman, a wife, she must learn to obey me. She threw water on me, all because I was looking at Alice's bottom, and you saw how Alice was sticking her bottom nearly into my face. And then even that one turned on me. Alice said I was just a man but that she and Hastings had been friends for a long time. Surely that makes no sense at all. Of course I am a man. What did she mean *just a man?* A man is a complete man, not *just* a man, whatever that means. And I am the master here, not some sort of low villain. All that is here is mine.

"What is going on, Trist? Mayhap I could have gone more gently with her, but I doubt it would have mattered. Besides, she deserved my force. And still she won't obey me. Still she said she hated me. Still she called me an animal. I saved her from Richard de Luci. Well, perhaps not exactly, but I would have if his assassin hadn't stabbed me before I could hunt the bastard down. Damnation, Trist, what have I done to deserve her woman's spleen?"

The marten closed his eyes and rested his head on his front paws.

Severin grunted and dressed in clean clothing, his tunic a rich pewter gray. He wished his damned squire, Mark, would come to help him. Mark treated his every word, his every request, with deference. Mark never goaded him or pushed him off his verbal course with wit. He would have to do something about Hastings. He just didn't know what yet.

Hastings remained in her chamber, sorting and mixing herbs, humming, as was her wont, for it calmed her. She wiped her brain clean of him, concentrating on the blossoms and stems on the flat board in front of her. Dame Agnes came in some moments later, bringing a tray. "You will eat something, Hastings. I will not have you sicken just because you do not know how to handle your husband."

Hastings was so startled she knocked over three foxglove stems, the blossoms thick and beautiful. She was on her knees in a moment, picking them up. She said without looking at her old nurse, "Did you know that the ancient Druids considered foxgloves their own flower? They believed that each blossom looked like a Druid hat."

"Enough of that nonsense, Hastings. You use your herbs and their lore to distract both yourself and the person you're speaking to, particularly if it isn't something you want to hear. I'll wager you even treat Lord Severin that way. He says something and you tell him a brief story about one of your plants." Dame Agnes frowned. "Why are you being so careful with the foxgloves? They're not good for anything, you know that. Why do you have them here with your healing herbs?"

"They're beautiful, no other reason."

Dame Agnes shook out her skirt, moved to smooth the cover on Hastings's bed, and turned, saying, "Listen to me. Everyone knows that Severin forced you. Alice informed even Eric the falconer, and you know that his mouth flaps looser than Belle's breasts. The lowest servant in the kitchen knew before the evening meal. There is no laughter, no loud conversation, no arguments below in the great hall. Severin's men have tried to be normal, but they are met with sullen silence. It is like someone has died. Their only sounds are slurping, chewing, and belching."

Hastings straightened. "I suppose Severin told you to fetch me down?"

"Oh no. I suspect your husband would just as soon leave Oxborough. Surely it is a great holding and he is now a man of wealth, but there is no pleasure in it for him. He eats, he even speaks occasionally to Eloise, but nothing else. The marten is stretched out beside him and stares at him, unblinking."

"There," Hastings said. "There is the truth for you. You act as if this is all my fault, but Trist knows better, he knows his master's cruelty, his lechery, his—"

"If you were a child, I would slap you. Unfortunately you are now a grown woman, indeed, the mistress of Oxborough and the three other keeps that now belong to Lord Severin. Listen to me, Hastings. You are a woman. You are not stupid. Alice told me how you have no notion of how to maneuver a man like Lord Severin into paths that are pleasing to you. She told me it smote her to see you floundering about like a fish in a net, insulting him for no good reason, enraging him until he had no choice but to punish you. And, of course, he did. Did he hurt you badly when he took you?"

Hastings felt the stiffness in her legs. She still felt a soft pulling deep inside. A man had come into her body. He'd touched her womb. He'd felt her belly and her hips to see if she would easily bear his children. The bastard. If only she told Dame Agnes what he'd done, she wouldn't be blaming Hastings for all this. But he had done so much more and Alice had told Dame Agnes. She couldn't believe Dame Agnes was speaking to her like this. Blaming her. It wasn't right. Surely she wasn't to blame for her new husband's actions, surely.

"Nay, he didn't hurt me, but that is not the point. I do not suppose that Alice admitted that Severin very nearly took her in his bedchamber, not ten feet from me?"

Dame Agnes laughed. She *laughed*. "Aye, she said she thought you'd gone behind the screen to dress. She said she was removing Severin's boots, bent over, her bottom to him, and showing him that she would bed him willingly if he chose. What is wrong with that, Hastings? Alice is a fine, strapping girl.''

"He is my husband.''

"I want you to put away your herbs. I want you to come and sit on your bed and listen to me.'' There was a light knock on the door.

"Enter,'' Hastings called.

It was Alice, and she was looking as unhappy as Hastings had ever seen her in her life. She looked furtively toward Dame Agnes.

Dame Agnes said, "Alice, would you like to help me give our mistress some instruction?''

Alice perked up at that. "Hastings? Are you all right? Did he hurt you? I don't see any bruises.''

This wasn't right. Hastings stared at two women she'd known all her life. He wasn't to blame unless he beat her? "He humiliated me.''

"What does that mean?'' Dame Agnes said, stepping close. "Humiliation? Men do that well as a rule. But what did Lord Severin do to you?''

"He measured me with his hand to see if I could easily birth babes.''

Dame Agnes nodded. "Aye, he would do that to prevent worry about you. You must needs have an heir quickly, Hastings, but he did this not to humiliate you but to assure himself that you would be able to birth them without dying. This is the humiliation? This is all that he did?''

"He was going to put his hands on Alice's bottom, then thought better of it.''

"Of course he would. You were standing there, weren't you? He spared you humiliation. It seems to me, Hastings, that you have sorely mistreated your new husband.''

Hastings squawked, opened the rose drawer, took out some of the drying blossoms, and ate them.

Alice said, lightly laying her fingers on Hastings's sleeve, "Men do not think clearly and sensibly as women do. They like to fight—to test their manhood and to clear their blood—to eat and drink, and to have sex as often as they can. There is little more to any of them.''

"That is an excellent description, Alice," Dame Agnes said, nodding in approval. "So, Hastings, you have really mucked things up here. You have taken a simple man whom you could have led about by the nose if you'd just thought about it. Instead you have treated him to fits of outrage and given him only quarrels. You have argued with him when there was no need. You have yelled and ranted and carried on at great length when all you would have had to do was smile."

Hastings grabbed another rose blossom and ate it, chewing viciously. "By Saint Godolphin's shins, he has never kissed me, not once. He doesn't like me. He thinks I'm ordinary, well, he did say that I was not an ordinary heiress."

"An ordinary heiress?" Alice repeated, frowning. "What does that mean?"

"It means that Severin always believed that an heiress would be ugly. I am not ugly, but I don't have anything else to please him. He doesn't like me, even after I saved his life. Bedding me is a duty, nothing more. You are wrong about him, Agnes. He does not want sex with me."

"Ah," Dame Agnes said.

"What does that mean?"

"It means, Hastings," Alice said with exaggerated slowness, "that you are angry because he did not show you proper gratitude. He is a man, a warrior. Such a man cannot tell a woman that she is brave and courageous and that he will revere her above all others for the rest of his life. Men are not like that."

"Aye," Dame Agnes said. "To be felled by an assassin, it probably shriveled his soul as well as his manhood. Then to have you save him, well, it is as Alice says. A man of his stature would find that more than difficult to accept."

"This is all very confusing," Hastings said, and took another bite of a rose blossom. Then she sighed and began to carefully wrap the foxglove blossoms in soft linen.

"And then you cured him."

"Aye, Agnes," Hastings said, jerking up. "That was a mighty crime on my part. Mayhap I should have kissed his feet instead? Mayhap I should have just leaned down and let him put his heel upon my neck."

"Do not become impertinent with me, Hastings. Now, sit down and eat the bread and stew Alice brought you. Rose blossoms are fine, but you need MacDear's stew."

Her nurse pointed to the bed, saying no more, until Hastings, shrugging her shoulders, sat down and allowed Alice to place the tray on her legs. She picked up the crusty bread and took a nice bite. Her stomach growled.

"You eat and we will talk. If you wish, you may ask questions. I wonder, Alice," Dame Agnes said, turning away from Hastings, "do you believe we should fetch Belle from the great hall? Her knowledge of men is legendary."

Belle, Hastings thought, her eyes widening. She was old, fat, and had scarce a tooth left in her mouth. Her hair was long and thick, however, very black with only a bit of gray showing. She had been wedded to four men, all of whom were dead now. However, Old Morric, the blacksmith, was casting his eyes in her direction and everyone poked everyone else with their elbows and whispered behind their hands, laughing. It was very confusing.

"If we discover that we need Belle, we will call her later," Dame Agnes said.

"Aye," Alice said. "I believe she was dallying with Morric. He looks besotted, his mouth hanging open, his eyes crossed. She will probably make him take wing tonight. I would not want him to shoe my horse on the morrow." Alice laughed. "He would likely put the shoe on the horse's rump. Aye, by the end of summer, he will be her fifth husband."

Hastings chewed on her bread, took a bit of the wondrously flavored beef stew with a thick sauce and onions and peas. It was salted to perfection. "MacDear has used sage in the stew. It adds a biting flavor. I like it."

Alice rolled her eyes.

Dame Agnes said, "Now, Hastings, this is what you will do. No, keep chewing your stew, I do not wish to hear any arguments from you. And aye, it is sage."

Nearly an hour later, Hastings was finally left alone in

the bedchamber, staring blankly at the two tapestries, one showing a banquet, the other a jousting tournament. At one corner of the tapestry there was a cup that Hastings knew held an infusion of flowers and leaves from the borage plant. It was believed to give courage to a man before he went into the tournament. If she squinted, she could see the tiny letters, b-o-r-a-g-e, in perfect stitches on the cup.

What was she to do? Was she to become a limp, well-washed rug and let him tread upon her? Was she to smile when he casually tossed out his insults? Was she to ignore his looks at Alice's bottom? Was she to ask him if he enjoyed himself when he took another woman to his bed? Was she to smile when he mounted her, told her that she was only adequate, and rutted on her like an animal?

No, she would kill him.

He didn't come to her. She quickly changed into her night shift, a loose cotton gown that came nearly to her knees. She crawled into bed, thinking, thinking. Could it be possible that she was in the wrong?

Alice had said slowly, as if instructing an idiot, "It is pleasant to have a man rut you if he goes slowly and easily, and knows what he is doing. I asked Gwent about his master's habits. He told me that Severin was usually very careful with a woman, that he enjoyed her and caressed her until she enjoyed him as well. Gwent said he does not understand why the two of you are prepared to slit each other's throats. He said it made no sense to him unless you were overly prideful, and such a thing in a woman would surely displease Severin."

Hastings couldn't believe that. Severin was careful with a woman? No, that couldn't be the truth. Nor could she believe that all the Oxborough people were discussing Severin and her. She wondered if Dame Agnes would demand to watch them mate to see how each of them behaved toward the other.

Saint Francis's staff, they should probably mate on one of the trestle tables with all their people looking on, offering advice, telling her how to arrange herself so that Severin would find the most enjoyment. She would never believe that a woman could possibly enjoy this mating.

She wasn't overly prideful.

She wasn't.

11

HASTINGS AWOKE EARLY THE FOLLOWING MORNING TO shouts from the inner bailey below the window. She jumped from the bed and ran to look down. There were Severin and at least twenty-five men—some men-at-arms from Oxborough and some Langthorne men. Where were they going? She realized then that he had not even slept in his bed last night. No, he had not come to her at all. Nor had Trist. She watched them ride out, Severin, garbed all in gray, his chain mail glittering in the early morning sun, at their fore.

He had not said a word to her.

She dressed quickly and ran down the solar stairs. Gwent was in the great hall, speaking to the steward, giving instructions to the thirty-some men-at-arms remaining at Oxborough. He looked up and smiled when he saw her.

"Severin is journeying to his other holdings. The castellans there must swear fealty to him. He will make certain there are no problems, no insurrections brewing."

"I should be with him. It is the way things are done. It is expected."

"He did not wish it. No one mentioned it except you. Why would you wish to be with him if you don't like him?"

"It is the way of things. Liking has nothing to do with it."

"Severin wished to go alone."

"I am not overly prideful, Gwent."

"Mayhap. Mayhap not."

"When will he return?"

"A fortnight, mayhap longer."

"Does he also journey to Langthorne?"

"Not as yet. This is more important." Gwent looked down at the cut on his forearm that did not seem to be healing. He'd been careless. During practice with the quintain, he had fallen and cut himself with his own sword.

"Let me see, Gwent."

He looked puzzled, then realized she'd followed his vision to his arm. There was a dirty rag tied around his forearm.

"It is nothing," he said, and rose. "I must work the men. It is what Severin wants."

Without thinking, Hastings shoved him back onto the bench. "You will go nowhere until I have seen what is wrong. I do not wish you to die, and that happens many times when there is an open wound. It is something about the blood that turns bad and poisons the body. Hold still, Gwent."

He suffered her. He didn't make a sound when she bathed the cut. It was deep and ugly. When she rubbed an infusion of chives and Saint-John's-wort onto the sore, he didn't even flinch. She knew that it hurt. "Listen to me, Gwent. You will keep this bandage clean. I will change it every evening until the wound is healed. If you do not obey me, there is every chance that you could die."

Gwent wanted to tell her that she was a woman and thus she saw every little cut or bruise as something to fell a man. But he kept still. Men did die too easily from wounds. Also, she was the mistress of Oxborough, Severin's wife, and he rather liked her. He had never seen his master so utterly baffled in his life. She had right upended him and he had said to Gwent that if he didn't learn to control her he might thrash her and then she would make his bowels turn to water and what man wanted that?

Gwent rose, smiled down at her, and said, "My thanks, Hastings. Worry not about Severin. If there is any trouble at the keeps, he will send a message to me. Ah, Hastings, since you have cured my arm, I agree. I don't really believe you are overly prideful."

"Keep the bandage clean, Gwent."

"Aye," he said, then turned to see Torric the steward standing there. "Ah, I believe it is the worm who has crawled into the hall to see if I have yet realized that he is a miserable cheat. By Saint Andrew's teeth, I hate cheats."

Torric was a cheat? He had been with her father for five years now. Her father had trusted him. They were rich, all their holdings prospering. Gwent believed he was cheating? That meant that Severin believed it too. She had never paid any attention to the steward's varied tasks about Oxborough. She only knew that Torric performed all his duties well, was usually fair with all their people, and smiled perhaps not as much as a man should, but it wasn't all that important. Perhaps she should begin to pay a bit more attention.

During the second week of Severin's absence, on a hot and dusty afternoon, Alart, the porter, yelled that a company of men were approaching. Since Oxborough rose above the surrounding countryside, they could see all who approached from great distances. These men were still some miles away.

Hastings saw the king's standard. Surely King Edward was not arriving for a visit. But still, Hastings quickly changed her gown, combed her hair, and braided it neatly about her head, and grabbed Eloise's hand to stand in front of the keep.

It was the chancellor of England, Robert Burnell, King Edward's secretary and most trusted advisor. He looked as if his bones had been rattled into dust. He didn't ride well. His face looked drawn and tired, yet they were but a three-day ride from London. Riding beside the chancellor on a bay palfrey with white stockings was one of the most beautiful women Hastings had ever seen in her life. She was so fair, her hair shone nearly white in the sunlight. She was wearing a white wimple that fastened beneath her chin. She was young, not more than five years older than Hastings, and she rode her palfrey well. She was wearing a soft green gown with long, loose sleeves that fell nearly to the ground. Burnell slowly dismounted. Then he shook himself, looked up at her, and nodded. He handed the reins of his horse to one of the Oxborough stable lads.

"My lady," Burnell said, giving Hastings a fat smile, for he'd known her since she was born, though he'd seen her only rarely during the past ten years, "this is Lady Marjorie, widow of Sir Mark Outbraith. King Edward has sent her to you to care for Eloise of Sedgewick. This is the child?"

The child pressed herself against Hastings's side.

"Eloise," Hastings said, "my dear, this is a very nice man who serves our king. He isn't here to hurt you."

"What is wrong with her?" Robert Burnell asked, one eye on Eloise, who refused to release Hastings's leg.

"Her father beat her and her mother set her on her knees most of the day to pray. She is much more at ease now, but it will take time."

"Ah, the little girl," Lady Marjorie said, and without paying any attention to the dirt on the keep steps, she dropped to her knees and looked straight into Eloise's pale blue eyes.

"You and I," she said very slowly and quietly, "will become great friends. You may call me Marjorie." She reached into the pocket of her beautiful cloak and withdrew a cloth. Slowly, knowing Eloise was staring down at that cloth, she unwrapped it. Inside were almonds covered with honey. "Just one, Eloise, just one. That way they will last a long time and you will have something to look forward to."

Eloise very slowly reached out and took an almond. She studied it. Then she eased it into her mouth. Almost immediately she closed her eyes in ecstasy.

Marjorie smiled and rose. "You are Hastings of Oxborough?"

"Aye. You have come quickly."

Robert Burnell said, "We will remain until tomorrow, Hastings, then go to Sedgewick. Lady Marjorie will be the child's guardian until she comes of age. Where is Lord Severin?"

"He is away visiting his other holdings."

The evening meal was an odd affair. Robert Burnell sat in Severin's chair, Lady Marjorie sat in Eloise's chair with Eloise on her lap. "She is so very thin," Marjorie said.

"You should have seen her when she first arrived at Oxborough."

"All of this is very strange. However, I fancy that at Sedgewick, everything will soon be all right again."

What am I, Hastings thought, a witch to terrify and starve the child? She realized she didn't want Eloise to return to Sedgewick. Beale was there. Both Hastings and Eloise were afraid of Beale, probably with good reason. When she spoke of this to Robert Burnell after the long dinner, he was silent for a long moment. Then he shrugged. "I will hang the woman. Then there will be no problem. You did say that she threatened you, did you not, Hastings?"

"Aye, I did, but sir, surely hanging is a bit too severe, even for Beale. Cannot Eloise simply remain here? It is kind of Lady Marjorie to come to her, but I can be Eloise's guardian until she is of marriageable age. Severin will protect her and her holdings."

"I am sorry, but His Majesty is set on this course. Besides, you are newly wedded. You and Severin will have babes. What need do you have of a child not your own?"

"I like Eloise. She has not had an easy life. I cannot believe she would be happy if she went with a stranger back to Sedgewick. Please, sir—"

"Hastings, you don't understand. His Majesty is indebted to Sir Mark Outbraith. Some four years ago he rallied to the king's side during an ambush near to Jerusalem. We heard that he was killed in a squabble with his neighbor some six months ago. Lady Marjorie is his widow. He left her with nothing. His Majesty thus decided that to repay his debt he would make her the child's guardian."

"But she is so young."

Robert Burnell laughed in that raw way of his that made him sound out of practice. "You are but eighteen, Hastings. Lady Marjorie is twenty-three. Leave be. See to your own affairs. Eloise is no longer your responsibility." He took a deep drink of wine and sighed deeply. "If I mistake it not, this is from Lord Graelam. From his father-in-law's vineyard in Aquitaine?"

"Aye, it is. Would you like another goblet, sir?"

Burnell drank deeply, then said slowly, "I had hoped to see Severin, yet it is wise of him to see to his holdings immediately. I am surprised that you did not accompany him."

"He did not wish me to."

"Is he to your liking, Hastings?"

"He appears to be a brave warrior, sir. If you would know the truth, he does not like me. But then again, I suppose many husbands don't like their wives. I know that I am not particularly fond of him."

Robert Burnell waved an indifferent hand. "You are both young. You will change. Once you begin having children, you will see him in a different light. I understand that Richard de Luci poisoned his wife so he could take you and wed you? That he failed because the poor lady didn't die speedily enough?"

"So I have been told. Lord Graelam said he slipped on a rabbit bone and hit his head. He is dead."

"Excellent. You have grown up well, Hastings. You are comely and you fed me an excellent meal. The keep is sound and well managed. You and Severin should try to model yourselves upon our blessed king and queen. Aye, it is a pleasure to serve our king and queen. Their affection for each other is a constant in this chaos of men's affairs. Fret not, Hastings. You are young. You will bend, as you should to your husband."

Did everyone want her to become a sheep in women's clothing?

"And Severin? What will he do, sir?"

"He is a lusty young man. He will teach you to enjoy lust and to laugh."

She sipped at the wonderful Aquitaine wine. It warmed the belly. It also made her feel easy and smile a lot, despite the fact that Robert Burnell was again telling her it was she who had to change, not Severin. She smiled now at Robert Burnell. "How long will you remain at Oxborough, sir?"

"Ah, I must take Lady Marjorie and the child back to Sedgewick on the morrow, as I told you. As to this woman Beale, I will see the extent of her madness, for mad she must be to hold a knife to the child's throat and try to escape with her. You are not to worry about the child. Look at the lady. Already the child is smiling and holding her hand."

It was true, Hastings thought. Eloise had gone to Majorie with scarce a thought to Hastings. She felt betrayed and a bit jealous of the beautiful woman. She did not like that in herself but it did not seem to matter if she liked it or not. It was there, that jealousy. Why had Eloise gone so quickly over to her?

Severin returned to Oxborough three days later, a fortnight to the very day. Hastings was standing on the top steps of the keep watching him and his men ride into the inner bailey. Children and animals scattered out of the way. She watched him dismount and hand the reins to Mark, his squire, who was patting his warhorse's sweating neck, speaking to him, Hastings thought, telling him about the delicious carrots from her garden. She liked Mark. It was just that he couldn't bring himself to speak to her. All he did was open his mouth, stutter, then shut it again.

Severin was bareheaded. His gray tunic and chain mail shone brightly beneath the noonday sun. He looked in her direction then and she saw the weariness in him. Still, his dark blue eyes seemed to brighten. Dame Agnes's advice sounded a litany in her head, advice soundly agreed to by Alice: "When your lord returns, you will smile at him and you will see to his needs. You will show your interest in him and you will applaud him in his recitals. You might consider kissing him, though knowing you, you would probably purse your mouth and make him prefer a sour apple.''

Kiss him. She'd thought a lot about that. She could do it, she knew she could. But what if he flung her away from him? What if he just looked at her and laughed, or told her she bored him or told her that her kiss was just ordinary?

"Severin!"

He looked around. She yelled his name again and he slewed about to look at her. His jaw dropped in utter surprise. She laughed aloud, picked up her skirts, and dashed down the deeply indented steps.

"I am glad you are home," she shouted, but didn't stop running. She ran right at him, jumping up to fling her arms around his neck and hug him until she wondered if she were not choking him. She was hanging there, her feet off the cobbled stones of the inner bailey. Then, slowly, finally, his arms came around her. He pressed her tightly against him.

"I am glad you are home," she said again, kissing his neck, his right ear. "I have missed you. It has been too many days without you. A fortnight. Too long. Welcome home, my lord." And she kissed his cheek, very close to his mouth.

Then his arms fell away. He clasped her upper arms and gently pulled her off him, setting her feet on the cobblestones. He stared down at her, stared at those damned eyes of hers that were sparkling with delight, that held no secrets to bring a man to his knees, at least that he could see. Aye, it was delight he saw, he wasn't blind or particularly stupid. And she was lightly flushed, as if embarrassed by her show of affection for him.

"What have you done?" he said finally, not releasing her upper arms. "Have you killed one of my men? Have you poisoned one of our people by mistake? Did MacDear cook Gilbert the goat thinking him a chicken? Will the damned goat have a boot in his mouth when he is brought out on a platter?"

She laughed and threw her arms around his chest, hugging him tightly. "Nay, I have just missed you. Did you not miss me? Just a bit?"

"Aye, mayhap a bit. I left Oxborough with a sour feeling in my belly. It lasted many days."

"I am sorry for it. Come, my lord, I have some wine for you and some delicious capon smothered in almonds. You will tell by the tenderness that it is not Gilbert the goat." She gave him a side look, then turned quickly, went onto her tiptoes, and kissed his mouth. She was a bit crooked, but it was his mouth. He tasted warm, his lips soft. She hadn't expected that, but then it was over and she wondered if she remembered aright.

She said, her breath warm against his chin, "Almonds, Severin. Do you not love almonds?"

He was staring at her mouth. "You have killed someone, haven't you? You have hung our priest. You have burned down the armory. You have destroyed all our winter storage."

She kissed him again. He was actually jesting with her, wasn't he? She kissed him again. She hadn't been wrong. His mouth was incredibly warm, as was his breath.

"Hastings," he said, then heard his men laughing behind him. He looked up to see Dame Agnes standing on the steps, smiling down at them. "You wish me to take you here in front of all our people?"

She kissed him once more, a fleeting kiss, a girl's kiss, as all her other kisses had been, at least those that had landed on his mouth, for indeed, she was naught more than a girl when it came to kisses, and smiled up at him. "Nay, I just wished to greet you as you deserve. Won't you kiss me, Severin? The kisses I gave you were my first. I know nothing about how it is done. But I like the taste of you. And your mouth is so very warm and soft."

He actually shuddered. He pulled her against him, grabbed the thick braid in his hand, and pulled her head back. He kissed her with all the hunger in him, and it was a lot. He felt surprise in her and shock. Not revulsion, just shock. He was going too fast, too hard. She had never been kissed before. He eased, just caressing her mouth now, and slowly he ran his tongue along her lower lip.

She made a strange noise. He lifted his head.

"That was your tongue," she said. "Surely it is an odd thing to do. Not that it wasn't nice, but still, Severin, are you certain that is done?"

"There are many things men and women do to each other that you would think odd right this moment, Hastings. But not tomorrow or the next day."

There was now a good deal of jesting and laughter all around them. "I think we have provided my men an entertainment that will have them giving me advice throughout the rest of the day and night." He cupped her face in his palm. "I do not understand this change in you, but I will accept it. It is pleasant."

She laughed, pulled away from him, and shouted to all his men, "Come into the great hall. MacDear has prepared bounty for all of you." She added low to Severin, "If you would come to our bedchamber, I will see to your bath."

His eyes nearly crossed. He'd been so weary he had thought he would fall out of his saddle, but no more. He wanted to grab her up into his arms and run up the solar stairs with her, kissing her and fondling her all the way until he had her on her back in the center of that big bed, and then he would pull off all her clothes and come into her and . . .

"My lord, welcome home."

He shook his head. His men laughed harder. His voice came out rough and mean. "Aye, Gwent, it is excellent to be back. All went well else you wouldn't be smiling like a buffoon. And Beamis, you have helped train all these louts?"

There was more laughter, Beamis and Gwent poking each other, insulting each other, and he was pleased that the two men had become friends. He suddenly saw in his mind's eye the young girl who had come to his bed at Fontivale keep some three days' ride from Oxborough. She was younger than Hastings and had known more than some of the women he had taken to his bed in the Holy Land. He swallowed, remembering how she'd been there in his bed, waiting for him, smiling, her arms ready to clasp him to her. She'd told him how magnificent he was, how he made her feel, and he remembered so clearly that he thought that this girl didn't think he was an animal. She'd made him feel strong and powerful. But then he'd seen Hastings clear in his mind in those moments when he'd come into Anne. He'd seen Hastings's face pale and set as he moved over her. He'd known that she hated this joining with him, he'd known it and hated her for her hatred of him. He'd taken Anne three times before he had fallen into an exhausted sleep. And then he had dreamed of Hastings, dreamed of that moment when she had saved him from death by the assassin's knife, how she had wiped him down when he had lain there roasting with the hellish fever. The coolness of her hands, the lightness of her touch.

He had felt immense guilt the next morning. At first he hadn't recognized it for what it was, but when he had, he'd hated himself for it. Guilt was the spawn of weakness. Guilt? Because he'd taken his pleasure with another woman? It was absurd. But he had left the next morning, a day earlier than he had planned, not seeing Anne again.

What had happened to Hastings? Why had she changed toward him? Had she dreamed about him? Did she feel guilty that she had not treated him as she should have?

He heard Gwent say quietly, "I do not yet know if Torric the steward is a thief. I do not calculate and figure as well as you do. You will have to see to it, Severin."

"Aye, I will see to it on the morrow. But today—"

"I know. Today and tonight it is your lady who will get all your attention." Gwent stared after her. "I wonder," he said slowly, "if your lady has experienced an epiphany."

"You mean, has a vision visited her and told her how to be a proper wife?"

"Something like that," Gwent said, still staring after that laughing girl he didn't know. "Don't muck up this miracle, Severin."

"But—"

"Bend as she has bent."

"Oh aye, but I'm too hard to bend, truth be told. She

kissed me, Gwent. It was a girl's kiss, for she doesn't know yet what to do with her mouth, but I will teach her, and it wasn't bad, all soft and warm, and—''

Gwent threw back his head and laughed deep and long. Other men joined in, not knowing why they laughed but seduced by the laugh from a man who could pound most of them into the ground in the practice field within a matter of minutes. Beamis laughed, picked up his little boy, whirled him over his head, then tossed him to one of his waiting men. The child shrieked and shrieked with laughter.

Severin punched Gwent hard and strode into the great hall.

Had Hastings really had an epiphany? Or had she let another man in her bed and felt guilty for it? Was that why she had run to him, hurled herself at him, and kissed him? No, not Hastings. Why had she changed toward him? Would it last, this change of hers, longer than a goblet of wine?

# 12

HASTINGS LAUGHED AS SHE LEANED OVER HIS BACK, A sponge filled with her lavender soap in her hand. His muscles were deep and hard. She was startled to find that she liked the feel of him, the texture of his flesh. He wasn't very dirty and she was surprised at that. Surely he had ridden hard many days he had been gone, surely he had not been near too many bathtubs.

"Ah, that is good," Severin said, leaning back against the edge of the tub, his eyes closed. Though at each of his keeps he had visited, the castellan's wife or one of the ladies had performed this ritual for him, this was different. The way she touched him was different. He didn't believe, at this moment, that he had enjoyed a scrubbing more. He wished it were her bare hand rather than the thick sponge.

"You are very big," she said at last, and her voice was just a bit thin. But then she laughed again. Mayhap that laugh was a bit on the thin side as well, but Severin didn't care. He turned and grabbed her wrist. "Hastings," he said. He saw indeed that her laughter was now forced, that her smile looked painful, her eyes a bit wild. She was chewing on her lower lip. This laughing bride of his wasn't all that certain of herself or the new role she was playing with him.

He thought of Gwent's awed words about an epiphany,

released her wrist, and said, "Kiss me and then leave me else we won't enjoy MacDear's capon until tomorrow."

Her eyes nearly crossed. Then she lightly touched her fingertips to his wet shoulders, leaned down, and kissed his closed mouth, her lips even more closed than his. Sewn together, he thought, but it didn't matter. He waved her away with the thick sponge.

Hastings closed the door behind her and slumped against it. She drew a deep breath. This was all very strange. Because she had met him with kisses and hugs, he seemed a different man. Could Dame Agnes and Alice be right? All she had to do was laugh and feed him well and kiss him and then he would not force her again? He would go gently with her? He would no longer yell at her or shake her until her head snapped on her neck? She pushed away from the wall and walked quickly down the solar stairs.

She wondered where Trist was. She had missed the marten. She would oversee boiling an egg for him herself.

Severin was wearing the new tunic she'd sewn for him. It was pale blue, soft as Trist's pelt, and beautifully made. It was too tight across his shoulders.

But he had worn it. To please her. She had left it smoothed out atop the bed and kept her fingers crossed. He had worn it. When she met his eyes, she smiled. Then, before she could lose her courage, she skipped to him, stroked her palms over the wondrous soft wool, and said, "You are magnificent. I am sorry, Severin, but I did not think you were so wide. I will make the next tunic larger." She measured him with her fingers, making the calculations in her head.

"It is a fine tunic," he said, and his voice was low and gruff. He looked as if he would say more, but both of them became aware that there was a growing silence in the great hall. Even Edgar the wolfhound, who had been barking his head off just a few moments before chasing one of the little girls about as she waved a ball of wool in his face, was silent, sitting on his haunches, staring toward them.

"I was wondering why you always wore gray."

"I believe it is because the women who did all the weaving and dyeing at Langthorne only knew how to dye gray. After I left, I suppose it was just a habit and I sought nothing but gray. You believed perhaps it was a superstition for me? Some sort of ritual?"

"Aye, perhaps. I know how to dye beautiful colors, Severin. May I sew you more tunics, each a different color?"

"You may do whatever you wish with my tunics. This one is very soft. I thank you."

"Everyone is wondering what has happened between us," Hastings said, and to prove to herself that she knew exactly what she was doing, she thrust her chin in the air and looked him right in his dark blue eyes.

"Shall I tell them that nothing has happened as yet?"

"But it has," she said, just a bit of desperation seeping into her voice.

"Aye, I much enjoy hearing you laugh. I have never heard you laugh before today."

"It is not ordinary?"

"Nay," he said, smiling down at her. Then he rubbed his knuckles lightly over her cheek. "You are so soft," he said, then leaned down, kissed her lightly. "Softer than my new tunic." He laughed at her stunned expression and strode to the lord's high-backed chair.

Trist had wrapped himself around Severin's wine goblet. He stretched out his arm to pet Trist, feeling the tightness of the material under his arm. Too, he wished the new tunic were more full-cut. He was hard and hurting. He quickly sat down. Trist unwrapped himself and came to rub his whiskers against Severin's hand.

He stroked the marten's soft fur until Hastings herself placed his pewter plate in front of him. There was a thick, rich slab of white bread and atop it was a capon, perfectly roasted, with honeyed almonds, peas, cabbage, and onions around it. He had been well fed in his three new keeps, but none could compare to MacDear. He fell to his meal, wanting to eat quickly so he could grab Hastings and haul her to their bedchamber. She wouldn't fight him tonight. She would smile. She would hold out her arms to him. Just as

Anne had. No, he wouldn't think about Anne, that woman child who had given him so much guilty pleasure that he'd almost swooned with it. No, he should not have felt guilt. Hastings was his wife, nothing more, nothing less.

There was nothing to change here. Except her. Aye, she had changed, and he was pleased. He hoped the changes continued.

He would not rub her nose in the dirt for bending to him. No, he would be magnanimous. He wondered what had happened to turn her from a bold-tongued shrew—who had helped him, he admitted that—into this lovely smiling girl who looked at him as if she were actually enjoying looking at him.

No, he would not muck up this miracle.

His men talked at him, around him, through him, but it made no difference, he merely nodded at them and ate. He knew MacDear's capon was delicious, but he didn't care. He didn't care about anything except shoveling down MacDear's food and getting to the bottom of that well-shined pewter plate.

The meal had just in fact well begun when he shoved back his chair and grabbed Hastings's hand.

Every head in the great hall slewed around to look at them. He felt Hastings grow stiff as the beautiful silver laver that had dents in it. He said out of the side of his mouth, "Ignore them. They have no idea what we are about." That was more surely the biggest lie he'd told in many a month. "Come, Hastings, I will please you."

Please her? She couldn't begin to imagine this pleasing thing, but she smiled and nodded and clasped his hand more tightly. Trist jumped up onto her shoulder and crept carefully around her neck until he was half on her shoulder and the other half of him was leaning against Severin's chest.

When the cheers started, Hastings thought she would sink into the rushes, not because she was embarrassed but because she was excited and she was afraid everyone saw it on her face. Everyone knew about this pleasure thing but her? She saw riddled old Belle, sitting at a trestle table, leaning heavily against Old Morric the blacksmith, who was feeding her bits of beef, one of his huge hands lightly caressing her breast. Why hadn't Hastings noticed this before? Belle winked at her. Hastings knew Dame Agnes and Alice were both grinning like fools, but she simply couldn't bring herself to look at them.

Just before they reached the solar stairs, Severin gave a shout of laughter, picked her up, and tossed her over his shoulder. Her long braids nearly brushed the floor.

Then he lightly slapped her bottom, making his men yowl with laughter. This is what it should have been like the night of their marriage.

He didn't let her down until he reached their bedchamber. Slowly, he eased her down his chest, feeling her breasts, her belly sliding against him, letting her feel the length of his body, and when her toes touched the floor, he pressed his hands against her bottom and brought her against him.

"Oh," Hastings said.

"Look at me, Hastings. That's right. Don't be frightened of me. Those other two nights, forget them. They were nothing, just bad dreams that will fade with time until they are no more. Will you try?"

"Aye, I will try."

They hadn't exactly been bad dreams for him because a man's lust was easily assuaged, though he had wished she wouldn't have fought him, that she would have welcomed him, at least a bit. That was over now. Now he had a girl who had bowed completely to him. He wasn't about to let her unbow.

Trist leapt from Hastings's shoulder to land on the bed. He stretched out his full length and stared at them, mewling loudly. Severin remembered Trist sitting beside him when Anne had been in his bed. The marten hadn't made a sound.

"Will you come willingly with me, Hastings?"

"Aye. You are breathing hard, Severin. Does MacDear's capon not sit well in your belly?"

He merely grinned down at her and gently pushed her back. She sat down on the bed, her hands folded in her lap, watching him intently, her lips slightly parted. So she wanted to see him, did she? If this was what it took not to muck up, then so be it.

He fumbled with his clothes, but finally it was done and he was naked, standing in front of her. He forced himself to keep his arms at his sides.

He would not muck up.

"You," she said finally, her eyes on his belly, "are beautiful, Severin. I've thought so before, but it was just a simple thought with nothing to go with it. I did not realize what your beauty would mean to me. Please, come closer. Mayhap even close enough so that I could touch you if I wished to."

Never had he stood before a woman naked, his sex swelled because he had no say in that, and he knew his sex would swell more and she would be afraid, but he prayed she would not be overly afraid. Just a bit. Aye, he wanted just a bit of hesitation in her when she looked at him. He stood directly in front of her. He watched her white hands reach out to lie palms flat against his belly. He shuddered and his sex hardened. He saw then that she had closed her eyes. She was feeling him, every bit of him, her fingers probing lightly into the muscles over his belly, moving slowly lower until her fingers tangled in the bush of hair at his groin. He wanted her to touch him so badly he thought he would howl if she didn't. Lightly, so very lightly, her fingers found him.

His flesh was alien to her, he knew that. She circled him, coming ever closer. He wondered how much longer he could stand it. Then her fingers closed around him. Her eyes opened and she stared at her hands and at him held between her hands.

"Don't be frightened, Hastings. Well, mayhap just a bit, so I will know that you admire my endowments."

She licked her tongue over her lips. He nearly leapt on her. He threw his head back, his hands dug into his flanks, his throat worked convulsively, striving for control. But there was very little left. He pulled slowly away from her.

To his shock, she didn't release him. She rose, still holding him, walking toward him even as he moved back.

He laughed, an agonizing laugh, but still a laugh because surely if one were to see this odd dance of theirs it would bring laughter and a bit of amazement.

He clasped her arms in his hands. "Release me, Hastings, else I will spill my seed on this beautiful carpet."

"It is from Flanders," she said, still holding him, her fingers stroking him slowly. "It is very old. Nay, not yet. Let me hold you longer. You're hot between my hands, Severin. Hot and smooth."

"You cannot. Please let me go, Hastings. It will be a close thing."

She sighed. "Very well." She released him. She sighed again, then said, "Will you help me, Severin?"

He was breathing so hard now, his chest was heaving. "Hastings, I cannot. If I do, I will rip your gown. Nay, sweeting, you do it. But be quick. I cannot wait."

This was not the same man who had shamed her those two nights. Not the same man who had insulted her, who had looked at her as if he didn't care if she were his wife or not. No, not the same man at all. She didn't understand this, but she realized that she hadn't wanted to release that male part of him that came inside her. She had liked to hold him. It made her feel incredibly strange, somehow urgent, mayhap even frantic. It also made her feel powerful. She wasn't aware that her own breathing had quickened, but Severin was. He sat on the bed, watching her as she had him. She was quicker, her gown and shift pulled over her head in but an instant of time. Then she was pulling free her garters and rolling down her stockings. She kicked her feet free of the pointed-toe slippers.

"Come here," he said.

She blinked at him, looked over her shoulder, looked back at him, and said, "All right."

"Is there someone behind you?"

"Nay, but I'm naked and I am not at all certain if I should be doing this."

"Do it. I did."

When she was standing in front of him, between his legs, he reached out his hands and cupped her breasts. Her flesh was soft and smooth, and she was so very white. He wanted to weep. She looked down to see him close his eyes. He wasn't looking at her. That was better. She moved a bit closer, resting her hands on his bare shoulders. The wound had healed nicely, the scar long and nearly flat.

His hands closed about her waist. He squeezed inward, his thumbs angling downward to touch her navel. His hands were large and dark against her white skin. Just looking at his hands on her made those odd urgent feelings grow stronger. She wanted him to touch her lower. It was that simple. She had held him and he had wanted her to hold him, she had realized that quickly enough. And now she wanted his fingers on her, where, exactly, she didn't know, but the feelings were beginning to pound into her now, and there was so much heat, liquid heat, and she could feel it in and on herself, but she didn't care.

"Severin," she said.

He didn't raise his head. He opened his eyes and stared at her belly, stared at his hands that were parting her woman's flesh now, staring at her, and she thought she would die from the incredible feelings that were roiling through her. Then his callused fingertips were touching her and she cried out, a low, hoarse cry that filled the bed-chamber, and her back arched, and she was pressing herself against those fingers of his, and her belly was nearly pressed against his face. Then to her utter shock, he held her parted with his fingers and touched her with his mouth.

She screamed, hard and loud, not caring if someone were passing outside the bedchamber to hear that scream and to wonder. Not with shock or embarrassment, but at the bolt of pressure that tore through her, very low, yet it seemed to be throughout her entire body, and somehow she knew there was more. But what he was doing to her, where his mouth nuzzled, she had never known, never imagined such a thing.

"Severin, I don't know—"

She felt his finger ease upward inside her even as he caressed her with his mouth, and it was all over for her. She crumbled over him as the pleasure took her, and he caught her and gently laid her on her back, his fingers on her now, stroking her, keeping the feelings churning and erupting in her, and she wondered how a woman could survive such a cataclysm. She closed her eyes, arched her back, and whispered, "Severin, this is like nothing in the world."

"No," he said, "it isn't. Hold still, I would come into you now." And he did, but slowly, easily, and he was hard and slick and she found herself lifting her hips to bring him more deeply into her. He felt wonderful, filling her, making her want to hold him so close he would meld into her even as his sex was deep and deeper still inside her belly. He shuddered and tensed and reared back, and she watched him take his release and it was a very different feeling she had watching him now than when she'd lain cold and angry beneath him before.

He was sweating, breathing heavily, his chest heaving, but he kept up on his elbows, looking down at her, and his eyes were vague, the dark blue warm and blurred, not cold as she had first believed when she saw him stride into Oxborough that day to marry her.

"You are not ordinary," he said, leaned down, and kissed her mouth. "Part your lips for me."

She did. He kissed her again and she felt his tongue glide over her lips, then ease inside her mouth. She made a tiny sound and he drew back to look down at her.

"This is all very strange," she said. "Is that Trist?"

"Aye, he is mewling so loudly it pains my ears."

She laughed, a sweet sound that made him kiss her again. Then he sighed and pulled away from her and rolled onto his back. He brought her with him, resting her face against his shoulder. Her palm lay over his heart.

"That is pleasure, Hastings."

He felt her lashes against his chest. He felt the warmth of her breath as she said, "It is something I could not have imagined."

"Few can until it overtakes them. You responded well to me."

"As you did to me, Severin." She pictured holding him as he backed away from her. She giggled.

She felt his hand stroking down her back, stroking over her hips. She pressed herself closer against him.

"You are filled with my seed."

There was such satisfaction in his voice that she bit him, then licked him. "Aye," she said against his warm flesh, "and I brought you into me and held you deep and close and filled you with myself."

He shuddered, then moaned. He said nothing more. She listened as his breathing slowed and evened into sleep.

Thank God for Dame Agnes and Alice.

Trist stretched out on Severin's chest, his paws over Hastings's hand.

How would one possibly have the strength to do this five times in the space of one day?

# B

SOMETHING WAS LIGHTLY SCRATCHING HER STOMACH. IT felt good. She sighed, stretched just a bit, then remembered the night before and opened her eyes.

She lifted the covers to see Trist curled next to her, his claws going up and down her belly. She petted him. "Where is your master?"

Trist opened his eyes, looked at her for a very long time, then stretched and slithered out from beneath the covers. He sniffed the air. Hastings sniffed the air too.

The air smelled of them. Of sex. She had smelled that before, but she hadn't known, hadn't really thought about it. She'd been a dunce. She'd been a blockhead.

She pushed back the covers and rose. She was sticky. His seed, she thought, as she bathed herself in the pewter basin of cool water.

Why had he left her? Why had he not awakened her so she could see to his morning meal? Perhaps this was the way men were supposed to behave after being with their wives for the night.

She saw the blue tunic she had made for him, laid out neatly on the end of the bed. There was a huge rent beneath the right arm. She remembered now that he'd ripped the tunic when he'd pulled it over his head the previous evening. She didn't mind at all that it was ripped. She believed she could add some more material to make it large enough for him. Aye, she could do that.

She was humming when she came into the great hall a short time later. There was Severin, seated between Gwent and Beamis, the two men listening intently to what he was saying. It was still very early. She felt wonderful.

She could not believe what had happened.

At that moment, Severin looked up and saw her. His face went very still. Then, slowly, he smiled. He raised his hand and called out, "Come here, Hastings. This almond bun is difficult to eat. I wish you to feed it to me."

She laughed and skipped toward him. She was filled with energy, filled with a lightness she hadn't felt in a very long time. She realized suddenly that she was happy.

He pulled her down onto his lap. "Now, this fool Gwent here has been instructing me on how to eat the bun but he does not do it well. My brain is weak from all your demands last night. Feed me, Hastings."

She pulled off part of the bun and eased it into his mouth. She was staring at his mouth as he chewed. She was staring at his throat as he swallowed.

"Now, kiss me."

"In front of Beamis and Gwent? In front of everyone? Everyone is watching us."

"Aye, I know it. Kiss me."

She did, a shy kiss, her lips closed, but he didn't care. It was a symbol, nay, more than a symbol, it was a vow, a promise, and all saw it. She was now his wife. There would be no more strife. She had bent to him. He let her feed him the rest of the bun. Then he lifted her off his lap, saying as he did so, "If you remain there, I will have to send my hand up your leg and pleasure you and that would shock our people for they believe you to be modest and bashful." He patted her buttocks.

"Now, I understand from Gwent that Eloise has returned to Sedgewick in the company of her new guardian and Sir Robert Burnell. I trust you treated the king's messenger properly?"

"Nay," Hastings said. "I kicked him in the shin, wept on his shirt when he said he was taking Eloise, and fed him a potion to make him fall in love with Edgar the wolf-hound."

He laughed. Perhaps before he would not have laughed. Perhaps before he would have drawn up tight as a bow, but not now. "I am sorry if you will miss the child. What did you think of her guardian? Gwent said she was the widow of a Sir Mark Outbraith, a man to whom the king owed a favor. Her name is Lady Marjorie?"

"Aye, that's the long and short of it. I was jealous, Severin. Eloise went to her immediately, left me as if I were naught but a slug to crawl along the ground." Hastings sighed.

"Aye, I can see that, but you will have your own babe soon, Hastings. In nine months."

She thought of his seed, deep within her. She turned red. He laughed. She cleared her throat and said, "That is what Sir Robert Burnell said, but I do miss her, Severin. She was still thin. Lady Marjorie acted as though I had starved her."

He rose from the trestle table, reached down so that Trist could easily climb up his arm, then said close to her ear, "I must practice with my men now, then Gwent wants me to go over the steward's records. That is why I left you this morning. If I had stayed, naught of anything would have been accomplished. Ah, but Hastings, after our meal, I can teach you something more about pleasure. There are many ways to reach the goal. Would you like that?"

She lowered her head. "Perhaps, but I might be too tired, Severin. Perhaps my legs are so sore that I cannot move them, perhaps—"

He touched his fingers to her mouth even as he lightly stroked his other hand down her back. "So soft," he said, leaned down, and kissed her. "Not so very ordinary after all." She felt his tongue slide over her bottom lip. "That feels very nice. But my tongue still wants to stay in my own mouth."

"A shy tongue, but that will change, you will see. Be about your duties, Hastings. Think of me and what I will do to you. Ah, be quiet, Trist, else I'll believe you some sort of magician.'' The marten was mewling so loudly that even Edgar the wolfhound heard him and was walking slowly toward them.

He hugged her to him, then, whistling, he strode out of the great hall, Gwent and Beamis on either side. He looked splendid. Hastings found that she didn't look away until he was gone from her sight.

"Well, I had believed you too stubborn, but you have proved me wrong, Hastings. I am pleased."

Hastings turned, grinning, to say to Dame Agnes, "You are pleased? You don't know what being pleased is." Then she too turned away, whistling as loudly as her husband, and made her way to her herb garden.

Alice said to Dame Agnes, "If there were no pleasure possible between men and women, can you begin to imagine the strife in the world?"

"War isn't enough for you, Alice? Men slaughtering men endlessly?"

"That is a good point. If women never received any pleasure, then they would likely slaughter the men. Soon there would be no one left except women. It would doubtless be a better life for us, but the boredom. I am just not certain."

Dame Agnes smiled and patted Alice's shoulder. "It is a mystery. However, for us here at Oxborough we will pray that both the lord and the lady continue to see each other through lust-filled eyes, at least until they discover that they quite like each other."

Hastings watched as Torric slowly walked toward Severin, who sat in his high-backed chair, the chair from which he judged local matters, the chair from which he faced a man he knew was cheating him. Gwent stood at his side.

Severin had asked her to come to the great hall to witness what he did. She was pleased that he had asked her. She was gravely disappointed that Torric had proved to be a thief. But she had seen the entries with her own eyes. Years upon years and he hadn't even made any attempt to hide it. The money was simply removed, no explanation, no reason given.

"Come closer, steward," Severin called. "I want to show you proof of your thievery."

Torric, his shoulders back, his head up, walked more quickly to Severin. "I am not a thief," he said in a loud voice that carried to every corner of the great hall. "What I am is a fool to have remained after Lord Fawke died."

"Well, you didn't flee. Now, steward, you will explain these entries you made. They go back many years. I do not understand why you did not even try to hide your thievery. Is your arrogance so great? You never believed that Lord Fawke would question you as I am now?"

Torric looked at the pages of parchment that showed his neatly entered numbers. He swallowed. "I have no arrogance, my lord. Nor am I a thief. It does not look good for me, does it, my lord?"

"I would say that Gwent is itching to hang you by your skinny neck."

Torric's hand went to his throat.

"What did you do with all that money, Torric? Is it buried beneath Hastings's herbal garden?"

"My lord, I swear it to you, to our God above, that I did not take any money from Lord Fawke. Oh dear, I suppose that I must speak now or suffer my own death."

"It is your best chance to survive this, steward. Make your tale plausible and interesting."

The steward appeared to be arguing silently with himself. Finally, he looked Severin straight in the eye and said, "Those figures are just as Lord Fawke ordered me to write in the records of Oxborough. I did nothing but what he bade me to do."

Her father cheated himself?

"That makes no sense, Torric," Severin said. "There is a small ransom gone from Oxborough. Because this is a wealthy holding, Oxborough has not suffered from the missing funds. But it will not continue. You steal what is mine now. Cease your lies and it will go easier for you."

But Torric held firm. "Nay, I am not lying. I have never

spoken of this before because I gave my sacred oath to Lord
Fawke. I entered the figures he told me to. I did nothing
more than what he bade me to do."

Gwent, unable to keep quiet, shouted at the steward,
"Stop your lying, you wretched bastard. The Devil's teeth,
I hate cheats and thieves. You will confess your crimes or
I will gullet you right here, right now."

Torric took a quick step back, only to feel the large hand
of one of the men-at-arms at his back. "Please, my lord,
I'm not lying. The money went south. Every three or four
months, Lord Fawke and three or four men took it there.
Did you not notice that all those entries appear very regu-
larly? I do not know who lived there or lives there now.
Only Lord Fawke knew. His men, if they knew, were sworn
to secrecy, as was I. All had Lord Fawke's trust. None ever
betrayed him. None until me, until now."

"But now he is dead and thus your silence matters no
more," Hastings said, stepping forward. "Why do I know
nothing of this holding you speak of, Torric?"

"You knew nothing of the man your father wedded you
to, Lady Hastings. Why should you know of this? I swear
it to you, I am not lying. I only did what your father ordered
me to do. I prayed that you wouldn't realize that there were
funds missing, Lord Severin. But I did realize that only a
fool would not readily realize that something was wrong. I
know you will kill me, but at least now you know the truth.
All the money went to a holding in the south."

"What is this holding called?"

"Rosehaven."

"Who lives at this place called Rosehaven? Who would
Lord Fawke send money to?"

"I do not know, I swear it."

"Let me gullet him now, Severin. The little puking bastard will just continue to lie until I do."

"Nay, Gwent, hold. This is proving interesting. Do we
have a mystery here, I wonder? Hastings, have you ever
heard the name Rosehaven?"

She shook her head. She said to Torric, "I remember
that my father left every few months. He always told me

he was visiting one of his holdings. Once or twice I asked to accompany him but he refused. Did he always carry the money to this Rosehaven?''

''Always. He told the men that if they failed to guard the pouch, there would be retribution. He was always gone for sixteen days, which meant he spent nine days at Rosehaven each time he journeyed there. The last time, he sent Beamis with a great deal of money because he realized that he was dying, a final payment, I suppose. I did not question him. He would have risen from his deathbed and killed me.''

Gwent turned to Severin. ''That is what alerted me immediately, Severin, that huge amount that was missing recently. Do you think the little bastard is telling the truth?''

''How long have you been at Oxborough, Torric?'' Severin asked, sitting forward in his great chair. Trist climbed out of Severin's tunic and slithered down his arm to stretch out his full length. He stared at the steward, his paws stretched out to cover Severin's fingers.

''For eleven years, my lord. I have toiled for Lord Fawke. I never cheated him. He paid me well. He trusted me. I prayed you would not discover the missing funds, but you have. Kill me, but it will not gain you any justice. Justice is down south at Rosehaven keep.''

''Where exactly?'' Hastings asked.

''On the coast, near Folkstone. It is nearly four days' hard riding from Oxborough.''

Severin was silent. He stroked Trist's back. Finally, he said, rising, ''We won't know the truth of the matter unless we go to this Rosehaven. Hastings, you will accompany me, as will you, Gwent. We will take fifteen men. We will leave in the morning.''

''Beamis knows the truth, Severin.''

''Aye, he knows. But I like mysteries. I want to visit this Rosehaven and juggle all the pieces of this mystery until I am able, by myself, to fit them all together. Torric, you will remain here. You will continue with your duties. I will have Beamis keep an eye on you with the instruction if you attempt to flee Oxborough, he will kill you. Do you understand me?"

"Aye, my lord. I understand you perfectly."

"Beamis has known me since I was born," Hastings said as she walked into the bedchamber just ahead of Severin. "He has never hinted anything. Nor has my father. What is going on here, Severin?"

He stopped her, his hands light on her upper arms. He turned her slowly. "I care not at this moment if he is keeping a bastard prince prisoner at this place called Rosehaven. Kiss me, Hastings."

She did, her mouth closed until she felt his tongue gliding along her bottom lip. She wrapped her arms around his neck, came up onto her tiptoes, and pressed herself against him. She said against his mouth, "I like that, Severin. Tell me what to do."

"Open your mouth, just a bit. That's it. Now, this is something men and women do. Don't be startled." She felt his tongue slowly slide into her mouth. She jumped and closed her mouth, holding his tongue inside.

He wanted to laugh but he couldn't. He stroked her tongue with his until she opened her mouth to show him her approval. And her growing enthusiasm.

"This is something I had not considered," she said, speaking, then kissing him, "something that should not be as exciting as it is—"

"Be quiet, Hastings." He locked his hands beneath her bottom and picked her up. He didn't stop kissing her even as he fell on top of her on the bed. Then she was laughing into his mouth. No woman had ever before laughed whilst he was kissing her. Severin drew up, balancing himself on his elbows. He stared down at her. "This is fun," she said, and chopped her hands against his arms. He fell on top of her. Soon he was laughing with her. They kissed and laughed even as they struggled out of their clothing.

When they were naked, he let her come down to her knees beside him. She immediately leaned down and kissed him, licked her tongue across his lips, then straightened again. She didn't wait this time, just clasped him between her hands, leaned down again, and took him in her mouth.

He nearly bowed off the bed. "Saint Andrew's toes, who told you to do that?"

She didn't release him, just said, her warm breath on him, "Dame Agnes and Alice both recommended this to me. I thought it sounded repellent, but they assured me that it was what a man wished above all things. Is that true, Severin?"

"I don't know. I am going to die."

When he finally had the resolve to shove her away, he prayed that she would release him. If she didn't, it would be all over for him. She did, finally, but it was slow and excruciatingly wonderful. He was moaning, his back arching, nearly beside himself. "You're not dead yet, Severin, but you sound very close."

Then she laughed, kissed his belly, and went back up on her knees to look down at what she had wrought. He sucked in air. He tried to slow his breathing. He felt her hand on his thigh moving upward and managed to whisper, "Nay, Hastings. I must recover for a moment, don't push me anymore."

She laughed again only to suck in her breath in surprise when he flipped her onto her back and came over her. "You bring a man to the brink of madness and laugh while you watch him teeter? You laugh to see what you have done with that mouth of yours? Well, Hastings, let's see how long your laughter lasts."

Her laughter didn't last five seconds. She was panting, heaving about, whimpering, her hands digging into his shoulders, when he raised his head, kissed her belly, and said, "Well? Are you teetering yet?"

She yanked his hair. He laughed and returned to her warm flesh. But he didn't give her release for a very long time. She finally shouted, "Severin, I cannot bear this. Get it done."

And he did. When she lay there, sucking in great breaths of air, quivering with pleasure, he was over her and coming into her."

She heard him laugh, then moan deeply. There were no more words between them, just passion that built and built until finally Severin shouted to the beamed ceiling.

He collapsed over her, kissing her until she had the strength to turn her face up to gain some kisses on her mouth.

"This is very tiring work, Severin."

"Aye," he said, nipping her bottom lip between his teeth, "would you believe me if I told you that most men would prefer battle to this wearisome job?"

Her laughter rang out. Trist raced up his bare master's back to peer down at her over Severin's shoulder.

"Aye, my lord, and most women would doubtless prefer shoveling ashes out of the ovens to this demanding task."

Trist mewled loudly. And Severin thought it was strange to be lying on top of a woman, laughing and speaking nonsense and enjoying it quite a lot.

## 14

THEY DIDN'T LEAVE FOR ROSEHAVEN THE FOLLOWING morning. A messenger arrived just as Hastings finished drinking a goblet of Gilbert the goat's milk. She rose quickly when she heard shouts from outside.

It was a messenger from Langthorne. Lord Severin's mother had disappeared.

He asked very softly, "How is this possible? My mother was guarded constantly. I selected the women myself before I came here to Oxborough. What happened?"

The messenger didn't like the lord's voice. He swallowed, got a grip on himself, and said, "It appears that one of the women became ill. Your mother asked to tend her and the other woman agreed. When she returned to the sick chamber, your mother was gone. I'm sorry, my lord. Sir Roger has mounted a search. His master-at-arms, your man Thurston, told me I should come to you. He is worried. Sir Roger did not wish to tell you yet, but Thurston said it was your right to know. By the time I left Langthorne, they had still not found her."

Severin stared at the man a moment, then waved him away. "Get him ale," he called to Alice. "His voice cracked from thirst even as he spoke to me."

Hastings knew, however, that the messenger's voice had

cracked because he'd been terrified that Severin would kill him.

"I fear I must go to Langthorne, Hastings. There is no time for this Rosehaven, no time for anything else."

"We will leave within the hour, Severin."

He arched a dark eyebrow. "I would make better time were I to have just men with me."

"You will see that I shan't slow you. Besides, when we find your mother, perhaps I could give her some herbs that would make her better. What is her illness, Severin?"

"She is mad."

Madness? Hastings wondered if her father had known about this. Surely he hadn't, else he would never have picked Severin to continue his line, not if there was madness in it. "Tell me more specifically what she does or says or how she acts."

"She can act very normally, converse with you like she is still the lady of the keep, then, suddenly, her eyes will go blank. She will say strange things. She will not know who she is or who you are. Several times I saw her throw herself to her knees and try to hit her head against the stones. Then she will sleep for many hours. When she wakes, she is usually normal again. But nothing is ever certain. That is why I had two women to keep close to her."

"Ah." It sounded like no madness Hastings had ever heard of. It sounded very strange indeed.

"What does that mean?"

"It means I must consult the Healer before we leave. Do you wish me to try to help her?"

"Very well, but Gwent and some of my men will accompany you. I don't want to take a chance on losing you."

She said nothing to that. She'd gone into the forest more times than she could count over the years to meet with the Healer. But now she was married and her husband wished to guard her. Protect her. Was he afraid that she would fall and hurt her toe? No, certainly not. She decided that protection from a man who made her feel as he did perhaps wasn't such a bad thing at all.

"Give me leave to worry about you now, Hastings."

She blinked up at him. "Do you now so easily read my mind, my lord?"

"Your thoughts are sometimes as clear to me as Edgar the wolfhound's."

That made her laugh. Without thought she kissed him, in front of the messenger, in front of all the people who were in the great hall.

"Aye, those thoughts of yours are simple and straightforward, but I mind not, Hastings. Take care and come back to me quickly."

She frowned, saying, "Why wouldn't this Sir Roger want you to know immediately that your mother had disappeared?"

"A very good question. I will look forward to his explanation."

Hastings imagined that Sir Roger had kept quiet because he had a healthy desire to keep his hide intact. He was doubtless praying that he would find his overlord's mother alive and thus escape Severin's anger. It was not to be.

Hastings had always believed that the Healer was older than the sessile oaks that grew thick and strong by her cottage—that, indeed, she had magically appeared on the earth at the same time those trees had burst through the soil. But her face was unlined, her skin soft, her hair was black with but a few strands of gray weaving through it. She always wore a dark brown wool gown with a rope tied around her waist. For as long as Hastings could remember, the Healer had always looked the same.

The Healer wasn't smiling at the group of men who rode to her cottage. She didn't smile either when she saw Hastings, just waited patiently, her hands very still at her sides.

"Healer," Hastings said as she dismounted her palfrey, Marella. "You look well. Ah, and here is Alfred." The huge brindle cat leapt into her arms, making her stagger back. Hastings heard the men's hoarse whispers. They were probably crossing themselves, for the cat surely had to be the largest in all of England. Hastings hugged Alfred, petted his big head, then set him down.

The Healer said, as she rubbed her bare toes against Alfred's fat side, "He eats all my food. I am now the skinny one. He will bury me when the time comes. Now, Hastings, come inside and tell me what it is you wish."

The smell within the small cottage nearly swamped the senses. There was basil, rosemary, foxglove, allium, hyssop, so many smells that collided with one another, blending and softening, forming new scents that dazzled the nose and made Hastings's eyes water.

Hastings sat on a small stool and waited for the Healer to give her a cup of her own private potion, a sweet yet tart brew that she much enjoyed, but the Healer would never give her the recipe or ever send her away with more than that one single cup. She watched the Healer give a large wooden bowl of the potion to Alfred. The cat's slurping was loud in the room.

"It is my lord's mother," Hastings said, then she told the Healer what Severin had told her. "He said she then would sleep. It seems to me that this sleeping is her mind's way of renewing her, perhaps. Have you something that could help such a strange malady?"

The Healer looked through the narrow open door at the men who were milling about. She winced as one of them, paying no attention, let his horse back into the wood pile and knock logs to the ground. "I have always disliked men," she said in that soft singsong voice of hers. "They tread upon my herbs because they never pay attention to anything that is beyond their noses. They belch and snore and their minds are lewd. Nay, I would rid the world of the animals if I could."

"My husband isn't like that."

"It is too soon for you to know that. I imagine you believed he was Satan's own spawn before you enjoyed pleasure with him. Aye, turn red, Hastings, but don't lie to yourself. Your father was like that, as was Sir Richard de Luci. Aye, that one was a pig who killed his wife to have you. I am glad he failed, Hastings. Nor am I displeased that he managed to kill off that miserable wife of his before he failed. I have heard talk that all is not well at Sedgewick. There are forces at work there that will bring tragedy.''

"You speak of Eloise?"

"Aye. Poor child. What chance could she have?"

"You heard that Lady Marjorie abuses Eloise?"

The Healer shrugged. "It would be nothing new, would it? But you will have a care, Hastings. Nothing is ever what it seems. Nothing. Don't ever forget that. Now, let me give you some herbs that might help your husband's mother. Ah yes, there are so many smiles and sighs now that you enjoy Lord Severin. Why did you bend, Hastings?"

"I do not like strife. I know nothing of men and thus I did not deal well with him. Dame Agnes and my serving girl, Alice, told me what to do. I decided to treat him well, nothing more, Healer."

"He probably brags to his men that he has brought you to heel."

"Perhaps I am the one who controls the heeling."

The Healer shook her head. She smiled, it was a small thing, stingy even, but it was a smile. "You are guileless, Hastings. That is why you must have a care. Go now, I have business with my plants. Alfred, you may have no more potion now. Go terrorize the men outside. Meow at them and stretch up on your hind paws. It will scare them witless. Mayhap they will flee screaming into the forest and lose themselves and get eaten by boars. They are all worthless loutheads."

Hastings touched her fingertips to the Healer's arm and took her leave. Gwent said as he helped her mount Marella, "A strange woman. As for that cat, the beast is large enough to have a seat at a trestle table."

"He eats enough for two men," Hastings said. "Give him two seats."

It rained all during the day, endless, ceaseless rain, turning the world gray, making them all miserable. There were twelve of them, all pressed against their horses' necks. Hastings was relieved that she'd brought most of her herbs.

Someone would surely sicken from this miserable weather. By six o'clock that first afternoon, Severin called a halt. In their path was Wigham Abbey, a stark gray-stone building built in the last century. It looked menacing in the dying afternoon light. Hastings shivered, not from the cold or the rain, but from the apprehensive feeling that pile of stones gave her.

The abbot, Father Michael, greeted Severin politely and welcomed them all into the cold great hall of the abbey. He was affable until he saw Hastings. He cleared his throat, saying, "My lord, your lady, of course, will not remain here. One of the brothers will escort her to another building, where she will remain until you are ready to resume your journey in the morning."

"I don't think so," Severin said, nothing more. Hastings didn't understand what was happening but she knew he was angry. So women weren't allowed with the monks. Why did this seem to anger Severin?

"It is the way of our order, my lord. She will be fed. But she is not allowed to remain here with the men. It is considered a sacrilege. It is not done. Our Lord would not look kindly upon us for breaking one of his sacred orders."

Hastings was on the point of telling her husband that she didn't care, she just wanted to change from her wet clothes, when Severin drew his dagger from the wide leather belt at his waist. In a quick, graceful movement, he put the point to the abbot's throat. "I know how you treat ladies, Father. I will not have my wife lying on a damp mattress with only a stingy thin blanket to cover her, shivering until her teeth chatter. I won't have her drinking cold, thin soup that some monk slips into her cell whilst she isn't looking. She will remain here, with me, with my men and your holy brothers."

Father Michael opened his mouth, both astonished and infuriated. Severin simply pressed the tip of his knife into his throat. A drop of blood appeared. "It will be as I say, Father. I will ensure that she doesn't send your monks into agonies of unfulfilled lust. She will remain at my side.

Think of her as another man. Think of her as a budding brother whose hair is but overlong.''

Above all, the abbot wasn't stupid. This man all garbed in gray didn't seem to care that he, Father Michael, abbot to this long-lived order of Benedictines, was God's emissary, that he would go to hell if he stuck that knife in the abbot's throat. Father Michael would have to give in, but it galled him. All the lord's men were wet to the bone, huddled together, but the woman, ah, that one standing there all proud, her long hair in damp masses down her back, as wet as the men were, he could still see how she was looking at him, at his helpless brothers. He knew she had put her husband up to this. She was a snare of the Devil. All females were. Seducers of honorable men, whores. She should be off by herself, away from men of goodwill and morality, she should—

"We are all wet, tired, and hungry. See to it, Father."

The abbot nodded, his mouth a tight, thin line, and turned to his cowled brothers. His thin face was red, the pulse pounding in his neck, just beside that speck of blood. Hastings saw him cuff one of the brothers. She said, staring at the holy man who had so carelessly struck another, "Is that true, Severin? Women are kept separate? They are not treated well? I did not know this."

Severin only shrugged. "It would not matter if the weather were warm and the sun bright in the sky. But in this dampness, you would surely become ill. I want you out of those wet clothes. Come along."

"Why is this a rule, Severin?"

"I have been told that the Church still debates whether or not a woman even has a soul. Think on that, Hastings. If you don't have a soul, then you should be forbidden the company of God's perfect male creatures. You are not worthy. You are no better than an animal, at least in God's eyes."

"That is very strange. Father Carreg never said any of this to me."

"Father Carreg isn't stupid. He probably believed you would make his bowels watery if he preached such a thing at Oxborough. But this is usually the way of things. It was my mother who told me of this. Travelers are welcome at religious houses, but women are to be set aside because the priests believe they will taint the very sacred air with their wickedness."

She looked perplexed until she smiled, a dimple appearing in her cheek. "I've tried to be wicked only with you."

He laughed, took her hand, and followed the silent brother, who led them to his own cell. Severin left her to change. "I will change with the other men. Dress warmly, Hastings."

The cell was dry and warm and smelled of sweet rosemary. When she returned to the main dining area, where there were six trestle tables set close together, she inhaled the odor of warm ale, fresh baked bread, and roasted chicken.

"This is not the normal fare for travelers," Severin said to her. "I have paid dearly for this meal. It had better taste as good as it smells. I told the abbot that the food had to find favor with my wife else I would be displeased. I then touched my fingers to my knife. I enjoyed watching him pale." He touched his palm to her cheek, then to her forehead. "You are warm to the touch. You feel all right?"

"Oh aye," she said, and touched him back. "And you, my lord?"

"I believe," he said slowly, looking down at her, "that if you continue as you are, all the brothers will gnaw their knuckles in the throes of lust. I promised the abbot that he was to think of you as just another man, a castrato, perhaps."

She giggled and raised her voice to a high, squeaky wail, "Very well, then, I can even sing for my dinner. I will not kiss you, but I want to, Severin. Your mouth pleases me."

"Stop it, Hastings. Ah, our meal is ready."

Hastings said after she bit into a chicken wing, "Don't stick your dagger through the abbot's neck, 'tis well enough prepared."

After dinner, Hastings checked all of the men. Tabar, one of the Oxborough men-at-arms, was overly warm, his chest heavy. Hastings mixed him a potion of warm milk and gentian and watched him drink it down. "Now, chew these columbine leaves if your throat becomes sore. Keep yourself warm, Tabar. Sleep close to the other men. Their body warmth will help."

One of the brothers, a small, wiry man with great purity of expression, came to her after she gave Tabar the herbs. His look was furtive. "I have a toothache, my lady. The tooth looks healthy, but it must be rotting from the inside. Have you perhaps anything that would help me?"

"Aye, Father. Mix these ground delphinium seeds into a mug of wine or ale. It will relieve you. But the tooth must be pulled, Father. If it pains you, it cannot be long until it will cause you such agony that you must pull it."

"Aye, I know it, but I am a coward. I would wait until the pain drives me into delirium. Then one of the other brothers could draw it for me."

Suddenly, the abbot was there. "You come to this woman? You speak to her? You take the Devil's evil potions from her?" He knocked the packet of delphinium seeds to the floor.

The brother looked ready to cry out his misery. He stared down at the scattered delphinium seeds beside his sandaled feet. "Father Michael," he whispered, "it is just a small thing for the pain in my tooth. The lady does nothing evil."

"What she gave you would produce evil visions in your sleep, Brother. You would dream of the flesh of women and this dream would corrupt you."

Hastings didn't say anything, but it was difficult. She wanted to kick the abbot. She wished he had the toothache. She wondered if he would suffer silently or chance dreaming of her.

"Come," Severin said quietly, walking to her. "You can do nothing for the brother. No, don't argue. The brother is a member of this order. He must follow the rules."

He took her hand when she lagged, looking back at the poor brother who was holding his palm to his cheek. He pulled and she had to skip to keep up with his long strides.

"I do not wish to fluster the poor brothers. We will lie

together as would a brother and his sister.'' No sooner had they settled themselves in blankets on the narrow cot in the brother's cell than there came a yell from the great hall.

Severin, whose hand had been on Hastings's breast, cursed, leapt to his feet, and pulled on his clothes. Sword in hand, he was gone within moments.

When Hastings came into the great hall, a blanket wrapped around her, there was the poor brother whose tooth had been paining him on his knees on the stone floor. He was moaning and pressing his hands against his jaw. Blood was dripping through his fingers. The abbot stood over him, holding the tooth in his hand, looking grim and pleased. ''It is done. Whine no more.''

''I could give him something to slow the bleeding,'' she said quietly to Severin.

''Nay, you cannot. The abbot would go into a frenzy of religious fervor were you to do anything.'' He sighed and ran his fingers through his hair. ''Let us sleep, Hastings. Morning will come early. Let us pray that the rain stops. I want to leave this place.''

The rain did stop near dawn the next morning. Severin awakened her with a kiss to her temple. She opened her eyes and looked up at him. She lifted her hand and lightly caressed her fingertips over his mouth, his nose, his cheeks. She smoothed his eyebrows. ''I am glad you kept me with you.''

''Aye, but there is no time to ask for more of a show of gratitude.'' He pulled off the blankets and rose.

Within the hour they were riding from Wigham Abbey. Hastings turned in Marella's saddle and stared back at the grim stone buildings. Even in the morning sunlight, it looked inhospitable. ''I wonder if convents are as depressing as that place.''

''Benedictines relish the torture of their flesh,'' Gwent said. ''Let them all rot. I do not imagine that it much pleases God, but who knows?''

Tabar was better. He was even whistling. He was effusive in his thanks to Hastings.

''He is young,'' Severin said. ''He will glow and squeal

his infatuation for you but then it will disappear. I will suffer him until he cures himself of you. If it is not soon, I will cuff him hard and that will clear out his wits.''

Hastings laughed. She poked her husband's arm. He smiled at her and stretched out his hand, gripping hers.

Gwent grunted and said under his breath, "He has not mucked up the miracle, praise be to God.'' He had never seen his master so at ease with a woman. Even with most men he was silent, his speech terse. He heard Severin laugh. It was indeed a miracle. All the men looked quite pleased.

# 15

THEY REACHED YORKSHIRE ON THE AFTERNOON OF THE fifth day. The weather remained warm and dry. They passed to the east of Leeds, on toward the coast, to the town of Hawksmere. Langthorne village lay just behind at the head of the estuary. Hastings was both excited to see Langthorne and anxious that her mother-in-law had been found by now. Poor woman. She prayed the Healer's herbs would help her. But sickness in the head was frightening simply because there were no sores, no fever, no broken bones. It was hidden. It was unknown. Thus it was to be feared and reviled.

Langthorne keep stood on a slight rise at the head of the estuary. It looked as old as the black rocks that poked up randomly in the fields. There were gouges in the outer walls, stones spilling out like waterfalls of rock. The fields surrounding the outer walls looked devastated, the people ragged and poor. She'd known that Severin had wedded her to gain money to renew his home, but she hadn't expected it to be quite so bad. His expression was set. He said nothing. He would have come here soon enough, but she was glad that it was sooner. There was much to be done to bring Langthorne back to its former glory, whatever that had been. It would be passed down to her sons and daughters. She didn't want it to be a ruin.

His mother was at Langthorne. Sir Roger's men had found her sitting on a branch in a tree, her bare legs dangling. She laughed as she waved to them.

"I regret, my lord, that it took us three days," Sir Roger said, all pleased with himself. There had been no surprise when their party had ridden into the inner bailey. It was obvious he had discovered that Severin was coming. He was a tall man, thinner than the legs of the trestle tables in the great hall of Langthorne. His hands moved constantly. She didn't know if he was naturally nervous or whether this nervousness was brought upon by Severin's presence and how Severin would deal with Sir Roger's lapse.

"Is she normal?"

"Aye, she appears so. She is quiet, so the women tell me. As I said, she was laughing and waving. That is the only way we found her. Who would think to search up in the trees?"

"May I see her, Severin?"

"Aye. Sir Roger, this is my lady wife, Lady Hastings."

"My lady. 'Tis an odd name you carry."

"But 'tis solid, Sir Roger. When you say my name you have no doubt that you have said it."

"I will believe what you have said though my wit must have more time to glean your meaning."

"She is like that," Severin said, and cuffed his wife's shoulder.

"I do not see Trist, my lord," Sir Roger said. "He is well?"

"My damned marten wasn't to be found when we left. I believe he is spending more time in the forest, perhaps mating. We will see."

Hastings followed Severin up the narrow stairs to the small chamber where Sir Roger had moved his mother a short time before when he had taken a mistress, thus needing the larger chamber. The new chamber, Sir Roger said, all affability, was quite adequate.

Adequate, hah, Hastings thought, when Severin unlocked and pushed open the door. The room was dark and narrow. It smelled of stale reeds and urine. There was one narrow window that had a square of bear skin over it. The reeds on the cold stone floor were filthy with rotted food and excrement. Hastings simply stood in the doorway, so dismayed that at first she didn't see the woman who was standing still as a pillar, her back pressed against the stone wall.

"Mother," Severin said, but made no move toward her.

The woman shook her head but didn't move. "Who is she?" She raised her arm and pointed at Hastings. "Why are you with this girl?"

"She is my wife. Her name is Hastings."

"I am not stupid. I remember now. She is the heiress, the one you had to marry to save us."

"Aye. I'm pleased you remember. How do you feel, Mother?"

"Feel? Are you blind? Just look at my feet. They hurt. Sir Roger's bitch made me flee the keep and I had to hide in the forest for nearly a week before I managed to gain the attention of the men-at-arms who were riding below. I had to hide in the tree so the wild animals wouldn't kill me. They said they were looking for me. The bitch must have gotten frightened that I would die and Sir Roger would be angry. Just look at my feet. No one cares about my feet."

"I do, madam," Hastings said. She turned to her husband. "Please have one of the men bring my trunk of herbs. May I speak to your mother, Severin?"

He was staring at his mother, clearly uncertain.

"I am larger than she is. If she becomes violent, I will be able to deal with her." She turned to the fat woman who was hovering behind them. "Bring me warm water, a bathing tub, and many bathing towels."

The woman's three chins wobbled. "Aye, my lady."

"This is one of the women you selected to see to your mother?"

"Aye, it is. She has gained more flesh than seems possible in such a short time. You will call me if you need anything. I will go into the hall and speak with Sir Roger. I would know more about this situation." He paused a moment and looked around him. "I do not like this chamber.

It would depress the spirit of a healthy man.''

"Aye, it would. We will speak of it later, my lord."

He was still frowning when he left her.

"My feet!" he heard his mother screech.

Hastings managed to get her mother-in-law to sit on the narrow, musty bed. The coverlets were thin and smelled dirty. When she saw her feet, she wanted to cry. They were torn and filthy, some sores crusted, others still oozing blood. She looked up at the now-silent woman whose dirty hair hung in strings to her meager breasts and said quietly, "Madam, allow me to take care of you."

The woman stretched out a dirty hand and lightly touched it to Hastings's cheek. "I was once pretty like you are. It was a very long time ago. There was a man I loved. He looked very much like the man who was standing in the doorway with you. He died, you know. It was a petty thing, the way he died. He was drunk and fell from his horse into a ditch. There was water in the ditch, just a small amount of water, but he landed facedown and drowned. Is that not petty?"

"Aye, it is. The man with me is your son, Severin."

"Severin? I wonder why he is named Severin. I would have called him William, after the great conqueror. I remember Severin. He was a quiet boy, but strong, so very strong. I remember how he once lifted me above his head with just one hand. Then he left. Ah, but my feet hurt."

Hastings tended her mother-in-law herself. She didn't want the fat woman in the same chamber with her. As for the second woman Severin had picked to care for his mother, she never saw her. It was some minutes before she thought to ask, "What is your name, madam?"

"I am Moraine. I was once pretty, like you are."

"You still are," Hastings said, her voice grim as she held Moraine's filthy, bleeding foot in her hands.

"Sir Roger says that my mother escaped when one of her women became ill, nothing more. He was very sorry for it. But he found her and she is safe. He apologized sincerely for not sending a messenger, but he did not wish to unduly alarm me. He did find her unharmed, so my trip is wasted. He promised to punish the man who rode to Oxborough. I told him that the man wasn't to be punished, that I had planned to come soon in any case.

"Then he said his mistress, Glenda, was always kind to my mother—indeed, that she would weep when my mother forgot who she was and where she was. He said my mother was very fond of Glenda when she wasn't succumbing to her madness. He seems very pleased with himself that he found her and that she's alive. As to her small chamber, as you know he sees nothing at all wrong with having moved her into it. After all, my mother is mad. Most of the time she isn't aware of where she is, thus why waste the large bedchamber on her?"

"Did you kill Sir Roger, Severin?"

Slowly, very slowly, the ferocious frown disappeared. He stopped his urgent pacing. He smiled down at her. "My blood was hot enough to do it, but I held back. Perhaps he deserves it, I'm not yet certain. But it amazed me, Hastings. I truly saw nothing at all wrong with what he has done. I believe he even expects me to reward him for finding her. When I would have questioned him more, he left the hall when my attention was elsewhere. By Saint Olaf's elbows, even the ale he served me tasted of piss."

"Let me kill him instead. I'll wager you will find out he does deserve it."

That brought him to a stop. He arched a black eyebrow. "You are but a girl, yet you speak like this?"

"Aye, a dagger through his black heart. As for this mistress of his, you heard what your mother said. Something about the bitch making her flee Langthorne. So Sir Roger denied that. I would like to know the truth of it as well. If the mistress had something to do with it, then I would like to tie her to a stake in the village and keep her there for all to see for at least a sennight. It would rain at least three times in that period."

"Why do we not simply tie both of them to the stake, naked, back to back?"

Her eyes glittered. "I like the way your mind snaps to

the perfect punishment. You said that Sir Roger sees nothing wrong with what he has done to your mother. I would imagine that because he treated her with indifference, the two women you picked to care for her became quickly hardened. I don't know where the second woman is. Your mother is very thin, Severin. Her feet are very bad—she was barefooted the entire time she was hiding in the forest—but I have treated them as best I can and bandaged them with clean linen. I have given her some of the potion the Healer prepared. She is sleeping now, in one of my night shifts. Her clothes were filthy. This fat woman probably ate all your mother's food.''

"Where have you put her?''

Hastings smiled slowly. "In the chamber Sir Roger moved her out of. In the lord's chamber. I had two of the servants move in a small cot for her. She is now sleeping on clean covers and she herself is now clean. Do you mind sharing with your mother?''

He shook his head.

"I, ah, had all of Sir Roger's clothing and possessions and those of his mistress moved to the small chamber where they had put your mother.''

"I like the way your brain works as well, Hastings. Excellent. I wish to question Sir Roger more closely. His mistress is visiting in the village, he told me, but she should return soon. Then, very briefly, before he escaped me, he complained that the money I have sent has not been enough to accomplish anything. It has bought only enough food to keep the people from starving. That isn't right." He stopped, cursed, then fell again to pacing.

Hastings looked about the hall. "This is very strange, Severin. Sir Roger is still gone. We are very nearly alone here. What is happening?''

"I don't know. Gwent and our men are looking about to see what needs to be done to the barracks, to the keep itself, and to the peasants' cottages and the fields. It doesn't look very hopeful, Hastings.''

"No matter. You will fix it. I wish the man would return so that you may question him.''

"We will see once he returns. I believe he was so surprised at my anger that he wanted to take himself off, perhaps speak to his mistress and decide how best to deal with
me. Aye, I shall tie them both to a stake in the village."

She laughed. It was the first sound Sir Roger heard when
he came into the dim hall, his mistress, Glenda, behind him.
All would be well. His heart slowed. He realized the moment the words had escaped his mouth that Lord Severin
wasn't pleased to hear him complain about the money he
had sent to Langthorne. Then he had seen Gwent just outside the hall and the look the lout had given him had shriveled him to his toes. Thurston had looked grim. That mangy
bastard betrayed him, had sent the messenger to Lord Severin. He could give him orders, but he could not have him
whipped. He was Lord Severin's man. Damnation.

It was true that he had panicked when Lord Severin had
come from seeing his mother. He had seemed angry. But
why? She was alive, wasn't she? He, Sir Roger, had found
her. The mad old woman wasn't worth more than a man's
spit. No, Lord Severin would have to reward him for finding that mad old crone. He would give him another bag of
coins. Aye, everything would be all right. Still, he thought
to pray as he moved forward.

"My lord, my lady," he called, his voice complacent
now, with more than enough deference to please the master.
"I am pleased that you are here, though your visit is a
surprise. Your dear mother is fine, just as I told you. The
women you selected have cared well for her, except that
the second one died so now there is just one."

"The fat one," Hastings said.

"She must have meat on her to deal with a madwoman."

Hastings wanted to choke his neck with her own hands.
His neck was skinny. She could choke him, she knew it.
She felt Severin close his hand over hers. It stilled her. She
realized she was breathing fast and forced herself to ease.
She saw the girl standing to Sir Roger's left side. She was
very young, plump, pretty, her hair light and thick, in fat
curls down her back, held with a gold net. There was such
a look of self-satisfaction on her face that Hastings's

breathing speeded up again. Sir Roger had just proven himself a fool.

"Glenda," Sir Roger said, "fetch our lord and lady some of the special wine and bread and cheese."

The girl gave him a sullen nod and left the hall. Perhaps, Hastings thought, Glenda had eaten her mother-in-law's food. Her bottom was good-sized. She would be as fat as that serving woman when she was twenty.

Sir Roger rubbed his hands together as he motioned Severin to the lord's chair, its beautiful carved arm posts dull and dirty. He looked at Hastings and shrugged.

"You may remain standing by your lord," he said to her.

"There is no lady's chair?" Severin asked.

"It is in the lord's bedchamber," Sir Roger said.

Severin patted his leg. "She will sit here until you have the lady's chair fetched for her, Sir Roger."

"Oh, aye, my lord." Sir Roger called to a ragged serving boy and spoke quietly to him. Then he straightened, his eyes going to Glenda, who was directing two servants who carried trays with wine, goblets, bread, and cheese.

The food was set upon a trestle table. Hastings rose and waited. Severin rose slowly, saying, "Sir Roger, bring my chair to the trestle table."

The man gaped at him, then managed to pull the large chair to the nearest end of the table. "My lord," he said. Severin knew exactly what he was thinking. He was a knight. What right did Lord Severin have ordering him to do a servant's task?

Hastings sat on the bench at her husband's right.

They drank the wine and ate the bread. No one said anything. Glenda sat herself at the other end of the trestle table beside Sir Roger.

"You told me that the money I have sent isn't enough," Severin said matter-of-factly. He tore a piece of bread off with his teeth.

"Aye, my lord. Mayhap I should not have mentioned it to you so soon after you arrived, but it is a concern. I have used the money wisely, but there is so much that needs to be done before Langthorne regains its previous grandeur.''

Hastings kicked up some of the dirty reeds with the toe of her boot. ''Aye, you are right, Sir Roger. I have always found that one must have money to keep a great hall clean. Sweeping up old reeds and replacing them must be more costly, though, than even I imagined.''

Sir Roger paid her little heed, merely shrugged and said, ''There are few enough servants and they are a surly lot. Some even escaped Langthorne after the marauders devastated the area and killed your brother. I didn't have enough men to catch them. My Glenda does her best with them, but it is difficult.''

''Aye, my lord,'' Glenda called out. ''The lot we have are pigs.''

She had a lovely musical voice. Her teeth were white and straight. She was rubbing herself against Sir Roger's arm. The man's eyes glazed. Sir Roger was an even bigger fool than Hastings imagined.

''There has been no work done on repairing the outer walls,'' Severin said as he pushed the pewter plate out of the way and leaned forward on the trestle table. ''Why?''

''There aren't enough men, my lord.''

''Gwent told me that you have nineteen men. What do they do all day?''

''They patrol the area and improve their skills on the practice field.''

''As of tomorrow, you will divide the men into three groups. Whilst one group practices, another will patrol, and the third group will begin repairs.''

Sir Roger gulped.

''The money I sent was enough to hire workers from the villages around here to assist in the repairs. What have you done with the money, Sir Roger?''

''As I told you, my lord, the funds were only sufficient to keep us clothed and fed.''

''I have remarked upon all the servants here. They are ragged and dirty. My own mother was wearing a rag. If the money went for clothing, then who is wearing it?''

''There was no reason for your dear mother to have new

gowns, my lord. She is mad. She would not know it if she were wearing a new gown or an old sack.''

Hastings said very quietly, "What happened to Lady Moraine's clothes? I could find only rags in that small trunk in the chamber.''

"Who is Lady Moraine?" Hastings heard Glenda ask Sir Roger.

"That is the woman of whom you are so very fond," Hasting said. "That is the poor madwoman with whom you are so very tender and loving.''

"Glenda simply did not know your mother's name, my lord. It is nothing more than that.''

"Where are Lady Moraine's clothes?" Severin asked.

It was in that instant that Hastings knew. "Ah," she said, in the mildest of voices, "I venture to say that perhaps her clothing is in one of the large trunks in the lord's bedchamber?''

"Aye, that's it," Glenda said. "There was no reason for the poor dear mad creature to wear the gowns, so I removed them so she wouldn't shred them.''

"I see that you are wearing one of them," Hastings said.

"Oh no," Glenda said. "I do not wear her gowns. The lady's clothing was old and ugly.''

"I wish to see an accounting of the money I sent you, Sir Roger. Now.''

"There is no steward, my lord.''

"Then you will show me what records you have kept.''

Sir Roger rose slowly. He was sweating. "Indeed, my lord, I have not yet spent all the money. I have held it close. I have not spent it on needless things. I want to use it wisely. I am a cautious man.''

Severin rose slowly to his feet. He pushed back the lord's chair. He stood there, tall, fierce, all in gray, his whip coiled about his hand, his expression unreadable even to Hastings. She fancied she could feel the fear rolling in waves off Sir Roger. She said not a word, just waited, watching her husband.

He strode to Sir Roger, leaned down, grabbed him about his tunic, and pulled his feet off the floor. He didn't release him. He said very quietly, "You will fetch the money right now. You will bring what records you have here to me."

He shook him, then released him. He turned to Glenda, who wasn't looking quite so complacent now. "You will bring me all the gowns you own. Now."

He didn't touch her, just watched her scramble from the bench and run toward the stairs.

To Hastings's surprise, Severin turned back to her and winked. "Soon," he said. "Soon we will have this mess cleared up."

Hastings suddenly remembered when she had first seen him standing in the great hall of Oxborough. He had terrified her with his stillness, his utter control. Ah, but now he was her husband, her lover. He had just scared two villains spitless and he had winked at her.

Her heart swelled.

# 16

GLENDA WASN'T STUPID. SHE HAD NOT LEFT HER GOWNS IN the lord's bedchamber. She knew the other servants hated her and thus would steal her precious clothes if they found them. She had kept them well hidden.

When she returned to the great hall with three gowns, several tunics, three shifts, and stockings, Severin merely turned to Hastings, who said, "I suggest, Glenda, that you bring the remainder of your clothes purchased with my lord's money. If you do not, it will not go well with you."

It was then that Glenda looked up at Severin, her blue eyes wet and bright with as yet unshed tears. "My lord," she whispered, "there are naught but two more gowns. Please, my lord, I cannot go naked." Her voice fell even lower. "I could please you, my lord, more than your lady does. She is a shrew with a loud voice. You wed her only to gain her father's land and money. All know of the sacrifice you have made. I could ease your trials, my lord."

Severin didn't have time to answer. In the next instant, Hastings was on the girl. She grabbed a handful of hair, pulled her head back, and put her face right into Glenda's. "Don't you ever speak to my husband like that again, do you hear me, girl? You believe me some dumb cow who will just stand about and be insulted by you? Aye, I am an heiress, but I am not at all ordinary. My lord will attest to that. You don't know that I am a healer, do you? That means I can also take my revenge upon someone who angers me. I can make your monthly flux never stop. You would bleed and bleed until you were white and drained. You want that, Glenda?''

That was a threat Severin would never have considered. Glenda's face was already leached of color. She looked terrified.

"Aye, my girl. Never forget that I am a shrew with a loud voice and you will be the first to hear it if you displease me again." She shoved Glenda away from her. "Go fetch the remainder of the gowns. Get them all or I will see to it that your bleeding begins today."

Severin watched the girl scurry toward the stairs like the Devil himself was after her. He turned to his wife, who was looking very strange. He expected her to be pleased with herself, but she didn't appear to be. She was pale, not as pale as Glenda, but still without color. Her eyes had darkened from that pure, soft green to nearly black. He took a step toward her. "What is wrong, Hastings?"

She waved her hands at him. She didn't want his questions. She just wanted to go bury herself. "It is nothing."

He drew her up against him. She felt his large hands stroking down her back. "Come, tell me the truth, or I will not be pleased with you."

She threw back her head. Her face was still pale, her expression pained. "I made a vow to the Healer. I was never to make a threat that I would mean."

He stared down at her, feeling like a fool. He said very slowly, "And this is the first time you have done it. That means that you would not have given me watery bowels?"

She shook her head. "I don't know how to. Nay, I wouldn't have done that to you, even had I known what herbs to mix together."

He cursed. "I don't even remember now why you made that threat, but you deserved what I wanted to do to you. But then I thought of my bowels and hunkering down next to the pig byre. I let you be. Saint Elrod's knees, why can

I not remember why I wanted to strangle you?''

"Mayhap it is no longer important."

He frowned down at her, those dark blue eyes of his looking directly into hers. She believed he would no longer chastise her? Did she not understand that she had bent so completely to him, he had not even thought about it, that there had been no need? Very simply she had not displeased him since she'd run into his arms upon his return from visiting his new properties.

Suddenly, she whispered, "I shall have to confess to the Healer when we return to Oxborough. She will probably make my bowels watery as a punishment."

That made him laugh, but he sobered quickly enough. "Then you really meant what you said to Glenda?"

She lowered her head and nodded. "Not now, but I meant it when I threatened her. She is a sly girl. Sir Roger is besotted with her."

"He's a fool."

"Aye. I only hope that he has not betrayed you because of Glenda."

Severin just shook his head, touched his fingers beneath her chin, and forced her face up. "This was some sort of vow you took to have the Healer teach you?"

She nodded, leaning her cheek against his palm. "The Healer has told me since I was just a little girl that I could not harm another person with my knowledge of herbs. She said that if I did, then all my potions would lose their efficacy."

"Then you will forget that you were serious in your threat. All is still well. You are right, Hastings. Sir Roger is a fool. Ah, here he comes. This should prove interesting."

Severin knew in his gut that there were coins missing from the thick leather pouch. He could see it in Sir Roger's eyes, see it in the nervous movements of his hand when he handed Severin the pouch, see his guilt in the sheen of sweat on his forehead. And, he supposed, that is what made up his mind. He counted out the coins on the trestle table and frowned down at them.

"What did you plan to do with the money?" Severin asked, not moving, just standing there tall and strong and dark-browed as the Devil himself.

"I was waiting, my lord, waiting to see what was really needed."

"Was I not very clear in my instructions? Have you not viewed the holes in the outer walls? Have you not seen the devastated fields? Have you not remarked the sullen faces all about you? By Saint Andrew's eyeballs, you have done nothing but clothe yourself and your mistress. You have not even limed the jakes. The stench is overwhelming. Damnation, man, you'd best pray that the meal you will feed us reflects your buying of decent food."

"I have held your money close, my lord," Sir Roger said, and he looked scared now, very scared. "I have waited, but what is wrong with that? I have been here but a month and a half. Surely that is a very short time to expect anything. Surely. Besides, you should not have come here for another half year, at least."

Glenda crept into the great hall. There were more clothes in her arms. She was not shaking like Sir Roger, but she looked as if she were on her way to judgment and knew herself guilty. She was.

"Hastings," Severin said. "I would that you examine all the clothing she has brought us and select those things you think would suit my mother."

Glenda squawked. "My lord, nay! Your esteemed mother is much thinner than I am. Your esteemed mother does not even know what her name is usually. There is no reason to give her lovely clothes. She would not know the difference. She would spit her food upon the gowns. She would piss on the shifts."

Severin said very quietly, "It matters not what you believe. You are speaking of my mother. If you ever speak about her like that again, I will ensure that Hastings makes you bleed your life away. See to the clothes, Hastings." He added to Glenda, "You will oversee the meal now. I assume that it is one of your tasks, to oversee the servants?"

She nodded, head down.

"Take Sir Roger with you. Sir Roger, make certain there are no stones in the flour. I like my bread to be soft on the inside. Ah, Gwent, I am glad you are come. We have much to discuss."

Gwent spat on the reeds as he watched Sir Roger and his mistress walk quickly from the great hall. "Will you skewer the mangy whoreson?"

"I am thinking about that." He pointed down to the piles of coins. "At least the fool did not spend it all on his mistress. But he did spend a goodly portion. I wonder why many men lose their wits over simple females?"

Gwent would not have gone near an answer to that inquiry. He merely looked grim, which is what he felt, and waited.

"What say you, Gwent, if Thurston takes over here?"

"He'll whip the arse of every healthy peasant in the area to rebuild Langthorne and plant the fields and repair their cottages. Aye, and they'll give him loyalty once their bellies are filled again and they have decent garments to wear on their backs."

"I think so as well."

That night, Severin looked down at his sleeping mother. He was surprised at how young she looked in her sleep, young and very clean. Hastings had combed her hair until it was dry, then braided it loosely. It looked soft and thick, a lovely pale brown. He said quietly as he backed away from the small cot, "I remember it was always thus. She would sleep and sleep and when she awoke, she would remember who she was and her mind would flow smoothly for a week or perhaps longer."

"We will see. The Healer did not know if her potion would help her. I have the girl Glenda sewing the gowns for your mother. She is skilled. It surprised me. Your mother will have a new gown to wear on the morrow. I am willing to wager that it will fit her nicely."

Severin walked to the bed, sat on the edge, and sighed. "Thurston is a good man. He will do his best, but it isn't enough, Hastings. What he needs is a good wife. Perhaps soon he can gain a knighthood.''

"Can you see that he is knighted?''

"Aye, I can.''

"If you knight him, then I will find him a wife who will see that the reeds are sweet-smelling, the meals are prepared well, the jakes are limed, and everyone goes about their duties without sullen faces.''

"Ah, and where will you find this paragon?''

She examined her fingernails. She was humming softly. "Hastings?''

"I am thinking,'' she said. "Perhaps your mother will have a proper lady in mind when she awakens.''

"Think you she sleeps too heavily?''

"Aye, the potion is strong.''

He nodded, rose, and began to remove his clothes. "Can you keep your screams in your throat?''

She gave him a slow smile. "And you, my lord? You bellow like a bull.''

He grinned at her. "We will do our best, but I must have you. It has been a very long time.''

Since the previous night, she thought, very pleased. The evening had been warm, the stars had filled the heavens, slanting light down through the oak branches. He'd led her into that ancient oak forest after they'd eaten roasted rabbit by the camp fire. There they'd caressed each other until Hastings had gasped, "Please, Severin, come to me else I'll expire.''

But he hadn't. When finally she had cried out, he gently reached his hand up and closed it over her mouth. When she had eased a bit he'd come into her and found his own pleasure.

"Aye,'' she said now, still studying her fingernails. "A very long time. I have felt neglected. I have felt like a cow left overlong in the pasture.''

"Now you want me to milk you? Your jest went a bit awry, Hastings.''

She grinned at him. He patted her cheek with his hand, leaned down, and kissed her. He was whistling when he began to unweave his cross garters. He was jesting with a woman. Nay, not just a woman. He was jesting with his wife. He had wanted to strangle her not that long ago. He had been strongly tempted to beat her. When he'd left Oxborough to visit his other holdings, he hadn't ever wanted to see the witch again. Then the miracle. The epiphany. He remembered when he had forced her. Nay, not really forced her, for he had used the cream, but still, she hadn't wanted him. She had hated him.

She no longer hated him. Why? he wondered. Now she smiled at him, welcomed him, and many times treated him as though he was the king. It made him feel very good.

He knew he should keep his mouth shut, should not question what God had wrought, but he didn't. He waited until she was on her back and he was balanced on one elbow over her. He was looking down at her breasts. Not ordinary breasts at all. They were full and white and so very soft. He was lightly rubbing his finger over that soft flesh of hers. "Why did you change toward me? You hated me. You said I was an animal. You wished I would disappear from your life."

She became utterly still.

"Hastings?"

"Will you push and push until you batter me down?"

"Nay, I am your husband. There should never be any need near for me to push you. It will be your joy to always tell me what it is I wish to know."

"Very well. I can see that you will be Edgar the wolfhound with a beef bone. Dame Agnes and Alice told me to. Dame Agnes said that I had not enough experience in a woman's ways to deal well with you. They told how this dealing worked with men. And since you are a man, they decided it would work with you as well. A smile and a kiss, and a show of interest in you, Severin, that is what they told me to do. I don't think Dame Agnes believed I would succeed though. I believe she thought I would bite you rather than kiss you. But I did kiss you and it was very nice. I believe I tasted your surprise."

He said in the most satisfied voice she had ever heard,

"You bent utterly to me. You accepted me as your lord and your master."

"I do not think it wise of you to draw such a drastic conclusion."

"Why? It is what resulted. They told you to give over to me, to stop setting yourself up against me. They told you to enjoy my man's body."

"Aye, they did say that. Alice told me that all the men knew you were not a pig with women, that you were gentle and kind and enjoyed a woman's pleasure. I did not believe that, for at that time I knew nothing of this pleasure they spoke about. But Alice was very certain. She said that if I wished it, she would bed you and discover for certain that it was true. I thanked her for offering herself as a sacrifice, but that I would try it myself. She said that I just might learn some very interesting things if I just allowed you to come to me without anger, if I just relaxed and didn't tighten myself when you came near."

"Dame Agnes and Alice told you all this? Which of my men did they speak to?"

"Alice never draws a conclusion without copious evidence, particularly, I think, if it concerns something men do or don't do. I would imagine it was a good many of your men. I do know she asked Gwent after your return. She said he would never lie, at least to her."

Severin fell over onto his back. He didn't know whether to feel like an ass or a man blessed. He had gained, not lost. He was satisfied with his wife, not in misery. She no longer lay beneath him like a dead log. She enjoyed him thoroughly, he knew it if he knew anything at all. "This is all very interesting. But heed me, Hastings, I treat you now the way I would have always treated you if you hadn't been such a—" He paused, which was fortunate because Hastings was above him now, and she was breathing fast and hard. "Aye, Severin? You wish to say more?"

He stilled. It was dark in the bedchamber. She couldn't see the wickedness on his face. "Aye, perhaps. Does 'shrew' fit your mouth? Or prefer you 'fishwife' or 'harridan'?"

"You are saying that it was all my fault, this rift between us?"

"Naturally it was all your fault. You're proud, Hastings, and stubborn as a stoat. I am a man of peace. I am reasonable in all my dealings, with both men and women. I wanted no battle with you, but you fought me for no reason that I can remember."

It was too much. She slammed her fist into his belly. He wasn't prepared for it and thus she did make him start at the jab of pain. He moaned, grabbed her, and pulled her down onto her stomach. He swung his legs over her and kept his hand on her neck to keep her down. He realized in an instant of time that his belly didn't hurt all that much at all. He realized in the instant just beyond that one that he was astride her white buttocks and both of them were naked. He eased his hand from her neck, down her back, until he held her in place with his hand pressing at her waist. He looked at her squirming beneath him and wanted to be inside her, then, no more words, no more fists to his belly. He was breathing hard. He jerked her onto her knees, ready to thrust into her, then he stopped. No, he couldn't. She wasn't ready for him. He would hurt her. She would call him an animal again. He would muck up the miracle.

He touched her soft flesh with his finger and was so grateful he nearly wept. She was ready for him. He slid his finger into her and to his utter, besotted surprise, she moaned. He was trembling with this response from her, so unexpected was it. "Hastings, what is this? How can you want me when I have not kissed you or fondled you?"

Her head was buried in her arms. She was embarrassed, but not so embarrassed that she wanted him to stop.

"Come into me, Severin. Now. Please."

It took no more than that, just those few simple words and he was above her, pushing into her, feeling her pull him deeper, feeling her delight in him and what he was doing. It was too much. He did try. He thought he'd die. He only yelled once, surely not such a loud yell, but it was a yell, and his lady mother jerked upright on her narrow cot and said, "By the Devil's cloven foot, are we under attack? Where is my husband? Where are my sons?"

Severin was throbbing deep inside her, his seed still spilling into her. He tried desperately to get a hold on himself, but he could barely breathe, much less talk.

Hastings said, her voice surprisingly even, "My lady, we are not under attack. It was simply your son, held for a brief moment in a dream. He will be all right shortly. He usually is."

"Ah, that is a relief." Lady Moraine fell back again, and in but a moment she was breathing low and even in sleep.

Severin pushed into her again, he couldn't help himself. He stayed within her, looking at himself joined into her. He leaned over to fondle her breasts, to knead her belly.

He had given her no pleasure. But he would. He was regaining his manly vigor. He pushed again, slowly, and was pleased that he was hard again. He withdrew, pulled her onto her back, and came over her again. He lay flat on top of her, his hands cupping her face, gently smoothing her hair from her forehead and eyes.

"I wish I could see you clearly. Do you want to hollow out my guts again with your fist? Do you believe me selfish? Do you believe Alice would find me unworthy?"

"Nay," she said, and brought his mouth down to hers. She felt his fingers smoothing over her belly, felt those fingers of his become damp with her as they stroked her. When she would have cried out in her pleasure, no thought of her mother-in-law twelve feet away from her, Severin covered her mouth with his and took her cries deep into him.

He said on the edge of sleep, "I will fix Langthorne on the outside if you will fix it on the inside."

"Aye, I will do that," she said, bit his shoulder, kissed the salty flesh she had bitten, and curled tightly against him. She said against his chest, "Haven't I brought you to heel very well, my lord?"

But Severin was asleep, at least she thought he was, at first. But was not that snore a bit too loud? Perhaps a bit contrived? Was his hand squeezing her buttock a bit hard?

He was a man she could get very used to having close by, she thought, and settled even closer. Her palm was splayed wide on his belly.

The following morning when Severin awoke, Hastings was gone. He saw that his mother still slept. It worried him until he lightly touched his fingertips to her throat. The beat was strong.

When he entered the great hall, his chair was seated at the trestle table, there was white linen covering the wood, and a pewter plate set in front of the chair. The hall was filled with men. There were at least four women serving dozens of loaves of bread, the smell rich and yeasty. There was butter and flagons of ale. There was even cold capon for him. He had told her to fix the inside of Langthorne. Evidently she had. But this quickly? Was she a witch? Where was she?

He ate, Gwent and Thurston on each side of him. Sir Roger sat beside Thurston, his look determined. Severin said nothing. He saw Glenda serving the men. She did not look happy but she was moving quickly, her movements graceful and efficient.

Where was Hastings?

He was nearly finished breaking his fast when there was a sudden silence in the great hall. He looked up to see Hastings standing beside his mother—aye, it was his mother, but he would not have believed it except Hastings was there as well. She was clean, her hair was combed and braided loosely about her head. She was wearing a gown fitted at the waist, the arms fitting tightly to the elbows, then flaring out so that they touched the ground when her arms were lowered. There was a set of keys on the gold chain about her waist. She was smiling. Then she looked up at Hastings and laughed at something she said. It wasn't a mad laugh, but a sweet, bright laugh.

She didn't look at all mad.

He felt a spurt of optimism, then shook his head. No, he remembered that she could be like this following those deep, long sleeps of hers. It was just a matter of time before her mind faded again and she would look at him as she would look at a stranger. He noticed she was limping slightly.

His mother smiled at everyone until she saw Glenda. She shrank against Hastings. Severin rose and strode to them.

"Mother?"

"Aye. My Severin. Is it really you?" She raised a thin, white hand and lightly stroked his face. "All the others are dead, your father, your brother, but you are not, thank the gracious Lord. You are very handsome, my son. I am glad you are home."

He hugged her, saying in her ear, "Don't be afraid of that plump wench over there. I will see to it that she never comes near you again."

"She is not a nice girl," Lady Moraine said, and hugged her son. "I am very hungry. Have you eaten everything or is there a heel of bread left for your poor mother?"

She was jesting with him. He looked over at Hastings, whose expression was unreadable. Why wasn't she smiling like a loon? What was wrong?

He escorted his mother to the high trestle table and sat her in the lady's chair beside him, a chair she had sat in her entire married life. He himself served her. He looked down and saw that Sir Roger was staring at her as if she were a ghost come to plague him. Clearly his mother had not done well here under his care. Had he never allowed her to eat in the great hall?

As for Glenda, that wench didn't seem to be paying any attention at all to the high table, her eyes on her wooden plate, her knife stabbing at the thick slice of bread. He would ask Hastings to get to the bottom of this. What had Glenda really done to his mother?

He himself found out the answer to that question that same afternoon when he chanced to leave the men who were working on the western outer wall to have Hastings bathe and bandage a cut he had on his thumb. Actually, it was Gwent who had told him to seek out his wife. "Aye, my lord," he had said, looking at that bleeding thumb, "your wife would have my toes for mulch were I not to send you to her."

And so here he was, standing in front of the open door to the lord's bedchamber. He heard voices from within. He started to open the door and stride in when he recognized his mother's voice, but not her voice from the previous evening. No, this voice was low and thin, a thread of fear in it, and it raised the hair on the back of his neck.

"I knew Sir Roger as a boy. He was sweet and slow and his father forced him to learn to be a knight. He had no chance against you. You have made a fool of him. You shan't have him. My son will not allow it. You thought I would die, didn't you, when you forced me into the forest with no cloak and no slippers?"

"Aye," Glenda said, and she didn't sound a bit scared. Indeed, there was venom and resolution in her voice. "I'll be rid of you again, you mad old woman. You don't belong here. As soon as Lord Severin and that bitch wife of his leave, I will take over again and you will see who is the real mistress of Langthorne. Until then I will bide my time. Aye, I will continue to sew more of my gowns for you since I have no choice, but when we are alone again, you old crone, then you will wear what you deserve to wear: rags and naught else. To waste clean water on the likes of you, it turns my belly. Aye, you'll see. It won't be long until your son leaves. You believe anyone will heed you? No, all wait for you to sink into your stupor of madness again. No one will believe you if you say anything against me."

Then he heard the sound of a hand slapping flesh. He opened the door to see Glenda over his mother, his mother sitting in a narrow chair, Glenda holding both her arms, leaning close to his mother until she was pressed against the back.

"Come on, you miserable hag. Why do you not start screaming now, you mad old woman?"

# 17

WHEN SEVERIN WAS AT HIS MOST FURIOUS HE LOOKED AS calm as King Edward's chancellor, Robert Burnell. He walked into the chamber, saw Glenda jerk about to see him, saw her face freeze. She slowly moved away from his mother. He said nothing, just smiled at his mother, walking straight to her.

"You are lovely, madam," he said, leaned down, and kissed her.

She looked terrified. He continued to smile at her and lightly stroke his fingertips over her pale cheek. He called over his shoulder, "Glenda, come here."

His mother paled even more. "I don't want her here," Moraine whispered. "Please, Severin, do not let her come close to me again."

"Ah, but I do want her to come here, Mother. Please do not worry. I want you to trust me." He turned to the young girl who was standing there beside him, her arms folded beneath her breasts, shoving them up and forward, for his pleasure, he supposed.

"I was standing outside the door. It was cracked open. I heard what you said to my mother."

The girl didn't move. She merely smiled up at him, clearly disbelieving him. "I just told her how very lovely she looked. I told her that it would give me great pleasure to sew more gowns for her. Surely this is what you heard, my lord.''

''My man Gwent hates cheats. I hate liars.'' He calmly grabbed Glenda's hand and dragged her to him. He stripped off the clothes she was wearing, new clothes, clothes she had not given over to Hastings the day before. He stripped her to her plump hide. He even pulled her out of her stockings and shoes.

''Now,'' he said, ''I believe there is something for you to wear in my mother's old trunk. If you don't wish to wear the rags you made her wear, then you may travel from Langthorne naked. It matters not to me.''

''My lord, you cannot mean this. Surely, I cannot go out of here naked. The men would ravish me, they would—''

''That is likely,'' Severin said, sounding bored. ''Do what you want, Glenda. I just want you gone by the midday bells.''

He watched Glenda scurry from the bedchamber. He turned to his mother and smiled. ''No one will ever torment you again. No one. I give you my oath on it.''

Lady Moraine was wringing her hands. ''She is cunning, Severin. Sir Roger had no chance. He did not know that she dragged me from Langthorne and left me to die in the forest.''

''He should have known. He is a man. He is responsible for Langthorne and all its people. A man must be responsible for his actions. I will send Hastings to you. I wish to see color in your cheeks.''

Not only was Glenda gone by midday, but Sir Roger was also, the pouch of coins gone as well.

''Shall I find them, my lord?'' Gwent asked, and rubbed his gnarled hands together.

''Aye, Gwent, find them, take the pouch, then let them go. I fear Sir Roger will not be long pleased with his actions. I rather believe he deserves what will happen to him. I think it more a punishment than simply killing the fool.''

''It is an idea that had not occurred to me, my lord,''

Gwent said. "There is the feel of a never-ending pain for Sir Roger in it. Aye, it's good." He strode from the great hall.

Severin turned to see Hastings walking slowly, her head down, toward him. She frowned as she kicked dirty rushes out of her path. And he saw her clearly thinking that she had forgotten the rushes. Then, when she saw him, she stopped and turned red in the face.

He raised a thick black eyebrow at her. "What have you done, Hastings? Worry not about the rushes, you will change them quickly enough. It matters not."

She stared at him and suddenly she was again as clear to him as Edgar the wolfhound. He laughed. It was too much, she ran at him, pounding her fists against his chest, which gave him no pause at all. He continued to laugh until he realized that his men were looking at him, utterly bewildered. He brought her fists down in his large hands and held them at her sides. "What is wrong, sweeting? Has someone offended you? Why did your face turn red when you saw me?" Then he said, very close to her ear, "Ah. I plan to take you in a very different way tonight. I want you to think about it, Hastings. All the ways a man and a woman can come together. We will do all of them and I vow you will like them, each and every one."

She whispered against his chest, "But my bottom was in the air."

"Aye, I just wish there had been some more light. All I could do was feel you. A lot of soft, extraordinary flesh, Hastings. Your bottom pleases me. I told you that it did, do you not remember?"

She groaned, then pulled back in the circle of his arms. "You will mock me until I will want to kill you, Severin. Now, I heard what Gwent said. I think you are wise. As for what you did to Glenda, I trust you did not enjoy it as you stripped her."

"Not at all," he said. "I have scarce ever been so angry before in my life, except those times with you, of course." And she knew it was true because he was looking toward

Thurston, thoroughly distracted. "Go, my lady. I have much to do before our meal."

It was one week later that Lady Moraine, not quite so pale and thin now, said in a clear, crisp voice, "I know who Thurston must marry."

Knives and spoons clattered to plates. There was utter silence in the great hall. Severin wasn't yet used to his mother being with him in her mind, but she had been, with no relapses since Hastings had begun giving her the Healer's potion. She drank a bit of it every morning.

"Who is it, Mother?"

"He must have sons, thus I cannot wed him, but I know of a proper girl, daughter of Sir William Dorset. He has a small keep near Hawksmere. She should be of marriageable age now. What say you, Thurston?"

Thurston was trembling. He was now Sir Thurston of Hornsby, his father's small keep near Kentleby. He was going to be Lord Severin's castellan at Langthorne and now he was going to have a wife. A wife. He wasn't ready for this. He said, "I—I do not know, my lady. A wife would be a lady and she would expect me to know how to act and speak and I could not belch or make other noises that would offend and—" His eyes rolled back in his head.

Lady Moraine said in that same crisp, clear voice, "Hastings, perhaps Thurston needs some of the Healer's potion to steady him. Have I enough to share with him?"

Thurston persevered. He wedded Blanche, the nineteen-year-old daughter of Sir William Dorset, exactly one week after Lady Moraine had made her announcement. Hastings was pleased. Blanche had, as had Hastings, run her father's keep since the age of twelve. She would see that everything stayed aright.

Lady Moraine remained clearheaded. She put on flesh. She smiled and jested. Severin had stopped shaking his head whenever he happened to look at her. He was getting used to a mother who was as she once was. Still he worried. "You believe the Healer's potion has really worked, Hastings? You believe this miracle will remain?''

"I don't know, Severin."

"I want my mother to return with us to Oxborough."

She gave him a big smile and hugged him. "I was praying you would want that," she said, and came up on her tiptoes and kissed his mouth. He went silent, still surprised when she showed him affection anywhere outside their bedchamber.

Gwent had remarked one day that it appeared to him that Severin was a happy man, a man more than content with his beautiful wife.

"Beautiful? Hastings? Nay, Gwent, she is but ordinary, in her looks and in her intelligence. Her nature is even ordinary and—''

Hastings had yelled, flying at him, but he was ready. He caught her, lifted her beneath her arms, and held her high, laughing up at her. "That will teach you for listening to others' conversations, madam."

Gwent had stared at the two of them. He slowly shook his head. He turned and walked away, for surely Severin would kiss his wife in but a moment. He prayed that nothing would happen to ruin the contentment.

The next morning they left Langthorne to return to Oxborough. Gwent lifted Lady Moraine onto her palfrey. He'd told Severin that he would watch out for his mother. He would tell Severin if anything untoward occurred because he knew Severin was worried. His mother had been very quiet since the day before.

Severin turned his head one last time to see the place of his birth. Langthorne would regain its power in the region, he would see to it. Thurston was rubbing his hands together, for now he was married, and evidently he had enjoyed the pleasures of the marriage bed. Hastings had spoken privately to Blanche and been pleased. "Everything will go well. You spoke to Thurston, Severin? You told him to be gentle and kind with his bride?"

Severin was frowning. "Aye, I did tell him that. He told me just before we left that I had been wrong in my advice. Then he gave me this huge smile and said that his bride was a tigress and she wanted no gentleness from him.''

Hastings stared at her husband. ''I don't understand.''

''There are some ladies, Hastings, who enjoy a man who's fierce with them, a man who enjoys rough play, a man who holds them down and pretends to conquer them. Your sweet-faced, gentle Blanche is one of these women. He said she was beyond wild even before he tore through her maidenhead. He said after he did that, she mounted him, pummeling him, nearly killing him by dawn.''

''I had not thought of this. Mayhap you will explain this wildness to me, Severin.''

''I think not, sweeting. All you are to remember is that when we are alone, you are free to do whatever you wish to, save gullet me with a knife if you happen to be angry with me.''

She said nothing to that, merely stared through Marella's ears, deep in thought. Severin dug his heels into his horse's sides and rode to the head of his men.

*Oxborough Castle, Five days later*

''We found Sir Roger and Glenda within two hours of their escape from Langthorne,'' Gwent was telling everyone in the great hall, clearly enjoying himself. Only Severin was already privy to the details, and he had told Gwent to keep all those delicious details to himself until he could entertain all their people. Hastings could see why he had wished to wait. He had an excellent audience. He cleared his throat again. ''Sir Roger had tried to cover their trail, but he is inept, the poor whoreson.'' Gwent spat into the clean rushes, looked up in horror at Hastings, then quickly said, ''The girl Glenda had wrapped all the clothes she could steal in an old blanket. She tried to tell me that it was just the rags you had allowed her, Severin. Sir Roger believed we would kill him. I will say this, he didn't whine like I expected him to. Nay, he sat straight on his horse and appeared to accept his death. When I asked him to give me the pouch of money, he stared at me. He shook his head. He swore he hadn't taken it. Then he turned pale. He looked to the girl and merely held out his hand.''

Gwent paused a moment to drink from his wine goblet. Everyone was attending him. There wasn't a sound in the great hall of Oxborough. He cleared his throat, this time speaking directly to Lady Moraine. "The girl Glenda said she didn't have any pouch. She didn't know what he was talking about. I merely took that stuffed dirty blanket from her and threw it to the ground. I opened it and kicked all the clothes away. And there was the pouch, wrapped in a shift.''

He paused and speared a piece of pork onto his knife. Lady Moraine placed her hand lightly on his forearm. "What happened, Gwent? Come, you have held it all in for far too long. My beloved son would not tell me anything. Tell us now.''

Gwent almost belched, but he managed to hold it in. Not in Lady Moraine's face, at least he knew not to do that. He cleared his throat yet again. "I dally not, my lady, it's just that what followed is best not told in your hearing.''

Lady Moraine lifted her eating knife and gently pressed the point against Gwent's neck, a clean neck since he had bathed just that afternoon, bless Saint Sebastian's arrow-pierced body. Gwent said quickly, "I stripped her naked just as Lord Severin had done. I took all the clothes and the pouch and brought them back to Langthorne. My men and I left her there with Sir Roger just staring down at her. The men would have taken her, but I did not allow it. No, we just left her there in the middle of the road. There was no love or lust in Sir Roger's eyes, my lady, when he looked down at her. None at all. I know not what happened, but I imagine that Sir Roger left her there.''

"You stripped off her shoes, Gwent?" Lady Moraine asked, leaning close.

"Aye, my lady, every stitch of covering.''

"That is good. You remember that Glenda took my shoes and forced me into the forest.''

Gwent laughed and rubbed his hands together. "A fitting punishment for her then, my lady."

And even as Hastings listened, laughed, and nodded with approval, she wasn't paying them much attention now. She was thinking instead of Lady Blanche. She was wondering how Lady Blanche knew about this wildness, how she, a lady, had known that she wanted to attack her husband and be attacked by him. It was confusing.

When she was at her bath a good hour later, she was still thinking of Lady Blanche. She turned to Dame Agnes. "We mayhap need Alice and Belle."

"Ah," said Dame Agnes with a goodly deal of satisfaction. "Your lord experiments, does he?"

"Aye, but that is not what I wish to ask about. You see, Sir Thurston's bride wanted rough play; she was fierce and was wild even when she was still a virgin. Afterward, she was wilder still. I have never heard of this. I do not understand it. And I want to."

Dame Agnes merely nodded. She left the bedchamber to return shortly with Alice. "We could not find Belle. Gwent said she was with the blacksmith, Old Morric, that the man is nearly dead he has drained him of so much of his vigor and seed. I have told Alice what you said. She said this is very common, that sometimes ladies—"

Alice cleared her throat, took the thick sponge from Dame Agnes, and began to rub soap over Hastings's back. "Some men think their wives should lie on their backs, close their eyes, and open their legs. That is all these men expect, all they want. Some men, though, obviously like this Sir Thurston and your Lord Severin, are more flexible in their views. I daresay if you were to mount your husband, even tie his hands to the headboard, even take him in your mouth, he would swoon with the pleasure of it."

"What do you mean, take him in my mouth? What him?"

"Don't be obtuse, Hastings. His rod," Dame Agnes said.

"Oh. I have done that once. I thought he would expire. You are right. It appeared to be something a man would beg for."

"Hmmm," Dame Agnes said. "Things are progressing well. You will simply learn this wildness, Hastings. It is not a sin; it could bring you great pleasure if you let your husband know that you might enjoy it."

"I could not," Hastings said. "I could not. He would laugh at me. He would think—"

"What he would think," Severin said from the doorway, standing there all tall and relaxed, his eyes as dark as the night, his arms crossed over his chest, "is that your women can leave you now."

Alice handed him the soapy sponge as she passed him. She was whistling. Dame Agnes merely looked as satisfied as MacDear when he had baked a pheasant to perfection.

Severin didn't move until he was alone with her. Slowly, he turned to shut the door to the bedchamber. He turned the key in the lock. When he turned to face her again, Hastings was sitting in her bathwater, feeling like a rabbit in the sights of a hunter's arrow.

"You should have asked me if you wanted to know more about this rough play, Hastings."

"I did but you would not tell me anything."

"I still won't, but I will show you." He held out his hand to her. Slowly, she rose in her bathwater and he held her there. "Stand there for a moment, I would look at you."

"The water is chilled."

Slowly, reluctantly, he handed her a drying cloth. He couldn't wait to get her onto the bed.

"Mayhap this wildness isn't really me, Severin."

He merely grunted, thinking if she were any wilder, he would be a very happy dead man. When she was dry, when she turned to face him, he was standing naked by the bed, smiling at her, his hand held out. "Drop the drying cloth and come here. We will soon see just how much of this wildness is in your blood."

"How will you know? Will I shriek and writhe about? Must I draw your blood?"

"Nay, you will mount me and I will let you plunder me."

She looked at him very straightly, dropped the towel, and said, ''And after I have plundered you, may I take you in my mouth again?''

She thought he would leap on her, but he managed to hold himself back. He was breathing fast and hard. His man's sex was ready for her, she knew that, but it was more than that, it was the words she'd just said to him.

She gave him a siren's smile and walked toward him.

# 18

THE HEALER FELT LADY MORAINE'S HEAD, HER LONG NAR-row fingers gentle and light, covering every bit of her skull. "Ah," she said, pressed Lady Moraine's head back, and looked closely into her eyes. She pulled up the eyelids and looked some more. She hummed as she smoothed her fingers over Lady Moraine's ears, twisting and turning them, pulling them away from her head and peering inside.

Hastings began to fidget.

Lady Moraine did nothing at all, merely stroked Alfred's length in long, slow strokes. He was hanging over her lap, purring so loudly Hastings wondered if it didn't distract the Healer.

Evidently not.

The Healer finally turned to Hastings and said simply, "I am the most skilled healer in all of Britain. The potion I gave your husband's mother has cleared out the clogged pathways in her brain and balanced her humors once again."

Lady Moraine cleared her throat even as she petted Alfred, who was now purring so loudly she had to speak louder than normal. "Healer, I thank you. Will I take your potion the rest of my days?"

"Aye, my lady, I think it wise. I do not know if the

potion has permanently removed all the clogging from your brain or if it will return if you cease the potion.''

"I will take it even when I am on my deathbed.''

"Aye, you want to be full-witted when you prepare to leave this earth. Now, Hastings told me that one of the wounds on your left foot hasn't healed properly.''

Alfred had to leave the goddess, though it was obvious he didn't want to. Hastings hadn't realized her mother-in-law was so strong. She actually lifted Alfred and set him on the cottage floor. His huge tail whipped the air. He meowed loudly, then nudged over his bowl with his nose, sending it careening out the front of the cottage.

The Healer laughed even as she lifted Lady Moraine's foot and closely examined it. She felt every toe, pulling them apart to peer closely between them. The Healer said, "Does this hurt, lady? No? Very good. Ah, here is the problem. Just a pinch of patel root and saffron strands mixed in a bit of hot water will heal this. Ah, lady, you clean well between your toes. This is good. It keeps lice and ticks away.'' She looked to see Alfred, looking ready to leap at Hastings, adding, "It will not, however, keep Alfred at bay.''

Alfred leapt. Hastings staggered backward, clutching the cat in her arms.

When Hastings and Lady Moraine left the Healer, after giving her three fresh pheasants for her cook pot, two of them for Alfred, Gwent and his two men did not at first react. They were staring at Alfred, who did at that moment look like the Devil's familiar. He was seated in the open doorway of the cottage, nearly as tall as Edgar the wolf-hound, cleaning his teeth with the claws of his left paw.

"That beast came from a witch's brew," he said under his breath, but Alfred snapped his tail hair, stared hard at Gwent, and looked very pleased with himself when Gwent jumped a good two feet into the air.

"That damnable beast," Gwent yelled, angry with himself for reacting so strongly. One of the men dared to laugh. Gwent turned on him, giving him so mean a look that the man paled and shrank down in his saddle.

"You are well, Lady Moraine?" he asked, as he assisted her into her palfrey's saddle.

"I will remain sane, Gwent, and thus able to give my son endless advice on the running of Oxborough. What think you of that?"

Gwent smiled widely. "I believe Lord Severin will be so pleased we will have a feast to celebrate. As for advice, lady, you will have to contend with Hastings."

"I will never contend with Hastings. She is the most perfect of daughters."

Hastings blinked at that, opened her mouth to stammer some sort of profound delight, when Lady Moraine added, "Then again, Gwent, she is very young and doubtless needs my advice more than does my son. I saw him frowning over naught just this morning. What had she done to bring that frown to his beautiful face? I will find out and teach her."

"You will have to contend with Dame Agnes and Alice, my lady," Hastings said, and laughed. "Aye, they have endless advice, and I vow that much of it pleases me." She laughed again.

Lady Moraine waved good-bye to Alfred, lightly kicked her heels into her palfrey's sides, and laughed over her shoulder at Gwent, who was still looking at the damned cat, who was now waving its huge paw. The Healer stood in the open doorway, her arms crossed over her chest, just staring at them.

He shook his head. "Nothing is as it should be in this place."

The ride back to Oxborough took only fifteen minutes. There were dark clouds lowered in the sky, the air was thick and cooling rapidly. The men didn't want to get wet, but Hastings wasn't uncomfortable, nor did she worry about the rain pouring down, as it would, surely, in the next few minutes. No, she was thinking of her husband, blessing again Dame Agnes and Alice, who had told her how to deal with a man.

She had dealt with him very well the previous night. He'd let her do just as she pleased, as he had promised.

She had explored his hard body, tracing each of the scars with a light touch, then kissing each of them, spending the most time on the scar that had slashed the inside of his right thigh. That thigh was thick, covered with a light furring of black hair, and she loved to knead the muscles, to stroke him as Lady Moraine had done Alfred.

When she had loved him with her mouth, he had bowed off the bed, moaning and thrashing until she was heady with success. She did not care that she received no pleasure, for his had peaked into such intense release that she had found herself drawn into it, watching him as he shook and twisted, then freezing with the utter force of his release. And she thought, as she saw his dark eyes fix on her face with unleashed wildness, that surely he was a man to love, a man to protect, a man to trust, for all her life.

He had grabbed her waist and pulled her down close to his face. He had held her there until he could breathe and speak again.

"Think you to control me?"

"Nay, I think to enjoy your pleasure."

"I gave you nothing, yet you smile at me and you still caress me with your hand on my shoulder. I do not understand you, Hastings."

"Must I be as carnal as a man all the time?"

"Aye," he said, his voice stark and deep. He pulled her onto her back and didn't leave her until she had moaned into his mouth.

Hastings shook slightly with the power of that memory. She imagined that she would renew that powerful memory at least once a week for the rest of her life. Mayhap fewer days than an entire week. She felt a stab of sheer lust when she pictured him yet again on his back, his man's rod in her mouth. A storm could blow in from the sea and it wouldn't gain her attention.

She heard a laugh and turned to see Lady Moraine place her hand on Gwent's arm as he pulled his horse closer to her palfrey. "Alfred is just a cat, Gwent, not a monster, though he does purr louder than a man snores."

And Hastings watched Gwent and Lady Moraine,

watched them ride together ahead of her and the two other men, heard them laughing, saw Gwent reach out quickly to grab her palfrey's reins when the mare stumbled. She prayed with everything in her that the Healer was right, that Severin's mother was well again, that her madness had disappeared with the Healer's potion.

Then she saw her husband, garbed only in a loin cloth, working side by side with twenty men on the eastern wall of Oxborough. Sweat glistened off his chest and arms, his dark hair was plastered to his head, and she wanted to throw herself against him and ask him, very quietly, if he would come with her to create more of the wildness of the night before, if he would let her take him again as she wished.

She sighed, knowing he could not leave his men. Unless the rain came down in torrents. She closed her eyes a moment and prayed hard. When she looked up again, she swallowed. He looked hard and lean and healthy, a man with strength, a man with a wife who very much appreciated him. By Saint Catherine's knees, she prayed that one day he would come to feel about her the way she felt about him. She shook her head, leaning closer to Marella's neck. No, she couldn't love him. It wasn't done. Theirs had been like most marriages, fashioned of money and possessions and power. They each had a role to play. It was just that there were some roles she enjoyed playing more than others.

She thought again of looking down at his face even as she moved over him, and shuddered with the memory of those minutes. She did not think, though, that she had shown true wildness in her blood when he had brought her to pleasure. She had not bitten him or raked his back with her short fingernails. She had just yelled a bit, as she always did. As for Severin, she did not know how he could ever be wilder than he seemed to be naturally.

Perhaps she would ask Dame Agnes and Alice about this. But it wasn't quite time. Severin waved to her and she waved back. They rode into the inner bailey and she gave Marella over to Tuggle, who immediately crooned a litany of strange sounds to Marella, who butted her head into his chest.

A bit later she saw Dame Agnes with Lady Moraine and—what was that all about?—there was Alice with Gwent. Now, what was Alice saying to him? Was it more about this wildness in the blood? Aye, she thought, the previous night had been a revelation—but was it really a revelation or merely another diversion that men and women shared? She would see.

What was Alice speaking to Gwent about?

Severin did not come to their bedchamber until far into the night. He did not awaken Hastings. But he was there early the next morning when she woke up, lightly caressing her shoulders, the hollows, the bones, kissing the pulsing cord in her throat.

"You did not come to me," she said, smiled up at him, and touched her fingertips to his mouth.

"Nay," he said. He fell onto his back and stared at the ceiling, now visible in the early dawn light. "The storm has passed."

She said nothing, knowing there was something on his mind, content to wait.

"I must travel to this Rosehaven place. None knows what or who is there. Your father went there three or four times a year, taking money with him each time. I will leave this morning."

"I went with you to Langthorne, Severin. Did you wish that I had not gone there with you?"

He was silent. Finally, he turned to face her. "I do not know what to expect at this Rosehaven. I do not wish to place you in any danger."

"How can I be in danger if you are beside me?"

"You are flattering me, Hastings, to gain your own ends. Tell me, why do you wish to go to this place?"

"I want to know who is there. I want to know why my father journeyed there for so many years, faithfully, time after time. Something drew him. Is it a debt to King Edward? A debt to a friend about whom I know nothing? Is there a mistress there?''

"I think I will find a mistress. She cannot be young and still winsome, for he has gone there so many years. Or perhaps he kept many mistresses there, ridding himself of an old one, replacing her with a young one. But why not simply enjoy his mistress here at Oxborough? I do not know. But I do believe it must be a mistress that drew him back again and again. There is no other reasonable answer.''

She said very quietly, "I cannot remain here without you. I have an appetite for you that you must attend to, for surely it is one of your husband's duties.''

He stared at her, then laughed. "So that is how you will bend me so that I will give you what you want. Very well, Hastings, I will take you to this Rosehaven so that you will be satisfied in your woman's appetites.''

"And Trist will accompany us? I missed him for the time we were at Langthorne.''

"I will discuss the matter thoroughly with him.''

Then he kissed her and came into her very slowly. He did not finish until he heard the servants moving about outside their bedchamber door. She remembered that Trist hadn't been with them when Severin had shown her his wildness in the blood.

"This is what you must have, Hastings?''

"Aye, my lord. You are gracious. You are generous. I am the most blessed of women.''

He threw his new blue tunic at her, which she caught and immediately smoothed out. "It will fit you now,'' she said, very pleased with herself, and handed it to him.

His wife had made the tunic for him, he thought as he dressed. The wool was fine and very soft. Trist would like the feel of that tunic. He wondered where the marten was. He hadn't slept with them the night before. Ah, the tunic did fit him. He left her, whistling, saying over his shoulder, "We will leave by the noon bells.''

But they didn't leave Oxborough at the noon bells.

• • •

"My lord," Alart called down from his tower on the ramparts, "men from Sedgewick are nearing Oxborough."

"Sedgewick," Severin said, frowning. "I wonder what they want. I wonder if Sir Alan is in any difficulties."

Severin had known the man who led the men-at-arms for many years. His name was Remis. He was getting old, but he was still strong, trustworthy, loyal. The group remained a goodly distance from the outer wall. Remis rode just a bit closer, drew in his horse, and called out, "My lord, there is the sweating sickness at Sedgewick. I have brought the child Eloise and her guardian, Lady Marjorie, and ten men, none of us as yet ill. Sir Alan insisted on remaining. He was not yet ill when he ordered us to come here."

Trist poked his head out of Severin's tunic. He sniffed the air and pressed his face against Severin's neck. "You have done well, Remis. Who else is still at the castle?"

"Sir Alan has men guarding the bulwarks, my lord. None wished to remain within the castle or the walls. If outlaws come to plunder, the men will kill them. Sir Alan is a brave man."

Hastings stepped forward. "Remis, to be certain that none of you brought the sweating sickness here to Oxborough, I believe it wise for you to camp outside the outer wall for at least three days. No more. Ask Lady Marjorie if she needs anything."

Remis returned to the group of men who were surrounding the woman and child. There was discussion. Then he returned.

He shouted up to the ramparts, "The lady brought all we would need. She foresaw that we should not immediately enter Oxborough. We will remain without."

"If anyone sickens, I will put a potion outside the walls."

"My thanks, Lady Hastings."

Severin was frowning. "This is a pity. Sir Alan is my friend. It is unlikely that he will survive. Should I go prepare him a proper burial?" Trist continued to stare at Remis. He made a soft growling sound deep in his throat, then pulled back.

She shook her head. "You might not get ill if you travel to Sedgewick, but if you did, I do not know if I could save you, Severin."

He was already nodding. "I will keep Sedgewick closed for a week more. Do you think that is enough time, Hastings?"

"A fortnight, at least, perhaps more. I will discuss this with the Healer."

In the three days that followed, none of the Sedgewick people who had come to Oxborough became ill. Father Carreg gave long and grateful thanks to God. Trist stayed close, never once going out of the keep. Whenever Hastings wanted to hug her husband, she had to see first if Trist was sleeping inside his tunic, against his chest.

Hastings stood next to her husband on the great front stone steps of Oxborough keep when the Sedgewick people rode through the gates into the inner bailey. Remis gave his horse over to a stable lad, then came to bow before Severin.

"My lord. My lady. God has blessed us. He has allowed us to live. My lord, I do not believe that you were at Oxborough when Lady Marjorie arrived to take Eloise back to Sedgewick." He turned and smiled at the woman. She walked gracefully to where Severin and Hastings stood. Slowly, she raised her head and pulled back her veil.

Severin turned to stone.

Hastings did not at first notice. She saw now that the woman was even more beautiful than she remembered. "My lord," she said, "this is Lady Marjorie."

That beautiful melodious voice said, "Ah, Severin. It has been many years since I have seen you."

Hastings blinked at this as she turned to her husband. He was staring at Lady Marjorie, just staring, unmoving, staring as if she were a phantom. He looked frozen; red stained his cheeks. He said finally in a hoarse, very deep voice, "Is it really you, Marjorie?"

"Aye, Severin. I am a widow now, twice over. You remember that my father forced me to marry that filthy old Baron Lipwait? He died and my brother forced me to wed

Baron Outbraith, a young man who was pleasing enough.''

"I was told that Eloise's new guardian was a widow of a knight who had once saved Edward's life. What is this, Marjorie?''

"It is true. King Edward owed my husband his life and thus he repaid him by giving me the guardianship of Richard de Luci's daughter. I am content. I live well at Sedgewick. It is good to see you again, Severin.''

Hastings said in an overly loud voice, "Why did you not tell me, Lady Marjorie, when you first arrived to take Eloise away, that you knew my husband? You said nothing at all.''

Marjorie gave her a beautiful, soft smile, dimples deepening in her cheeks. "I had not believed it important, my lady. What was important was the child. Eloise, come here and bid hello to Lady Hastings and Lord Severin.''

Eloise had gained flesh. Her round face shone with health. Her braids no longer looked skinny and dull. She tightly clasped Marjorie's hand. Marjorie leaned down and whispered something to her. Eloise smiled at Severin, nodded to Hastings, and gave them a lovely curtsy.

Hastings wanted to hug the child to her and tell her how very beautiful she was, but Eloise immediately pressed against Lady Marjorie's side.

Trist came again out of Severin's tunic and stared at the woman and the child. He extended a paw toward Eloise.

She laughed and said to Marjorie, "He is Trist and he is Lord Severin's marten. He is beautiful.''

"Aye, I believe he is fit to belong to his master," Marjorie said.

Trist continued to wave his paw toward Eloise. He did not turn to look at Marjorie, probably because, Hastings thought, her belly cold and knotted, the woman was so beautiful that it hurt even Trist's eyes to look upon her.

Torric the steward gave over his chamber to Lady Marjorie and Eloise. Hastings herself walked up the solar stairs to visit the small bedchamber to see that Lady Marjorie had everything she needed. She paused a moment at the door, which was open just a few inches, hearing Lady Marjorie saying to Eloise, "My sweeting, I know that you do not like being here. I know that Hastings treated you so very poorly before I arrived. But I will be here with you to protect you. You have naught to fear."

Hastings's heart pounded hard. She couldn't breathe. Eloise had told Marjorie that she had mistreated her? *Mistreated her!* Aye, Hastings had tried to force food down her throat. She had protected her from that awful woman, Beale.

"Nay, Marjorie, she was nice to me—"

"You do not remember correctly, Eloise," Marjorie said in a soft, soothing voice. Hastings could picture her lightly stroking her hand over Eloise's hair. "Aye, I remember your night dreams, how you woke up sobbing, your face all sweaty, tears streaming down your cheeks, crying of how miserable you had been here, how no one was kind to you. I will take care of you, no one else. Worry not."

"Aye, Marjorie. I love you."

"And I you, sweeting. I am the only one who loves you."

Hastings slowly backed away from the door. She did not know what to think. All she knew was that she wanted Lady Marjorie away from Oxborough as soon as possible. And she, damn Saint Oscar's knees, had told Severin it would not be safe to return to Sedgewick for at least two weeks.

She would go ask the Healer.

She prayed the Healer would have a shorter answer.

How did Severin and Marjorie know each other?

# 19

"WHY DID YOU NOT TELL ME LADY MARJORIE WAS ELOise's new guardian?" Severin's words hung heavy in the air as he drank deep from his goblet of ale, his eyes never leaving her face. He looked hard and remote, like the man she had married, the man who had stood in Oxborough's great hall saying nothing, just observing all of them. He was no longer the Severin she'd known since she had followed Dame Agnes's and Alice's advice and run down the keep steps and hurled herself into his arms many weeks before. She just stared at him, wondering what was in his mind.

"I did tell you," she said finally, leaning over to pat Trist, who was stretched his full length on the trestle table next to Severin's arm. He was washing his chin. "Do you not remember?"

"You should have said that she was young and the fairest lady you had ever seen. You should have told me that her hair is like spun silver and glitters in the sunlight. Then I would have known who she was. Why didn't you tell me, Hastings?"

It was her turn to pull back. "You believe I should have told you this woman had hair like spun silver? Would that not sound strange coming from my mouth? I remarked upon her beauty, but it wasn't my first concern."

He waved his hand at her. Trist mewled softly. Severin began stroking the marten's shining coat, long strokes, just like he had done on her back, from her neck to her thighs. Such long, soothing strokes. She stared at his hands. What was going on here?

"Who is this woman with hair like spun silver? I gather that you know her?"

"Aye, I have known her all her life. When I was seventeen I wanted to wed with her but I was only the second son and her father needed a rich man for her. When she wedded the old man, Baron Lipwait, I went crusading to the Holy Land. That is where I met Graelam and the king."

"Then that was fortunate, was it not? Because you met them, because they believe you honorable and strong, you are now one of the richest men in England."

He said nothing to that, merely continued to stroke Trist's fur.

"So you have not seen her for eight years. That is a long time, Severin. People change. Their feelings change. Haven't yours changed?"

Gwent came into the great hall, Beamis at his side. They were arguing about something.

"My lord," Beamis called out, "Lady Marjorie wishes to ride with the child. What say you?"

Severin rose so quickly from his lord's chair, Edgar the wolfhound raised his head and barked. Severin seemed unaware that Hastings stood not three feet from him. "They need protection. I will ride with them." He said nothing more, merely strode from the great hall.

Some time later, Hastings said to Dame Agnes and Alice, "I don't know what to make of this, but Severin changed toward me the moment he saw that woman." She was sewing a tunic for Severin of soft, warm gray. The wool was of the finest. She was pleased that her hands were steady, her voice calm. But she was cold, very cold, on the inside, where there was no warmth to be found, save from Severin. "He is riding with her and the child. He appears to worship Marjorie. He said her hair is like spun silver and shimmers in the sunlight. Lord Severin has never spoken like that since I have known him.''

''It means nothing,'' Dame Agnes said, flapping her hands at the young girl she had known since she had pulled her from her mother's womb nearly nineteen years before, the young girl who had become a fine lady, strong and kind. She was now pale and wooden. ''You just sewed a crooked stitch, Hastings. Why do you not stop that whilst we talk?''

Hastings laid the tunic over her legs, smoothing the material, paying no attention, really, just smoothing it, staring straight ahead of her. ''The look on his face was worshipful. Thus, would that not mean that he worships her? He loved her as a boy, Agnes, but he could not have her since he was a second son and had no dowry to offer her father. He loves her still.''

''Nay, I doubt that. Mayhap he still sees her through the boy's eyes, but that will not last, Hastings. Lord Severin is not a foolish man like Sir Roger. He has given himself to you. You are his wife. You will bear his children. You are the heiress of Oxborough. Without you, he would have nothing save his strong arm, and that arm would be in the service of other masters. He is now his own man. You have given him everything, a future, the ability to restore his lands. You have given him back his mother. Do not discount this, Hastings. This Lady Marjorie—bah, she is nothing, merely a memory sewn from unreal cloth, a chimera, a dream from a boy's past.''

''When you speak thusly, it makes so much sense.'' Hastings raised her face to Dame Agnes. ''But you did not see him just an hour ago when he spoke of her. You did not see how quickly he left the great hall to ride with her. There is so much work to be done, but he gave it not a thought. I saw the look on Gwent's face. He was shocked that his master would act thusly. He would not meet my eyes. He was embarrassed.''

''We will see. You will not carp at him. You will observe and you will bide your time. You will be patient.''

''I have never been patient in my life.''

"Aye, I know it. But you will begin now. Also, you will try to be gracious."

"Gracious? To that woman I heard lying to Eloise? It will be difficult, Agnes, very difficult. Ah, here is Lady Moraine. Do come in, my lady. Agnes and I were just discussing my crooked stitches."

Lady Moraine picked up her son's tunic and examined the sewing. "Aye," she said, "it appears that something bothered you just as you set this stitch right here." She pointed and handed the tunic back to Hastings. "My foot is healed. Did you not notice that I no longer limp?"

Hastings nodded.

"I went with Gwent to see the Healer again. Alfred jumped in the poor man's arms. I thought Gwent would faint. At least the cat didn't knock him over. The Healer told me to give you this." Lady Moraine handed Hastings a small vial. It was filled with a milky white liquid that looked very thick. "She said you were to pour a small amount into your husband's wine. She said it would improve Severin's vision of you, that it would make him feel about you as you do about him."

Hastings realized then that it was a love potion, probably made up of ground mandrake. How had the Healer found out so quickly about Lady Marjorie and Severin?

It was humiliating. She took the vial and slipped it into the pocket of her gown.

As Dame Agnes and Lady Moraine were leaving the bed-chamber, Agnes said over her shoulder, "Remember what I said, Hastings. I would not use that vial as yet. I believe there will be no reason to."

But what did Dame Agnes know of a pain that seemed to fill every nook in her body? What did she know about a woman whose hair was so silvery and shimmery that a man looked at her and his mouth was suddenly overflowing with a troubadour's poetry? She shook the vial, watching the cloudy white liquid darken just a bit.

Was Dame Agnes possibly right? Was Severin simply seeing Marjorie through a boy's eyes?

She went to see Father Carreg, who was reading in the

corner of the great hall, Edgar the wolfhound's head resting on his leather shoes. She merely nodded at him and sat at his feet next to Edgar.

Only Gwent was silent at the evening meal. Like Hastings, he was observing, eating steadily, but Hastings knew he was watching his master watch that glorious woman who seemed oblivious of Severin, all her attention focused on the child and on each dainty bite she took.

Trist was sprawled over Severin's shoulder, looking to be asleep. Hastings had offered him some roasted pork, a special dish made just for him by MacDear. Trist had eaten two bites from her fingers, stretched, and mewled softly in his throat, and shoved her hand away with his paw.

He had made no more movements toward Eloise.

"I trust you like MacDear's civet of hare," she said to her husband, who was pushing the food about the thick pewter plate with his knife.

"Aye," Severin said finally, "it is tasty. You had the rushes changed, Hastings. They are sweet-smelling."

He had noticed something other than the glorious Marjorie, praise be to Saint Ethelbert's knees.

"It is the rosemary you smell. Mixed with just a bit of ground roses, it fills the air with sweetness."

What an utterly boring thing to say to a husband she wanted to kiss and caress and demand to love her and only her and not that other woman from his boy's dreams.

She took a bite of chicken mixed with rice and almonds. It tasted like the rushes covering the cold stone floor. She thought about the vial in her pocket. It nestled there, ready for her to use, yet she hesitated. She didn't want to drug her husband. She didn't want the mandrake to make him turn back to her. No, she wanted him to do it of his own volition. She wanted him to want her as he had before he had laid eyes on Marjorie, who was still giving all her attention to Eloise.

Why could Marjorie not be a bitch?

Why could she not rub Hastings's nose in her power?

Hastings sighed, leaned over, and lightly stroked her hand over Trist's head. He mewled loudly, raised his head, looked at her for a good long time, then laid one of his paws over her hand.

"Trist has mated, I am certain of it," Severin said, his first unsolicited words to her.

"He seems content," she said.

"He has mated, thus he will show no more real interest until his babes are born. Then he will journey back into the forest to see that they are raised properly."

"Is that what you will do if I now carry your babe?"

He jumped. He stared at her face, then his eyes dropped to her belly. "Are you with child? Have you ceased your monthly flux?"

How to answer him? She had never known when her monthly flux would come. It had been many weeks, but she had no idea if his seed had made a babe in her womb.

"I do not know." Perhaps she should have lied. Perhaps if he believed his babe was in her womb, he would turn back to her. He was honorable—she cursed.

"What did you say, Hastings?"

"I remarked that Saint Osbert's elbows were perhaps too knobby. I cursed, Severin."

But he did not reply. She followed his line of vision. He was staring at Marjorie, who had leaned down to pick something from the floor. Her hair, loose and flowing, was a silver curtain, shimmering with light. She hated the woman.

She saw his hand tighten about the stem of his goblet. She wasn't blind. She saw the hunger in his dark eyes. He wanted Marjorie, wanted her as he had wanted his wife just two nights before. Had he wanted her as much as he wanted Marjorie, whom he had craved and loved since his seventeenth year?

Hastings had held his affection for less than three months. And what was that affection? A willing woman who freely gave him her body? Aye, naught more.

Marjorie had been in his mind for more than eight years.

Hastings didn't stand a chance. She fingered the vial.

No, not yet. She couldn't bear to resort to that damned vial.

She had already seen that he had not worn one of the tunics she had sewn for him.

She wished she could stick her knife through Marjorie's heart. The thought was deep within her and hard and real. Hastings knew then that she would never be destined for sainthood. She would be fortunate to gain a long purgatory.

A jongleur appeared, flinging five leather balls into the air, catching them, then tossing them upward, all of them in the air at the same time. He was speaking as he threw the balls in a circle around his head. He was singing. She saw that Belle was leaning heavily against the blacksmith, whose eyes were sated, his eyelids heavy. Belle was eyeing the jongleur with growing interest. Old Morric wore a witless smile.

She had seen Severin with such a witless smile.

The jongleur finished juggling the balls. He came forward to praise Lord Severin, the man who had singlehandedly killed sixty Saracens near Acre, the mighty warrior whom King Edward had begged to remain at his side but stay away from his beautiful queen Eleanor.

Marjorie's bright laughter turned many eyes toward her.

The jongleur then turned to Hastings. He struck a pose, studying her. Then he sang:

> "The Lady Hastings gave Lord Severin the world.
> She is gracious and wise, healing all who are ill.
> She is above ordinary, it is said, giving her loyalty
> to her lord, who now owns his fill."

She saw Severin flinch. Where had the jongleur heard about her being ordinary? Obviously one of the men had overheard his master and repeated it to the fellow.

Then, as if he couldn't help himself, the jongleur turned to Marjorie, and stared at her, his hand over his breast. He sighed deeply.

*"Such grace, such beauty, such silver hair*
*that makes men weep. The Lady Marjorie surpasses all*
*ladies. She is a goddess. She is a beautiful creature*
*that will make men dream throughout eternity."*

Hastings wanted to scream. She looked at Severin, who was staring fixedly at Marjorie. Could he not tell that the jongleur's rhyme hadn't rhymed?

Marjorie was laughing, waving her hand in dismissal to the troubadour.

The jongleur bowed deeply to Severin, then to Hastings, and finally, he fell to his knees before Marjorie, but she was just laughing at him, waving him away, shaking her beautiful head.

Hastings wanted to die.

But first she wanted to kill that beautiful creature who made men dream throughout eternity.

But even before that, she would kill the damned jongleur.

Severin came to their bed very late. She was still awake. She said nothing, just listened to him strip off his clothes—she heard every movement he made. She saw him in her mind's eye. He was naked, beautifully naked, hard and lean. He did not touch her.

She felt Trist snuggle against her back.

Just before dawn, she awoke to warmth, a man's warmth. She sighed deeply. He had come to her. She opened her eyes, expecting to see him over her, but Severin was lying on his side, still deeply asleep. She was pressed against his back, Trist against hers.

She eased her hand around his flank and pressed her palm against his belly. Then lower until she held him in her hand. He turned onto his back, arching up slightly.

He kissed her even as she continued to caress him. He said into her mouth, "Ah, Marjorie."

Hastings dropped him, leaned close to his face, and yelled, "You whoreson! You kiss me as I caress you and speak her name? May you rot in hell, Severin!"

She jerked the blankets off him, sending Trist scampering to the foot of the bed, and rolled off the other side. She wrapped herself tightly in the blankets and ran from the bedchamber.

The jongleur was in the great hall, leaning against one of the stone walls, eating MacDear's fresh black bread, doubtless writing a poem to Lady Marjorie's exquisite ears. She ordered him to leave Oxborough after he had chewed that last bite of bread. She didn't believe she could bear seeing him fall again on his knees in front of Marjorie.

She was thinking hard. She must be patient, that's what Dame Agnes had told her. How could she not do something when he whispered that woman's name into Hastings's mouth?

She looked up to see Severin standing at her elbow, looking down at her.

"You pulled the blankets from me and ran away. Why?"

"If I had a sword, I would have sent it through your belly."

"I have told you before, Hastings, before you had bent your will to mine, that a wife doesn't threaten her husband."

"Nay, you did not ever say that."

"If I did not, then I should have. I will say it now. Never threaten me, Hastings."

"Even when you whisper another woman's name into my mouth?"

Severin picked up her goblet and drank the rest of Gilbert the goat's milk. He set it down and wiped the back of his hand across his mouth. He shrugged. He had the gall to just shrug, as if what he had done was nothing at all.

"It makes no matter if I yelled the Virgin Mary's name. You will not act the shrew again with me. Fetch me bread and cheese. Ah, and some of that beef MacDear made last night. I am hungry."

Trist poked his head out of Severin's tunic, one of the tunics Hastings had made for him. He stuck his paw toward her and Hastings, smiling in spite of herself, shook his paw.

She rose from the trestle table bench. She tightened the blankets around her. She leaned down to pat Edgar the wolfhound's head. She accepted the lick on her palm. "I do not think so, Severin. However, I will tell one of the women to serve you.''

She began to whistle, though it was difficult to get enough spittle in her mouth. She strolled from the great hall, knowing he was staring at her, wondering if he would yell at her.

He remained silent. Did he feel guilty?

She did not tell any of the women to serve him.

That afternoon, she rode Marella into the village of Oxborough to visit her friend Ellen, baker Thomas's daughter. As she pulled her palfrey up in a side alley, she heard the veriest whisper of a sound, but it was just strange enough, just loud enough so that she looked up. A huge saddle balanced precariously on a window opening. She had no time. The saddle hurtled down, striking her on her head and shoulder, flinging her into a pile of refuse.

She looked up. She saw no one, save a shadow. She felt the pain swamp her. She called Ellen's name, then sighed softly and let herself fall into oblivion.

# 20

SOMEONE WAS LICKING HER.

No, it wasn't a someone. It was Alfred. Why was she at the Healer's cottage?

Hastings forced her eyes to open.

"Ah, finally she is awake," the Healer said, so close to her face that Hastings's eyes crossed. "Can you hear me?"

"Aye, I can even see you, Healer."

"Good. I'm going to lift your head and you will drink. It is not too foul a drink so do not complain."

Was that a man's chuckle she heard?

She obediently raised her head and downed the liquid. It tasted of strawberries. "It is delicious," she whispered, caught a shaft of black pain through her head just from those few words, and moaned.

"It is good you don't see the color," the Healer said. Hastings heard her say to someone else, "The potion will relieve her of the nausea and lessen the pain in her head and shoulder. I have examined her. She will not sing for a while, but she will mend."

"What else is in it, Healer?"

"A bit of ground gentian to calm your belly and just a small chunk of pounded iris root."

Hastings nodded, closing her eyes against a sudden shaft

of pain. Alfred's scratchy tongue on her cheek felt good. It tickled. She even managed a small smile.

She heard the man say, "I will leave her here then. I have duties that must be attended to. I will fetch her this afternoon."

"Aye, that will be fine, my lord."

My lord? It was Severin. She tried to raise her head to see him, but the dizziness forced her back down.

"Do not move, Hastings. You should know better than to try that."

"I just wanted to see Severin."

"You will see him later. You heard what he said. Duties. Men—I learned when I was just a little nit—they always have duties. What are duties, I ask you? Aye, duties are drinking and wenching and slicing each other with their swords and carving each other with their axes. Severin is no different. They are a wicked breed. I would say a worthless breed, but since they are necessary so that the next generation of them may be spawned, it would be going too far. Aye, a pity we cannot bring them all together and let them fight each other off a cliff. Close your eyes, Hastings, and rest. Alfred will lick you to sleep."

The damned cat did lick her to sleep.

When she next opened her eyes, the pain in her head was only a dull throb. She felt only tightness in her shoulder. Her belly was calm. Severin was staring down at her.

He lightly touched his palm to her forehead, then to each cheek. He sat down beside her. "You feel cool to the touch. The Healer says you will be fine. Do you remember what happened?"

The hazy fog lifted in her mind and she nodded slowly. "Aye, I remember now. I rode into Oxborough village to visit Ellen, Thomas the baker's daughter. I was going to tether Marella in the alleyway. A saddle fell on me from an upper window. I don't remember anything else. No, I remember that I fell into a pile of refuse. It smelled very bad."

"It is a very strange coincidence. It was one of my saddles that hit you. Gwent had taken it to Robert the leatherer to mend it. It is big, fashioned for a warhorse. You were lucky it didn't strike you directly on your head. Also, you no longer smell of refuse. The Healer bathed you. It is a relief. Ellen found you. She ran to the keep and fetched me. I brought you to the Healer.''

"But why would your saddle—of all saddles—fall on me? Nothing like that has ever happened before.''

He shrugged, but he was frowning even as he patted Alfred, who was standing on his hind paws, his front paws on Severin's leg. "I don't know as yet, but I will find out.''

Suddenly there was a ferocious hiss. Alfred froze, his tail bushed out, his fur sticking up from his body. He was staring at Severin even as he dug his claws into Severin's leg. No, it was Trist he was staring at. Trist calmly regarded the giant cat, sniffed the air, looked at Hastings, then retreated back into Severin's tunic.

Severin patted the lump in his tunic, saying low, "Stay there, Trist. That cat could eat four of you.''

Trist rumbled against his chest. Severin smiled. "He is trying to convince me he isn't afraid of Alfred.''

It was the first smile she had seen on his mouth for two days, since Marjorie's arrival at Oxborough.

Marjorie.

"I would go home now, Severin.''

"Only if the Healer says you are well enough.''

The Healer agreed but told her to remain in her bed for the remainder of the day, to eat a light broth, and to sleep for as long as she could.

"Be patient, Hastings,'' the Healer called after her, Alfred weaving in and out between her legs.

Hastings had wanted Severin to hold her, but not like this, not when her head was aching more ferociously now, and her belly wasn't all that calm now with the swaying of his mighty warhorse, despite the Healer's potion.

He was holding her in his arms, her head against his chest. Her belly quieted. She sighed and, surprisingly, slept the short ride to the castle.

She awoke to see Lady Marjorie standing on the top stone step of the keep, Eloise at her side. "Ah, my lord, you have brought her home. Carry her immediately to her bedchamber. That's right. Be careful now.''

She sounds like the mistress of Oxborough, Hastings thought, feeling strangely detached. Then she drifted away again from another potion the Healer had given her to drink just before she and Severin left her cottage.

When she awoke, Dame Agnes was seated beside her bed, sewing. There were three lit candles casting slivers of light through the shadows in the large room.

"My little pet, you're awake. Good. I will send for your broth. MacDear was very worried that it would not be exactly as the Healer wished it to be.''

Hastings said nothing. She was here alone in the bedchamber with Dame Agnes. Where was Severin? Where was Marjorie?

When she finally swallowed the delicious broth, flavored lightly with chicken and almonds, she heard herself ask, "Where is my lord?''

"He is in the great hall with all his men.''

"And Lady Marjorie.''

"Aye, I suppose so. What does that matter? All that is important is that you mend.''

"Why would Severin's saddle fall from a window onto my head, Agnes?'' Slowly, she continued eating the broth. Her stomach remained calm. She knew she had to eat. She had to regain her strength.

Dame Agnes straightened the sleeve of her gown. She studied the thumbnail on her left hand. She frowned at the brown spots on the back of her hands. She would have to see the Healer. "No one knows, Hastings. Lord Severin questioned everyone. The window from which the saddle fell was in the leatherer's shop, but you knew that. It certainly wouldn't fall from the baker's house. That second floor is a sleeping area for Thomas's three apprentices as well as a storage place for goods waiting to be mended, and raw materials. All believe it was an accident. That sweet Ellen ran all the way from the village to the keep. She is a good girl.''

"I would go downstairs now, Agnes.''

"You are not yet well enough, Hastings."

Hastings ignored her. She rose slowly, very carefully. Pain bolted through her head, but it wasn't too bad. Her shoulders were knotted and stiff. She could bear it.

She was wearing only her night shift. She smiled at Dame Agnes. "Please help me with my clothes. I must go to the great hall, I must."

Dame Agnes nodded.

Six bells were ringing when Hastings stood at the base of the solar stairs and looked over the great hall. She knew what she would see, but still, seeing Lady Marjorie seated in her chair next to Severin, Eloise beside her, nearly brought her to her knees. Marjorie was laughing at something Severin said. Everyone was laughing, arguing, eating with great appetite. No one seemed to find anything amiss. Everything was perfectly normal save that the mistress of the castle wasn't in her rightful place.

Marjorie was.

Hastings weaved where she stood. She felt Dame Agnes's hand beneath her elbow.

"She has taken my place," Hastings said.

"No. It seems that the smaller chair where she has sat had a broken leg. There was no choice but for her to sit in your chair. It means nothing, Hastings. You are ill and not thinking clearly."

"No, I suppose I am not thinking at all." Ah, but the pain she felt. It was bowing her inward, threatening to bring her to her knees.

"I will go back to my bedchamber now," she said calmly. She turned one last time to see Severin staring toward her. He half rose in his chair, then turned to look at Marjorie as she said something to him. Hastings saw him stare at those white fingers on the sleeve of his tunic.

"It is too much," Hastings said, and made her way up the stairs like a bent old woman.

She did not rise from her bed the following morning. Her head still pounded, the muscles in her shoulders knotted and burned. Severin had not come to the bedchamber the previous night.

He had slept with Marjorie, she knew it.

She ate fresh white bread spread with thick butter, and a large bowl of chicken broth, with just a hint of rosemary. Alice brought her chunks of sweet Oxborough cheese.

Alice patted her hand. "Do not worry, Hastings. All goes well. Everyone knows what is to be done. Everyone is very worried about you. I believe Lord Severin rode once again to the village to question all the apprentices again at Robert the leatherer's house. Still, it seems an accident, though I do wonder how Lord Severin's saddle could possibly fall on you. It bothers Gwent too. He keeps scratching his head and staring up at nothing at all."

Hastings knew why that saddle had fallen on her. Marjorie had hired someone to hurl that saddle down on her, Marjorie, the woman who would take her place as mistress of Oxborough were Hastings to die. But a saddle surely wasn't a very certain way to ensure another's demise. And why Severin's saddle? Unless it was Severin himself who had shoved the saddle from the open window down upon her.

She sighed. It made no sense. It had to be an accident. Still, she remained in bed all that day, just staring at the tapestry her grandmother had sewn for thirty years, according to Hastings's mother.

When Severin came into the bedchamber, looking healthy, windblown, as strong as an oak tree, she just closed her eyes. It hurt too much to look at him.

She said only, "Have you mended Marjorie's chair leg?"

He frowned at her. "Are you all right, Hastings? Are you thinking clearly? What is this about a chair leg?"

She looked at him straightly, watching him as he strode across the room to come stand beside her bed. "She was seated in my chair last night because, I was told, hers was broken. Is it fixed?"

"I do not know. No one spoke of it to me. I wish you to rise now. You will grow mold if you remain in bed much longer. Come, there are duties you must attend to. The

Healer said you were to rest, not sink into the folds of the mattress.''

"Mayhap later," she said. "I am very tired. I wish to sleep."

He looked down at her, studying her pale face. "I do not like this, Hastings," he said, then turned on his heel and left her. Trist crawled out of Severin's tunic and leapt upon the bed.

"Where did your master sleep last night?" she asked as she stroked the marten's soft fur. "Were you with him? Was he with her?"

Trist poked his head beneath her chin, opened his mouth, and bit her.

"So you believe I am foolish, do you? You are not a man, Trist, so I suppose she is just another female to you. Her silvery hair doesn't make your eyes crazed with lust."

Trist bit her again, this time just a little harder. She laughed. She couldn't help herself.

She slept throughout the afternoon, Trist beside her.

"Wake up, Hastings. You will bathe. I have had the lads bring the water. Come now, no more acting like the swooning lady of the keep."

Hastings allowed Dame Agnes to bathe her. She sat docilely while she dressed her and brushed her hair. She wasn't surprised when Alice slipped into the bedchamber.

"I have a pot of margolis," she said. "It will add a bit of color to your cheeks. I think your lips need a smear of it as well."

Hastings allowed herself to be painted. She said nothing when they garbed her in the gown she had worn on her wedding day. Finally, it was done.

"You are beautiful," Dame Agnes said, stepping back and looking at her charge up and down, rubbing her arthritic hands together. "Do you not agree, Alice?"

"Aye, the loveliest lady in the land."

"Was the chair leg mended, Agnes?"

"I saw to it personally," Agnes said. "Someone had

worked the leg loose. It was not an accident, but now it is fixed.''

"A chair leg and Severin's saddle," Hastings said. "How odd this all is.''

When Hastings entered the great hall, she saw that Severin was holding out her chair for Marjorie.

Hastings called out, "Good evening, my lord.''

Everyone turned to look at her. She saw Severin's hand still on her chair back. She saw that Marjorie was just smiling toward her. She said something to Severin, then returned to her own chair, leaning over to pat Eloise's hand.

Severin now held the chair for her, for his wife. He even pushed it closer to the trestle table when she was seated. He even touched his fingertips to her shoulder.

"You look well," he said, seating himself beside her. "By Saint Andrew's teeth, what is that red on your cheeks and mouth? Do you have the fever?''

"No, it is Alice's attempt to make me less ordinary.''

"I do not like it. You look like a camp trollop." He picked up the corner of the soft linen spread and pulled it toward her. "Wipe it off.''

She did.

"Now you look pale, but at least you once more look like yourself.''

"Aye. Myself.''

Marjorie leaned toward Hastings. "I was worried about you, but your women did not think you should have too many people coming into your bedchamber. You look much better, Hastings. I was very distressed when Severin brought you home yesterday. All were.''

"Thank you, Marjorie." She ate a bite of cherry potage. She tasted the rich red wine MacDear had poured into the thick soup.

"MacDear made the potage just for you. I asked him what your favorite dishes were, and he said this was one of them and he had not prepared it for you in a very long time. The dear man even allowed me and Eloise to remain in the kitchen to help him. He yells louder than any man I have heard in my life.''

Hastings looked beyond Marjorie to Eloise, whose head was down. She wasn't eating, just shoving her food about on the pewter plate. ''Eloise? Did you help MacDear like you did before when you lived here?''

''I did not know you had helped MacDear before,'' Marjorie said, covering Eloise's small hand with hers.

''I did not. Hastings wanted me to but it was too hot in the kitchens. Everyone yelled. That fat man yelled. I did not remain.''

Hastings gasped. ''That isn't true, Eloise. You even sat on MacDear's lap. Don't you remember?''

''I remember that you made me sit on his lap. He smelled and he yelled. I hated it.''

''Then why did you go back today?''

''Because Marjorie was with me. She didn't make me do anything I did not want to do. I ate cherries.''

''Aye, you did, sweeting. You still have a red tongue.''

Eloise stuck out her tongue at Marjorie, then laughed and pressed herself against Marjorie's side. Marjorie said to Hastings, ''My little sweeting here will give me gray hairs before I am even an old woman.''

''You will never be old,'' Eloise said. ''You are the most beautiful lady in all the world.''

Lady Marjorie tweaked Eloise's nose, laughing all the while. ''You are shameless, Eloise, flattering me until I will grow so large a head it will not fit through our bedchamber door.''

Eloise laughed. Hastings stared. It was the first time she had seen the child so gay. Trist mewled and climbed up onto Hastings's shoulder. She winced because of the knotted muscles, then began to relax when the marten's body heat began to seep into her.

She turned to her husband, who was staring down at his soup. ''You do not care for the cherries, Severin?''

He looked clearly distracted. ''What? Aye, Hastings. It is tasty.''

''Will you sleep in your own bedchamber tonight?''

He cocked his head at her. "If you are well enough. I did not want to take the chance last night that I would roll on you and mayhap hurt you."

"I am well enough. Where did you sleep last night?"

"Here in the great hall, wrapped in a blanket, listening to my men snore. Edgar the wolfhound curled up next to me."

Mayhap he had. Surely he couldn't have bedded Marjorie with Eloise in the same chamber. She began to feel better.

Eloise said, "I did not sleep well last night with Dame Agnes because she snores too. She's not like Marjorie. She's bony and her breath isn't sweet."

Hastings saw the great hall, all its people, through a haze of misery. Severin had bedded her. He had bedded another woman as his wife had slept in his bedchamber close by. It was too much.

She feared what she would do. Her fist closed about her knife. Slowly, she rose. Trist mewled but remained on her shoulder, wrapping himself now around her neck.

She said nothing to either her husband or anyone else, just walked slowly across that huge expanse that was filled with laughing people until she reached the solar stairs.

Then she heard Severin call out, "Trist, come back here. You have not eaten enough as yet."

But Trist didn't move.

Severin did not come after her.

But Marjorie came. She knocked softly on the bedchamber door. Hastings believed it would be Dame Agnes and called for her to enter. When she saw it was Marjorie, wearing an exquisite gown of saffron wool that Hastings had worn only one time before, she wanted to yell for the woman to leave her alone. But she didn't. She remained silent, watching her walk gracefully to the bed.

"Are you feeling all right, Hastings? Severin asked me to see you. He is concerned."

Hastings just stared at her. "Why are you wearing my gown?"

"I did not wish to but Severin insisted. I was not able to bring many things from Sedgewick, and naturally I wanted Eloise to have enough. I had only two gowns and they were both quite dirty. He insisted I wear one of yours. Do you mind? If you do, I will remove it immediately.''

"Aye, I mind. Will you remove it here in my bedchamber, Marjorie? Or will you wait to remove it in your own bedchamber whilst Eloise sleeps with Dame Agnes?''

"Ah,'' Marjorie said, as she ran her white fingers through her incredible silver hair. ''So that is the reason you left the great hall. The reason Eloise slept with Dame Agnes was because I had a cough that kept awakening her. It was irritating. I wanted Eloise to sleep, not just lie there, listening to me cough and cough.''

Hastings looked beyond her to her grandmother's tapestry. How clear and vivid the colors still were. She said nothing.

"I will go to my bedchamber now and remove this gown. I am sorry that I did not ask you if you minded. You were sleeping and Severin just gave it to me. I had no idea the gown was so important to you.''

"Aye, it is.''

"Then I will leave you. I will return the gown very soon. I hope you will be well tomorrow, Hastings.''

"Aye, I do too. I did not hear you cough at all downstairs, Marjorie.''

"No, it went away this afternoon.''

"Marjorie! What are you doing here?''

It was Severin, standing in the open doorway, looking large and intimidating, and Hastings hated him more at that moment than she ever had, even when he'd held her down and forced her.

"I am just speaking to Hastings. I will leave now and remove the gown. I will return it shortly.''

"What are you talking about?''

But Marjorie just smiled, shaking her head. Severin turned to watch her leave the bedchamber. When he turned back, he said, ''Why did you walk away from your dinner? Why did you take Trist with you? I called for him but you wouldn't let him come back to me. What is this about a gown? Hastings?''

# 21

SHE WISHED SHE HAD HER KNIFE, BUT ALAS, ALL SHE HAD was Trist draped over her shoulder. She said, not really wanting to look at him, but unable to look away, "Her chair was mended. Did you know that someone had twisted that leg off? Do you not find that strange? Why would anyone do that, Severin? Why were you going to seat her in my chair again?"

He plowed his hand through his hair. He looked utterly baffled, then impatient. "This is nonsense. What is wrong with you? The Healer did not describe such symptoms to me that you now seem to have."

"I am feeling just fine now. Did you discover any more about your saddle flying out of that window?"

"My saddle, aye, it was my saddle, wasn't it?" He stared at her, stared at Trist, who was looking intently at his master from his perch on her sore shoulder. "You believe I had someone throw my saddle down on you?"

"No, that is too devious. If you wanted me dead, you would simply throttle me."

"Aye, and I have wanted to throttle you more times than I can count." He turned away from her and began to take off his clothes. She turned her back to him. She felt the bed give when he eased down on it. He blew out the candles. The bedchamber was plunged into darkness.

"What was all that about Marjorie's gown?"

"It isn't Marjorie's gown. It is my gown and she will return it. She said you gave it to her."

"Aye, to wear since she had nothing left. Dame Agnes saw nothing amiss with lending her the gown. Why would you care, Hastings?"

"I do not want her to take what is mine."

"It is naught but a silly piece of clothing."

She said nothing. She heard him breathe, heard his breath ease and slow into sleep.

"This is damnable, Trist," she whispered, petting the marten's head. "Just damnable. What am I to do?" She was not exercising patience as Dame Agnes had advised her to do. She'd blurted out everything. And Severin had looked at her as if she were as mad as his mother had once been.

Two days later, Hastings rode Marella into Oxborough village. She did not tether her palfrey in the alleyway. She left her directly in front of Thomas the baker's shop. Ellen raced to see her, hugging her close, telling her she had been terrified that she was dead when she first saw her.

"I did not know what to do. My father picked you up and brought you into the shop. I ran to the castle. Lord Severin came immediately. He even let me ride pillion with him."

"Thank you, Ellen. Did you know that it was Lord Severin's saddle that fell on me?"

Ellen knew that. Hastings imagined that everyone in the village knew that and wondered about it, aloud. Aye, he was a man who had married an heiress and now there was a beautiful creature living at Oxborough. And his wife, the heiress whom he didn't need anymore. Hastings could almost hear them discussing this. It made her belly cramp. She shook it off. "I want to find out what happened. How could a saddle simply fall from a window? It makes no sense."

Ellen saw her mother look up from her baking in the

corner of the shop and lowered her voice. "You believe someone did it on purpose? To kill you? With a saddle? Come, Hastings, that is silly. No one really thinks that is possible. Perhaps some believe it a willful act, but not everyone does. Nay, not more than half the people think it was done apurpose."

A willful act. Done apurpose. But not to kill her. Then to what? Scare her? Why?

"You mean that the person found himself or herself there by the window with the saddle nearby and I happened to be beneath the window quite by chance, and thus, the saddle comes flying out to land on my head." It did sound remarkably silly. But still. "I want to speak to the apprentices."

"Very well, I will go with you."

Robert the leatherer's shop smelled of sweet oils, tanned hides, soft leather, and sweat. Master Robert had one journeyman and three apprentices, all of them working in the shop. Master Robert, short, a filthy apron wrapped around his fat belly, bustled forward, bowing even as he said, "Lady Hastings, dear child, I am so happy to see you well again. To think it was your lord's saddle that fell on you! Imagine that. I am devastated it was from my window that saddle fell. I will do anything, lady, anything. Just tell me your wish and I am your slave."

Well used to Master Robert from her earliest memories, Hastings merely nodded in that haughty way she knew would silence him, at least for a few moments.

"I would speak to your people, Master Robert. That is my wish."

An hour later, Hastings was chewing on an almond bun that Thomas the baker had given her fresh from one of his ovens. "No one saw anything. It seems that there were a half dozen men-at-arms from the castle at the leatherer's that day. I suppose that I will have to speak to Gwent."

"Aye, he is a good man," Thomas said, "Eat another bun, Hastings. You are nearly as skinny as the handle on my oven paddle."

Hastings returned to the castle to see Severin riding out with Marjorie. Where was Eloise?

At least Marjorie wasn't wearing another of her gowns. She had finally laundered one of her own? Hastings was truly supposed to be patient? She was tempted to ride after them, but she did not. There were duties that awaited her. Real duties, not trysts with a lover. She also wanted to speak to Gwent.

When she found Gwent, he said, "Severin has already questioned the men who were at the leatherer's shop that day. None saw anything. It was an accident, there is no other possibility."

"You, Gwent, were not the one struck down by that saddle."

"Aye, 'tis true enough," he said, then turned to wave to Alice. "But the facts remain the same, Hastings. Forget about it."

Hastings spent the next hour with Lady Moraine. Edgar the wolfhound lay with his head and wide, scored paws on Lady Moraine's feet.

"I am making you a gown, Hastings," she said. "It is the softest green. You will look rather lovely in it. Severin was right last evening. You should not wear the red cream on your mouth or smear it on your cheeks. Your features are too fine. Do you like the gown? It will be finished by tomorrow afternoon."

"Forgive me, Lady Moraine, but I heard Lord Severin tell Marjorie that the gown would be hers."

It was Eloise, standing off to one side, obviously listening to their conversation.

"Did you really, Eloise?" Lady Moraine said before Hastings could open her mouth. "When did my son say this?"

"I believe it was this morning, madam. He said the material would make her look like a goddess. She is a goddess and so very beautiful. She deserves to have splendid clothing." Eloise stared at Hastings.

"Well, no matter what you heard, Eloise," Lady Moraine said brusquely. "The gown is for Hastings. Now, child, would you like to sit with us and sew?''

But Eloise just shook her head and skipped away.

"How very odd," Lady Moraine said, staring after the child. "I did not pull out this material until this afternoon. The child lied. Why would she do that?"

"She loves Marjorie very much. Perhaps she sees that Marjorie wants to take my place and is thus very willing to assist her."

"Venom from a child is unpleasant, worse than from a grown man or woman. I will think about this. Ah, I must see the Healer today. My potion is nearly gone."

That evening, garbed in a lovely gown Hastings had never seen before, Lady Marjorie came into the great hall, greeting everyone graciously, smiling, her white hands fluttering. Her hair was loose silver waves down her back, held back from her forehead with a gold band. Severin stared at her.

It happened midway through the long meal. Marjorie's nose began to swell and turn red.

Hastings blinked, not believing her eyes. She opened her mouth, felt meanness flow through her, and shut it.

Marjorie's nose swelled to an even greater size and turned a brighter red. Soon people were staring at her, talking behind their hands. As for Severin, he had been feeding Trist. When finally he looked past Hastings to Marjorie, he gasped. Then he threw back his head and laughed aloud.

Soon the entire great hall was laughing and pointing.

Eloise burst into tears. Slowly, the hall quieted. And into that silence, everyone heard Marjorie ask, "Sweeting, why are you crying? What is wrong, Eloise?"

"Everyone is laughing at you, Marjorie. It's your nose."

Marjorie's hand flew to her nose. She felt it, horror nearly crossing her beautiful blue eyes. "Oh no, what is wrong?"

"It is swelled and very red," Hastings said. "Perhaps you would like to come with me, Marjorie. I will mix some herbs that will reduce the swelling and take away the redness."

Hastings had never seen Marjorie move so quickly.

There was no talk, no laughter. It seemed that everyone understood that the exquisite Lady Marjorie was humiliated.

"What could bring this on?" Marjorie asked, seated on a low stool while Hastings mixed mugwort and primrose with three spoonfuls of vinegar. She had looked into the small mirror Hastings's father had given his wife many years before. She hadn't shrieked, just stared at herself and lightly touched her fingertips to her nose.

Hastings knew very well what had brought this on, but she just shook her head. "It is very likely a poisoning from some food that your body does not like. This drink will cure it quickly, you will see."

"But what food? I have never had this happen before."

Hastings shrugged and mixed, keeping her head down. She poured in just a bit of goat urine, said to be very efficacious in matters of swelling. She felt wicked, but at least she would cure Marjorie. She wasn't that mean. Sometimes it was difficult being a healer. "Mayhap it is some herb MacDear uses that no other cook knows about. Mayhap it is not wise for you to continue to eat his food."

She handed her the small cup filled with thick liquid. "Drink it quickly, Marjorie."

Marjorie drank it straight down, then turned white and held her stomach.

"Nay, do not retch, else you will have to drink it again. This will pass. Just think about your nose being small and white again. Aye, see it already passes."

Marjorie's nose returned to normal within the hour but she would not return to the great hall.

Hastings fetched Eloise from the great hall, then returned to her own bedchamber, smiling and humming.

I am truly wicked, she thought. But then again, so was her dear mother-in-law.

Hastings felt queasy. She pressed her palm against her stomach, wondering. She raised her hands and cupped her breasts, squeezing them. They were sore. She had not suffered her monthly flux in many weeks.

She was with child, Severin's child.

She wondered if Marjorie would soon also carry Severin's child.

She shook her head, raced from the keep to the stable, and asked Tuggle to saddle Marella.

When she pulled her palfrey up in front of the Healer's small cottage, the woman was on her knees in front of her herb patch, whistling. Alfred was stretched out his full length in the sword of sun that shone through the thick branches of the sessile oak trees.

"Hastings," the Healer said, sitting back on her heels. "Look at this. It is a new sort of daisy. I have worked it and worked it and now I am certain that when I pound the flowers into powder and mix them with wine, it will ensure that Lady Moraine stays well in her head." The Healer paused, then grinned. "I believe it will also cure warts. I tried it already on two of the village boys. The warts were gone in three days. The boys will tell their mothers and sisters, and soon I will have more goods from the village than I will ever need. We live amongst a very warty people. And now I can remove them. I am the greatest healer in Britain. What think you of that?"

"I think I am carrying Severin's child."

The Healer rose slowly, wiping her hands on her skirts. She stepped to Hastings and merely looked at her. She reached out her hand and laid it on Hastings's belly. She looked at her tongue. She lightly scratched the skin on the backs of Hastings's hands, then looked at her fingernails.

Then she stepped back. Alfred stretched and rose. He meowed loudly and prepared to jump into Hastings's arms.

"No," the Healer said sharply. Alfred frowned at his mistress. Hastings had never before seen a cat frown, but Alfred did. He swished his tail and ran to the nearest sessile oak tree and was gone into the thick green leaves in but moments.

"Have you vomited?"

Hastings shook her head. "I do feel queasy sometimes. Not just at a certain time of the day, but it just comes and goes. I cannot predict it."

"Aye, I would say you carry his child. He is a potent man. Most of the churls are potent, and thus women are cursed to have their wombs filled whether they wish it or not. Aye, men—the blight of our land. Would that I could poison all of them, but then again, women like you wouldn't be pleased were your husband to crumble into dust."

"I would not be too certain of that right now, Healer."

"So he is acting more faithless, is he?" Then she grinned, showing very white, very even teeth. "Bring me this Marjorie and let me see what she is about."

"She is always very nice to me," Hastings said, so depressed she kicked her toe into a rock and gasped from the sharp pain. "She is also very beautiful except for last night when her nose swelled and turned red. I mixed a drink for her and it went away."

"Perhaps you should have waited, Hastings. The swelling would have gone away by the next morning."

"I know that, but I was weak. I didn't let her suffer. However, I did add goat urine to the mixture. She drank it."

The Healer laughed and patted her face. "Well done. You have turned into a fine woman, Hastings. Now, did I tell you what I learned from a monk who happened to visit me two days ago? If I grind up columbine leaves and add saffron, it will cure jaundice. What do you think of that?"

Hastings was excited, she couldn't help it. "Show me how to do it, Healer. I must know."

The Healer laughed. "If you and your husband had been married for more than a year and your womb was still empty, I would give you the distilled water of wallflowers to drink twice a day for four weeks. Unfortunately, Lord Severin is like most men, he plows and plows and his seed sinks immediately into fertile ground. Such a pity. Come with me, Hastings, and I will give you just a bit of my special mixture—no, I will not tell you the ingredients. It will keep you smiling and your belly calm."

• • •

Severin shoved the door inward. His skin felt tight, his loins were heavy, his wife hadn't spoken to him for well onto three days, and he was furious.

Hastings was standing over a narrow table mixing some of her damnable herbs. She looked up, then immediately back down to the mixture in a wooden bowl. "Did I ever tell you that MacDear will gently shred columbine flowers onto the platters that hold the meat? He says it makes the food look more appetizing. He prefers the red columbine, he says it adds—"

"I am sick of this, Hastings. You have changed again. You have returned to the woman I married. You have not treated me well. You have ignored me. The miracle has ended. I did not muck it up. I do not know why you have changed, but you once more have your shrew's mouth. If you wish to go back to the way we were, then so be it. However, you will see to me, your husband. My man's need is great. I would have you now and I will tolerate no arguments."

"Did you know that the name 'columbine' is from Latin and means dove? You see, people believed the plant looked like doves' heads."

He was on her in a moment. The pulse was pounding wildly in his neck. Trist wasn't with him.

"You will force me, Severin?"

"Aye, if I must."

"What is wrong with Marjorie? Is it her monthly flux or is she tired of you? Are you not moving quickly enough to remove me from Oxborough so that you can wed her?"

He jerked back as if she had struck him. "You are mad," he said, and ripped her gown from neck to waist. "Don't speak such nonsense again. I cannot have Marjorie. Fate saw to that many years ago." He ripped open her shift, baring her breasts.

"You will not force me again, Severin."

"I will do as I please with you, Hastings." He picked her up and threw her onto her back on the bed. He was over her in a moment, pulling up her skirts, opening his breeches. He was breathing hard.

She stared up at him and said, "Would you risk harming your child?"

He froze over her. "You carry my babe? A new lie, Hastings, but not a very good one. I haven't touched you for a very long time."

"Aye, and surely that is my fault."

"I have had other things on my mind. Now I want to relieve myself."

She bucked and heaved, so furious that she wanted to kill him. He lowered his face to kiss her and she tried to bite his mouth. He couldn't believe that she had tried to bite him. He reared back, forced her legs wide, and came into her hard and deep. She yelled, more with anger than with the pain of it.

"You animal," she screamed at him, not caring if a servant was outside the bedchamber door to hear her. "I hate you. I wish your saddle had hit you on the head. Maybe everything would be different, maybe—"

He was deep now, pushing against her womb, breathing hard as he heaved over her.

When he reached his release, he froze over her. As she felt his seed inside her, she said, "I will never forgive you this, Severin. You have betrayed me. I would that you never touch me again. Go back to your Marjorie and leave me be."

"Aye," he said, heaving and jerking, so spent he could barely speak, "mayhap I will. She always has smiles for me. She always welcomes me, just as she did when she was a young girl. Why did you humiliate her?"

"What are you talking about?"

"Her nose."

"I did nothing. I did fix her goddess's nose though."

"It matters not if you lie to me. Why will you not bend to me again? Why do you compel me to force you? Why will you not smile at me again? Why won't you let me kiss you or caress you? Why won't you let me give you pleasure?"

"I did smile at you until she came and you looked at her like a lovesick boy. You don't care if I smile or if I cry. All you care about is staring at her, riding with her, seating her in my chair. Your desire for her is clear for everyone to see.''

He pulled out of her and stood beside the bed, staring down at her. Her legs were sprawled open but she didn't care. She watched him straighten his clothes.

''I am with child. If I were not a healer perhaps I would destroy it, for I want nothing from you. Nothing.''

He was over her in an instant, his hands around her neck. ''You will not speak like that. It is blasphemy. A man would be justified to kill a wife who killed his child. Ah, but you aren't with child, are you?'' He released her throat and fell onto his back again. He sighed. ''Lie no more, Hastings. You know I will go easy with you if you will but bend to me again. You also know I will take you whenever I wish to. That is the way of it. Don't fight me. There is no need. Smile at me again, caress me with your hands, kiss me in front of our people. There was no reason for you to stop that.''

''Where did you ride with Marjorie this morning?''

''I showed her the marsh just beyond the northern estuary. Why? Come, Hastings, do not be jealous. It doesn't become you. Let me come to you the way I did before. You enjoyed my body. You yelled your pleasure. Do not continue this madness. I told you, Marjorie was lost to me years ago. It is over. It is done.''

Where had Marjorie gotten that new gown? Rot the woman and rot Severin. ''You think it your right to betray me? To have two women in the same keep? Or will another saddle fall upon my head?''

He stared down at her, his face white. He opened his mouth, but she raised her hand to stop him. ''No, Severin, no lies. I can bear no more lies.''

She saw that he was as angry as he had been so long before, when they had first wedded. He came over her again, shoved into her, and moved over her until once again he reached his release.

He held her arms above her head, speaking even as his breathing still hitched. ''No lies, Hastings. I will tell you the truth. You are pathetic. Look at yourself. Ranting at me, lying there with nothing to give me but your damned anger that I do not deserve. It is you who have mucked up the miracle, not I. I will not accept this, Hastings. Damn you, become the way you were a week ago. Look to Marjorie, she is sweet and gentle, an angel who walks in the sunlight even when it is night. Aye, try to mold yourself into Marjorie's likeness.''

He jerked off her. As he walked from the bedchamber, she yelled at him, ''I wish your saddle had fallen on you! All that was between us was a lie. I was never anything to you save a convenience. Damn you, I am not pathetic! I would rather mold myself in Satan's likeness than Marjorie's.''

He slammed the door behind him. She lay there for but a few moments, then rose to bathe herself. It was at that moment that Hastings made her decision.

# 22

"I ASK IT AS A FAVOR TO MY FATHER. PLEASE, BEAMIS, don't say no."

Beamis scratched his armpit, looked everywhere but at his mistress's face, and wished Gwent would magically appear, overhear what she wanted him to do, and forbid it without hesitation and with great force of voice.

Hastings tugged at his sleeve. "Listen, Beamis, you know my father traveled to this place three or four times a year. Don't shake your head. Surely you knew of it. You were his master-at-arms. You did, did you not? Of course you did. You accompanied him."

He nodded finally, praying that if Gwent didn't come then Lord Severin would appear. No, he would not pray for that. All knew that Lord Severin had mucked things up again with his wife. All knew that he desired Lady Marjorie, an exquisite wench with exquisite silver hair that a man wanted to stroke and rub against. But, Beamis thought, she was still just a wench like any other wench. Hair wasn't all that important.

Hastings was an heiress and a healer, only a wench secondarily. "I can't," he said finally, and wanted to cry.

Her hand was still on his arm, tugging now frantically

at his sleeve. "Beamis, I cannot remain here and watch her take my place."

"I cannot, Hastings. Please, do not ask this of me. It is impossible. I cannot."

He was miserable, she could see that, but she didn't care. She said very quietly, "The saddle that fell on me—Lord Severin's own saddle. You know it was not an accident. Do you wish Fawke of Trent's daughter to be killed? If I remain here, it could happen and you know it, Beamis."

Beamis groaned. Half the men thought it had been an accident. The other half wondered aloud, but Beamis knew what they thought. They believed that someone wanted Lady Marjorie to take Hastings's place as mistress of Oxborough. But who? The lady herself? How could someone so beautiful, with such exquisite hair, be so treacherous?

He was suddenly struck with inspiration. "No one will kill you. I will taste your food." He beamed at her. There was a wide space between his two front teeth. He habitually cleaned between those teeth with his tongue. "No one can poison you if I taste your food before you do."

She sighed and turned away, saying over her shoulder, "I am with child, Beamis. You wish my child to die as well? Lord Fawke's grandson?"

He cursed, spat in a mud puddle, kicked a roving chicken, and cursed some more at Gilbert the goat, who was chewing on a long strap of old leather. He wanted to strangle that goat with that leather strap. But the goat gave milk. Hastings would need the milk so the child would remain healthy in her womb.

He plowed his thick fingers through grizzled black hair. "I would be undone. Lord Severin would kill me were he to find out. And how would he not know? You would be gone from Oxborough and so would I. The roads are dangerous. There are more outlaws between here and the southern coast than men guarding King Edward. I could not sufficiently protect you. Besides, I would be dead because Lord Severin would kill me."

Hastings didn't believe Severin would precisely kill Beamis, but what could she say to that? She would have to travel alone. But she didn't know where Rosehaven was.

She patted Beamis's arm as she said, "You are right. I did not think this through. I will not ask you again. It was not fair of me."

Beamis wasn't stupid. He had known Hastings since she was a child. He'd watched her grow up. He looked thoroughly alarmed. "You will not go by yourself, will you, Hastings? By Saint Albert's toenails, promise me you'll not go to this Rosehaven alone."

"How could I? I have no idea where Rosehaven is." Well, she did know that it was near Canterbury, but that was all. There was probably quite a lot near Canterbury.

He looked vastly relieved. "No, you do not." He even looked skyward and she imagined he was giving thanks to God.

She found Severin with Torric the steward. There was no longer any distrust between them since Torric had told him about Rosehaven. Severin looked up, recognized that stubborn look on her face, and sighed. He left Torric, took her arm, and walked beside her outside the keep into the inner bailey. "You wish to apologize to me? You wish to kiss me again in front of our people and Gilbert the goat? Mayhap you could caress me with your hands?"

Severin rather thought she would do none of these things. She looked more likely to spit in his eye. She said, "You know that it is not safe for the Sedgewick people to return yet. It is another sennight, at least, to be safe."

"Aye."

"I know you do not wish to leave Lady Marjorie. Thus I would ask that you allow me to take some of your men and travel to Rosehaven. I will find out who is living there and what hold there was over my father."

"Why would I not wish to leave Lady Marjorie?"

"Because you doubtless love her."

"I do not love any woman, Hastings. You know that. I would have given my life for her at one time, but I was only a boy. I have not enjoyed her for many years. Aye, then she was a boy's dream."

He had joined to her when he had been just a boy? Before he had gone to the Holy Land? "Do not lie to me, Severin. There is no need. I merely wish to leave. You can seat her in my place and give her my gowns. She can sleep with you in my bed."

"I can do that with you here. No. You will remain at Oxborough and see to your duties. When I decide we will go to Rosehaven, then we will go."

He turned from her and walked back into the keep. She didn't think, just picked up a stone that lay near her feet and hurled it at him. It missed him, but not by much, loudly striking the stone wall of the keep and cracking in two. He turned more quickly than she believed a man could move. He already held a knife poised in his hand. He stared at her, stared down at the stone that had come close to striking him in the back.

She was breathing hard. She hadn't been aware before, but she was now. There were people about them, all staring now, even the chickens and dogs quiet.

He sheathed his knife again at his waist and slowly walked back to her.

He stopped just inches from her. She didn't move. "Did you not believe me before, Hastings?"

She stared at his throat.

"You dared to threaten me again?"

"I wish I had struck you."

He grabbed her arm and strode out of the inner bailey, walking so quickly he was dragging her. She pulled and jerked but it did no good. The sleeve of her gown ripped from the shoulder. He merely closed his hand around her bare upper arm and walked more quickly. When he reached the stable, he yelled for Tuggle to saddle his horse.

He stopped then, stared down at her, and shook his head. "I am going to take you down to the beach and beat you. I should beat you here, before all our people so they will know that I am the lord here, but I do not want to test their loyalties. MacDear might poison me."

"You mean to beat me to death as my father did my mother? Go ahead, Severin. And what will you give as your reason? You know that my father found my mother in the falconer's bed. In this case, it is you in Marjorie's bed. It is I who should beat you to death."

He actually growled deep in his throat. "You will not learn to keep your tongue behind your teeth, will you?"

Tuggle led out Severin's huge warhorse, stamping and snorting.

He picked Hastings up and threw her over the horse's saddle, then leapt up behind her. He forced her to remain facedown over his legs.

Gwent came running toward them, yelling, "My lord, do you wish me to accompany you? Where do you go?"

"I find it amazing that a man who owes me his loyalty tries to protect you."

"I will vomit if you make me remain like this, Severin."

"I am taking her to the beach to speak in private to her, Gwent. Leave go." Severin flattened his palm against the small of her back and kicked his horse in its sides. The last person Hastings saw was Lady Marjorie, standing on the keep steps.

Hastings didn't vomit. She became dizzy, but it passed when Severin pulled his stallion to a halt at the top of the cliff edge beside the path that led to the beach. He dragged her to the ground.

"Do not fight me," he said, and shook her. "Come."

He forced her before him down the narrow cliff path. She stumbled twice. Both times he caught her.

When she reached the sand beach, she pretended to crumble. He eased his hold. She jerked her arm free of his hand and ran. Her foot hit a piece of driftwood and pain shot through her toes. But she didn't slow. It was then, of course, that she began to think clearly again. There was no other way back up the cliff save that single narrow path. She was running her heart out and there was nothing in front of her but barren rocks and smooth-faced cliff face. Rocks. She'd hit him with one this time.

She stopped abruptly and turned. He was walking slowly toward her, knowing she was trapped, not exerting himself. She picked up a rock and waited.

He saw what she had done. It didn't slow him. Perhaps he even began to walk faster.

"Put down the rock, Hastings," he called, his voice loud and strong over the gentle waves that washed onto the shore not more than a dozen feet from them. It was chilly here, the breeze off the sea tangling through her hair, pressing her gown against her legs. She was breathing hard.

She held the rock more tightly. Surely there must be something she could do, save stand here like a fool ready to hurl a rock at him that he would easily duck.

What to do?

She refused to wait here like a goat tethered to a stake, refused to let him so easily take her and beat her. She could see the anger in him, see it in the starkness of his eyes, see it in the cords that stood out in his neck. But he had never struck her, never. But now there was Marjorie. And there had been his saddle, hurled down on her.

"You would beat me and harm your child?"

He waved away her words. "Do not try that tale with me again, Hastings. Marjorie told me you had begun your monthly flux on the day of her arrival at Oxborough. That is why I kept away from you."

"She lies."

He just shook his head and kept coming. The sun suddenly disappeared beneath a passing cloud. She shivered. She wasn't breathing hard anymore. She held that rock. She waited.

It was then she knew she would not remain there for him to beat her. She dropped the rock, turned, lifted her gown above her knees, and ran into the surf.

"Hastings!"

The water was so cold she felt her breath freeze in her chest. No, she would make it. She was a strong swimmer, Beamis had seen to that when she was a child. She would swim around the side of the wall of rocks and boulders to the beach just beyond. There was another path, much rougher than this one, dangerous to someone who didn't know it well, as she did. The water swirled about her knees. Just as she was about to dive into the next wave, she felt his arms close around her waist, lifting her free of the water, carrying her back to the shore.

She fought him, finally sinking her teeth into his arm. He dropped her onto the dry sand, stood over her, legs spread, rubbing his arm.

"You are a fool, Hastings. That water would freeze the heart in your chest."

"No it wouldn't. I have swum in it before."

"Did you seek to drown yourself?"

She lay there on her back, looking up at him. He was blocking the sun. She shivered, but not from her wet feet, not from the cold, but from the sight of him.

She saw him over her such a short time before, smiling, leaning down to kiss her, to nibble her earlobe, to kiss her breasts even as he eased into her. And she had held him close, her eyes meeting his, filled with him, and they had been together, and she had believed it would be like this forever.

She laughed aloud at her own stupidity.

He still had not moved.

She rolled onto her side, holding her stomach, still laughing. She heard herself hiccup. She felt tears burning her eyes. Stupid tears.

He came down over her, pulling her onto her back.

She whipped her legs up suddenly and drove her feet into his groin. He stared at her for an instant, knowing the grinding pain would be upon him in but a moment, knowing he would want to die, knowing he wanted to kill her. She was a red haze, nothing more than that, a red haze that dissolved quickly enough into such pain that he knew he would vomit.

"I wish you had not done that," he said, and sank to his knees, holding himself. He was gasping with pain now, rolling onto his side.

She jumped to her feet and ran back to the path.

Gwent was waiting at the top, his hands on his hips. "You should not have done that, Hastings. Now he will have to

retaliate. Are you mad? How will he sire a child if you
unman him?''

"He has already sired a child only he is too stupid to
believe it.''

"By Saint Sebert's nose, why did you have to strike him
there? I will try to explain to him that your mind is disor-
dered, that you need some of his mother's potion. Are you
certain you are with child?''

She nodded. She felt very tired.

Gwent cursed. "Get you back to Oxborough. I will help
Severin.''

"I will give you a rock.''


"You look dreadful, Hastings.''

"Thank you, Marjorie. You look like a goddess.''

"You are all wet and there is sand on your gown. Your
sleeve is torn from your shoulder. Your feet and gown are
wet. Did Severin beat you? He did not hit your face. That
is wise. It could anger some of the Oxborough people who
still feel some loyalty to you.''

Hastings smiled. "I doubt he will be of much use to you
tonight, Marjorie.''

"Severin is the lord of Oxborough. He is of use to me
only because he protects Eloise.''

"Was he so very clumsy then when he took you as a
boy, Marjorie?''

"He should not have told you that. We were very young,
both of us. I did not wish to be wedded to that old man,
to have him take my virginity, thus I gave it to Severin.
That was many years ago.''

Hastings didn't say anything more, just pushed past Marjorie and ran up the solar stairs. She needed clothes—not
gowns, but a boy's garb. She didn't care about the bandits
on the roads. Nothing could be as bad as remaining here,
for she knew when Severin recovered sufficiently, he would
return and beat her.

She could lose her babe.

She walked head high to the stable, ordered Marella to

be saddled, then, while Tuggle was seeing to her palfrey, she eased into the small area where all the boys slept. All the clothes she picked up were too small and filthy beyond anything she could imagine.

She just smiled at Alart, the porter, telling him she was riding into the village. He waved her off, though he was frowning.

She rode directly to the leatherer's shop and asked Master Robert once again to see the chamber from which the saddle had been hurled down upon her. Ah, she thought, as she rifled through his apprentices' trunks that were stacked in the corner of the room. She took what she wanted, stuffed them beneath her gown, and took her leave of Master Robert, who was in the midst of praising the gloriousness of the damned day.

She rode into Beethorpe Forest and changed into the boys' clothes. She hadn't estimated properly. The trousers were very tight. As for the tunic, it at least bagged enough to cover most of her to her thighs. She fastened cross garters, pulled on the supple leather boots.

She remounted Marella.

She had no money, no food, no weapon.

Where was she to go?

She just sat there on Marella's back. She deserved to be beaten, but not because she had angered Severin. No, she deserved it because she was so stupid.

She rode back to the village and managed to find Ellen alone, weeding her mother's small garden at the back of the baker's shop.

When she rode out of the village a few minutes later, she had a bow and six arrows, a knife, three loaves of bread wrapped in a big cloth, and a blanket.

*"You what?"*

"She is the mistress of Oxborough. She rides frequently to the village. I had to allow her to leave, my lord."

Severin cracked his palm over his own forehead. He'd come back to strangle her. At the very least he would have yelled at her until he was cleansed of his rage. That was what he had planned to do with her on the beach, just the two of them alone, but he hadn't had the chance. Damn her, she'd planned to swim to the next beach. Then she had unmanned him. Only now could he stand up straight. He drank down the ale Alice handed to him.

He gave Alice a sour look. "I don't suppose you know anything about this?"

She poured him more ale as she said, "If I did, I would tell you nothing, my lord. I do not want her or the babe harmed."

Severin smashed his fist on the trestle table. "She is not with child!"

"If she said she was, then she is."

"Did she tell you that she was?"

"No, but Dame Agnes wonders. She said she knew Hastings was queasy in her belly and that her appetite wasn't right. Hastings is very private. She waits before she speaks."

"She didn't wait before she kicked my manhood into oblivion."

Alice opened her mouth, caught the warning head shake from Gwent, and closed it again.

Severin said more to himself than to Gwent or Alice or the other dozen servants milling about, hoping to overhear something, "I wanted only to talk to her privately. You know there is no privacy here. She even picked up a stone again once she escaped me on the beach."

Gwent cleared his throat. He saw Lady Marjorie from the corner of his eye. He knew at any moment that Severin would leap from his chair and want to leave Oxborough on the instant. That was the way he was. He was brooding now, and that boded well for Hastings. It gave her time so that before Severin caught her, he would be relieved of most of his bile.

Time. By Saint Ethelbert's nose, they had best be after her. But where had she gone?

Gwent cleared his throat again. Lady Marjorie was nearly upon them.

"My lord."

Severin continued to frown down at the trestle table. He drank the rest of the ale and wiped the back of his hand over his mouth. "Damn her, now I must take time and men to find her. I wanted to finish the work on the eastern wall today. If she picks up another rock to hurl at me, Gwent, I will surely . . . We leave at once."

"Aye, my lord."

"My lord, what has happened?"

"Eh? Oh, it's you, Marjorie. Where is the child?"

"Eloise is with Dame Agnes."

"I am away to find my wife and bring her home."

"She attacked you, Severin. All saw it. Will you kill her?"

"Now, that is a thought," he said, nodded to Alice, who looked ready to leap for his throat, and strode up the solar stairs.

He met his mother near the jakes.

"You had best hurry, Severin. Hastings has been gone close to an hour."

"I will find her, Mother."

"She isn't happy, Severin."

"Neither am I. I am now one of the richest men in England and I vow a toad is happier than I am. That's what she believes me to be—a toad."

"Surely she would not liken you to a toad."

"She said I had the feelings of a toad. Ah, Trist, you wish to come with me? You must swear you won't try to protect her."

Trist had stuck his head out of Severin's tunic. He mewled and hung on.

Lady Moraine watched her son stride into his bedchamber and fling the heavy wooden door shut. She hurried down the stairs to find Gwent, the small vial held tightly in her hand.

Marjorie met her at the bottom of the solar stairs, a cool smile on her beautiful face.

# 23

"YOU LOOK FATIGUED, LADY MORAINE," MARJORIE SAID, so beautiful surely God had fashioned her after his angels. "Would you care to have a cup of milk with me?"

Lady Moraine shook her head, looking frantically about for Gwent.

"I believe perhaps your eyes look a bit wild. Perhaps you are not thinking clearly? Perhaps you need to rest? Let me help you, Lady Moraine. Let me take you to your chamber. Some time alone would refresh you."

"Alice!"

Marjorie lowered her eyes to her white hands. She stepped back when Alice nearly ran her down getting to Lord Severin's mother.

"I need to find Gwent," Lady Moraine whispered, but Marjorie heard her. She also saw that vial in the woman's hand. She knew what was in that vial. Eloise had overheard the women talking of it and had told her.

All three women whipped about when Severin pounded down the solar stairs. He carried a fat blanket that was tightly knotted.

"Mother," he said, leaned down, and kissed her. "I will return as quickly as possible. Ah, Beamis, you and Lady

Marjorie will be in charge of Oxborough whilst I am away. Mother, take care.''

He was gone.

It was too late. Lady Moraine slipped the vial into the pocket of her gown. When he brought his wife back, then she would pour the potion into his wine. He was very angry. What had she done to him? And he had left Marjorie to be mistress of Oxborough in his absence. She sighed. She supposed she couldn't blame him for not trusting that her wits would not wander. At least not yet.

Lady Marjorie turned to Alice, smiled brightly, and said, ''What has MacDear planned for our midday dinner?''

A sharp evening wind came up just when the sun was beginning to set. Hastings had ridden Marella hard for the past three hours. She'd seen two farmers, one of them sitting in an old cart pulled by a swaybacked mare who snorted with every step she took, the other walking bent over, a thicket of cut hay strapped to his back.

Neither of them paid her any attention. The one farmer did look at Marella, a combination of wistfulness and greed in his eyes. She didn't blame him.

Her bow and six arrows were snug against her side. She had practiced a good dozen times to get her bow notched quickly were outlaws to attack her. She was fast now.

She slowed Marella. She had come to the top of a small rise. Nestled in the valley below was a village filled with small thatch-roofed cottages. She would simply have to go around it.

Marella, sensing that a warm stable was near, was none too happy to be steered away from the village. She reared on her hind feet, but Hastings, well used to her palfrey's ways, wasn't moved. ''All right, we'll stop soon. It grows late. We're both hungry. Aye, I'll find you a nice stream and thick grass. Trust me, Marella, you do not wish Lord Severin to catch up with us.''

The cold wind eased off a bit. Then it just became a mild breeze. This was not the England she knew. Perhaps this was a sign that good luck would follow her. Perhaps she would find this Rosehaven before any outlaws found her.

But what about Severin?

She shuddered, remembering clearly what it felt like to shove her feet into his groin. She'd felt his shock in that instant, his disbelief, the quivering of coming pain.

He had deserved it. He would have hurt her and probably her babe as well.

She found a perfect place to tether Marella some thirty minutes later. After seeing to her horse, she spread the blanket on the grassy slope that rolled gently to the stream and went through her belongings. Not much.

Three loaves of bread.

The bread was delicious. She forced herself to eat only one loaf, then slid down the slope to drink the cold water.

Night was falling fast.

She left Marella saddled, just in case, apologizing to her all the while. She gathered her bow and arrows close, closed her hand over the knife handle, and pulled the blanket around her.

"Wot's a mere lad doing with a mare like that? Think ye the little blighter thieved her?"

Hastings was awake in an instant, frozen still at the sound of the man's voice. He was whispering, but the night was very still. She heard every word. She could practically see another man shrugging. How many were there?

"Ease yer knife in his ribs and let's take the mare."

"Ye saw, he's a pretty boy. We can sell him."

"Lookee, we watched him, believing his kin were close, but there's no one here but the boy. Let him be. He'd be too much trouble. I jest want the mare."

There were just two of them.

Not that it would matter. Her luck had run out.

They were too close for her to use her bow and arrows.

Slowly, holding her breath, Hastings closed her hand around the knife handle. It wasn't well balanced, a perfect weapon for killing, like Severin's was. No, it belonged to

Master Thomas the baker. She just prayed it would slice a man as well as it did bread.

She felt the ground moving as one of the men walked to her. Just one, thank God. She waited, ready.

She opened her eyes, saw him over her, staring down at her, the knife raised.

"So ye're awake, are ye?"

"Aye, you filth." She brought the knife up, felt it slide so easily into his belly, felt the vomit rise in her throat, and quickly jerked the knife out of him. He was still over her, staring down at her, so surprised that he opened his mouth but only blood came out, not words.

"Ye done with the boy?"

She had no choice. She plunged the knife in again, this time higher, into his chest. The knife point hit a rib and wouldn't go any farther. The man howled, twisted over, and fell to his side.

"Wot's the matter?" The other man was at his side. As for Hastings, she was on her feet, running to Marella.

The man wheezed out, "The little whoreson struck me down and kilt me."

Hastings was on Marella's back in an instant. The other man was running toward her, yelling curses. Marella reared on her hind legs and struck the man hard in the chest. He went over backward with a grunt.

It was at that moment that she heard more curses. Hideous curses curdled with the names of body parts and animals. This man wasn't whispering. He was roaring.

She recognized that voice.

She kicked Marella's fat sides. Her palfrey couldn't move. There were three men on horseback blocking her. Hastings whipped her about to see Severin sitting on his horse behind her, three more men at his back. How had he positioned his men so quickly? Curse him.

She slid off Marella's back, ducked around a stallion, and ran into the forest, Severin's curses following her.

The curses stopped. The feet pounding the ground behind her didn't.

Something huge and hard hit her square in the back,

flinging her forward. She fell flat on her face, the boulder flattening her down.

"I should let you play the fool in my castle," he said close to her ear. "My men would never stop their laughter. All you would have to do is recount what you have done this day, Hastings, nothing more."

He was breaking her back, but she didn't say a word. It would have been difficult because her mouth was pressed into the earth.

Severin rolled off her and came up to sit beside her. At least there was a half-moon. She didn't move for the longest time, just lay there. He knew he hadn't killed her with his lunge because her ribs were going in and out. Her face was flat down. Good, he hoped she had a mouth of earth. Mayhap a worm or two.

Then, finally, she pulled herself back onto her knees. Her head was down and she was breathing slowly, with difficulty. He merely watched her, saying nothing.

She sat back on her heels. She said at last, "No matter what you had done, I doubt I would have stuck Master Thomas's knife in your belly. You're my husband, after all."

"Where would you have stuck Master Thomas's knife?"

She just shook her head. "I don't know."

"I didn't have time to save you." He sounded incredibly angry.

"I didn't need your help."

"No, you didn't, did you?" He sounded even angrier. Why? "What if there had been a third man?"

She would be dead, she thought, but didn't say it aloud. "I would have dealt with him as well."

Severin got to his feet, brushed himself down, then just stood there, staring down at her.

She felt suddenly very weak. Why was that? She started to rise but discovered she couldn't. She felt a wave of dizziness. She looked down to see the knife on the ground where Severin had thrown her down. She had been carrying the knife.

She'd fallen on it.

She touched her fingertips to her side. They were wet and sticky. She looked up at him.

"You expect me to help you rise? See to yourself, madam."

He turned to walk away from her, then said over his shoulder, "If you run again, I will surely make you regret it more than you can imagine."

"I won't run again."

"Come then. I am tired and hungry. Then I will deal with you."

She tried again to rise. Slowly, slowly, she got to her feet. Even more slowly, she turned to face him. "I can't come, Severin. You can just leave me here. It doesn't matter. You have Oxborough, you have Marjorie. Aye, just leave me here."

He took a step toward her, his feet planted right in front of her. His hands were on his hips. He sounded like he was ready to do murder. "Do you wish me to strangle you right here, Hastings?"

Such anger in his voice, she thought, but it didn't really touch her. All that touched her now were sharp jabs of pain that went deeper with each moment that passed. She felt light-headed. She felt dizzier. The pain was bowing her forward, folding her in on herself.

"Aye, mayhap it would be better than this," she said, and with a sigh, she fell to the ground at his feet.

She heard him cursing again, the ripest words woven with animal parts. Then she felt his warm breath on her face, felt his hand on her side. She made a small sound deep in her throat and was gone from him.

"Drink this. Don't turn your head away, Hastings. Drink, you need this."

Need what? she wondered, and opened her mouth. It was warm ale with something in it, what, she didn't know. It tasted wonderful. Until the pain came and she choked, the ale running down her chin onto her chest. She heaved with the pain, jerking upward, then twisting onto her side, anything to avoid it. But she couldn't. It held her close.

"Did you poison me?" she whispered. "Is that what I tasted in the wine? Poison?"

"Shut your mouth. Gwent, help me hold her down. She'll make the bleeding start again."

"Carlic swears the chives he found near the stream will staunch the bleeding. He said he would have bled to death once if his grandmother hadn't ground it up and fed it to him. We'll see. No, Hastings, try not to jerk away from me."

His face was close to hers now. "Listen to me. Don't drag air into your throat, it will just make the pain worse. Breathe lightly. That's right. Focus on my face. No, don't look away from me, Hastings."

"The babe?"

It was at that moment that he knew he'd been a fool, knew he could have harmed her and his babe when he threw her over his saddle, when he had shoved her down the path to the beach, but he hadn't believed her.

But he did now.

He had gotten her with child. He felt a burst of satisfaction deep within him, a feeling he had never before experienced. It was satisfaction and something else, something else that was deep and now a part of him. He shook his head, leaned close to her, and said, "The babe is fine. The knife went through the fleshy part of your side. There was a lot of bleeding but the wound didn't go deep. I cleaned it through with hot water. Besides the chives for the bleeding, Carlic found some delphiniums. He said his grandmother gave it to him for toothache, but pain was pain."

"Not poison."

"No, not poison."

She tried to nod, but the pain ground her down. "Severin." His name was a whisper of sound.

"Aye?"

"Have you ever beaten or strangled a woman?"

"No. In fact I only began talking about it when I married you. It seems to relieve my spleen."

She laughed. It was too much. She gripped his hand,

feeling a wave of pain brim through her body. Then, suddenly, it lessened. "The delphiniums," she whispered, "they are good. I will speak to Carlic about this."

"Not just yet."

"Mayhap his grandmother still lives."

"Mayhap. Sleep now, Hastings."

She slipped away, but not for very long. He lifted up the bandage on her side. The wound was bleeding sluggishly. It needed to be stitched. He said to Gwent, "Take two men and go to that village we passed. I don't want to carry her there, it's too dangerous. Get me needles and thread, Gwent."

The big man shuddered. "I'll bring what else I can find as well."

Severin covered the wound with a pad of clean gray wool. Almost clean wool. Now the second sleeve of his tunic was gone. He hunkered down beside her. When she awoke, he would have her drink more of Carlic's potion. He looked up to see that his men had made a small fire and were roasting several rabbits. The smell made his stomach sing out. His men had buried the two outlaws. They had found nothing worth keeping on the men.

She remained awake, of course.

He cursed.

"Those animal parts I had never before considered."

"They're useful," he said, then leaned close. "You know that when Gwent returns with the needle that I must stitch the wound, Hastings. Is there anything I can do so the pain will not be so bad?"

"Rub some of the delphinium root over it. It will help deaden it."

He called to Carlic, who immediately was at his side, the long slender root held out in his hand. "Just rub it on her as it is?"

"Clean it first in the stream, then hold it close to the fire. It will warm the root and soften its flesh."

Severin rubbed it lightly over the skin around the wound. Then he drew in his breath and rubbed it directly into the tear.

He gave her more of the potion to drink. An hour later Gwent returned with a roll of clean white linen, a skin filled with rich ale, and needles.

"I am sorry, Hastings. I could get only black thread."

She laughed and moaned at the same time.

"Get it done," she said to Severin, and turned her head away from him.

"If you would faint, Hastings, I would be pleased."

But she didn't. He rubbed the delphinium root on the wound again.

To his relief, she barely jerked when he sank the needle into her flesh. He continued quickly. It did not take long. When he was done, he poured hot ale over the wound, then patted her dry. He made a thick pad of the white linen and pressed it against her. He tied the rest of it around her belly.

He looked at her belly. She was flat.

"When will the babe make you round?"

"By the fall," she said. "Thank you, Severin."

He did not sleep for a very long time. He sat crosslegged, watching the fire burn itself into embers. His men all slept, many of them snoring as loud as Edgar the wolfhound. His wife was with child. He still could not quite grasp it.

She moaned, turning onto her side.

He gently pressed her again onto her back. Her eyes opened. She raised her hand, lightly touching her fingertips to his jaw.

"I don't know what to do, Severin. I had not meant to stab myself with the knife. I do not think I am able to run from you now."

"I hope you will not want to run from me ever again."

She could only stare at him. "Marjorie will not continue to be your mistress, Severin. She wants my place."

"She is not my mistress."

Hastings closed her eyes and turned her head away from him.

# 24

"YOU HAVE LOVED ME SINCE I WAS TWELVE YEARS OLD."

"Aye, I loved you with a boy's unformed passion."

"Your passion was not unformed when you took my virginity."

He remembered, she saw it in his dark eyes. He remembered and he wanted her again. Severin gently kicked his horse's sides. Marjorie called after him, "Did you know your child was in my womb when I married that old man?"

He whirled around in the saddle.

"Aye, it's true. When that filthy old whoreson discovered that I wasn't a virgin, he beat me. I lost the babe. He enjoyed that. Perhaps now I am barren, for my second husband never got me with child."

"You were only married to him for two years. That is too short a time to be sure of such a thing."

"His name was Keith. I hated that name. He was not like you are, Severin. He was weak and easily led. His father criticized him constantly. Both of them died within months of each other. I was glad, but I was left with nothing. If the king had forgotten that he was indebted to Keith, then I would be some man's leman now, just to survive. You should not have left me, Severin. I should have been your wife, not this one at Oxborough."

"I could do nothing else. Had I taken you with me all those years ago, we would not have survived. I was a boy, strong for my age, skilled in weaponry, and loyal, but I had nothing, Marjorie. Nothing. I had to make my own way, you know that. Even when I returned, it was to find my lands devastated. I still had little enough. Were it not for the king and Lord Graelam de Moreton, I would not now be the Earl of Oxborough."

"You still love me."

"I thought that I loved you when I was a boy, but I have learned it is folly to believe in such a thing. There is lust. That commodity flourishes everywhere. It is what makes men behave like fools, witness what Sir Roger did at Langthorne. He betrayed me because of his lust for this girl. Aye, there is nothing more than lust. It can be controlled if a man manages not to forget who and what he is. And there is responsibility and duty. There is rarely peace at Oxborough, but then again, there is rarely boredom either."

"It is because of her that there is no peace."

"Aye, you're right about that. I am married to her, Marjorie. It is done. Why did you tell me that Hastings had begun her monthly flux?"

"I did not. I merely told you that she complained of belly cramps and said she had to change her gown. It is obvious, is it not?"

"Evidently not. Hastings is with child."

"So," Marjorie said very slowly, looking out over the sea, glimmering bright green today beneath a golden sun, her hand shading her eyes, "that is how she plans to hold you. That is why you are withdrawing from me."

Severin leaned forward to pat his warhorse's neck. "I do not believe that Hastings has any particular wish to hold me at the moment. Nor did I ever believe that a woman could make herself pregnant just by wishing it so."

"Ah, but she could seduce you to her bed and that is what she has done."

Severin only stared at her, remembering those precious few times Hastings had come to him, kissing him, telling him how she wanted him. There had been too few times.

"She is jealous of me. She knows that it is I you would prefer to have as your wife."

"Aye, she is jealous of you. Once you return to Sedgewick she will forget. As to her being with child, why, that is one of my responsibilities. I must have an heir."

"Will you visit me at Sedgewick?"

He stared at her, remembering when he had been deep inside her body. He remembered those moments as vividly as any in his entire life. She'd trusted him, loved him, given herself to him. Now she was alone. She was still so very beautiful, so soft, so gentle. He shook with the thoughts. "It is time to return to Oxborough," he said.

She threw back her head and laughed aloud. Her incredible silver hair rippled down her back. She wheeled her palfrey about, kicking her in her sides and calling out to him over her shoulder, "I have not forgotten the boy in the man, no more than you have forgotten the girl in the woman. You will come back to me, I know it."

When Severin finally returned to the castle, Hastings was sitting on the top step leading into the great hall. Her arms were wrapped around her knees.

They had been home for eight days. She was mending well. The wound hadn't become poisoned. Trist was stretched out on his belly beside her, watching his master approach.

"It is time," she said when Severin reached her.

"For what?"

"For the Sedgewick people to return home."

"I forgot to tell you. There were more cases of the sweating illness. A messenger came two days ago to tell me. It still is not safe. I fear it will be an empty keep once the illness is past. However, Sir Alan still thrives, thank God."

Hastings cursed.

"I believe I heard an animal part."

"Aye," she said, and rose slowly and very carefully.

"I would that you go rest now, Hastings. Alice told me that you have been on your feet for four hours now."

"I am not on my feet."

Severin picked up Trist, slung him over his shoulder, and began to rub his chin.

"I had to get out of bed because Trist would not leave me. He is growing fat and lazy. Just look at his stomach, Severin. He is a pig, not a marten."

Trist batted his paw at her. She laughed, a bright sound Severin hadn't heard in too long a time.

As quickly as it came, the laughter disappeared. "You rode with Marjorie. She enjoyed telling me about it."

"Oh? What did she tell you?"

"That you talked about the past, when the two of you were very young. She spoke about how much you wanted her, how much you loved her."

"Aye, that is true enough."

Hastings turned on her heel and stomped into the great hall.

"But it is not the entire truth," he called after her. She didn't turn, just got stiffer, her head higher. He just shook his head. What did Hastings wish him to do? Return Marjorie to Sedgewick, taking the risk she would catch the sweating sickness? No, he could not do that, but he would have to do something.

He followed his wife to their bedchamber. He paused at the door, believing someone was with her. She was saying, "I will be as fat as you are by the fall and then what will I do? I'll be a prisoner here at Oxborough. He can do just as he pleases, not that he hasn't always done what he wished to do. Especially with me. What am I to do?"

"You can begin by trusting me, Hastings."

She looked up to see him standing in the doorway. Trist, on his back beside her on the bed, twisted to see his master, and immediately flipped over and slithered to the floor. He raced across the bedchamber, climbed Severin's leg, and curled himself around his neck. Severin began to rub his chin.

She said nothing.

"I have come to look at the wound in your side. You have kept me away from you for a full seven days and nights. I want to see how well you are healing."

"Ah, won't Marjorie let you come to her? You wish to relieve your man's lust, Severin?"

"In part," he said, and that surprised her. "But more important, I want to see how you are doing. You told me you had healed and there was no poisoning. I want to see for myself."

"The Healer said I am nearly well. You do not believe her?"

"Lie down, Hastings."

He had not given her orders for a sennight. Of course there hadn't been too many orders to give her since that night she'd stabbed herself. He'd told her to stay in bed. She'd nearly grown mold in that bed.

To his surprise, she did lie down. He sat down beside her and pulled up her gown. "Keep your arms at your sides. I don't need your help."

"I am not helping you, Severin. I want to hit you."

"Trist, go sit on her chest."

The marten unwound himself from his master's neck and laid himself across Hastings's chest. He stared at her. She couldn't help herself. She laughed.

"That's better." He continued his undressing of her in silence. Finally, he said, "Your belly is still flat. I don't ask for much, Hastings, but perhaps just a slight curve would be enough to content me."

"You still do not believe that I am with child?"

"You have lost your humor, unlike I, who have gained in mine. That was a jest."

She chewed her bottom lip. Trist mewled, tapping his left paw against her chin.

"Now, I'm going to change the bandage. How much longer will you have to have the thick pad there?"

She was naked from her waist to her toes. He'd even pulled off her cotton socks and shoes. She wished . . . no, she wasn't about to wish for anything like that.

She felt his warm hand rest for a moment on the top of her thigh. "Now I see how you have tied this knot." He worked it loose, then let the narrow binding cloth fall loose to her sides. Slowly, very carefully, he raised the thick white linen pad. It lifted up easily.

There were only six stitches. They weren't badly done, but that damned black thread looked obscene against her white flesh. There was a lot more white flesh on her flat belly. His breathing hitched. He hadn't forgotten. He supposed he'd only suspended his memory of the way her flesh warmed when he touched her, the smoothness of her, the way her muscles tightened when he had caressed her with his mouth. He shuddered.

"When can the stitches be cut out?" His voice sounded odd, as if he were in pain.

"In two or three days. What is wrong with you, Severin?"

"Nothing really, but you are naked and I am trying to concentrate on your wound. Perhaps it is a bit difficult, Hastings."

"Try."

"The flesh is healthy-looking. Have you any medicine for me to rub on it?"

"Aye, over there, atop the chest. The small jar on the left."

He lifted the lid and sniffed it. "What is it?"

"That is Saint-John's-wort mixed with different salves into a cream. The Healer gave it to me. I have been rubbing the wound with it since we returned to Oxborough. The Healer said it would prevent scarring. It also makes my skin very soft."

"Your skin was already soft. Why did you not ask me to do it for you?"

"I don't want to lie here naked, Severin. You might forget the black thread in my side."

He grunted at that.

"I wouldn't be able to fight you for fear of tearing the wound open."

"You mean you would lie there like a sacrifice and not try to kick me loose from my manhood?"

"I would have to."

He said nothing to that. He watched her close her eyes

when he touched her with the cool, white cream. He felt her ease, for his touch was light.

"I hate to see the thread in your body. It brings back that night."

At last he was preparing to yell at her. How long could a man keep his bile swallowed, particularly a man of Severin's passions? "You will now tell me that I am a fool and threaten me and—"

"Hush." He was thorough, she would give him that. More than thorough. She had never stroked her own fingers over the wound to such pleasant effect.

"I do not need a bandage."

His fingers stilled. "You are certain?"

"Aye, I looked at the wound this morning."

He flattened his palm over her belly. His hand was large, nearly spanning her. He said mildly, "If I threatened to beat you now, you would not believe me."

"No. You would do nothing to harm your babe."

He cursed. She said nothing, just looked at him. He was still staring down at her. She didn't like this at all. She was naked and he was touching her and looking at her and she knew that she should draw away from him, but she didn't.

Trist was lying flat on her chest. Surely Trist was heavy enough to hold her down for a few moments longer.

Severin raised his hand and pulled down her clothes. He lay a blanket over her, pulling it to her waist. He said nothing. There was a line of sweat on his brow.

Ever since their return he had held his temper, coming to the bedchamber to see her every day, sometimes taking his dinner with her. But he did not sleep with her at night.

Not once had he yelled at her for fleeing Oxborough. Not once had he even growled or looked mean. Not once had he threatened to strangle her.

Why hadn't he at least yelled at her? Why hadn't he even spoken of it to her? It had been seven very long days and nights. Not a word remotely irate had spewed from his mouth. The good Lord knew that Dame Agnes, Gwent, and Beamis had all burned her ears, but Severin hadn't said a single thing. Neither had the pulse pounded in his neck nor had his face turned red.

It was driving her mad. She couldn't stand it another minute.

"I was just traveling to Rosehaven," she blurted out when he continued to be silent. "Beamis wouldn't take me because he was afraid you would kill him. I promised him you wouldn't really kill him, that you were just and fair, and perhaps you would pound him just a bit, but he still wouldn't do it. I do know that this Rosehaven is near to Canterbury. I would have found it. Did you not see that I was dressed like a boy? I looked like a boy. Even you would not have recognized me, Severin. I was safe enough. Well, there was obviously one problem and that was Marella. Those men wanted her, not me."

He said nothing.

She slammed her fist onto the bed beside her. "I have waited seven long days and nights for you to yell at me, Severin, yet you haven't said a single word. Surely you have not swallowed your bile. You have never swallowed your bile for as long as I've known you."

He said in the calmest voice she'd ever heard out of his mouth, "Why are you spitting all this out, Hastings? It is true I haven't said anything. It would seem to me that you would be pleased with yourself, that you would believe you had escaped my wrath and a fair and just punishment for what you did. You did say just a moment ago that I was fair and just, did you not? Aye, you did, do not shake your head at me. You are guilty, Hastings, so guilty my head aches with it. But still I hardly expected you to chirp it out like a guilty magpie."

"I am not a bird, nor am I guilty."

"I had no need to threaten you. Would you like to continue with your confession? Feel free to add all sorts of trappings you believe excuse what you did."

"Damn you, Severin, why can you not just yell and be done with it?"

"You truly want me to chastise you now?"

"Well, I don't like the way you said 'wrath' and spoke

of punishment. Is not a bout of yelling sufficient to make you forget everything?''

Severin bent over to stroke Trist's back. He mewled and stretched until his front and back paws were hanging off Hastings's chest.

Severin said finally, straightening, ''When I remove that black thread, you will receive your punishment. You will rest now, Hastings. Trist, come with me.'' He snapped his fingers. Trist looked up at him, stretched even more, then in the fastest move Hastings had ever seen, he rolled off her and bounded from the edge of the bed onto Severin's shoulder.

''Sleep, Hastings,'' he said over his shoulder as he left the bedchamber.

What had he and Marjorie talked about during their ride? Marjorie had seemed very sure of herself when she'd stopped to speak to Hastings in that sweet voice of hers, that damned sweet voice she could still hear clear as a clanging bell inside her head.

''Did I tell you that Severin loved me even before I passed out of my girlhood? How much he has always wanted me?''

''I don't believe you were ever a girl, Marjorie. That would have meant that you were occasionally graceless, mayhap even clumsy and had spots on your face. No, you were never a girl.''

''It pleases you to jest. Look at you, pale and thin, your hair in those tight braids. Do you honestly believe Severin could ever be content with you?''

''Aye.'' Hastings's side began to hurt.

''Content, you are right. But there is more, Hastings, and you will never have it from him. He will bed you when he must because he knows he must have heirs.'' She shrugged. ''He is a man. A man will also bed whatever is available to them, unless he has great affection for his wife. Severin has none for you.'' Marjorie gave her a gentle smile even as she touched her fingertips to her hair. ''I believe I will wash my hair. Severin stares at my hair, have you seen him do that?''

"I have. You have beautiful hair. But I do begin to wonder about your insides, Marjorie."

"What do you mean, my insides?"

Her voice sounded more sharp than sweet now. "I just wonder how far you would go to gain your way."

Marjorie laughed. "You do jest well, but nothing else. Poor Hastings, you move about like an old woman."

Hastings didn't sleep as Severin had ordered her to. No, she worried. She wondered about Marjorie's insides. She realized that all she'd gained from her attempted escape from Oxborough was a knife wound in her side and a husband who was treating her very strangely. He wanted to wait until the black thread was out of her flesh to punish her.

Tomorrow, she would make certain that Marjorie would no longer be in control of Oxborough. When she had brought it up two days ago, Severin had merely frowned at her and told her to rest. Well, Oxborough was her home. These were her people, not Marjorie's. She would show everyone that she was well again, that she was once again ready to be mistress.

She was bathed and dressed in her favorite saffron wool gown, fitted at her waist with a narrow golden belt, the sleeves fitted down to her elbows, then flaring out, falling beyond her fingertips. She felt beautiful. Even her hair was shining clean. There would be nothing Marjorie could possibly say.

Her side ached, but it was nothing, really. She did not walk like an old woman.

Her chair was empty. That was a relief. Marjorie sat in her place beside Eloise. Lady Moraine was speaking to her son. Gwent punched Beamis's arm. There was loud talk, as usual, ale splashing over the sides of the goblets from enthusiastic toasts. All in all, everything looked to be normal. Edgar the wolfhound was gnawing on a bone that Severin had tossed to him.

"Welcome, Hastings," Marjorie called to her. She leaned over and patted the arm of her chair. "I have had

MacDear prepare your favorite dishes. He even prepared some rose pudding. He said it was a favorite of your mother's."

*Her mother.* Hastings said aloud, "Yes, my mother was very fond of rose pudding. I believe it was she who gave MacDear the recipe when she first came to Oxborough."

Hastings wanted to tell Marjorie right then that she would never enter Oxborough's kitchens again.

"I heard that your mother was so evil and lewd that your father had her beaten to death," said Eloise.

It was bad enough to hear her husband's mistress speak of her mother, but that she'd poisoned Eloise was too much to be borne. She opened her mouth, but Marjorie forestalled her. "Nay, Eloise, those are just mean stories that you should never speak of yourself. Neither you nor I know anything of Hastings's mother. Now, come close and let me serve you some of these garden peas that Hastings grew herself.

"Forgive Eloise, Hastings," Marjorie said more quietly as Hastings passed her chair. "It is true that your mother is sometimes spoken of, but it was not well done of her to speak to you of it. You look pale, Hastings. Now that I see you more closely, you don't look well enough to be here in the great hall. Perhaps you should return to your bedchamber. Aye, you are very pale, Hastings. You still walk bowed over, your shoulders rounded, like an old crone."

Hastings hurt, but not from the healing wound in her side. She wanted to pick Eloise up and shake her until . . . until what? Until she pleaded with Hastings to forgive her. As for Marjorie, Hastings said nothing. Her eyes were on Severin. He finished speaking to his mother, looked up, and merely waved his knife at her. She was at her chair when he rose to pull it back for her.

She said to him, "Thank you for not shaming me in front of all our people." She sat down. She felt a particularly vicious pull in her side.

"What, I wonder, does that mean?" Severin said, a black eyebrow arched upward.

"I mean it is kind of you to allow me to sit in my own chair."

"Eloise has prayed for you every day," Marjorie said in that sweet voice of hers.

Hastings smiled at the child as she scooped up the rose pudding with her spoon. "I hope your knees are well healed, Eloise."

The child shrugged, not looking at Hastings. "I do not like rose pudding."

"Then you do not have to eat any," Marjorie said, scraping the small portion from Eloise's trencher.

Lady Moraine said, "You look lovely, daughter. I like the braids plaited with the yellow ribbons. Your eyes look greener. Aye, you are worthy to be my daughter."

Hastings laughed and lifted her goblet to toast her mother-in-law. But she had not wiped all the cream off her hands after she'd patted it on her wound because, as she'd told Severin, it softened her skin. Her hands were slippery still. The goblet slid from her fingers, falling on its side, the rich sweet red burgundy flowing onto the white tablecloth.

Trist raised his head, saw the red wine flowing toward him, and slapped at it with his paw. Then he sniffed his paw and licked it. He stuck his paw in the wine a second time, then licked it. Suddenly, his entire body stiffened, his back arched. He mewled loud and long, then suddenly he collapsed onto his belly.

Severin was on his feet in an instant. "Trist! Damn you, what is wrong?"

The marten lay unmoving.

"Oh no," Hastings whispered, "oh no."

"What is it? What is wrong with Trist?"

"The wine, he licked it twice off his paws. There must be something wrong with it. Oh no." Without thought, she grabbed the marten, holding him close to her chest, and ran from the great hall.

"MY LORD!" MARJORIE WAS ON HER FEET. "WHAT IS THIS? She is mad! What is she doing? The animal is dead, we all saw it collapse. Where is she taking it?"

Severin said to Gwent over his shoulder as he raced after Hastings, "The wine. Let no one touch it."

He caught her at the stables. He grabbed Trist and shoved him into his tunic. "He will be warmer there. No, I'm being a fool. It is no use, Hastings. Marjorie is right. He is dead."

"No, he is not. We will take him to the Healer. Quickly, Severin."

The Healer looked as she always did in the dying afternoon light, slightly sour in her expression, her feet bare, Alfred meowing around her.

"The marten," Hastings yelled even as she was sliding from Marella's back. "He drank some wine that was mayhap poisoned."

Severin pulled Trist from his tunic. He was limp. He looked quite dead. Severin's hand was shaking. He looked at the Healer. "Please," he said. "I do not wish to lose him."

"I have no knowledge of this animal. I am a healer of people. Go away."

"Healer, please." Hastings didn't realize tears were

streaming down her face. "Please, help him. He is dear to both of us."

"Oh very well," the Healer said, took the limp marten from Severin, and carried him inside her cottage.

Alfred snapped his tail but didn't make a sound.

Severin went after her, but the Healer shouted, "Nay, stay out, my lord. Hastings, help me." But Severin ignored her. He stood behind Hastings, his face tense and white.

"Open his mouth, Hastings, wide, and keep it wide."

Severin said, "What will you do?"

"I will make him vomit, just as I would do to a human. Will it be enough? Does this animal even vomit? I do not know, my lord. Go outside. You fill up too much of my cottage."

"Your cat is outside. There is now enough room for me."

The Healer actually smiled, then she snapped at Hastings, "Wider, Hastings. That's right. Now, let me get this down his throat."

Trist didn't move. The Healer continued to spoon the liquid down his throat.

Time passed. It seemed an eternity. The marten's body was still and limp. Hastings was feeling for his heart. She found it. "He's alive," she whispered. "Here, Severin, feel."

Severin slipped his hand beneath Trist's body and held it close to him. He thought there was a slight beat but he couldn't be sure. He looked at his wife, at the tears that were still dripping down her face. She was unaware that she was crying.

Suddenly, the Healer took Trist, raised him in front of her, and began to shake him. Then she laid him again atop the small scarred table and began to press into his body, pressing, then moving upward in a long, single motion. Again and again.

"I do not know where the creature's belly is. It must be somewhere along my path."

The marten jerked.

A paw slid over to Severin's hand.

The marten bunched up onto himself, then heaved forward. Food and liquid flew from his mouth. His small body shuddered and he twisted and heaved again and again.

"He'll heave himself to death."

"It's the only way, Hastings. If he can vomit up the poison, then he has a chance."

Severin reached down and began to press lightly on Trist's belly, pushing upward.

The marten continued to vomit until at last he simply fell flat, still as death.

The Healer raised his head with her hands and stared at his face. Then she lifted each of his front paws. She slid her hand beneath him, searching for a heartbeat.

She straightened, shaking her head. She looked at Severin, then at Hastings. "I am sorry, my lord, Hastings. The animal is so very small. He fought, but it was not enough. He is dead."

Severin was white and still, staring down at Trist. Then he raised his head and yelled, "No!"

He lifted the marten in one large hand and pressed him against his chest inside his tunic. He smoothed Trist against his own heart, stroking his fur, lightly squeezing the long body, again and again, whispering to the marten, saying over and over, "You cannot leave me, Trist. No, you will not die. You cannot."

He continued to rub his hands over the marten. The Healer said nothing, merely cleaned up the animal's vomit. Hastings felt bowed down with the pain of it.

Alfred came into the cottage. He looked at each of the occupants and meowed loudly. He jumped onto the table, turned to look at Severin, and meowed even more loudly. He stood on his hind paws and steadied himself against Severin's stomach. He was sniffing. He meowed again.

Suddenly Hastings saw a movement against Severin's tunic.

She was afraid to move, afraid to hope.

Alfred raised a front paw and swatted at the lump in Severin's tunic.

He meowed loudly.

Then, in the quiet of the small cottage, they all heard a faint mewl. A paw pressed against the inside of Severin's tunic.

Alfred swatted at the paw.

The mewl was a bit louder.

"My little baby saved the marten," the Healer said, and managed to pull Alfred off the table.

Slowly, as if he were afraid he'd kill Trist, Severin eased him out of his tunic.

He stretched Trist out along his chest, cradling him in his hands.

Trist mewled.

"Aye, tell me how rotten you feel," Severin said. "Just keep talking to me."

Trist vomited on Severin's tunic.

"There is no more wine," the Healer said. "There is hardly anything at all. I and my Alfred have saved him."

Hastings lightly stroked her hand over Trist's back. "You will rest, sweeting. You will be all right now. Perhaps by tomorrow you will be able to thank Alfred properly." She looked up at Severin. She raised her hand and lightly touched her fingertips to his cheek. "You are crying."

"Not as much as you are," he said, leaned down, and kissed her mouth.

"Have you hurt your side, Hastings?"

"Nay, Healer."

Severin frowned. He said to the Healer, "Have her lie down. Please look at the wound. I did this morning and it looks healthy. I rubbed more of the cream on her."

"And then what happened, my lord?"

Severin raised a black eyebrow at her. "Look at Hastings's side," he said again, continuing all the while to stroke Trist's back, feeling as if his heart would burst when Trist's paws closed around one of his fingers.

"All right, Hastings. Lift your gown and shift. I need to look at your belly anyway."

Hastings saw no way out of it and lay on the Healer's

narrow cot, her clothes again at her waist. "I do not like this, Healer."

"Why? He is your husband. Besides he does not care what you look like. All his attention is on that damned marten. As for Alfred, he does look interested, but for what reason, I don't know."

Finally, the Healer stood up. She walked to her small fire and poked at the embers, making threads of flame shoot upward. "I am hungry now and you should leave."

"That is all you have to say?"

The Healer laughed at the outrage in the lord's voice. "Very well. I believe you should be more gentle with your wife, my lord. Play is one thing and many women find it pleasant enough. I never did, but I have heard that some women have this weakness. However, this went beyond play. If you must chase her down, don't hurl yourself at her back when she is carrying a knife. She is healing well. The babe is fine. I will remove the stitches in two days' time. Now, as for the animal, give him milk to drink. It will dissolve any remaining poison in his belly. Tell MacDear to prepare a very light chicken broth for him."

"He won't eat chicken. He will only eat pork."

"Pork then, it won't matter. It's nourishing."

The Healer shrugged, frowning at the animal, whose head was resting against Severin's shoulder. "Tell Mac-Dear to prepare invalid food as if Trist were a human for at least two more days. Hastings, just dab a bit of horehound juice mixed with very old wine onto his tongue. It will also help eliminate all the poison from his body. Not too much now, he's very small."

Trist mewled, but didn't move.

Alfred bunched himself and jumped into Hastings's arms, knocking her back onto the Healer's cot.

Severin slept with his wife. Between them lay Trist, still weak, his breathing not always even, which scared Severin. He kept his hand pressed lightly against Trist's belly.

"He will eat on the morrow, Severin. For now the milk

is enough. I would not want to eat after vomiting up my innards as he did.''

''Still—''

''I believe you worry more for him than you did for me.''

''You're too mean to die.''

She was silent for a very long time. Then, she said quietly, ''I hope you are right. Had I drunk that wine, then we would have seen just how mean I really am.''

She thought he tensed.

''I didn't want to think about that just yet. Gwent said that amongst the four of us who were drinking from the wine goblets, only you and I had not yet drunk. He has kept my wine and your empty goblet. Also, he has kept the cloth the wine spilled on. Will you examine it on the morrow?''

''Aye, but you know what I will find, Severin. It is just a question of what sort of poison. Mayhap hemlock or a distillation of poppies. Perhaps foxglove, though there is argument about that plant and what it does. I would have to ask the Healer. Where would the poison come from?''

''So many strange and exotic foods and spices, aye, and poisons as well, came back with crusaders from the Holy Land.''

She started to say, *Who would want me dead?* but she simply couldn't say it aloud. It would make it real. It would make it very close to her, at her right hand, near to sitting on her shoulder. The saddle could have been an accident, but not this—oh no, not this.

If she hadn't rubbed her hands with the cream to make them soft, the goblet wouldn't have slipped from her fingers. She would have drunk from the goblet and she would have died.

She touched her fingers lightly to Trist's sides. He still breathed.

''I don't like this, Hastings.'' Severin's voice was low and deep.

She wondered if she had died, if he would have cried for her. If he would have howled ''No!'' as he had for Trist.

"Nor do I," she said.

"Your food will be tasted from now on. Your wine will be sipped first by someone else. I will announce this to everyone tomorrow. Whoever put the poison in your wine should not have any interest in poisoning someone other than you."

Lady Moraine said, "I have removed the marten's vomit from Severin's tunic but the smell remains. What can I do, Hastings?"

"I will give you some ground daisies in cold water. That will remove the smell. At least it sometimes does."

"You know that silver-haired bitch poisoned you. What will you do about her?"

"I will see that she and all the Sedgewick people return as soon as possible. Severin and some of his men are riding there today to see what is happening. Hopefully, the sweating illness has run its course. I pray that some have survived it. As of our last word, Sir Alan is still well."

"She wants my son. She won't give up. I think we should poison her instead."

Hastings stared at her mother-in-law, so lovely really, with her light hair scarce touched with gray, her slender body, her soft, dark eyes. Her hands were now soft and white, as well as her feet. "You believe me mad again?"

"Nay, I believe you ruthless, as is your son."

"She wants to replace you. If you hadn't spilled the wine, you would be dead."

"I know."

"At least Severin has told everyone that someone will taste your food and drink your wine before you do. I like that he said he would select a different person before each meal. Thus no one would know when they would be asked."

"It is a good plan. There are still saddles, however."

Lady Moraine gave a lusty sigh. "Aye, I know it. Gwent frets about it. I think you should consider poisoning the silver-haired bitch first."

Hastings fetched her mother-in-law some ground daisies

mixed in cold water. She was feeling a bit queasy and quickly mixed a bit of rosemary with honey. It tasted sweet and calmed her belly.

She found Marjorie in the great hall, seated in front of the empty fireplace, sewing a gown. Where had the material come from? Eloise was on the floor beside her, sewing on a small piece of white linen. She heard Marjorie say, "Those are fine stitches, Eloise. You are far more talented than I am."

"Nay, Marjorie, you are perfect."

Her laughter rang out. Several servants turned at the sound. Two of them were men. They looked utterly besotted.

"Flatter me not, sweeting, else I might grow ugly just to spite you."

"Like that night your nose got all big and red?"

"That was something else, sweeting, something I ate that did not agree with me. Ah, Hastings, does Severin's marten still survive?"

"Aye. Severin keeps Trist with him constantly. He is still weak, but he improves."

"He is just a silly animal," Eloise said.

"I thought you believed Trist to be beautiful," Hastings said, her voice steady.

"I am grown older. I have changed my opinions."

"Would you like to come riding with me, Eloise?" It was the last olive branch, Hastings thought. She had to try.

There was a leap of excitement in Eloise's eyes, Hastings wasn't mistaken about that. She twisted about to look up at Marjorie.

"I think that is an excellent idea, sweeting. Hastings can show you all the places she knew as a child."

Severin walked into the great hall, drawing off his gauntlets, looking at Hastings. He nodded to Marjorie, but said to his wife, "Gwent just told me that the tablecloth with the spilled wine on it and the remaining wine from my goblet are missing. Whoever took them wasn't seen."

"Now we will never know," Hastings said, as she looked directly at Marjorie. "It had to be poison, probably it was liquid of poppies. Just a touch of it masks pain. More than a touch brings death. Trist was very lucky.''

"It was you who saved him, Hastings. It was you who took him to the Healer." There was a soft mewl from within Severin's tunic. Severin smiled and patted the lump. "He ate MacDear's broth this morning. He did not vomit it up."

"I know. MacDear was so pleased he had to tell me himself."

"He would not leave until he saw that Trist ate the broth."

Trist mewled again. A paw appeared from between the laces of Severin's tunic. Hastings laughed, lightly touching her fingertips to Trist's paw.

"Eloise and I are going riding," Hastings said.

"Nay, I have no wish to go now," Eloise said. "My belly hurts."

"Oh no, sweeting," Marjorie said, immediately dropping her sewing. She lightly placed her palm on Eloise's forehead. "What did you eat this morning?"

"Some of MacDear's bread. It didn't taste very good. It left my tongue sour."

It was such an obvious lie that Hastings wanted to slap the child. "The bread tasted fine to me, Eloise. However, if your belly does hurt, then let me give you just a bit of—"

"I would not want to have anything you prepared," Eloise said, and took a step back. Edgar the wolfhound growled.

"Why not?" Hastings spoke calmly, slowly. What was going on here? Why had Eloise changed so utterly toward her? Eloise's vicious words about her mother had been one thing, but this was going too far.

"I believe you stole the wine and the tablecloth so no one would ever know what kind of poison you used. I think you added the poison to your wine yourself. I saw you drop something into your goblet. You just didn't have time to keep Trist from licking it from the cloth."

"Ah," Severin said, and stroked his chin. "That is

something that did not occur to me. Tell me, Eloise, why would Hastings poison her own wine?''

Eloise was standing very straight, her face white, her shoulders back. Marjorie was looking down at the sewing in her lap. She said nothing.

"Why, Eloise?'' Severin asked again.

The child shouted, ''Hastings knows you love Marjorie! She had to do something so you would pity her, so you would cease looking at Marjorie!''

Trist's head appeared in the opening of Severin's tunic. He stared at Eloise. The child backed up another step, nearly stumbling. Edgar the wolfhound growled again. ''It's true!'' Eloise yelled. ''I am not lying. I saw her put the poison in her own goblet!''

She ran from the great hall.

''Who,'' Hastings said, still looking directly at Marjorie, ''who stole the poisoned wine and the tablecloth?'' And why, she wondered, as she walked up the solar stairs. All knew it was poison, so why steal it?

# 26

"WHY DID THE CHILD LIE?" SEVERIN ASKED LATER THAT day.

Marjorie looked straight at Severin. "She did not lie. She told me what she had seen right after you and Hastings ran from the great hall with the marten yesterday."

"That is absurd," Hastings said over her shoulder as she paced back and forth before Edgar the wolfhound.

"Then why did she not say anything to me?" Severin said.

Marjorie shrugged. "The child still frightens easily. As you know, her father abused her. Her mother treated her as if she were Satan's get. She was afraid to say anything. She did not understand until later what Hastings had done. She thought nothing about it when she saw Hastings pour some liquid into the goblet. But later—" Marjorie shrugged again. "As I said, she was afraid."

"I did not pour any liquid into my goblet," Hastings said, still now, stiff as a pole. "That makes not a whit of sense. I would not kill myself. Does that also mean that I stole the wine and the stained tablecloth?" She was shaking her head. "I am the only one who could have possibly determined what kind of poison was in the wine."

"Or the Healer," Marjorie said.

Severin waved his hand for silence. "Tell me, Marjorie, when did Eloise say that Hastings had done this?"

"I do not know. It was near to the dinner hour, I suppose. Hastings, wait, I cannot allow you to hurt Eloise."

Hastings whirled about, hands fisted at her sides. "Hurt her? Why would I hurt the child? I just want to talk to her."

"Wait, Hastings," Severin said, "both of us will speak to Eloise. I want to understand this."

Trist balled himself up inside Severin's tunic, mewling softly.

They did not speak to Eloise because they could not find her.

"Later, then," Severin said. He lightly tapped his fingertip against Hastings's nose. "The child is mistaken, worry not overly about it."

"The child lied, Severin."

"Aye, that is also possible. I must return to the practice field. Remember, I wish to speak to Eloise with you."

He was afraid that she would hurt the child? Hastings pressed her hands against her belly. She felt a moment of dizziness. She grabbed the high back of Severin's chair. She said nothing as she watched him stride out of the great hall. She walked slowly outside, down the deep, indented steps. The sun was bright overhead. The day should bring her contentment, but it didn't.

Marjorie said from behind her, "You saved his marten. You gained more by doing that than by sipping the wine, becoming ill, and gaining pity for yourself."

She turned to see Marjorie standing beside her, her glorious silver hair loose down her back, sunlight shifting through it. She was so beautiful it hurt to look at her. "What did you say, Marjorie?"

"If Eloise was right, and I do believe her, aye, I certainly do, then you gained more than pity. You saved that damned animal of his. After you dropped the goblet you allowed the marten to drink some of the poisoned wine. You took a chance, Hastings. A big one."

"You honestly believe I would poison Trist? Marjorie, he could easily have died."

"A jealous woman will go to any lengths to defeat her rival. Mayhap even risking harm to the babe in her womb, but of course you did spill the wine, didn't you? You never had any intention of drinking it."

Hastings leaned down to pet Gilbert the goat's head. He was chewing on a leather strap that Hastings knew belonged to the armorer. She would have to tell him not to kill the goat. It was possible that she would need Gilbert's milk for her child. The child Marjorie believed she could possibly risk harming? The thought made her utterly cold inside.

She looked up at Marjorie. "You know, Marjorie, it's true. I am jealous of you. I do not like myself for it, but it is there, nonetheless. However, soon you will be gone. Soon Eloise's lie will be shown for what it is—a lie by a child who happens to adore you. She sees that you want to take my place. She would do anything to help you, even deliver this lie. But attend me. You are not my rival. I am the Countess of Oxborough. You are not. Do you wish to be Severin's leman? If so, that is all you will ever be. Can you be content with that?"

Marjorie laughed, a beautiful, clear laugh. Was there nothing ugly about the woman? Aye, her insides were in question.

"Hastings, Eloise is not the only one who adores me. She is not the only one to wish to make me happy. You believe I will truly go back to Sedgewick?"

"Aye, I do."

"We will see, will we not? But that is not important. You are looking less old and pale today. Are you ready to resume your duties as mistress of Oxborough?"

"I already have, Marjorie."

"Ah, here comes Severin's mad old mother."

"She is not mad. She is quite recovered now. Even the Healer does not know if it was really madness that afflicted her. It does not matter. Now she is well again."

"No, she is not. You have not observed her as I have.

There is wildness in her eyes. Her movements are clumsy, frenzied. She needs to be locked away.''

"Your insides are becoming clearer to me now, Marjorie. They are twisted and very black. Mayhap you poisoned my wine.''

For the first time, Marjorie looked as if she would like to strike Hastings. She was breathing hard, her beautiful white hands fists at her sides. "Does Severin tell you how much he loves you when he is deep inside you?'' she asked. "Does he kiss your ear as he tells you how beautiful you are? Does he tell you how much he needs you, how much pleasure you give him?''

Hastings turned on her heel and walked toward Lady Moraine. She thought of the vial that sat behind her herb jars in their bedchamber. She would pour the love potion into Severin's goblet at the evening meal.

"I hear that the silver-haired bitch has come out of the shadows and speaks quite openly to you now, Hastings.''

"Aye, she speaks her mind.''

"Did she promise that she would continue her efforts to murder you so she could marry Severin and take your place here at Oxborough?''

"Nay, the child Eloise accuses me of knocking over the wine goblet and poisoning Trist on purpose. Marjorie said I did it because I believed I would gain Severin's pity.''

She leaned down to pat Gilbert the goat's head. He had eaten nearly all the leather. "Hurry,'' she said to him. "The armorer could come upon you at any time.''

She straightened, pushing the hair back from her forehead. The afternoon was cool, a clean breeze blowing from the sea. "I have decided to pour the potion into Severin's wine goblet this evening.''

"Good. Odd, isn't it, that I never knew of this passion Severin had for Marjorie? Of course, my husband kept me away from my boys, said he didn't want them softened. That was before my brains curdled.''

"Your brains were never curdled. It was something else. But I pray the potion continues to work.''

Lady Moraine laughed and lightly slapped Hastings's

arm. "The Healer can do anything. You have always trusted her. Don't cease now."

But Hastings was shaking her head. "Nay, I won't. Do you know that I don't believe I will use the love potion just yet. Maybe not ever. What I've got to do is get Marjorie returned to Sedgewick."

Hastings saw to her household duties, directing the servants to lime the jakes, which had grown particularly noxious with the wind blowing from the east. She oversaw the wool weaving by three women of excellent skill who had been trained by her mother so many years before; she spoke to MacDear of the meals they would have for the next several days; she pulled up weeds in her herb garden and tied up her columbine. The sun was bright and hot overhead. Her side hurt just a bit; she rose to stretch. MacDear, who scarce ever left the kitchen, was at her elbow, his huge bulk blocking out the sun. "The marten ate all the broth, but still I worry. He does not run as quickly as he used to. Is he all right, Hastings?"

She smiled up at him, feeling the pulling lessen in her side. "Aye, he grows stronger, even from this morning until now. He ate all of your broth, you saw that, and he ate a bit of Severin's bread. Severin will not let him out of his sight. I believe he even practices with his javelin with Trist burrowed deep in his tunic. He will be racing again very soon."

MacDear fidgeted a moment, leaning down to lightly touch his big fingers to some allium. "It is good to have you back, Hastings."

"Aye. Did you not work well with Marjorie?"

MacDear sighed and clapped his palms over his chest. "Ah, that one is more glorious than the first evening star."

*Even you, MacDear,* she thought, and wanted to cry.

"But you know, Hastings, she is cold, that one. She plots and schemes and smiles that beautiful smile all the while." He leaned closer, but not that much closer because his belly was so big. "Watch her, Hastings. All know of the poisoned wine. Many believe she put the poison in your goblet, despite her beauty."

"I don't want to watch her. I want her to leave."

MacDear shrugged, turned, and yelled at one of the kitchen boys who was coming toward him, carrying a loaf of bread, "Hugh, you cocky little maggot, did you burn that bread?" He said to Hastings in a much lower voice, "Then send her back. Do it, Hastings. Do it today."

As she walked back into the great hall, her head bowed, deep in thought, she realized she wanted Severin to love her, regardless of Marjorie or any other glorious creature who just might cross his path. She wanted him to see only her. And she didn't want to use a damned love potion to bring that about.

Her side still hurt. Too much bending and stretching in her garden. She hugged herself as she walked up the solar stairs to her bedchamber. Two more days and the Healer would cut out the black stitches. Then Severin would punish her for running away from Oxborough. Perhaps then too he would come back to her bed.

Severin sat in his high-backed chair. He looked imperious. He looked cold and stern. Normally when he dealt with Eloise, he came down on his haunches to be at her eye level; he softened his voice. Not this time.

He said, "Come here, Eloise. Don't dawdle. I have not much time to spend with you."

He said nothing more, merely began to tap his fingertips against the arms of his chair. Hastings sat beside him, her hands in her lap. She saw Marjorie in the shadows of the great hall just beyond the mammoth fireplace. Severin had told her that he wanted to speak to Eloise alone.

She had merely nodded, not arguing with him.

Hastings waited.

Eloise crept several feet closer, her head down. She was twisting her fingers together. Severin did not appear to be moved by the child's obvious distress.

"You accused my wife of poisoning herself. You will tell me why you said this."

The child began to shake. She sobbed.

"Enough!" Severin roared. "I will not have any more

of your nonsense, Eloise. You made a grave charge against Hastings. You will answer it or else you will displease me mightily.''

To Hastings's surprise, Eloise hiccuped once, then raised her head. She stared at Hastings. Her young face, so smooth and clear, suddenly twisted. ''I saw her,'' she yelled, pointing her finger at Hastings. ''Aye, I saw her sneak into the hall, looking to see if anyone was about, then she poured this powder into her own goblet.''

''When?'' Severin asked, sitting forward in his chair. ''When did you observe Hastings doing this?''

''Yesterday, just before the dinner.''

''What was she wearing when she did this?''

''Wearing?'' Eloise suddenly jerked about to search out Marjorie.

''What, Eloise? Look at me!''

The child looked ready to burst into tears. She looked ready to flee.

''I don't remember,'' Eloise whispered, her head down, her feet scuffing the reeds.

Edgar the wolfhound snarled, then quieted again.

''It was only yesterday, Eloise.''

''She was wearing the gown she wore to the meal. Aye, that was it. It was that yellow color that makes her look sallow.''

Severin leaned forward only to have Eloise shrink back. ''Hold still,'' he barked at her. ''Now, you will listen to me, Eloise. I have never seen this hall empty of people. You say that no one was in the great hall, no one except you and Hastings?''

''Aye, that's true. She didn't see me. I was hiding.''

Severin rubbed his jaw. Then he called out, ''Dame Agnes, please come forward.'' When she was standing next to Eloise, he continued. ''Tell me of Hastings's movements just before the dinner meal yesterday.''

''She was with me, your mother, and Alice. We were dressing her in the saffron gown. She was with us until all of us came down into the great hall together for the evening meal.''

Severin said to Eloise, "Do you wish to hear the same words from my mother? From Alice?"

"I hate you! I hate Hastings! I want to go home with Marjorie." The child turned and ran to Marjorie, throwing herself against her, burying her head in her skirts.

"I am sorry, Hastings. This has not been pleasant for you." He stilled, turning to look at Marjorie, who was gently rocking Eloise against her. By Saint Albert's knees, she was so beautiful it made his groin tighten to look upon her. What groin would not tighten? At that moment, Marjorie raised her head and looked squarely at him.

"You may take the child to your bedchamber," he called. "You will speak to her about the evils of lying. I am very displeased with your tutelage, Marjorie. The child has changed since she was here in Hastings's charge. She is sly, her nature is unpleasant, and she has proven to be a liar. I do not like it."

Hastings could but stare at her husband. He was actually criticizing his goddess? But everything he said was true. Eloise was very different now. She was mean-spirited. Had Marjorie alone brought about the changes in the child? She did not believe that Eloise could possibly have known to say that her saffron gown had made her look sallow. What child knew that word? No, that had come from Marjorie, and Eloise was just repeating it. It was hurtful and Eloise knew well it was hurtful.

Severin waved Marjorie and Eloise away. "You will take the evening meal in your bedchamber," he called after them. Marjorie didn't say anything, nor did she turn to acknowledge his order. Her head was high. Her glorious hair floated down her back to her hips.

Hastings could throw the bloody potion down the jakes. She wanted to throw herself in her husband's arms. She wanted to dance, mayhap even juggle some leather balls as the jongleur had done. Severin had made his choice. He would return them very soon now to Sedgewick.

Then Severin turned to her and said, "I trust Dame Agnes isn't the liar here. As for my mother, she would say anything to protect you. Alice as well."

From one instant to the next, she thought, as her hand closed about the silver laver that stood next to her chair. It was filled with clean water. She picked it up, rose, and hurled it at him.

"You whoreson," she shrieked at him, but it was difficult because she was panting as if she had run ten miles. Water dripped off his face and his tunic. Trist poked his head out, his face wet. He was staring at Hastings, then twisting about to look up at Severin.

Severin had managed to block the laver with his arm and it was on the floor, more dents in the beautiful polished silver. Edgar the wolfhound was lapping water from an indentation in one of the floor stones.

Severin rose very slowly. Hastings didn't like the look in his eye. She tried to duck past him, but only got about three feet. He grabbed her about her waist, quickly moved his arm upward away from the wound, and pulled her back. He turned her around to face him. She was still panting hard. He might want to beat her, but he wouldn't. She was carrying his child. The stitches were still in her side.

He was not more than three inches from her. He was silent, just staring down at her.

He closed his hands around her neck, lifting her chin with his thumbs. "You fear me and then you do not," he said in the calmest voice she'd ever heard out of him. "But no matter, you continue to make a fool of me whenever it suits you."

"You called me a liar. You called your own mother a liar. What would you expect me to do, sit here with my head downcast and let you fling out your insults?"

"I would expect you to speak to me about my opinions, not attack me. I have allowed you too much freedom, Hastings. It is time to rein you in."

"What do you mean?" Her mouth felt dry, drier still as she watched the drops of water roll down his face.

"You are without control. You do not govern yourself. You do whatever comes to your woman's brain without thinking about your actions. I cannot allow this to continue. I will not allow it to continue. For the next two evenings, you will eat your meal seated beside Edgar the wolfhound. To assure myself that you will not leap up and strike me with a chair or a knife or the laver again, I will tie you to Edgar." He released her and stepped back.

"Mayhap you should not wear your best clothes. Edgar slobbers a lot. And Hastings, do not try to flee me again, else you will not like the consequences."

He turned on his heel and strode out of the great hall, not looking back.

"No!" she screamed after him.

Dame Agnes was just shaking her head. "Must I teach you everything again and again, Hastings? No, do not rant at me about the unfairness of what your husband has ordered. You amaze me. You actually threw the laver at him! He did not retaliate because, unlike you, Hastings, Lord Severin understands the results of his actions. He does not want to hurt you physically or hurt the babe. Evidently you don't care if you break his head. Ah, that I would have to see this. You will learn control or I imagine you will spend the next three months next to that wolfhound."

Dame Agnes, still shaking her head, left the great hall. Servants were staring at her. Men-at-arms were staring at her. Edgar the wolfhound barked and nuzzled against her hand.

Lady Moraine brought an old gown to her bedchamber before the evening meal. "It is but for two nights. It is not a bad punishment. Do not—"

"He humiliates me beyond what I can stand. He called me a liar. He called you a liar. Does that not bother you?"

"You will run away again?"

"I cannot. None of his men would let me even go into the outer bailey. On his command. I hate your son, my lady."

"You threw the laver at him, Hastings. Not so long ago you sent your knee into his manhood. How many other times have you attacked him?"

"He deserved it. Did you not hear him? He accused me of lying. He accused you and Agnes and Alice as well. Did that not make you want to hit him? Why do you just ignore it?''

Lady Moraine sighed. ''He is my son. Wear the gown.'' She smiled suddenly. ''He was also right. I would say anything to protect you.'' She hugged Hastings tightly to her chest, then released her, patting her cheek. ''Just two nights and it is over.''

When Hastings came into the great hall there was immediate silence. Everyone knew what had happened and knew what would happen now. She stared straight ahead. Severin rose. In his hand he held a rope.

He said nothing, merely motioned her to the fireplace where Edgar the wolfhound was staring at her with unblinking eyes.

''Sit down,'' he said.

She sat in the rushes.

He tied the rope around her ankle, the other end around Edgar's neck. He motioned for Alice to serve her. He returned to his chair.

''Your food has been tasted. Your wine has been sipped.''

''Why bother with the tasting when you believe I poisoned the wine myself?''

''Enough, Hastings.''

And that was that. Talk was slow to resume. All the people she had known since she was born did not meet her eyes. She knew they were wary, mayhap even scared of their new lord. She ate a bite, then turned when she heard Gwent say something.

She heard a slurp. Edgar the wolfhound was swallowing the large hunk of fish he'd stolen from her trencher.

She heard a laugh. It was Lady Moraine, curse her. Evidently her wonderful son had jested with her.

At least Marjorie wasn't there.

But she would be the following night.

Hastings said nothing to anyone. Some time later she was dozing, her back against Edgar, when she felt the knot being unfastened about her ankle.

''Come to bed, Hastings.'' He was holding out his hand to her. She ignored him, rose slowly, and walked past him to the solar stairs. He did not come after her.

# 27

"Everyone saw him tie you to that filthy wolf-hound, like an animal, tethered in the rushes. I believe I can still smell the wolfhound on you. Do you also have fleas and lice?"

Marjorie gave her the sweetest smile.

"Aye, it is a difficult odor to get rid of," Hastings said, and ate another bite of sweet yellow cheese. "But the rushes were fresh with rosemary. There were no fleas or lice."

"It is interesting that Severin ordered me to my bed-chamber, yet he tied you to the wolfhound for all to see. I was told you threw the laver at him. You are not very wise, Hastings. A woman who is not particularly beautiful should learn wisdom."

"You are right about that." Hastings drank the rest of Gilbert the goat's milk. She had awakened feeling queasy that morning, but now she was filled with energy, her step light, her heart so heavy she didn't think she could bear it. And here was Marjorie laying her sneers on with a trowel.

"I will enjoy seeing you tied to the wolfhound this eve-ning meal. I wonder if Severin will invite me to sit in your chair?"

"If he does—" Hastings broke off. Severin came into

the great hall. He was sweating, his hair plastered to his skull. There was blood on his clothes. He was grinning, Gwent just behind him, slapping his shoulder.

"I have killed a boar and given it to MacDear. See to its preparation, Hastings. Alice! Bring us ale!"

Hastings left the great hall without another word. Later she went to her bedchamber to fetch the vial. She would take him a goblet of sweet wine that Lord Graelam had brought to Oxborough and in it would be the love potion. She would make sure there was no other woman around. She would sweetly beg his pardon for hurling the laver at him. She would try not to choke on her words as she spoke them.

She had failed, she thought, as she searched behind the herb jars for the vial. She was preparing to drug her husband so that he would love her. She was pathetic.

In the end it didn't matter.

The vial was gone.

Severin stood in the bedchamber door, the rope in his hand. "Come, Hastings."

She was sitting on the bed. She didn't look at him, just shook her head.

"You will come willingly or I will carry you. This is your final night. Anger me not."

"Nay. I cannot bear it. I will not willingly let you tie me to Edgar again. I will not do it."

His eyes darkened as he walked quickly to her. He picked her up in his arms and carried her down the solar stairs. "Now," he said close to her ear, "do you wish everyone to see you being hauled here or will you walk to the hearth and accept your punishment?"

She swallowed. "I will walk."

He set her down, watched her straighten the old gown, and walk, head high, to the hearth. Edgar the wolfhound looked up and barked, his huge tail wagging.

She heard Marjorie laugh. She heard Eloise giggle.

"Sit down, Hastings."

She sat, not moving even after he had once again tied

the rope about her ankle and the other end around Edgar's thick neck. "Take care Edgar doesn't steal your dinner tonight."

Then he was gone, striding to the high table where Alice stood beside his chair, holding a large platter piled high with boar steaks.

When Alice brought her trencher, she whispered, "Only tonight, Hastings, then it will be over. Everyone is angry about it, but none know what to do. Gwent said he would have knocked his axe along Severin's head if he had called him a liar. Then he added that you had kicked Severin in his manhood. That, he said, was worthy of your punishment. That and you ran away from Oxborough and stabbed yourself with that knife. Gwent tasted your food and sipped your wine. It is fine. Eat, Hastings, and soon this will be over."

But she didn't. She didn't look toward the tables. She knew Marjorie would turn and wave to her or just look at her. She heard her bright laughter, knew she was speaking to Severin. Finally, she couldn't help herself. She looked up to see Marjorie leaning across Hastings's empty chair. She was holding up her wine goblet. She heard her say to Severin, "My lord, do taste my wine. I had it brought from Sedgewick. Perhaps you will enjoy it."

It was in that instant that Hastings knew that Marjorie had stolen the vial. She had poured the Healer's love potion into the goblet, drunk from it, and was now giving it to Severin. If he drank it, then he would love Marjorie.

She leapt to her feet, only to have Edgar leap to his also, barking loudly, believing it a game.

She watched Severin bring the goblet to his mouth. She saw Marjorie's white fingers on his sleeve, tugging at him. He drank the wine even as he was looking at her.

Hastings sat back down. Edgar put his massive head in her lap. She looked up to see Trist running through the rushes to get to her. He ran right up Edgar's back and sprawled on top of the wolfhound's head.

She reached out to pct him. Edgar slobbered on her hand. "It is too late, Trist. She has won." She leaned down and laid her head next to Edgar's. She felt Trist drape himself over her shoulders.

She awoke the following morning to see Severin standing, fully dressed, by the bed. Trist was on his shoulder, licking his whiskers. He still looked thin, his stomach caved in, but he was fast improving.

"I carried you up last night," Severin said. "You never awoke. Dress yourself, I am taking you to see the Healer. She said she could cut out the stitches today."

He looked just the same. Of course, she had yet to see him with Marjorie. She was certain he would gaze upon Marjorie and look besotted.

"I do not need you with me, Severin. Surely you have many important things to do. The stitches are nothing."

"Dress yourself, Hastings. I will not tell you again."

Why did he care? She pulled back the covers only to realize that she was quite naked. Her eyes flew to his. She grabbed the covers and jerked them to her neck.

He sighed and turned on his heel, saying over his shoulder, "I will see you in the hall. You will break your fast before we leave."

Why would he take off her clothes if he was besotted now with Marjorie?

The Healer lightly pressed her fingertips against the wound. Her head was back, her eyes closed.

"Well?" Severin said.

"Oh, you are still here, my lord?" The Healer turned and gave him a sour look. "I do not like you in my cottage. You are too big. Like most men, you take up too much room. My poor Alfred must remain outside whilst you are here. Now, take Hastings home. She is fit. The wound has healed very nicely. If it pleases her, you can play your games with her again. As I have told Hastings, these games are not to my liking, but she is young and does not know better. Aye, take her away from here."

"The babe is well?"

"The babe is resting comfortably. Worry not. Men never worry about the babes in their wives' wombs. They care only when a boy is produced. All this worry—it might be a girl, my lord, then you would have wasted all this concern.''

''You are wrong, Healer,'' he said. He leaned down and straightened Hastings's shift and gown. He offered her his hand. ''Come, let us go home.''

When Severin was ready to lift her onto Marella's back, Hastings said, ''Oh, I am sorry. I must ask the Healer a question. I will return shortly, Severin.''

He waited for her outside the cottage, staring at Alfred, who was sitting in the center of a pool of sunlight, lazily bathing himself.

''Healer, it was the woman Marjorie who gave Severin the potion. She drank of it, then handed it to him, and he drank as well, all the while they were looking at each other.''

''You have ruined this royally, Hastings. By Saint Ethelbert's teeth, you have just given your husband to another woman.''

''You are certain that the potion will result in their loving each other?''

''Naturally I am certain. Ah, Hastings, I should strangle you for your carelessness. She stole the potion, didn't she? Nay, don't bother to make excuses. Well, it is over for you. Even when you get her back at Sedgewick, he will follow her there. He will be unable not to. I am sorry, Hastings.'' She turned away from Hastings, shaking her head even as she began to stir the pot over the fire.

''What did you want from the Healer?'' Severin asked.

Hastings didn't realize that tears were pooling in her eyes.

''You are very pale, Hastings. Damnation, you are crying. What is wrong? Is it the babe?''

She couldn't speak. She shook her head, letting him help her onto Marella's back. ''It is nothing, Severin. Nothing at all.''

It was late that afternoon when Marjorie found her. She hadn't truly been hiding from her, but the spinning shed had become her refuge in but two short days.

"Hastings, aye, I see you are here. Many wonder where you are. I simply said that you were still embarrassed from your humiliation the past two evenings. Everyone understood that. All hope you are duly chastised." She laughed as she lightly stroked her fingers over some newly spun wool, a coarse gray to be sewn into tunics and gowns for the castle servants.

"What do you want, Marjorie?"

"Nothing, really. Did you see Severin? He and I took some bread and cheese and wine to the beach. It is a lovely day, the sun bright, the sea a vivid blue. We much enjoyed ourselves, but you knew that would happen."

Hastings felt a bolt of pain in her belly.

"I will not be returning to Sedgewick, Hastings."

It was too much. Hastings rose slowly from her stool, handing the spindle back to Mara the spinner. She left the weaving shed, Marjorie behind her.

"Such a coward you are, Hastings. You are like a whipped dog. You slink away."

Hastings knew in that instant that she wouldn't have stopped herself even if she thought about it for a long year. She whirled about and threw herself at Marjorie, grabbing her glorious silvery hair and pulling with all her strength. "Bitch! You damnable bitch!"

Marjorie wasn't a weakling. Soon the women were rolling in the dirt, shrieking at each other, poking each other, but it was Hastings who did not release Marjorie's hair. She scratched Hastings's face, kicked her in the belly, managed to roll over on top of her, all the while trying to get her hair free of Hastings's fist.

Severin couldn't believe his eyes. None of the men could. Severin cursed even as he ran to them, waving Gwent back. He clamped his hands under Marjorie's armpits and lifted her off Hastings. Still Hastings didn't let go of her hair. Marjorie shrieked in pain and kicked out, hitting Hastings in the belly again.

"Let her go, Hastings! Damnation, don't hurt the babe."

Hastings saw her husband over her, holding Marjorie,

and without a word she released the hair. She was left with a good-sized tangle in her hand. That pleased her.

Severin set Marjorie on her feet.

"What is happening here?"

Slowly Hastings rose. Her sleeve was torn free from her gown. She was filthy, but on the other hand, so was Marjorie.

She felt the small rivulets of blood streaking down her left cheek. It was nothing. She had a fistful of Marjorie's hair. She smiled at the woman and tossed the wad of hair into a mud puddle beside her.

She said in a voice bright as the sun overhead, "Why, my lord, Marjorie wants to return to Sedgewick. She is unhappy here. When I told her that I wanted her to remain, that you as well wished her to stay, she became angry. She values her independence; she values caring for Eloise by herself. She wants to leave."

"I am tired of your lies, Hastings." He turned to Marjorie, whose lip was bleeding and swelled. That made Hastings feel very good as well.

Hastings said, "Are you not used to all my lies by now, Severin? Can you not picture me pouring poison into my own wine goblet? Can you not imagine that I spilled it on purpose for Trist to drink?"

Severin whirled about to face her, his hands on his hips. "Be quiet, Hastings. Hold your sharp tongue. What happened? Why are you like two fishwives trying to kill each other?"

Marjorie only shrugged. "It is a private matter, my lord, nothing to concern you. Your wife has no control. You have remarked on that before. Indeed, you punished her for being so ungoverned. She has not learned. Mayhap she needs more nights next to Edgar."

Hastings took a step toward her. Severin quickly stepped between them. "No, no more. There will be no more fighting between the two of you, else I will punish both of you. Go now. You are both filthy as Edgar after a boar hunt."

Marjorie was whistling as she walked through the great hall.

"Hastings, wait a moment."

She turned to see Gwent staring at her, his distress evident. He walked to her. "I have come to a decision, Hastings," he said, lightly touching her shoulder. "I will see that the woman is returned to Sedgewick. All want peace again at Oxborough. There will be none as long as the woman remains here. You are not able to deal well with her. You carry the lord's heir. I will see to it."

"Severin will not let her go," Hastings said, shrugged, and walked up the solar stairs.

"Aye, he will," Gwent called after her. "I have spoken to Lady Moraine and she has told her son what he must do."

As if that would make any difference, Hastings thought, wincing at a pain in her left leg. When had Marjorie kicked her in the leg?

In the dark of the night, Hastings was in a deep sleep, dreaming of the lupine that bloomed so vividly in her garden, and how the lupine was really a deadly poison and someone was going to pour it into Severin's goblet. Then something wasn't right. There were no more lupines. There was the light touch of a hand on her belly. The hand was pressing ever so gently, lightly, stroking her belly, touching the pelvic bones, gently rubbing over the scar from her wound.

She placed her hand over the one on her belly. The hand stilled, then she slipped her own beneath it. She was touching her own flesh. She was naked. What had happened to her night shift? But she didn't really care. The hand was caressing around hers, fingers sliding beneath her palm, between her flesh and her hand.

Her brain was still heavy with sleep. She knew she should pull away, but she didn't. Fingers splayed lower. It was Severin. His hand, his fingers, his touch that made her feel so urgent. Aye, Severin. He parted her flesh and was touching her, lightly rubbing, finding a rhythm that she'd forgotten existed. It had been so long, too long.

"What are you doing here?"

His fingers stilled. "This is my bed and you are in it,"

he said, and started his rhythm again. She tried to pull away from him, but he pressed his other hand against her, holding her still on her back. He was on his knees between her legs.

She didn't understand why he was touching her like this. Then his fingers went lower, opening her, easing inside her, and she arched her back. She didn't want to, but she moaned. Her own moan brought her fully awake. She knew what he was doing to her, but she didn't care. She wanted more. She wanted pleasure and she wanted him even though she knew that soon enough he would be gone from her.

"That is good," he said very quietly, even as she felt his warm breath against her flesh. He blew against her, and she shuddered like a leaf in an autumn storm. Then his fingers delved deep inside her, even as he touched her with his mouth.

She cried out, thrashing beneath him, her fingers digging frantically into his naked shoulders. She screamed, "Severin!"

"Aye," he said, his breath hot against her flesh. "Take your pleasure, Hastings. Now."

And she did. She welcomed him wildly when he came into her, shoving deep, high inside her. She locked her legs about his flanks, drawing him deep and deeper still, and when his fingers eased between their bodies to touch her, she felt again the rippling pleasure building and building until soon she could no more control that pleasure that swamped her than she could have prevented herself from throwing the laver at him.

When her pleasure crested, his did just a moment later, and she gasped into his mouth, "I love you, Severin. I've loved you for a very long time."

He froze over her, then shoved hard and fast until he fell over her, panting hard.

Her wits came back slowly. She couldn't take the words back. The words lay between them, hard and real and immense in their power.

He now knew that he need worry about her no longer.

She leaned up and bit his shoulder. He probably believed

it a loving gesture, but it wasn't. She wished she could bite him to the bone for what had come out of her mouth. Unplanned, all of it unplanned, just because he'd awakened her, loving her, making her lose herself in the passion, in the closeness to him.

She bit him again. He reared up on his elbows, looking down at her. "You must give me a few minutes before I can pleasure you again, Hastings," he said, rolled off her, and within moments she heard his deep, even breathing. He'd come to her simply because she was here and available to him. But why hadn't he gone to Marjorie? He'd drunk the love potion, after all. Surely it was Marjorie he wanted, only Marjorie, yet he'd come to her. She was already carrying a babe. Why?

She, lackwit that she was, she'd opened herself to him, given herself completely over to him, told him she loved him. She was an incredible fool.

She cursed. It was the use of the animal parts that made her feel better.

# 28

ALICE SAW MARJORIE PACING BACK AND FORTH, BACK AND forth, in front of Hastings's bedchamber.

She stepped down a few steps and waited. What did the woman want? She heard the thick oak door open, heard voices.

It was Lord Severin. She heard the door pulled shut.

It was the master Marjorie had been waiting for. Alice wasn't surprised, but she did think that the woman was luckier than she deserved. What would she have done if Hastings had come out or if they'd come out together? Ah, but that one was just full of stories and her wits worked quickly.

Without hesitation, Alice pressed herself against the solar stair wall, making no sound, and listened.

"I have waited for you, Severin."

"It is very early, Marjorie. What is it you wish?"

"I wish for us to ride to the beach. The morning is warm, the sun bright. I wish to speak of the future."

Alice thought she'd choke. The bitch, the damnable bitch. Coming right out with it. She sounded utterly confident. Mayhap, Alice thought, she should get some of the love potion for herself from the Healer. Marjorie certainly believed it worked. Just listen to her. Alice would pour a goblet of it into Beamis's ale, the blind oaf.

She heard a deep sigh from Lord Severin. Fight against it, she wanted to shout at him, but she held her tongue, hearing him say at last, "Very well."

She heard Marjorie's skirts swish, and she heard a quiet moan. The woman was kissing him or caressing him with her hand, Alice didn't know which. She began to whistle, very loudly, and clopped up the few stairs.

The noises stopped.

Lord Severin was standing with his back against the closed bedchamber door when Alice came into view. He was holding Marjorie away from him. At least he still had some shame or perhaps the potion wasn't such a miracle after all.

"Good morning, my lord," Alice said, sounding happy as a gull who'd just snaffled a fish from the sea. She merely nodded to Marjorie. "Is Hastings awake, my lord? I wish to speak to her."

"Hastings is within. She is grinding some felwort, she told me."

"Then I will see to her." Alice knocked on the door, did not wait for a reply, and walked in, still whistling.

She didn't close the door completely, and remained close, listening. She held her finger over her lips when Hastings looked up and opened her mouth to speak.

"I must speak to you, Severin. Away from here. Away from her. Come with me now."

Alice began to whistle loudly. She clopped her feet right next to the door.

Then she flung the door open. "Ah, my lady wishes to speak to you, my lord. The Healer gave her a mixture of herbs to feed to the marten. It will complete his healing."

Hastings just stared. Then she saw Marjorie standing next to her husband, just outside the bedchamber door.

She called out, her voice as cold as the frozen water in the jugs during winter, "My lord, do you have Trist?"

The marten poked his head out of Severin's tunic. Severin merely looked down at Marjorie, raised his hand, then lowered it. "Aye, here he is. I'm bringing him."

Once Severin had left the bedchamber, leaving Trist sniffing in the various open jars of herbs, Alice grabbed Hastings's sleeve. "She attacked him, Hastings. I saw it. It is she who searches him out. Not the other way around."

"He did not push her away, did he?"

"Don't sound like a beaten dog! I know you believe the love potion makes him unable to resist her, but I don't believe it. He did resist her. I heard him speak. He sounded like he just wanted to get away from her. Listen to me, Hastings, Severin's mother, Dame Agnes, and I have all discussed it, and we've decided that it is time to take care of Marjorie once and for all."

"Kill her?" Her voice was wistful, then she shook her head. "I cannot do that. I would like to, but I cannot. The king would be displeased if he had to find Eloise another guardian."

Alice laughed. "That was a good jest, Hastings. Perhaps your humors are returning to their proper balance. No, it is not our idea to lay an axe on her neck. No, we want you to do something else. Something very basic, well, perhaps more than basic. Lady Moraine said it was the most elemental of strategies and the most advanced of strategies as well. Now, tell me what you think of our idea."

A shadow fell over her columbine. His voice, deep and smooth, said, "I must punish you, Hastings."

She whirled about so quickly she fell on her bottom. She had pulled up a primrose by accident he had startled her so. "Oh, dear, I would not have picked it so soon. But still, it is very lovely." She began stroking the primrose as if she were its lover. Severin stared at that damned flower and felt his loins tighten. She stared up at him. "I don't wish to be punished, Severin. I wish you would go off and fight with one of our neighbors or join the king against the Scots or the Welsh. Surely that would take your mind off me."

He appeared to ponder that quite seriously. "There are no enemies right now of any count. Aye, you're right, long stretches of peace are difficult. Do not you fear that I might fall in a battle?''

She hadn't thought of that when the words jumped out of her mouth. ''Nay, I do not wish you to get hurt. I might not be near enough to you to heal you.''

''It pleases me that you do not want me dead.''

''You are known. Why would I prefer the unknown?''

He pictured another man as her husband. It didn't please Severin, particularly if he were dead. ''You have spoken all around the core of the apple, Hastings. It must be done. Do not try to dissuade me.''

''No, I shan't try that. You are more single-minded than Gilbert the goat. Ah, you have the rope, Severin?''

He shook his head. ''Nay, my father always said that a man should not repeat his punishments. To use your own words, it is the matter of the known as opposed to the unknown. The fear of a punishment diminishes if it is known. Damn you, Hastings. Don't you dare pretend that I'm abusing you. You know that I put off punishing you until after the stitches were cut out of you. You know that you deserve it. You escaped Oxborough, put yourself in grave danger, and wasted my time finding you.''

''That is my biggest crime, is it not? Wasting your valuable time?''

''Give over, Hastings. I will not allow you to anger me, not today.''

''Why not today? Perhaps you are riding with Marjorie? Mayhap to the beach where you can discuss the future? You want to be certain that your bile is sweet and gently flowing?''

How did she know what Marjorie had said? Alice, doubtless Alice had overheard them. He shook his head and lightly laid his hand on her shoulder. ''No, I do not have the time. I asked her if she would like Gwent to accompany her, but she refused. I suppose I must speak to her soon, however.''

He did not sound like a man so smitten by passion that his eyes were nearly crossed with it. No, he merely sounded harassed. Mayhap Alice had been right. Mayhap the love potion didn't work. She brightened. Mayhap their plan would also work. She was still a bit taken aback that it was her mother-in-law who had decided upon this particular advanced strategy. She had no particular faith in it, but she would try. By Saint Ethelbert's elbows, she would certainly enjoy trying. She was more adept now. She knew what to do. There would be no fumbling about, no guessing. She would know quickly enough if it was working.

"Why do you look so pleased with yourself when I am trying to decide on how to punish you?"

She lightly stroked the primrose against her cheek. Like the softest velvet, she thought. Rich enough for the king himself. She looked up at him through her lashes. "I enjoyed your mouth on me last night, Severin."

He froze to the spot. He was staring at her mouth.

"Aye, and when you came inside me and I pushed my hips up against you, you came deeper and deeper. You made me want to weep with the pleasure that you—my husband and known to me—gave me."

He ran his tongue over his lips. He was still staring at her mouth. "You are with child," he said finally.

"Aye, were I not, then I would be now. You were inside of me, Severin, inside my body, touching my womb. It is a feeling that makes me want to hold you even now and stroke you with my hands and bring you into me again. I am truly sorry that you have no time."

"By Saint Eggbert's nose, you will kill me with your thoughts. Nay, continue to think, it will not harm me, but perhaps it isn't wise for you to speak your thoughts aloud. What did you say you wanted me to do to you?"

"It's what I want to do to you. Let me touch you with my mouth again just as you touched me last night. Remember when I held you in my hand and wouldn't let you go?"

He actually shook as she spoke. "Aye, I remember. I would have laughed had I not hurt so much. I remember that first time you took me into your mouth. It"—he swallowed, feeling awash with lust—"pleased me."

She rose slowly, gently laying the primrose against his chest. She pressed herself against him. She slipped her hand between them and found him. He was already hard as the wooden stake that held up her irises.

She outlined him with her fingers. "I should like to do that again, Severin. Soon now, very soon."

He shifted his weight from one leg to the other. He thought he'd die. "Do what exactly?"

"My hands on you, my mouth on you, everything."

He grabbed her wrist. He pulled her hand away, but he didn't want to. By Saint Elbert's toes, he didn't want to. "Many of our people are doubtless watching."

She leaned up on her tiptoes, whispering into his mouth, her hands clasped behind his neck, "Take me into the forest and punish me as you will there."

His dark blue eyes dilated.

Lady Moraine and Alice stood on the narrow ramparts, watching Hastings and Lord Severin ride from the castle. Alice laughed. "They are riding so hard their mounts must believe they are going into battle."

"Aye, a battle of sorts. They are going to the forest, just as we'd hoped. Hastings asked us why our strategy is always the same—well, a bit more skill we are requiring of her now—but still the end is always the same." Lady Moraine just shook her head. "She is very young, but she is learning. I liked what you told her, Alice."

"Aye," Alice said, looking quite smug. "It is true. Men are simple in their needs and wants. Coming into a woman is the first thought in their heads in the morning and the last thought in their heads at night. Once Hastings has mastered that, she will seldom have another frown from your son."

"That is true," Lady Moraine said. "And I am pleased that she loves Severin. Oh aye, Alice, she loves him very much. She would not be able to employ the strategy if she did not love him. As for him, well, we'll see. A man is very different from us. Love doesn't come to him all of a moment. He must exercise his lust, ruminate upon all facets of his situation. He must be made comfortable in what he has before he can come to appreciate it with his heart as well as his head. Now, watch your step, Alice. The wind is heavy and could blow you off.''

Alice gripped the wooden railing on the inside of the ramparts' walk. ''Saint Peter's bones, I know Hastings will succeed. She will also enjoy herself immensely.''

''It pleases me that she agreed to our plan even when she was certain that Severin was bedding Marjorie. She is very hardheaded, my daughter-in-law.''

''As you said, she loves your son. Doubtless, when they are not shrieking at each other, she also enjoys his man's body. I also believe that the Healer made a mistake. That potion didn't blind Severin to all save Marjorie. I vow he doesn't have a thought for her.''

''Thank the Lord for that. I wonder how he will punish Hastings.''

Alice laughed so loud, Auric, one of the men-at-arms on guard at the corner tower, stared over at them. Alice raised her hand and waved at him. He gave her a wide grin, showing his remaining six teeth.

Hastings and Severin did not return until it was time for the dinner meal. They tried to slip up the solar stairs unnoticed, but it didn't work. Gwent shouted, ''My lord, the wind has died down. The temperature has dropped. A storm is blowing up. Beamis agrees with me. All the horses and other animals are safely in their sheds. Most all our people are already within the great hall, as you can see, as they can see you. As everyone who is not blind can see you and Hastings.''

Hastings tugged on his hand, grinning up at him. ''We are the butt of their jests, my lord,'' she said.

''You have twigs and leaves in your hair, your gown is ripped beneath your right arm—''

''That was the arm that reached nearly everything of interest, my lord,'' she said, and giggled again. ''Remember when you had me reach up and hold to that branch over my head? I believe that is when it ripped.'' She raised her hand and pulled a leaf from his dark hair.

He wanted to tug at his tunic, to swipe at his hair, but he forced himself to be still.

"Mayhap, my lord," Beamis called out, "you wish time to bathe before we eat?"

"Their jests become riper," Hastings said as she picked a leaf out of her own tangled hair.

"Alice," Severin called out, "serve ale. It will close the mouths of these louts."

When Severin and Hastings walked into the great hall close to an hour later, it was to loud singing, laughter, Edgar the wolfhound barking loudly as he chased after a bone one of the men-at-arms threw for him, and several amorous bouts, the most interesting between Belle and the armorer.

"I wonder if there is a drop of ale left at Oxborough," Hastings said, grinning up at her husband.

He paused a moment, oblivious of the nearly sixty people, all watching them now. "I have yet to punish you, Hastings." He lightly touched his fingers to her cheek. She turned her head and kissed his palm.

"Mayhap you should wait until our child is born."

He lightly touched her stomach. "Give me a curve here, Hastings. Something to show me that my child is within."

"Soon," she said. "Soon."

They took their chairs, answering jests coming from Gwent and Beamis. Hastings started to take a bite of her stewed onions and cabbage when Severin grabbed her hand. "It must be tasted first."

He turned to Marjorie. "Give Hastings your trencher and you take hers."

Marjorie looked pinched. Her face was pale, her eyes darkened with pain, with deep anger—Hastings didn't know—but she said nothing. Eloise was silent and slouched down in her chair beside her.

"Give her your goblet also."

Marjorie continued silent, simply doing as he bade.

The laughter and jests continued long after the sun set, the storm blew in, and the wind howled around the castle, making the tapestries billow against the stone walls that faced the sea.

"You have won."

Hastings drank the last of her wine before turning to Marjorie. "Won?" she repeated slowly. Severin was in close conversation with Gwent, Trist on his shoulder. "Won? This was never a contest, Marjorie. Severin is my husband, not yours. The love potion you stole from my bedchamber did not work. Listen to me. I merely want peace again. I want my husband with me. I don't even want you dead. I merely want you gone from Oxborough."

Marjorie was staring hard at Hastings. "I have studied you. You are comely, but no more than that. I am more beautiful than any other lady I have ever seen. Severin wanted me, adored me, gawked at me even. He kissed me, touched me, caressed me until I opened myself to him. Even though you used your body to distract him today, it should not have worked. Oh aye, his crazy mother delighted in telling me that he had taken you into the forest. To frolic, she said, and she laughed at me. He should have gone with me, not you. I do not understand."

"Mayhap there are qualities Severin cherishes other than just a beautiful face and silvery hair. Mayhap there is honor and caring. Mayhap he got a glimpse of your insides, Marjorie. Did you try to poison me?"

She shrugged, picked up a piece of warm bread, and began to chew on it. "We will return to Sedgewick on the morrow."

"I will be pleased to see the back of you."

"Would be that you had drunk from the goblet and not dropped it. Would that the marten had died."


Hastings was on her knees, pulling weeds from between her lupines and her foxgloves. She was humming. The air was fresh from the storm the night before. The sun was high in the sky.

And Marjorie was gone. Thank the good Lord.

She sat back on her heels, a weed in her hand, shaking it free of rich, black dirt. Severin had spoken quietly to Marjorie before he'd lifted her onto her palfrey's back.

What had he said to her?

She tossed the weed over her shoulder and gently pushed a stake more deeply into the ground. She tied the iris closer to the stake with a short length of thick wool thread. The columbine was blooming madly, bright yellow flowers. She would begin harvesting them soon. She turned at a soft mewling sound.

Trist moved onto her thighs and butted his head against her stomach. She stroked his soft fur, back and forth, back and forth. "Will you have babes soon, Trist? Severin told me that you had been gone, back to the forest, he believed. Did you find a mate? If so, then why did you leave her?"

He mewled, wrapping his paws around the chain of keys that hung from her waist.

"Your belly is fat again." She paused, leaning over to gather the marten against her. "I would have been very unhappy if you had died, Trist."

A shadow fell over her shoulder. She knew it was Severin. She was smiling even as she raised her face to him. He had come to her again. He had known she would be here in her garden.

"Have you come to take me for another walk in the forest? Will you press me against a tree and jerk up my gown as you did yesterday? Then will you lift my legs around your waist and come into me?"

He stumbled, nearly falling over her patch of blooming daisies, all of them with bright yellow centers and stark white ray flowers.

Trist batted a paw at him. He came down onto his haunches, stroking Trist's chin.

"The forest, Hastings? You wish to do more than take a simple walk?"

She leaned closer to him. "What I truly wish to do is strip off all your clothes, press you down upon your back against the soft green moss, and mayhap then I would recite poetry to you."

She giggled even as she leaned against him. "I would see the effect of my words upon you."

He leaned over and kissed her. "After you'd given me your best words, Hastings, I would bring you over me and let you take me. Would you like that? It would free my hands to stroke you.''

She became very still, her eyes steady on his face. ''You will stay with me, Severin?''

''Aye, I will stay with you forever. You are my wife.''

She wanted also to be his love, but that could wait, she supposed. One day he would love her. Surely he already admired her insides.

They rode again into the forest.


''Mayhap it will become a habit,'' Gwent said to Beamis, shading his eyes with his hand, watching until Severin and Hastings disappeared from view.

''Aye, if the master doesn't muck it up again. At least the beautiful wench is gone, praise the saints. Lord Severin did not keep her. He will not go to Sedgewick to see her. I know when a man has made a decision.''

''I agree with you and that pleases me as well. The boy shows good sense.''

''I thought you told me once that Hastings threatened to make his bowels watery if he deceived her.''

Gwent laughed. ''I wonder if she would do that. It would bring any man low.''

Lady Moraine said some time later to Alice as she polished the laver, ''We will all become well used to my dearest son and Hastings disappearing in the middle of the day.''

''Aye,'' Alice said, staring over at Beamis, who was wiping the back of his hand across his mouth after drinking his ale. ''I wonder if Beamis has ever disappeared in the middle of the day in his bloody life?''

At the evening meal Severin did not ask anyone to taste Hastings's food. No one marveled at that. There was a lightness in the air, an ease in all the talk now that the Sedgewick people were gone. Now that Marjorie was no longer here to attack the mistress and seduce the master. And the child who had accused Hastings of pretending to poison herself to gain Lord Severin's pity. Eloise wasn't missed either.

The talk that night was about the place called Rosehaven. What would they find? It was a mystery that teased every brain.

The following Monday morning they left for Rosehaven.

# 29

"WILL YOU SEE MARJORIE AGAIN, SEVERIN?"

He turned to face her in their nest of blankets. It was a cool night, the air heavy with an approaching storm. It was their second night away from Oxborough. By tomorrow night, given no accidents or outlaws or rain—which was too much to ask of the gods—they would reach Canterbury. "No," he said, reaching out to touch her belly. She was wearing her gown since she, Severin, and twelve of the men were all lying about the dying camp fire, each wrapped in blankets. She felt his hand on her bare thigh, moving up, then resting on her leg, waiting. He eased his hand onto her belly. "Lie on your back so I can rest my hand on my child."

She turned to her back. His hand was warm, his fingers callused.

"I did not mean to ask, it just came out of my mouth." She sighed. "I have never known such jealousy, such helplessness. It is not a nice thing. I hated the feelings, sometimes even more than I wanted to kick Marjorie."

"I know," he said. His hand began to rub lightly over her stomach. "It was difficult for me, Hastings. She is so beautiful, perhaps even more so now than when she was a girl. I saw her through my boy's memories, all of them radiant with worship for her. When I left her all those years ago, I was bowed with grief. Then, suddenly, she was with me again. I was overwhelmed.

"Nay, do not pull away from me, Hastings. It is difficult for me to speak of, but I owe it to you. Because of who she was, because of who I had been, I mucked up my miracle."

"You what? What is this? *What* miracle?"

He laughed quietly. "Never mind. Even in my besotted state I came to realize she was dangerous to you. Finally, I came to realize also that she had changed over the years. I swear to you that when she was young, there was no meanness in her."

Hastings didn't disagree. On the other hand, she would never have laid a wager on the absence of meanness in Marjorie, at any age.

"The child, Eloise. I am not certain, but I wonder if Marjorie has stoked a black fire in that child's heart. She did lie about you."

Hastings wanted to howl yes, Marjorie was ruining Eloise, but she kept her mouth shut. Now was not the moment. For the first time, he was speaking frankly to her. She was also very aware of Severin's hand lying quietly in the hollow of her belly. She heard several of the men snoring. One grunted in his sleep. There was some quiet conversation on the other side of the fire, an occasional chuckle.

"What will happen, Severin?"

"What do you mean? To us, Hastings?"

"Aye, to us."

"Why, you will bear my sons and daughters and we will build a great dynasty. Our name will pass through the centuries, known and respected."

"That is not quite the magnificence I wished to hear about."

He leaned down and kissed her. "No? Then I will take you to that forest and we will lie on every patch of ground where the sunlight forks through the oak trees. Nay, not now, when we are home again, home at Oxborough."

She fell asleep with his hand resting lightly on her belly.

• • •

"That small jewel of a keep is Rosehaven," Gwent said, pointing to the golden-stoned castle that stood at the end of a promontory that reached like a long bony finger well into the River Glin.

"Lord Brenfavern said it was owned by the Earl of Oxborough," Severin said. "He had not yet heard of the old earl's death. It is guarded by men-at-arms hired from all around these parts. They take turns. There has never been any trouble since all the men-at-arms perform duties here at one time or another during the year. An interesting strategy."

"But who lives there?"

"We will find out in a very little while," Severin said. "Lord Brenfavern didn't know." He kicked his warhorse in his sides.

"Carry our standard high," Gwent called to the man carrying the Oxborough crest. "We want no surprises and no arrows raining down upon us."

There was neither surprise nor arrows.

The guard immediately recognized the Oxborough standard and waved. They heard men shouting. Without challenge, the guard opened the double gates that led into the small outer courtyard. There were at least a dozen soldiers standing about, several horses, and an armorer pounding on a helmet. The men called out welcome, making no moves at all toward their weapons. Severin motioned Gwent and the other men to remain in the outer courtyard.

He and Hastings rode slowly into the inner bailey. Severin came to an abrupt halt at Hastings's gasp. There were gardens surrounding the inner walls of the keep, filled with vividly blooming flowers, so many of them, and on one wall was a trellised rosebush that spilled huge red blooms from near to the top of the wall to the ground and beyond. Beautiful stone fountains stood in the center of clusters of flowers. The sound of flowing water filled the air. Severin heard a bird twittering. There were wide walkways so that no one trampled the gardens. Hastings sniffed roses strong in the air.

"It's a castle for a princess," she said, flinging her arms wide. "Just look at it."

"Your father's mistress, Hastings. Prepare yourself for it. He has treated her very well. He created this special place just for her."

Hastings heard the children's shouts before she saw them. Then four girls came running from one of the gardens, all laughing, shouting, calling to each other. Two women were trying to keep up with them.

The oldest of the girls appeared to be no more than ten years old, the youngest only four or five years old. They came to a surprised halt, staring up at the man and woman.

Her father's bastards? Hastings felt a cramp forming low in her belly. She wasn't sure now that she should have come. Her father had obviously deceived her for years, had kept a mistress ever since he'd murdered her mother, and she had borne him all these girl children.

The oldest girl called out, "You must dismount. Mother does not like the gardens to be trampled. Did not Gergen tell you? You must leave your horses in the outer courtyard. Mother will be displeased if you harm her flowers."

Severin nodded and dismounted. He turned and lifted Hastings down from Marella.

"What is your name?" Hastings called to the girl.

"I am Marella."

"That is my palfrey's name!"

The girl laughed. "Your mare is very pretty. I do not mind having her name at all. But it is also the name of William's prized mare. It is said that when the mare died, William mourned her for a week and buried her beneath his bedchamber window."

"That is quite true," Hastings said. "It is also true that William's mare had a white stocking, just like my Marella."

"Aye, that's what Papa said."

The youngest girl, all blond and white and skinny, ran through her sisters to Severin. She had not one whit of fear. But the women did. They were shouting at her, but she paid them no heed.

Severin came down on his haunches. "And who are you?"

"I, my lord? I am Matilda."

"A famous name."

"Aye," the little girl said, flinging her head back in a gesture that Severin recognized, not certain how he did, but knowing that he had seen that gesture before. "She was William's wife. She was short and perhaps a bit plump, but she was brave and loyal and the most beautiful woman in Normandy. Just as I am, except I was born in England and will likely remain here. My mama says I will be short as well. Who are you, my lord?"

"I am the Earl of Oxborough. This is my wife, Hastings."

"I wanted to be named Hastings," another girl of about seven said, stepping forward, "but Father said it wasn't possible, that another girl already had that name. My name is Normandy. That is where William came from."

"You can't be the Earl of Oxborough," Marella said, grabbing Matilda's hand and pulling her back. "My father is the Earl of Oxborough. You are lying."

"Oh dear," Hastings said.

"He will come and take you away," Matilda said. "Papa wouldn't let anyone harm us."

Suddenly a woman's voice rang through the children's chatter. "Who are you, sir? What is going on here? Why did my men allow you to enter?"

Hastings turned slowly at the woman's voice. Oh God, memories flooded through her mind. She remembered that voice. The woman was standing in the pure sunlight, tall and straight, no gray in her rich chestnut hair, her eyes still a vivid green. She was heavier, but still she was beautiful, her dark green wool gown falling in graceful folds to the ground.

Hastings took a step toward her. She stretched out her hand, staring, disbelieving. No, it was impossible. She wet her lips. "Mama?"

The woman froze. She moaned softly, then picked up her skirts and ran to Hastings. She grabbed her arms and shook her. "Is it possible? Is it really you, Hastings? Oh my baby, my baby! Oh God, you're here!"

"I don't understand this," Gwent said, coming up to stand beside Severin.

"I don't either," Marella said.

"Come here, Harlette," one of the women called to a dark-haired little girl who had sidled up to Gwent.

"Who is Harlette?" Gwent asked.

"She was William's mother," the little girl said. "She was the most beautiful lady in all of Normandy, before Matilda. But who is *she*?"

"She," Severin said slowly, watching his wife hug the woman who was her mother, "she is my wife. She is the Countess of Oxborough."

"But Mama is the Countess of Oxborough," Normandy said.

"I don't understand," Marella said. "They are different women."

No one would ever deny that they were mother and daughter, the resemblance was so marked.

"But you were beaten to death," Hastings said yet again as her mother continued to cry and hug her. "Father didn't want me to see it so I was taken away, but Dame Agnes told me you were dead. She held me when I wept. She took care of me."

"Ah, Agnes. How I have missed her. Aye, your father had me beaten. When I fell unconscious from the lash he had me taken away. He proclaimed to all that I was dead. Actually he took me to the Healer in the forest. When I was well, he said he could not allow me to resume my place at Oxborough. He would be shamed if he allowed it, for I had dared to cuckold him. But he could not live without me, he said, and he cried, Hastings. He cried and cried, begging me to forgive him.

"I refused. I told him he was an animal. I told him I would never forgive him. He brought me here to this small keep that sits on this point into the River Glin. It was a pitiful pile of stones then. But I planted my gardens. I gave it life. I named it Rosehaven and it became a place of beauty. You will see all the roses later. I named one Hastings, after you. There has never been violence here.'' Her mother paused, staring at her daughter, who was exactly her same height. ''You are beautiful, Hastings, more beautiful than the rose named after you. I always knew you would grow up well. And just look at you. As each of my other daughters was born, I looked for you in her, and always there was something to remind me of you. A shrug, perhaps, or the way Marella laughs, the way Matilda flings her head back, all have something of you in them. Ah, but I have missed you, wondered about you, wondered if you ever thought of me and what you thought. Did you believe me evil? Sinful?''

Hastings shook her head. She couldn't speak, the tears were too full in her throat.

''I begged him to let me see you, but he refused. He said that if you knew I still lived, that he still lived with me, that you would not be able to keep the secret.''

''When he was dying, I wonder why he did not tell either of us,'' Severin said, rubbing his chin.

''My husband was not overly encumbered with scruples,'' Hastings's mother said. ''So he is dead.''

''Aye, many months now. He made Severin his heir; we were married when he was dying. I'm sorry, Mother.''

Lady Janet said nothing for a very long time. She stared toward the small larch that grew in the middle of one of the gardens. ''He wasn't a bad man. I imagine I will miss him. I came to accept him, for I had no choice. But he loved his daughters—all of you—and he saw to it that no neighbor ever coveted Rosehaven. You say he never told you. Well, I doubt he wanted to face your recriminations on his deathbed, Hastings. Now, come into the keep. I will serve you some sweet wine and some cakes that my cook does very well.''

The great hall of Rosehaven wasn't very grand. It was more like a manor house, not fashioned for war or siege. The walls were all the same pink stone with beautiful thick tapestries covering them. There were only four trestle tables, each cleaner than the next. There was a small fireplace that had no black soot on it. Fresh rushes were scattered on the stone floor. They smelled strongly of rosemary. It was a keep for a princess.

After they were served wine and cakes, Lady Janet said, "Your father had the tapestries sent from Flanders."

"They are lovely," Hastings said. "They must keep you warm in the winter."

"Not really, but they are lovely to look at."

Trist poked his head out of Severin's tunic.

Matilda gasped and pointed. Harlette shouted, "Look, Lord Severin carries an animal in his tunic."

Hastings looked at the line of girls. "You are all my sisters," she said, still unable to take it all in, still distrusting her own eyes. Her mother lived and she had four more daughters. She got a hold on herself. "Ah, this is Trist. He is a marten. If you are gentle and you don't yell too loudly, he will come out and play with you."

Trist worked his way out of Severin's tunic and jumped to a trestle table. He eyed each of the girls. He held out his paw to Normandy. She squealed. Trist mewled and turned onto his back, waving his thick tail at them.

"What is your mother's name?" Severin asked quietly as he watched the girls sidle nearer and nearer to Trist, who was putting on a fine entertainment for them.

"Janet. Her father was the Earl of Monmouth. He died some two years before my father supposedly had her beaten for her faithlessness."

"Ah, so he had no fear of retribution."

"No, my mother's younger brother became earl, but he was too young to seek retribution. I have never seen my uncle."

Lady Janet handed Severin another goblet of wine. "I trust you will like this one. It isn't so sweet as the first. Naturally it comes from Normandy, though I did not realize any grapes would grow in that northerly climate."

"Father lied," Hastings said, sipping the new wine. "The wine comes from Aquitaine. I faced him with it several years ago after speaking with a wine merchant." She laughed. "Anything and everything from William the Con-

queror or Normandy, Father wanted to claim as his own.
Just look at all our names."

"It is a tradition of long standing," Lady Janet said.
"Mayhap it is written of somewhere at Oxborough and we
will find it someday. It is time for dinner. I hope you will
enjoy our cook's food, Hastings. She isn't MacDear, but I
have taught her well."

All the Oxborough men-at-arms were on their best be-
havior. There was no spitting into the rushes, no pummeling
the dog, whose place was beside the fireplace, no belching.
The meal was quite good. But conversation was difficult.
Hastings was relieved when it was over.

The four girls were delighted to give their chamber to
their sister and her husband. All of them wanted to sleep
with their mother, a treat rarely granted.

"This is all very strange," Severin said as he stripped
off his clothing. The bedchamber was small but beautifully
furnished with four trunks, each one covered with a thick
brocade with a girl's name on it. There were rugs on the
floor. There was a screen in the corner and behind it a
bathing tub. The bed was narrow, covered with a thick bear
fur.

Severin was so self-sufficient, Hastings thought, watching him. Most men must have their page to assist them. He
was also beautiful. She wondered if he was also thinking
of what Rosehaven meant to him and his future.

"Aye," she said, her fingers on the laces of her gown.
"I have four sisters."

"Why didn't he tell me?"

"Shame? Mayhap he believed all would think him weak
if they knew he hadn't really killed his wife, but took her
elsewhere and stayed with her."

"It teases my brain, Hastings. But he must have realized
that I would learn of this."

"I must suppose that he believed a dead man wouldn't
care if he were reviled or praised. Shame would not be able
to touch him."

He grunted and climbed naked into the sweet-smelling
bed. She pulled her gown over her head. "Where is Trist?"

"With the girls. I hope he does not swoon with all the adoration he is receiving with those four."

She slipped into bed beside him.

"Why are you wearing your shift?"

"Your mind is far away from carnal thoughts, Severin. I did not wish to tempt you."

He laughed and helped her pull the shift over her head. He threw it onto the floor. He was always very neat with his own clothing, but with hers—she sighed and curled up next to him.

"Tell me what we are going to do," she said, kissing his shoulder.

"Rosehaven," he said, even as he began to stroke her hair. "She named it Rosehaven because of her flowers. She gave you her joy and ability with herbs and plants."

"Aye. Tomorrow she wants to show me the rose she named after me."

"It has thorns, I doubt it not. Big ones."

"I would not want to be a boring, placid sort of flower."

"A thorn in my side," he said, turning to face her. "Your mother has lived here for nearly ten years. It is her home. It is well protected. I have no idea what to do, Hastings."

"We will ask her," Hastings said. She didn't stroke her hands over her husband. Indeed, her fists were against his chest. "My mother never cried when she heard my father was dead," she said. "She did not even seem to care."

"You do not know that. Today everything is too new to both of you. It will take time for you to know each other's hearts again. Fret not about it now, Hastings, and love your husband."

She did with pleasing enthusiasm.

"I have four sisters," Hastings said against his throat before she fell asleep some time later.

And I will have to dower all of them, Severin thought, then smiled. He had never before had sisters and now he had four of them. He decided then that he wanted them to come back to Oxborough. He wanted to be surrounded by family. He wanted to be responsible for them, to protect them. Aye, he liked the thought of four little sisters.

"This is my home. I cannot leave Rosehaven."

Lady Janet was serene, calm, all those tranquil and even-tempered qualities Hastings didn't have and would probably never have.

She sat forward, saying earnestly, "Mother, we cannot allow you to remain here. I have found you after nearly ten years. I have found my sisters. You must come back to Oxborough. It is your first home."

"I do not want the memories that would be there, lurking, waiting to hurt me."

"There are no more bad memories. Severin cast them all out when he came."

Severin looked back and forth between mother and daughter. He knew what Hastings would look like now in her older years and it pleased him. Ah, but he prayed she wouldn't become the placid woman her mother was. No, he wanted her passion, her laughter, her yelling when she wanted to kill him. He wanted their children.

He prayed he would never see Marjorie again. He would never tell Hastings that he had once come close to taking her. It was that second night when he'd tied Hastings by that damnable rope to Edgar the wolfhound. But he hadn't gone with Marjorie. He had looked over at his sleeping wife, her head against Edgar's neck, and had managed to deny himself. The next morning it had been easier. Then Hastings had seduced him.

A wife seducing her husband. Surely it did not happen all that often. But she had. He swallowed, remembering that afternoon spent in the forest. It had left only her in his mind.

"I know!"

He was jerked out of his thoughts at Harlette's shout. Trist was wrapped around her skinny neck, but she was grinning widely.

"Mother does not want to leave her gardens."

"But we want her to," Marella said, rubbing Trist's chin just as Severin had showed her.

"That's right," Matilda said, sidling up to Severin. "We don't want Mother to give all her time to her flowers. We want her to give her time to us."

Normandy stood there, arms folded over her chest. She was a beautiful girl and would soon grow to be a beautiful woman. She would, Severin thought, grow to look just like Hastings.

"Mother," Normandy said very slowly, very calmly. Completely unlike Hastings, Severin thought. "I agree with my sisters. You spend too many of your hours plucking at your blooms. We learned that we only have you in the winter. This isn't good. We have spoken of it and would like to return to Oxborough. Our brother"—she nodded to Severin—"has agreed to let you have two gardens within the inner bailey."

Severin had agreed to no such thing. He said without hesitation, "It is true, my lady. Your blooms are welcome next to Hastings's. She must needs still learn from you. I saw that her columbine wasn't what it should be. Her lupine isn't as vivid as yours."

Lady Janet looked at each of her daughters in turn. Then she frowned at Hastings, "You, my daughter, are the mistress of Oxborough. I fear I could not settle to be an adjunct to your household. I have controlled Rosehaven entirely for nearly ten years, since your father was not often here. Even when he was here, his mind was not on castle matters. I am used to doing things as I wish them to be done. I am needed here."

The four girls sighed and looked wistfully at Severin and Hastings.

Two days later a compromise was reached. Lady Janet and her daughters would spend the winter months at Oxborough. "After all," Harlette said, "we all flourish in the winter, unlike the flowers. We will have her all to ourselves."

"I want to be with Trist," Normandy said, rubbing her cheek against Trist's chin.

"What about me?" Hastings asked to no one in particular.

"You will have your husband," Severin said. He added to his mother-in-law, "You will wish to be with Hastings when she births our first child this winter."

Lady Janet's eyes widened. She clapped her hands and shouted, "I will have a grandson or granddaughter who will not be named after William the Conqueror or his wife or his mother."

"Mother," Marella said. "I am named after a horse. But I have accepted it. It was William's favorite mare. Father once told me that not only did William love that mare, he always rode her when he visited Matilda. He said that William would say that the mare's scent reminded him of Matilda's."

"How very odd," Hastings said. "Surely he didn't mean it like that."

Marella shrugged. "Father said that Bishop Odo wanted the mare but William would not give her up."

Lady Janet flung out her hands. There was, Severin saw, dirt beneath her fingernails. "Enough, Marella. I just wish Severin to promise me that he will not name his son Odo or Rolf or Grayson, the young man who was William's groom. He came to a very bad end."

"I swear it," Severin said. "What do you say, Hastings?"

"I was thinking more of calling our son Lupine or perhaps Foxglove."

Severin grabbed her and kissed her hard in front of her four sisters and her mother. When he allowed her a breath, Hastings grinned up at him and said, "How do you like Primrose, my lord, if we have a daughter?"

# 30

THERE WASN'T A CLOUD IN THE SKY WHEN DISASTER struck. The air was warm and the breeze from the sea some five miles distant was balmy when the first man fell off his horse, crying out as he clutched his belly.

It was over in minutes. Gwent was the last man to fall, his face contorted, his huge body heaving with pain.

Only Hastings and Severin were left.

The horses neighed, stomping, some of them rearing in fright.

Severin leapt off his horse, running to Gwent. "What happened? What is this, Gwent?"

"I do not know," he said, struggling with the pain, "I do not know." Then his head fell back over Severin's arm. Severin cried out. Hastings was beside him in a moment.

"He's not dead, Severin. Just a moment." She checked the other men. "None are dead, but all are now unconscious. It has to be some sort of poison. It makes no sense. How could they be poisoned and not us?"

Severin sat back on his heels. "I know," he said slowly. "Aye, I know. When we stopped at that village fair, the men all wanted ale. You and I wandered about for a little while and then you wanted to visit the forest nearby. Neither of us ate or drank anything. Just the men."

"But who would do this? Do you think everyone at the fair was struck down?"

"I don't know, but now I am concerned that it will be fatal." He rose, grabbed his horse's reins, and led him off the rutted road, tethering him to a tree. "We must get them all comfortable. Will it hurt the babe if you help me move them, Hastings?"

"Not at all. Let's move quickly."

He let Hastings carry the feet of two men who were too large for him to carry. The others he simply slung over his shoulder. They set up a camp not far off the road beside a small meadow filled with daisies and daffodils.

Hastings came down on her knees to examine Gwent. She raised his eyelids, smelled his breath, felt his heart, pressed her fingers against the pulse in his throat. "I just don't know what it is, Severin."

"I'm certain that my dear Marjorie could tell you, Hastings."

Severin's sword was out of its sheath in an instant, his muscles tensed, ready to fight, but he didn't have the chance. They were surrounded by a dozen men all armed with swords and bows and arrows. In their center was Richard de Luci, his arms crossed over his chest. He looked about at all the unconscious men. He looked amused.

"You're dead," Severin said, staring at the man. "Lord Graelam de Moreton told me you were dead. You slipped on a rabbit bone and struck your head."

"But you never found my body, did you? I heard about that and laughed and laughed. I have wondered what to do about you, Severin of Louges—"

Severin raised his head unconsciously. "I am now the Earl of Oxborough as well."

"Aye, you got to her first." Richard de Luci turned his attention to Hastings, who was kneeling beside Gwent.

"On the contrary," Severin said, his hand tightening about his sword handle, "her father wanted me. Had he wanted you, doubtless he would have asked you. You were never meant to be anything other than what you are."

Suddenly, without warning, de Luci was panting, his face

suffused with rage. "You damned whoreson! That's a lie. The old man was witless. I know that Graelam de Moreton pushed him to select you, aye, I know it well. You, Hastings, should have been wedded to me. I should have become the Earl of Oxborough. All that property, all the farms and villages that belong to you now, Severin. Was that filthy old man as rich as believed?"

"Aye, even richer," Severin said, not moving a muscle, eyeing de Luci closely, seeing the rage diminishing slowly, thinking, thinking.

"Whoreson," de Luci said again, his hand going to his sword. Then he stopped. He shook his head. He appeared a different man now, calm, still, his eyes no longer hungry and dead. He said in a thoughtful voice, "I have thought and thought about this. I reasoned at first that even with you dead, I would gain naught. The king would take Oxborough and all its properties and possessions. He would wed Hastings to another man of his choosing. Even if I were to wed Hastings after I killed you, the king might be angered beyond reason. He might seek retribution. Ah, but I have found the solution to the problem."

"There is no solution. I won Hastings. All is mine. All will remain mine. Everything you reasoned is true. You poisoned my men. Will they live?"

"Aye, why not? Marjorie said it would just bring them low for a day or so. I asked her how she knew so much about poisons. She told me that she read many of Hastings's herbal manuscripts. Well, she read about poisons. I nearly strangled her when I learned from one of my men that she had poisoned you, Hastings. But you escaped death and so did Marjorie.

"You two were to be unconscious as well. Actually, nearly everyone in that village will be vilely ill for a day. We didn't know which ale stall you and your men would visit, so Marjorie had to poison all the ale. It wasn't difficult to do, yet you two escaped. How?"

Hastings looked him straight in the eye. "You are a wicked man. You will gain naught from this save my husband's enmity for the rest of time. I suggest that you flee like the coward you are. King Edward will never allow you back at Sedgewick. You will live and die an outlaw."

"She is right," Severin said. "Why have you attacked us? As you said, it will gain you naught. As for your solution, you haven't one. Why?"

Richard de Luci crossed his arms over his chest. He looked beyond Hastings to the dozen men stretched on their backs, all unconscious, some snorting, some moaning and twitching. They were all covered with their blankets.

"It is difficult," he said slowly, his eyes on Severin again, hatred deep in them. "My Marjorie wants you, Severin. But not just you, of course. She wants Oxborough as well as you. She wants to be a countess. She fears poverty, for her second husband left her with nothing. I have led her on, for she is a fine piece in my bed. Ah, but you, Hastings. I have determined that there is but one road for me to travel, and it will be my solution and my salvation. I will kill Severin, wed you, and take you into hiding until you are with child. I ask you, what would King Edward do then? Kill me, the man who sired the brat in your womb? I don't think so."

"He would kill you," Severin said. "Even if you could weasel your way out of the king's wrath, Lord Graelam de Moreton would kill you."

"Not if I had Hastings, Severin. She is the key to everything. She and her womb."

"You are too late."

"Shut up, Hastings." Severin spoke low, but one of de Luci's men heard her and shouted, "My lord, I don't understand, but she says you are too late."

"Too late for what, Hastings?" Richard de Luci walked toward her, smiling at her, sheathing his sword. "What?"

"I will kill you if you harm Severin. That is why you are too late. I love my husband and I will kill you."

"Ah, so that is it. Well, we will see." De Luci nodded to his men. Their sword tips were on Hastings in but a moment. "Now, my lord Severin," de Luci said, "throw down your sword and your knife and let my men bind your hands."

There was no hope for it. He saw the tip of one man's
sword pressed lightly against Hastings's throat. He would
kill that man. But now, he couldn't do anything. Severin
hated it, but there was no choice. There would be another
time. He would see to that. But not now. Now, de Luci
held control. De Luci took Hastings's arm and pulled her
away from Severin.

"You harm her in any way and I'll kill you."

"My lord Severin, both you and your wife are so taken
with each other. Am I to believe that you want her for more
than the wealth she brought you?"

Severin stared at the man, saying nothing. He wouldn't
give him the satisfaction. De Luci raised his hand. In the
next instant, one of his men brought the butt of his sword
down on Severin's head. He collapsed where he stood. Trist
mewled loudly and slithered from beneath his master.

The men jumped back.

"What is it? It is a weasel!"

"Mayhap it is a Devil's familiar."

"Don't be absurd," Hastings said, all the contempt and
scorn she could muster in her voice, for she didn't want
Trist to be harmed. "He is a marten and a pet. Trist, come
here."

Trist ran to her, climbed her gown, and settled himself
on her shoulder. He raised a paw toward Severin. "It's all
right, Trist. Severin will be all right. Just stay with me."

Trist turned and rubbed his whiskers against her chin.

De Luci said, "Hastings, you may ride your own palfrey.
Let us go."

They left the Oxborough men lying unconscious.

When Severin regained consciousness a short time later,
he found himself tied facedown over his warhorse, his
hands bound behind him. De Luci saw he was conscious
immediately and merely raised his hand to acknowledge
him.

"You may remain thus for a while, my lord. It should
give you a taste of humility." Then he laughed. "No, I
won't kill you, at least not yet. You have your uses, my
lord. Marjorie told me that Hastings was a bitch. I told

Marjorie I would have you ready at hand to torture if Hastings did not perform as I bade her.''

He reined in beside Hastings. He was still laughing.

''You are pathetic,'' she said, staring between Marella's ears.

He was silent in an instant. He said very slowly, with utter calm, ''What did you say to me?''

''I said,'' she repeated, turning now to face him, ''that you are pathetic. You keep your distance, have one of your men strike him down, you tie him to his horse, and now you laugh because he is helpless. I doubt you would ever want to face Severin by yourself. He would kill you very quickly, for you are naught but a puking coward.''

De Luci's face was suffused with rage, then slowly, very slowly, even as his eyes became utterly black, his face paled to white. ''Oh yes, Marjorie said you were a bitch,'' he said slowly. ''I told her that I could control you. It was just a matter of knowing what to do and the exact moment to do it.'' He raised his hand and slapped her hard across her cheek, nearly knocking her off Marella. Trist mewled loudly, barely hanging on.

He saw it in her eyes and yelled at his man, ''Ibac, hold her!''

She was lurching out of her saddle, ready to throw herself on de Luci, when a huge hand grabbed her arm and pulled her back. She moaned with the pain of it, then shut her mouth, furious with herself that she had made a sound. She was panting hard. ''I will get you, you miserable whoreson.''

He didn't hit her again. She saw from the corner of her eye that he was stroking his short beard with his gloved hand.

The rest of de Luci's men were silent. Finally, the man Ibac said low to Hastings, ''You would have thrown yourself upon him had I not stopped you. You have no weapon, you are naught but a woman. Lord Richard is a man of violent and unpredictable actions. He could smile at you one moment and stick a knife in your ribs in the next. He is as calm as a monk, then strikes out like a wild man. I do not understand you.''

Hastings smiled at the man Ibac. ''I see that you speak in a near whisper. You fear this madman?''

''I did not say he was mad,'' Ibac said, his tongue flicking over his dry mouth. ''Nay, never mad. It is simply not wise to anger him. Take care, lady.''

De Luci called a halt just as twilight was darkening to night. The men moved quickly about their tasks.

''Untie him,'' Hastings said, as she moved to stand beside Severin.

De Luci nodded. ''He is sly. Do not let him out of your sight. It matters not that he is bound. Tie him to the tree yon and two of you remain close to watch him.''

Severin thought his stomach would heave out his guts. He stood very still for a moment, regaining his balance and a calm belly. He drew in deep breaths.

''You are all right, my lord?''

He couldn't yet speak. He merely nodded.

Trist jumped from her shoulder to Severin's. He eased himself down into Severin's tunic.

It was dark, the only light coming from the fire, when one of the men handed Hastings a piece of roasted rabbit. Hastings thanked him and offered it to Severin.

''Nay,'' he said. ''You carry my babe. Feed him.''

''I will feed the father first. Open your mouth.''

After she'd fed him his fill, she simply looked at the man Ibac and then at the flaming pieces of rabbit still roasting over the fire.

She fed Trist, who looked distinctly unhappy, then ate two pieces, each burned black, each tasting delicious. ''I'm sorry, Trist. I know you do not care for rabbit, but it is not such a bad taste, is it?''

The marten was cleaning his face. He merely looked at her a moment and went back to his bath. Hastings couldn't help it. She laughed. ''He is insulted,'' she said to Severin. ''Insulted.''

Severin laughed as well. He didn't know there could possibly be any laughter anywhere in his body, but there was.

De Luci looked over at them, frowning. He opened his mouth, then closed it. He resumed eating and speaking to several of his men, one of them Ibac.

Hastings told Severin what the man had said to her. He didn't seem to hear her, just stared at her a moment, then said in a low, utterly enraged voice, "How dare you, Hastings. By Saint Peter's staff, you could have killed yourself, he could have struck you—"

"I didn't think," she said, splaying her hands in front of her. "He is mad, at least he is uncontrolled, and surely that must play to our advantage."

He looked at her oddly, wishing he could touch her, wishing he could pull her against him and press her face against his heart. He swallowed, looking away. De Luci could not allow him to live. He must think of something, and yet here was Hastings, speaking of their advantage. "You are right," he said quietly. "We must determine how to exploit this weakness of his."

"I will control myself," she said with such utter conviction that once again Severin laughed.

De Luci yelled, "Get her away from the whoreson. Bring her to me."

Hastings slowly rose when one of the men came to her. "It is all right, Severin. I will control myself and I will learn what he is planning."

But she didn't learn a thing. He gave her a cup of ale and she was thirsty. She didn't think, just drank from the cup. In moments, she sagged to the ground.

She didn't know that Severin, drinking from the same cup before her, was also unconscious, Trist patting his face, staying close to warm him.

Hastings awoke to see Eloise staring down at her, her thin face as blank as a death mask, her eyes opaque and dull.

"You didn't die."

"No, I did not. We are at Sedgewick, Eloise?"

"Aye, my father brought you and Lord Severin here. My father was worried when you did not wake up. Lord Severin yelled and screamed, but it did no good. My father merely cuffed him with his sword. But now you are awake. I will call Marjorie."

"Eloise?"

The child turned slowly, as if she didn't want to.

"Your father is planning to kill Lord Severin and—"

"Ah, Hastings, you are awake and already trying to talk someone over to your side. Eloise, my sweeting, fetch a cup of milk from the kitchen. It will clean out Hastings's insides. Your father doesn't want her to die just yet."

"Marjorie, how pleasant to see you."

"Be quiet, Hastings." Marjorie said nothing more until Eloise was gone from the small bedchamber. "Listen to me. I did not realize what Richard planned. I merely wanted you gone so that I could have Severin. But Richard wants Oxborough and the only way he can gain all that wealth is to wed you."

Hastings marveled at her. "That makes no sense, Marjorie. You knew that de Luci wanted Oxborough. The only way he could have it was to kill Severin. You would have realized that if you had but used that brain of yours that must lie beneath that beautiful hair."

Marjorie was silent for a very long time. Finally, she nodded, saying, "Aye, I suppose I did know it, but you see, he promised me, Hastings. He promised he wouldn't kill Severin. He promised he would give Severin to me and a lot of gold so that we could live in France."

"But Severin would still be the lord of Oxborough."

"Not if—"

"De Luci will kill him. I care not about myself. If you can, save Severin. Take him to France. Take him anywhere, just save him."

Marjorie gave her a twisted smile. "You are weak, Hastings, begging me to save Severin. I doubt he would beg me to save you. Have you not seen that men are greedy creatures? They think only of themselves, only how to make themselves more important. But Severin, I had believed he was different. Aye, he wanted all your father's possessions, but only because he wanted to save his father's devastated lands and keep and take care of that miserable mad mother of his.

"But now I see that he has changed. He has grown accustomed to the power that wedding you brought him. He will become as greedy and selfish as the rest of them."

"He is not selfish and you know it, Marjorie. Now, why did you not tell de Luci that I carried Severin's child?"

Marjorie shrugged. "I started to, then changed my mind. It is something he doesn't know. Perhaps I will find a way to make use of it. I don't have much of anything, but that is something. I know you will not tell him."

"Stop this blindness, Marjorie. Just stop it. De Luci intends to kill Severin. If he doesn't, then he will have no chance of ever gaining anything."

"Do not be too certain of that," Marjorie said. "There are other ways."

Hastings started to demand what she meant when Ibac suddenly appeared in the doorway. "The child fetched me. My lord told me the moment Lady Hastings recovered she was to come to the great hall." He gave Hastings a worried look. "Can you walk? Shall I carry you?"

Hastings shook her head and slowly, very slowly, rose, swinging her legs over the side of the bed. She was dizzy, but it was passing. She felt weak and wondered how long she had been unconscious. Eloise appeared in the doorway, a goblet in her hand.

Marjorie took the goblet and gave it to Hastings. "It will give you strength. Drink it."

"More poison, Marjorie?"

Ibac sucked in his breath, staring at the beautiful silver-haired woman with consternation. Like every other man-at-arms, he'd looked at her as he would look at a statue of the Virgin Mary, with reverent awe. What was this about poison? No, surely the Lady Hastings was wrong.

Marjorie said nothing, merely smiled as Hastings drank from the goblet. It was goat's milk, sweet and strong. She felt strength flowing back into her body. Trist, who had been lying beside her, now jumped onto her shoulder.

Ibac stayed close, his hand up, ready to steady her, but

Hastings wasn't going to collapse. No, she was thinking
furiously. Severin had to be all right. She had to think of
a way to save him.

The great hall of Sedgewick had blackened beams,
greasy, scarred trestle tables, benches that were so filthy
she didn't want to sit on one. The rushes smelled stale. The
vague odor of urine hung in the air. A half dozen wolfhounds lay in the matted rushes near the huge fireplace.
How long had Richard de Luci been here? More than a
week, she guessed, for everything to be so filthy and neglected. Sir Alan would have never allowed that.

In the lord's chair sat Richard de Luci.

She called out, "Where is Sir Alan?"

De Luci merely smiled at her. "In the dungeon with your
husband and his men that were here at Sedgewick. A pity
he didn't die of the sweating sickness, but he survived intact. He hasn't enjoyed my dungeon. Come here now, Hastings, and let me look at you."

She didn't want to get near him, but Ibac's hand was
nudging against her back and she was forced forward.

"You look like a witch. You smell like the wolfhounds."

She looked around with contempt, then turned back and
said, "If I were forced to remain here with you and Marjorie in charge, I should smell as vile as this great hall
within a week. Be thankful I will be gone long before that
happens."

Richard de Luci leapt from his chair and strode to her,
his fist raised. "You damnable bitch!"

He was shaking he was so furious. Ibac sucked in his
breath and stepped in front of her. "She is still weak and
ill, my lord. She will become more submissive as she regains her wits."

Hastings believed that de Luci would kill Ibac, but at the
last moment, he pulled back his fist.

"Bring Lord Severin. I would tell him what is going to
happen."

Marjorie was standing silently, staring at Richard de
Luci. Eloise was, Hastings saw, hiding beneath one of the
trestle tables. Had her father abused her again?

"I have been wondering," de Luci said slowly, looking at Hastings's breasts, "if I should rape you in front of Severin. Think you that he would even bother looking if he had Marjorie in his arms at the same time?"

# 31

HASTINGS DIDN'T PAUSE, THOUGH THE PAIN THAT IMAGE brought lanced through her. She said without hesitation and with perfect honesty, "I do not know. But know this, de Luci, if you touch me, I will kill you." She heard Ibac moan behind her. She had no time to move. De Luci was on her in a moment. He backhanded her, knocking her onto the filthy rushes. He raised his foot to kick her, then leaned down and grabbed her arm, jerking her upright again.

"You will not speak to me like that again, my lady." He grabbed the front of her gown and jerked it outward. The soft wool parted easily. He grunted at the sight of her shift beneath, grabbed it, and ripped it.

"I had not believed you would be so well endowed," he said, staring at her. He reached out his hand to cup her breast. "Marjorie told me you were nothing compared to her. How odd that she would lie to me. I will have to speak to her about that. Women are meant to obey."

"Don't touch me."

"If you move, I will strip you naked right here in front of all my men."

She felt his fingers lightly touch her breast.

Severin yowled louder than Edgar the wolfhound. "Take your hand off her or I'll kill you!"

Richard de Luci turned, smiling. "Ah, you have brought him. Now that we are all together, and my poor Marjorie has seen that her beloved prefers his wife to her charms, mayhap she will not be too distressed when she learns that you are to die."

Marjorie quivered, Hastings saw it. Mayhap Marjorie could save Severin. She'd spoken of those other things, whatever that meant. De Luci turned his attention to Severin. Slowly, Hastings raised her hand to pull the rent material over her breasts. She wanted no more of Richard de Luci's attention until she was ready. He turned to walk back to his chair. He paused a moment, seeing Eloise cowering beneath a trestle table. He said very softly, "Come out, Eloise, or it will go badly for you."

The child slithered from beneath the table.

"Stand up."

Eloise managed to lock her knees and stood.

"You look like your miserable mother, your face all pale and gaunt, your hair thin and ugly. I would have gotten Hastings if your mother had not taken so long to die." Quick rage deadened his eyes. He calmly raised his hand and slapped Eloise so hard that she was hurled a good six feet, only to land against one of the wolfhounds.

"No!" Marjorie was at the child's side in an instant, touching her, clutching her to her breasts, stroking her hair.

Hastings said, "I wonder which man or woman will kill you. We will have to wager to see who will win the honor of sending you to hell."

"All you can speak about is violence? You believe you or your husband over there can kill me? You bore me with all these threats—all the same. I know they are empty. When I take you, you will see how helpless you are." De Luci sank down into his lord's chair. "I am hungry. It is time for the evening meal."

Hastings realized that his violence against Eloise had temporarily relieved him of his rage. He terrified her. "I want you bathed and perfumed for me. Marjorie has told me that you have all sorts of herbs and perfumes. You will set about to please me, Hastings, or I will kill this whoreson husband of yours without another moment passing."

"I will please you," Hastings said, and now, for the first time, she looked at her husband. Severin was standing between two of Lord Richard's men, his hands bound behind him. He was dirty, his clothes ripped, but they hadn't beaten him. She continued to stare at him, praying he would not respond to her words. Severin said nothing. He kept his eyes on Richard de Luci, not on her.

Severin said, even as he began to move his fingers, to regain feeling, to step from one leg to the other, to gain strength, "Do your men know that they will all die if you continue with your madness?"

"My men are loyal to me," Lord Richard said, but he stared hard at Ibac, who stood at Severin's right elbow. "They will follow my commands even to hell if need be."

"It will need be," Severin said. "I can promise you that."

Hastings saw the rage rising again in de Luci. Severin was helpless. He could not protect himself. She quickly stepped forward, her fingers lightly touching de Luci's sleeve.

Unfortunately when he turned to look at her, she didn't know what to say. She wanted to kill him, but surely it wouldn't be wise to tell him that. Not again.

"I am thirsty," she said. "I would like some wine."

De Luci relented, then called to a plump girl who was standing in the shadows, "Bring the wine. Do not add water to it or I will slit your dirty throat. If you dare to steal a drink, I will also know, for I will smell your breath."

He turned back to Hastings, catching sight of his daughter, still in Marjorie's arms. "Why do you comfort the scrap? She is as evil as her mother ever was. She will turn on you in time, Marjorie. I have told you that. Even though she is young, she is evil."

Hastings thought if Eloise had any evil in her it had to have come from her father. She looked at Severin. She could tell by the darkness of his eyes that he was thinking furiously. But what could any of them do?

Then Hastings knew. She would have to kill de Luci, or

die trying, otherwise Severin would be killed. She shook
her head even as she thought it. No, she would never let
that happen.

When Hastings was sipping the sour wine the servant
girl had brought, she watched other servants bring in platters of food for the late afternoon dinner. Men-at-arms came
into the great hall, shuffling and silent, none of them looking toward their lord. Ibac moved Severin to a table and
let him sit on the long bench. Then, to Hastings's surprise,
he untied his hands so he could feed himself.

She saw the leap of surprise on Severin's face as well,
then the utter joy, quickly masked. She felt calm flow
through her.

The roasted wild boar steaks were dry and stiff as Marella's new saddle, the onions and cabbage were mushy and
had no salt. The bread was grainy. Hastings hoped de Luci
would choke on it, but he ate with enthusiasm, his entire
attention on his trencher.

Severin ate slowly, feeling the food, as bad as it was,
give him needed strength. No sooner had he drained his
mug than de Luci yelled, "Bind him again. I trust him
not."

He had no chance, for de Luci had pulled a dagger from
his belt and held it to Hastings's breast. At least he had
feeling back in his hands. It would take a while for the tight
ropes to numb them again.

He couldn't stop looking at Hastings. De Luci had lowered the knife, but he was looking at the torn material over
her breasts. Once he reached toward her, but withdrew his
hand when Marjorie said something to him, something
about the child. De Luci laughed. Severin wondered about
Gwent and his men. He prayed they would survive, that
outlaws wouldn't find them and kill them. Gwent would
realize soon enough who it was who had taken them. There
was no one else except de Luci. He would reason quickly
enough that de Luci must have survived. Then Gwent
would know they were here at Sedgewick. If he was able,
he would come.

It darkened in the hall. Candles were lit, but the shadows

in the corners were thick and black. It became quickly colder after the sun set. Soon de Luci rose and stretched. He said to Marjorie, "You will attend me tonight for a final time." He yelled down to Severin, "I know you bedded her when you were but a lad. She is still beyond beautiful. I like her to lie on her back, her hair spread all about her white body. Aye, she pleases me, but not as much as Hastings will." He leaned down to grab Marjorie and kissed her hard on her mouth. Eloise cried out.

De Luci straightened, his fist held out toward his daughter. "Be quiet, you little halfwit. By Saint George's toes, you offend me. Go to my chamber, Marjorie, and prepare yourself whilst I speak to my future bride."

He had changed his mind. Hastings kept her face blank, but it was difficult. He was slippery, so very unpredictable. She knew she wouldn't bathe or change her gown or brush her hair unless forced to.

Marjorie merely nodded. She and Eloise left the hall. De Luci stared about, looking very pleased with himself. "Aye," he said, belching, "I will enjoy the first woman you bedded, Severin. Would you like to see me take Marjorie? She swore to me that you hadn't bedded her at Oxborough. Is that true, I wonder? I can't imagine a man not taking her if she asked for it.

"No matter. Then I will take your wife. She is not as beautiful as Marjorie, but her possessions make her beyond what any man could wish for. I wonder if she will struggle once I begin caressing her. Most women cease struggling quickly. Will Hastings? We will see.

"Then, my fine lord, I will kill you. It will make a fitting ending to the week."

He didn't believe her, Hastings thought, staring at him. He believed he could rape her with impunity. He was mad. She said, "I would speak to my husband."

De Luci laughed. "I think not, my lady." To Ibac, he said, "Take him back to the dungeon. He has eaten his fill. Hastings sees that I do not torture or starve him. Now I fancy she knows that I will if she does fight me. Aye, Hastings, I will keep him alive to ensure that you cooperate with me.''

Hastings saw Trist slither inside Severin's tunic as he slowly rose. She had never been so afraid in her life. It was a suffocating fear that numbed her brain. All she could see was Severin, bound, pushed in front of two soldiers from the hall.

She lay on the narrow bed, smelling the dead air, wishing for just a single window, but there wasn't one. There were no rushes on the stone floor, which relieved her. They would be as foul as the ones in the hall.

Ibac had left her unbound, but the door was locked, and it was the only way out.

She lightly caressed her belly. There was a slight curve now, and she smiled, despite her numbing fear. Their babe was within and he was growing. She desperately wanted him to live, to know both her and his father.

De Luci had forced her to bathe. He'd said, "If I still need relief after I have taken Marjorie, I will come to you, Hastings. I want you prepared for me." She was wearing a clean night shift, one that de Luci had taken from Marjorie's trunk. It only came to the top of her thighs. Her hair was nearly dry now, spread about her head.

When the door rattled, she thought she'd faint. Dear God, de Luci was here. No, it was so very late now. Surely he wouldn't come, not this late. There was nothing she could use to protect herself. Nothing.

Her only chance was surprise. She forced herself to lie perfectly still on her back, her eyes tightly closed.

She heard the door open slowly, felt the narrow shaft of light slice through the darkness in the small chamber.

Her hands were fists at her sides. She couldn't seem to swallow. She wanted to scream and hurl herself at him at the same time. No, no, she had to wait, she had to be patient. She had to gain an advantage.

Then, suddenly, his hand came over her mouth. She tried to lurch up but couldn't move.

Then she heard the most beautiful voice in the world

whispering next to her ear, "Hold still, Hastings, and I will get you out of here."

"Severin?"

"Aye, I'm here. I am your knight. Finally, I am going to rescue you as a knight should a damsel."

She nodded as she stared up at him. "I love you, Severin. I was so frightened. Aye, you are my knight."

"Trist would not let me leave you." He smiled down at her, quickly kissed her, and lifted her from the bed.

He stood by the chamber door as she pulled on her old, dirty clothing. "Can we not kill him whilst we are here?"

He shook his head. "I would like to but I cannot risk you, Hastings. He has three of his men guarding his bedchamber. I cannot risk our babe. Come now."

Trist poked his head out of Severin's tunic and batted his paw at her.

"He is in a hurry. He knows since he released me that de Luci will want to kill him as well."

"That is why Trist left me to go to you."

"Aye, he chewed through the ropes on my wrists. I have released Alan and his twelve men as well. They will come with us, though it will be difficult. They are sick and weak. Several have died. If they were able, we would fight, but they are not."

Hastings could not imagine how Severin would get them all free of Sedgewick, but she said nothing. "Be my shadow," he said over his shoulder.

At least thirty men were sleeping in the hall, wrapped in their blankets, snoring as loudly as the wolfhounds.

Hastings had never before in her life wondered about silence, but now it was all she could think of. They could not make a sound. If one of the soldiers awoke, all would be lost.

When Severin reached the wide double doors, he turned and motioned her to follow him. He led her down a narrow corridor and opened a short, thick door. It led into a small granary. There was another door.

Once they were in the inner bailey, pressed against the side of the keep, deep in the shadows, he whispered, "I learned everything about Sedgewick when I gave it over to Sir Alan. He and his men should be within the stables just beyond. Then we will lead the horses through the postern gate.''

''But the horses—''

''I know. Alan has told all his men to hold their nostrils so they won't neigh. We need luck in this, Hastings.''

And she thought: I have you, what need I of luck?

But she was soon to change her mind. She heard a man shout.

Severin simply pressed her behind him, whispered for her to stay close. He raced toward the single scream. Just inside the stable door a man was on his knees, Sir Alan over him, a dagger pressed against his neck.

''The fool screamed. I will kill him.'' With no more words, the knife went into the man's throat. He gurgled loudly, then fell onto his side.

''The other stable lads are bound and gagged. Let us go, my lord, and quickly. My lady, I am glad to see you well.''

Hastings followed Severin, her fingers securely fastened against Marella's nostrils. She kept tossing her head, but Hastings knew that one neigh might do them all in. She didn't know how she did it, but she kept hold.

Slowly, it took so very long for them to go through the postern gate in a single line. Many of the men were staggering with illness but they knew now that they had a chance to live. None fell. None spoke. They all just moved slowly forward, one after the other, until Sir Alan, the last man through the postern gate, turned and quietly closed it.

Still they walked the horses until Severin raised a hand. ''Quietly,'' he called out. ''Quietly.''

He lifted Hastings onto Marella's bare back, then swung onto his stallion. The moment the horses' nostrils were released, three animals neighed loudly.

''Onward!'' Severin shouted.

They were away. They rode hard until the horses were lathered and panting. Severin then called a halt. ''All of you remain here, rest your mounts.'' He nodded to Sir Alan and they rode back along the narrow rutted wagon trail.

Hastings was patting Marella's neck, speaking softly to her and telling her how brave she was, when Severin pulled his horse beside hers. "No one follows. By now de Luci must know of our escape. But he isn't a complete fool. He knows that we can reach Oxborough before he can catch up to us."

He leaned over, kissed her hard, then patted his palm to her cheek. "You have done well, wife," he said, then kicked his stallion in his heavy sides.

They were safely within Oxborough's gates before dawn.

It wasn't until they were in the great hall that they discovered that someone else from Sedgewick had escaped with them.

# 32

"MY LORD," LOTHAR SAID, STEPPING FORWARD, "I HAVE something to tell you."

Severin, tired, hungry, and so weary he wanted to lie down beside Edgar the wolfhound, turned to the large burly soldier who was one of Sir Alan's trusted men. "Aye, what is it, Lothar?"

"You see that I am very healthy, my lord, my three friends as well. It is not because of chance that this is so. It is because of something entirely different, something that I ask you think about carefully before—"

"Speak, man!"

"Lord Severin, Lothar brought me with him."

Eloise came from behind one of the other men. She was dressed like a little boy.

"She saved us, my lord. Before Lord Richard came upon us with stealth, the child was friendly to me. When I was thrown into the dungeon, she brought me food. I shared the food with the men close enough to me that I could reach them. We all survived. We are well. Eloise couldn't feed all the men else de Luci would suspect."

Hastings walked slowly to Eloise, pulled back the coarse woolen hood. She smoothed the child's braids. She lightly ran her fingertips over her thin cheeks.

"I do not understand, Eloise. Come drink some milk and eat, then you will tell Lord Severin and me everything."

Eloise spoke even as she stuffed MacDear's sweet white bread into her mouth. "He told Marjorie he would kill me if she did not do just as he said. He hurt her as much as he hurt me. She tried to protect me. I thought if I left, then he could not force her."

Lady Moraine, who was pressed tightly against her son, afraid to let him go to the jakes by himself for fear he would disappear, said, "I will take care of you, Eloise, but you must promise me something."

The child was chewing more slowly now on a piece of mutton. She nodded.

"You will not treat Hastings badly."

Eloise bowed her head. When she looked up, Trist was sitting on the trestle table in front of her. He reached out his paw and patted the back of her thin hand.

Eloise burst into tears, sobbing and hiccuping. "I want Marjorie!"

Hastings looked toward Severin, who was chewing a big hunk of yellow sweet cheese. She didn't like this one bit. Now she had to feel sorry for Marjorie? That damnable witch with the black insides? It was not to be borne. "We have to rescue her?" she said, barely above a whisper.

"I will think about that," Severin said.

Lady Moraine looked up at Hastings, then drew the child to her. She rocked her against her. Then she pressed her back at arm's length. "It is difficult, Eloise, for anyone to want to help her. Marjorie tried to poison Hastings."

"No, no, she did not." Eloise brushed her hand over her eyes. She drew back her shoulders and took a deep breath. "It was I who put the powder in Hastings's wine. And it wasn't poison. It wouldn't have killed her. I just wanted to punish her for making Marjorie's nose grow large and red. Marjorie knew but she took the blame for me."

"I really don't like this," Hastings said.

Severin was on his feet. "I don't either. As I said, I will think about all this. I must go now, Hastings."

"To find Gwent and our men?"

"Aye, I have prayed myself numb. They have to be alive. They have to be. When we are all together again, then we will make plans."

She did not demand to accompany him. In truth she was exhausted, the babe making her nearly dizzy with fatigue. "You will be home soon," she said a short time later when she stood in the outer bailey, waiting for all the men to mount.

"Aye, as quickly as possible. Sir Alan will take care of Oxborough. If Richard de Luci tries treachery, he will not succeed. You will consider Oxborough under siege until I return."

She nodded, stood on her tiptoes, and wrapped her arms about his neck. "Be careful, Severin."

He brought her close, his breath warm against her hair. "We will get through this, Hastings. You will see."

"I know," she said, and kissed him. "I know," she said again against his open mouth. She felt a shudder go through him and kissed him yet again.

He stepped back, his breathing quick and hard. He smiled down at her, his eyes dark and vibrant. "I have sent a man to Lord Graelam de Moreton in Cornwall. God knows how long it will take for him to come, or even if he is able to come."

"He will come. Will you send a messenger to the king?"

Severin shook his head. "No, I don't wish to take a chance on Edward's whim. I want Richard de Luci killed before any learn that he is still alive. All will be as we believed it to be before the madman came back from the dead."

"My lord," Sir Alan said, striding up to Severin, who was now holding Hastings in the circle of his arms. "Our messengers to your other keeps are well on their way. Men will begin arriving within two days. I doubt we will need Graelam de Moreton."

"I know," Severin said, pulling Hastings against him once more, as he could not prevent himself from doing so. "It is just that I promised him. He told me if I did not and he heard that I was ever in grave danger, he would stake me out in the middle of a practice field and ride his war-horse over me." He kissed Hastings's nose, then grinned at Alan. "I believe him. I am not a fool."

Hastings laughed. It felt wonderful to laugh, even for a moment.

"I must go. Take care of our babe and Alan will see to your safety."

He slammed his fist into Sir Alan's shoulder, all in good humor, and said something low to him that Hastings could not hear. Sir Alan nodded solemnly. Severin waved yet again to Hastings and strode to his warhorse. Hastings watched him leap gracefully astride.

"God be with you, my lord," she called. He waved at her and was soon outside the massive Oxborough gates. She ran to the sturdy wooden ladder that led up to the ramparts. She watched him until he was gone from her sight.

When Alice came to her later, Hastings was on her knees beside a man whose belly was so shriveled he could only keep MacDear's lightest broth down without vomiting. She looked up, her head cocked to one side. Alice looked utterly bewildered.

"I do not believe this, Hastings."

"What is it?" She was on her feet in an instant. "What has happened?"

"We have a visitor. She has never come here. She has never left her cottage. All know she is a recluse. Yet she is here demanding to see you."

Hastings turned to see the Healer walk briskly into the great hall. She was wearing shoes. Hastings's own mouth dropped open at the sight of her.

The Healer waved everyone away, said nothing at all to anyone, and quickly knelt down beside a sick man. She continued silent, merely grunted at some of them, shook her head at one man who was already unconscious, and actually pinched another man's wrist who just happened to grin up at her.

"Where is Alfred?" Hastings asked for want of anything better. She was as bewildered as Alice.

"My beauty is sleeping soundly in the sun. I left him a roasted chicken if he awakes and is hungry."

"He is always hungry, Healer."

"Aye, he deserves to be, not like these louts sprawled about in your great hall, Hastings. Well, I've done what I can for them. The man yon will die soon. I cannot help him. The others will survive with your care."

"Healer, how did you know we needed you?"

Hastings stared at the Healer as the woman looked down at her long fingers, twisting the odd gold ring about on her finger, a magic ring perhaps, one older than England itself.

"Healer?"

Her braids flew as she raised her head. "Bedamned to you, Hastings! Where is Gwent? I had prayed he would be here, but he is not. Where is he?"

Gwent? The Healer despised men. All knew it. Gwent?

Hastings noticed for the first time that the Healer did not look quite like the ragged woman that she normally did. No, her gown was a soft yellow, she was wearing leather slippers, her thick, long hair was braided loosely and tied with a yellow ribbon. She looked remarkably young.

"My son has gone to find him and another dozen of our men," Lady Moraine said.

"He is a man but surely he would not lose himself apurpose."

"No, he and all the other men were drugged," Hastings said. "Richard de Luci swore that it would not kill them. But he captured us and we were forced to leave all of them unconscious on the ground. Severin is very worried. We will know by the end of the week."

"That dim-cockled lout," the Healer muttered to herself. "I warned him that this journey to Rosehaven would bring him low, but would he listen to me? Does any man ever listen? No, the cocky little bittle sticks just strut about and expect all to transpire as they wish it to. I told him not to go. Even Alfred jumped on him and tried to hold him down."

Hastings could but stare at her. "But you did not tell me

that the journey would bring me low, Healer. Yet you told Gwent. What is this?''

''I did not know about you, Hastings. You are here, after all, standing in front of me all smiling and well, and Gwent is likely in some dungeon somewhere rotting like a meat under maggots. By the Devil's shins, I will make the overgrown pus-head regret this once he returns.''

''Saint Catherine's eyebrows,'' Lady Moraine gasped, staring at the Healer, ''I see the truth now. You are besotted. You are acting just like Hastings does with my son. You and Gwent. But how can that be? He hates Alfred. I suspect he even fears him. He jumps whenever the cat leaps at him.''

The Healer's chin went up. Hastings saw that her neck was firm. No, the Healer wasn't old at all. Certainly no older than Lady Moraine or Hastings's own mother. ''Gwent now has great affection for Alfred. Alfred even once sat on Gwent's legs whilst he ate some of my special broth. Alfred did not try to steal the broth. There is now a bond between them. That miserable crockhead.''

''Healer,'' Alice said, ''Alfred would steal the meat off your plate. Surely he would not show pity to Gwent?''

The Healer turned on Alice. ''You will not talk about my tender Alfred like that. He is a sweeting. It is Gwent that is a hulking cretin, so sure of himself and his prowess that he must needs follow Lord Severin. Now he will die in a dungeon, rotting.''

''But I thought you hated men,'' Lady Moraine said.

''Of course I do,'' the Healer said, staring darkly at Lady Moraine. ''They are all useless, windy bladders, concerned only with themselves. But you, lady, you blather nonsense. You will say no more about it. I will leave now. I will return tomorrow to see if there is any news. That lackwitted oxhead had better return to Oxborough well enough so that I can fix him.''

Without another word, the Healer marched out of the great hall, everyone staring after her, even one man who was too weak a moment before to raise his head.

"Well," Hastings said, shaking her head, "this is a remarkable thing."

"Aye," said Alice, "more than remarkable. Gwent kept his distance from me when I told him I would consider bedding him and giving him a man's pleasure. He did not seem interested. Well, he was interested, but something held him back. I could not understand him. By the Devil's horns, does the wind blow that way?" She just shook her head and carried a mug of milk to one of the ill men, saying a silent prayer now for Beamis, who rode with Lord Severin.

Hastings was laughing even as she lightly rubbed her palm over her belly.

Within two days fifty men from Severin's other keeps had arrived at Oxborough.

"We will starve if they long remain," MacDear said as he stirred a giant caldron of stewed pheasant with cabbage, onions, and leeks.

Steam curled up about his massive head, wreathing him in gray mist.

"I will tell them they can only eat every other day," Hastings said, poked his huge arm, and returned to the great hall. The sick men were nearly well, the one man who had died shortly after the Healer had come had been buried in the Oxborough graveyard.

Sir Alan was dealing well with the three castellans, drawing Sedgewick keep on a large square of parchment so they could see what they would face as soon as Lord Severin returned.

The Healer returned the morning of the third day.

"I am sorry, Healer, but there is no word. But Severin said I was not to worry. He will bring them back safely."

"He is a man. His horse brings him back, not his small brain. Gwent's brain is even more shriveled. I will grind borla root and stir it into his ale. It will make his toes numb and his manhood as flaccid as the onions in MacDear's soup. I will tell my sweet Alfred to grant him the weight of all his affection."

Hastings was holding her stomach she was laughing so hard. "But Healer, if he is flaccid, then what pleasure is there for you?"

"You speak like that silver-haired bitch, failing to give me proper honor and respect."

"Oh nay, never that. Please remain, Healer. Please."

But the Healer had already turned on her heel. She raised a hand, but did not turn around.

Hastings was not laughing that afternoon as she lay in her bed, the cover pulled to her chin, staring up into the darkness. She could hear the wind howling, feel the coldness of it in her bones even though she was warm.

She missed Severin. She was afraid for him. What was happening?

Sir Alan had sent a dozen men to camp in the woods near Sedgewick to keep watch and report back if Richard de Luci did anything untoward. Another dozen men followed the route back to where Gwent and the other men had lain unconscious. The remainder were guarding Oxborough as if it were the king's residence.

As for Eloise, she did not leave Lady Moraine. She was pale and silent, a little ghost who missed that damnable Marjorie.

Hastings turned onto her side. Severin had wanted a curve in her belly—just a slight curve to please him, he'd told her—and now she had one for him to feel. She wanted his hand pressing lightly against her.

Suddenly, the bedchamber door burst open and Lady Moraine flew into the room, shouting, "They're back!"

# 33

"WHERE THE DEVIL IS GWENT?" SEVERIN ASKED AS HE strode into the great hall, Sir Alan by his side. "Alart told me he was riding into Pevensey Forest just a bit ago. Why would he leave? Where is he?"

Lady Moraine said with great composure, "He is visiting Alfred."

"What? That is unlikely, Mother. He is terrified of that beast."

"Very well, then, it is the Healer he visits."

"Why? He is well, he swore it to me. Come, Hastings, my mother is jesting with me. What is going on?"

"Gwent and the Healer are in love."

He stared at her, brought to an utter and complete silence. Then he began shaking his head. He reached inside his tunic and pulled Trist out. He began to stroke the marten's chin. Trist mewled. Severin just stood there, staring at nothing in particular.

"What is this?" Sir Alan asked, accepting a goblet of ale from Alice.

"The Healer hates men," Severin said finally.

"Mayhap that's true. You should have heard her cursing Gwent. She called him names that I have never even heard you use, Severin."

Severin shook his head, stuffed Trist back down into his tunic, and called out to his three castellans, "Everyone quench his thirst. We have a lot of talking to do before we leave in the morning."

It was only after he had settled all the men that he came to Hastings. He pulled her against him, saying nothing, just held her, his cheek against her hair. Hastings felt Trist between them. She said against his throat, "Truly, Gwent and all the men were in the forest near to Sedgewick?"

"Aye, they were trying to decide how to come inside to rescue me. They didn't know that I was no longer at Sedgewick. None suffered anything save watery bowels and headaches from the drug. Hastings, does Gwent really have tender feelings for the Healer?"

"I believe so. Do you believe he will live in the forest with her?"

"I still cannot believe it. Do not ask me such a question. Do we have any food left?"

She laughed, pulling back in the circle of his arms. Trist stuck his head out of Severin's tunic and mewled at her. "It is good that we will kill de Luci soon. All MacDear can talk about is that we will starve during the winter."

He pulled her again against him. Trist slithered out and wound himself around Severin's neck. "Severin?" Hastings said against his chin.

"Aye?"

"How will we kill de Luci?"

"I have decided to take Sedgewick. He has only twenty men at most. It should not take long with the men I have. I hope Graelam doesn't come with me, for we will have no need for them."

"And will you try to save Marjorie?"

He sighed, kissing her ear. "You know, Hastings, she is guilty only of wanting me. I am a brave knight, a man of fine parts, a man who gives of himself to a woman even when he is not completely aware of all his giving. I am magnificent in battle. Can you blame her for still desiring me beyond all reason?"

She had no leverage, but she tried. She shoved her fist

against his belly. He grunted for her, but his laughter didn't stop. "What do you say if I have her marry Sir Alan? With the king's approval, of course."

"Her silvery hair would still be very close to Oxborough."

"I prefer a wench with hair with so many shades I still have not managed to count all of them. Look at this—it's the color of dirt. Isn't that interesting?"

"My lord."

"Aye, Beamis? Speak, man. My wife here is bereft of words. It is unexpected, but I bask in it for the seconds it will last."

"My lord, you are jesting. All are wondering what will happen and here you are, jesting."

"Beamis, I will tighten my jaw very soon now. We will have our evening meal, then we will all come to agreement on Sedgewick."

"Come away, Beamis," Alice said, dragging at his tunic sleeve. "Leave them be. They are newly married—well, not that newly—and they wish to play for just a moment. Why don't you come with me and I will show you what this play is all about."

To Hastings's surprise, Beamis turned his ugly face upon Alice, found something akin to a smile, and gave her his hand. "Not too much play," they heard him say to her. "Lord Severin must have my head clear so that I may give him superior council."

Trist waved his paw after them.

When Severin and his soldiers arrived at Sedgewick the following afternoon, the keep was deserted. There were but a few servants milling about, a very old porter who scratched his bald head and muttered about the blackness of men's hearts, and a dozen chickens who were squawking loudly because they hadn't been fed. Children and women were nowhere to be seen.

Severin turned to Sir Alan as they came to a halt in the inner bailey.

"He is gone," Gwent called out. "He and all his men

are gone. The old porter tells me he rode out yesterday.''

"Was Lady Marjorie with him?''

"Aye, she was. Riding beside him, pale as an angel, the old man said.''

"Where would he go?'' Severin said aloud. Then he realized that he had left only twenty soldiers at Oxborough. Only twenty, but still it was enough. The gates were closed and barred. No one unknown could enter, no one.

Severin remembered that day so long before when two of de Luci's men had managed to get into the inner bailey. He had been stabbed in Hastings's herb garden. No, Beamis had orders. No one unknown would be allowed into Oxborough.

Still he worried. He worried more when they questioned some farmers on the return route to Oxborough and discovered that de Luci had come this way.

Severin cursed, plowing his fingers through his hair.

"My lord,'' Sir Alan said, ''de Luci can do nothing.''

"He is mad and he is smart. I don't trust him.''

"I hope he has not harmed Marjorie,'' Sir Alan said, and all could see that he was smitten.

They rode hard back to Oxborough.

"Please show me where the Healer lives, Hastings. My belly hurts and Lady Moraine told me that the Healer could make even a dying pig well again.''

"We can't leave Oxborough right now, Eloise,'' Hastings said, coming down to the little girl's eye level. "Lord Severin wants us to pretend that this is a siege. Now, let me try to make you feel better.''

But Eloise's bellyache went away before Hastings could give her a rather sweet-tasting potion of pounded daisy powder mixed with wine.

Hastings was mending one of Severin's tunics—a pale blue one—when Beamis came running into the great hall. Edgar the wolfhound raised his head and growled deep in his massive throat.

"It's the Healer,'' he shouted. "By Saint Ethelbert's elbows, de Luci has her!''

Hastings didn't at first understand, then she rose quickly, the tunic falling to the rushes at her feet. "Oh no," she said, "oh no."

"He is outside the walls, the Healer held in front of him on his warhorse. He has a rope around her waist and a knife held to her neck. He says he wants to speak to you or the Healer dies."

Hastings ran out of the great hall, through the inner bailey, to the outer bailey and up the wooden rampart stairs. She stared down at a sight that scared her to her toes. The Healer was seated tall and straight in front of de Luci. So, de Luci had decided that if he had threatened Marjorie, Hastings wouldn't have cared. He could be right about that. But the Healer . . .

"Healer," Hastings called down to her. "Are you all right?"

"Aye, Hastings," the Healer shouted. "This man is mad. You are not to trust him. Do not do anything he says."

For that, de Luci cuffed her hard against the side of her face.

"Don't touch her, you miserable whoreson!"

"Then you will give me what I want, Hastings, and you will do it now."

He wanted Eloise. No, she wouldn't give her up to that monster. "You may not have Eloise. You would only abuse her. She will remain within the walls, safe."

"I don't want that miserable little Devil's spawn. No, Hastings. I want you."

Hastings saw one of Beamis's men gently pull back on his bow. "No," she whispered, "no. You could harm the Healer. We can't take that chance."

Beamis shouted down, "Lady Hastings goes nowhere. You will take your wretched band of outlaws and leave Oxborough. Lord Severin will return soon."

"I count on that," de Luci shouted back. He then lifted the knife and set it against the Healer's neck. He sliced. A thin line of blood appeared, beading and flowing down into the Healer's gown.

The Healer didn't move. "Don't come out, Hastings," she shouted.

De Luci hit her again, this time knocking her unconscious. She sagged against him.

Hastings couldn't bear it. "I will come out if you will release her. I will also come out if you release Marjorie."

De Luci slewed his head upward at her words. "Marjorie? You want that bitch? She has done nothing but try to do you in. She hates you, she always will. But I will release her. I have no more use for her once I have you."

"I will come," Hastings called. "But hear me, de Luci, it will gain you naught. I am with child, Lord Severin's child. There is nothing for you here. Leave the Healer and take your leave."

De Luci shouted back, his voice clear and hard, "I know you are not with child. Marjorie told me. Do not lie. Come to me and the Healer goes free. Marjorie as well, if you really wish to have her near your food."

"I will come," Hastings called.

Beamis blocked her way. "No, Hastings, you will remain within the walls. If the Healer dies, then so be it, but Lord Severin will not return to find his wife gone."

"I do not intend to trade myself over like a helpless damsel, Beamis. I do not intend to place myself at de Luci's mercy, such as it is. No, I have a plan. I will have that monster's head on a plate before Severin returns."

"Lord Severin won't like it. He was furious when Lord Graelam denied him de Luci's death. Now you would do the same? I cannot allow it, Hastings. Damnation, why didn't the madman die when he tripped on those rabbit bones?"

But Hastings wasn't listening to him. "I must speak to Alice. I need her."

"Do what? Alice, you say? I don't want Alice involved in this, Hastings."

Hastings smiled behind her hand. "No, there won't be any chance of danger to Alice. After I've spoken to her, then I need to gain your agreement, Beamis."

Her heart was pounding as she ran up the solar stairs. So

the bastard still wanted her, did he? What on earth did he believe he would gain? He must know that Severin would hunt him down and kill him with savage pleasure.

But she didn't have time to put her plan into action. At that moment there were shouts and screams. By the time Hastings got to the ramparts to see what had happened, Eloise was already well within the ranks of de Luci's soldiers. Then she was in Marjorie's arms, clutching her fiercely.

Hastings cursed.

What to do now?

De Luci sounded like a happy man when he shouted up to her, the knife point still at the Healer's neck, "You see all that I have now, Hastings? Give over. Come to me and all three of them can come into Oxborough. They will all be safe from me."

"You may not go, Hastings, but I can."

She turned to see Lady Moraine. She was smiling even as she said, "You are very close to my plan. Come, we need to scheme very quickly. I do not want that madman to hurt the Healer more than he has already done."

They walked quickly toward the keep. Hastings had to duck around Gilbert the goat, who was chewing on an old gauntlet. Lady Moraine said as she took double steps to keep up, "Why did the child flee? Has she no wits at all?"

"She loves Marjorie very much. She must have become afraid for her when she saw her with de Luci. She escaped through the postern gate. Was no one guarding it?" There was no answer. Hastings hurried into the great hall, Lady Moraine on her heels. Hastings knew she didn't have long, knowing that de Luci would stick that knife point in the Healer's throat with as much indifference as he would dispatch a chicken.

Alice appeared at her side. "There must be something we can do, Hastings," she said as she looked toward the ramparts, at Beamis, who was staring down at de Luci. "I wanted the lout to give over, but now he fancies he owns me and can tell me what to do."

"He cannot say nay to my plan. Tell me what you think, Alice, Lady Moraine."

Twelve minutes later, the great gates of Oxborough swung outward, as did the narrow postern gate.

Seventeen cloaked and hooded women walked through the main gates and the postern gate, their heads down, their steps coming directly toward de Luci and his line of men.

De Luci howled. "I will not have this! Which one of you is Hastings? All of you, remove the cloaks and hoods! Do it now or I will kill all of you."

But the women just kept walking toward him. He shouted at his men to bring them all down, then knew that if Hastings were among them, he could kill her. She was his salvation, only she could protect him. He could not kill her, not until the king had given her to him, removed Severin as the Earl of Oxborough, and placed him in his stead.

Seventeen women! What was the meaning of this? "Hastings, come out! I won't stand for this. Leave the rest of the women and come to me. Come now or the Healer dies!"

But the women just kept walking toward him, steps unhurried, coming, coming. De Luci's horse fidgeted, rearing back, trembling with its master's fury and indecision. The men behind him were all yelling at the women, all of them sounding worried and frightened. Of seventeen women? De Luci snarled. He wouldn't stand for this. He hurled the Healer from his horse, sending her to roll away from him in the dirt. He rode his warhorse directly at the women. Not five feet from them, he heard a woman shout, then all of them threw back their hoods.

There were only three women. The rest were Oxborough men-at-arms. They raised their bows and arrows. De Luci yelled, whipped his warhorse about, and rode wildly back to his men. He grabbed Eloise from Marjorie and pulled her up in front of him. Arrows rained around him. He heard his men screaming in pain.

He grabbed the reins of Marjorie's palfrey, jerking them out of her hands, and rode away from Oxborough, toward the cliffs of the North Sea.

Hastings set her bow and arrow down at her feet. She'd brought down one of de Luci's men. "He has Eloise and Marjorie," she said, and felt like a failure. But the Healer was all right. She was standing now, brushing dirt from her gown. The yellow ribbon tying her thick braid had come unfastened and was dangling by her face.

Beamis came running full tilt to Hastings, shouting, "It worked. I knew it would work. You and Alice and Lady Moraine were well guarded. Aye, an excellent stratagem." He was rubbing his hands together. "Aye, now we will catch him, Hastings. How far can he get with the child and that unkind angel with her silver hair whom every man desires?"

Alice was with the Healer, helping her dust herself off. The Healer came to Hastings and said, "Listen to me, all of you. He is mad. His brain has given way to the red mist. It is rage and impotence that fill him now. He is very dangerous. He looks at you, Hastings, and sees you as his only hope. He believes you will guard him from the king's wrath. He will not give up until he is dead or he has you, Hastings. Do not let yourself get close to him. Once he realizes that you cannot save him, he will slit your throat." She lightly touched her fingertips against the thin line de Luci had drawn with his knife across her throat.

"I will not let him near me, Healer. Let us mount and go after him. I must get Eloise. Healer, please remain here to tell Severin what has happened if he returns."

# 34

SEVERIN SAW HER FACING DE LUCI AT THE CLIFF EDGE, HER cloak billowing out behind her, the harsh sea wind lifting her hair off her face. Marjorie and Eloise stood behind de Luci where he'd shoved them, close to the cliff's edge.

De Luci's four remaining men clustered around him, all armed, all ready. No one was moving. Hastings was speaking, but he was too far away to hear her words. He held up his hand, holding all his men silent and motionless.

"He has Marjorie," Sir Alan said.

Severin grunted. He didn't particularly care if de Luci took Marjorie to the Holy Land with him. If he never saw her again, he would count himself blessed. His eyes were on Hastings. What was she planning? He knew she was planning something. She occasionally thought of excellent strategies. He knew he would have to wait, but he didn't want to. He wanted to strangle both her and Beamis for allowing this, when it was over. Pray God that it would be over soon, that she would be all right. It seemed a desperate prayer, but there was nothing else for him.

Hastings said very slowly, "You can escape, Richard. I will allow the men to let you go if you release Marjorie and Eloise now. There is nothing for you here. You must forget about Oxborough. It will never belong to you. I cannot guard you. I cannot protect you. Do you understand me?''

But she saw the blank rage in his eyes, the mad hunger in his soul, knew that if she were closer, he would grab her, and in his madness, mayhap even hurl her over the cliff.

She spoke louder, to his men. ''Listen, all of you. There is nothing for you to do. Will you kill me? Lady Marjorie and Eloise? Why? It will gain you nothing but a deep pit in hell. Sheath your swords. Walk away from this.''

De Luci screamed, ''Any of you whoresons leave me and I'll flay the hide from your backs!''

Several of his men were backing away. His words didn't slow them. Hastings could see the impotent rage in his eyes, making him shake, and she knew deep down that he would never release his mad dream of what he believed should be his.

She felt the knife she held against her cloak. She wanted to go to him. She wanted the chance to stick her knife in his black heart, but she had promised Beamis to hold back.

It was at that moment that Hastings knew Severin was close. She knew he was waiting. He couldn't come closer, for it would probably mean Eloise's and Marjorie's death.

De Luci turned to say something low to Marjorie. She shook her head at him, and he raised his fist. Then, suddenly, before he could strike, Marjorie grabbed Eloise and pulled her to the ground at the cliff's edge. They rolled once, twice, Marjorie's arms around Eloise, then they disappeared over the edge, Eloise's single scream rending the silent sky. Hastings felt her blood riot in her body. Marjorie had killed the both of them? Oh God, she couldn't begin to bear this. She stared at de Luci, who had turned his head for a moment to look at where Marjorie and his daughter had stood. Then he shrugged. He merely shrugged. What had he said to Marjorie? What had she said to earn his fist? What threat had he made that had sent her and Eloise into oblivion?

Hastings could not have stopped herself even if she had thought deeply about it. De Luci had brought them to this.

He was responsible for all the misery that had come upon
them from the very beginning. He was a monster and he
was mad. She raised the knife and threw herself at him, the
knife coming down toward his chest in a high arc.

He grabbed her arm, but she was strong. Her rage made
her even stronger. Beamis was upon them, but they were
very close to the edge now, too close.

Beamis was yelling at Hastings to back off, to get away
from de Luci, but she couldn't. Both of them were locked
together now, even as the knife came down closer and
closer to his chest.

Suddenly, she felt the point ease through the cloth of his
tunic. So easily it slid in, but it didn't slow him. He was
yelling, his spittle flying into her face, raging at what she
had cost him, and now she had stabbed him and surely she
would die for it.

Suddenly, she felt something grab her ankle. Her eyes
flicked over the side of the cliff and what she saw astonished her. But de Luci grabbed her, jerking her close, and
she knew she would die. She shoved the knife deeper into
his chest. He jerked back with the agony of it, screaming,
and reeled off the edge of the cliff. At the last moment, he
grabbed her, pulling her, and she knew she had no purchase. She yelled Severin's name even as she went over.

Severin watched as de Luci and his wife, locked in a
death embrace, disappeared over the cliff.

"No!"

De Luci's few men had thrown down their weapons. But
it didn't matter. Beamis was enraged. The four men were
dead in but moments.

"No!"

Severin flung himself off his warhorse's back and ran to
the cliff edge. He knew what he would see. He would see
Hastings still locked against de Luci, both of them crushed
on the rocks below.

But he saw only de Luci. She must be beneath him, the
whoreson had her pinned beneath him. Severin could tell
that his neck was broken.

Severin was panting, heaving with the agony of it,

searching frantically for a path down to the beach and rocks below.

"Severin."

He shook his head back and forth, back and forth. No, it couldn't be true. Dear Jesus, he could hear her calling to him, but she was dead, locked beneath that madman. He felt shock pulling at his brain, felt helpless rage pouring through him like a wound that would bleed his very life away.

"Severin."

No, he was leaving himself now, going toward her, hearing her, wanting just to see her once more, just hold her once more.

"*Severin!*"

"My lord, it's Hastings! By Saint Anthony's blessings it's Hastings!"

Severin threw himself on his belly, leaning out over the cliff as far as he could without falling. He couldn't believe what he saw. A ledge jutted out some three feet below him. On the ledge Marjorie was stretched out her full length, her feet hooked beneath a narrow overhang. Eloise knelt beside her. They were both clinging to Hastings's arms as she dangled off the ledge.

"Severin," Marjorie shouted, "we aren't strong enough to pull her up! You must help us."

Within moments, men were holding a rope tied securely beneath Severin's arms. They lowered him until he was on the ledge. He grabbed Hastings's arms and dragged her up.

"You're alive," he whispered again and again in her dirty hair. "I couldn't have borne it if that whoreson had killed you. I'm going to strangle you when I get you home. I love you. At the very least I will beat you. You deserve that, Hastings. You deserve your last punishment that I never meted out to you either afternoon in the forest. By all that's holy, I love you."

"And I you," she whispered against his neck. She raised her eyes and he saw the blank shock in them. He stroked his large hands up and down her back even as she said in a singsong voice, "I killed him, Severin. I stuck my kni in his chest.'' She looked over at Marjorie, who was on her hands and knees, breathing heavily. ''Then something grabbed my ankle. I looked down and saw Marjorie on the ledge. She was trying to pull me over to save me. I shoved the knife deeper into his chest and he went over, but he grabbed me and I couldn't pull away. When I struck the ledge, I rolled off, but both Marjorie and Eloise grabbed my arms and held me. She and Eloise saved me.''

His hand was on her belly, lightly caressing. He said nothing. He let her talk—it would bring her back to him. He felt her give a great shudder, then she stilled.

''Our babe is all right,'' she said, lightly laying her hand over his fingers. ''He's all right, don't worry.''

Severin couldn't believe this. He shook his head. Marjorie, who hated Hastings, had saved her life? By all that was holy, it was beyond his comprehension. He sent Hastings up first. It never occurred to him to send up the child first. He wanted Hastings safe. At last.

It took some time to get all of them back to safety.

The instant he was on firm ground, Severin grabbed Hastings, pulled her against him, squeezing her so tightly she knew she heard her ribs groaning. ''Never again will I let you out of my sight,'' he said, then, ''Never again. I love you but you will fight no more of my battles. Never again. I have decided that if I do not control you, I will die of the strain of it. Aye, you will remain in our bedchamber. You may mix your herbs but nothing more. Perhaps soon I will allow you to come into the great hall, but only after I have ensured that it is safe for you, only after you have sworn to me that you will never stick a knife in another man's chest. Well, mayhap that would be acceptable, but you will do no knife sticking next to the edge of a damned cliff.

''Aye, and then you will only leave the great hall if I give you permission and then you will always have me with you. Do you understand me, Hastings? I will not let you out of my sight again. I love you and I will now strangle you. Come, we will go home now and I will strangle you and then the Healer will make certain that our babe is all right.''

She kissed his chin and tried to squeeze him as hard as he was squeezing her. "Just a moment, Severin. Marjorie and Eloise saved me. I must thank them."

He released her although he didn't want to. He watched her walk slowly to where Marjorie stood, alone, with Sir Alan some feet away from her, looking at her as if he wanted to consume her. Eloise was clutched against her side, crying. Marjorie was comforting her and doing a fine job of it, Hastings had to admit, though she didn't particularly want to.

"You saved me," Hastings said. "You didn't have to, yet you did. You grabbed my ankle. You let me know I could fall over and land on the ledge with you. You grabbed me when I fell with de Luci. You didn't let go. You also saved yourself and Eloise. That was excellent, Marjorie, though it pains me to have to say it. Aye, it was excellent."

"Thank you, Hastings. I am very tired of all this furor. My heart is still pounding with fright. Come, little sweeting, let me dry your tears. We are all safe and your father is finally dead." Then Marjorie raised her beautiful eyes to Hastings's face. She threw back her glorious silvery hair. "I had to save you, I had no choice."

"When you and Eloise disappeared over the cliff edge, I believed you were killing yourselves."

"Oh no, I saw the ledge. I prayed, Hastings. I prayed more in those seconds than I have ever prayed in my life. I nearly lost Eloise, but I managed to get her onto the ledge. When I grabbed your ankle, I wanted you to know that we were there and you would be all right. I am glad we managed to hold on to you until Severin came. Since I had my feet beneath that overhang, I was in no danger of being pulled over with you."

"I hate this," Hastings said, scuffing the toe of her shoe. "I really do hate this, but I will say it again. Thank you, Marjorie, for saving me. I really didn't make your nose swell or turn red."

"I know. It was Lady Moraine. She was trying to protect you. Her punishment gained my respect."

"What think you of marrying Sir Alan and remaining at Sedgewick? Severin must ask the king, but he will probably agree. Perhaps you could visit Oxborough once every five years."

Marjorie laughed. "Aye, that is an acceptable idea. Sir Alan pleases me sufficiently."

"You will never have to worry again that you will starve."

"No, I daresay that I won't. And I will have my Eloise forever."

Severin couldn't stand it anymore. He was upon them in an instant. He picked Hastings up in his arms and strode away with her, calling over his shoulder, "I will send a messenger to the king on the morrow. Sir Alan, see to Lady Marjorie and Eloise. I believe we would like you to return immediately to Sedgewick. All your men as well. Ah, before you leave, bury de Luci's men. Leave him on the beach below, I care not."

Hastings said, as she nibbled his earlobe, "At least I won't have to see her silvery hair for five years."

It was very late. The castle was quiet save for the snores of the men sleeping in the great hall, and Belle, who could make noises louder than any man-at-arms at Oxborough. Beside her the armorer was sleeping blissfully. He was sprawled out on his back and he looked dead.

In their bedchamber, Severin was over his wife, deep inside her, staring down at her face in the dim light of the single candle.

"No, Hastings, don't move. I just want to remain here for a while, just feel you and know that I am feeling you without lust rampaging through my body. I want you to feel my love for you, which at this moment is greater than my lust, but I cannot promise that it will last much longer." He leaned down and kissed her. He said into her mouth, "You are mine now, damn you. No more strife between us, no more believing it is another woman I want. I want only you. Will you strive to believe me?"

"You mean that I cannot yell at you when you vex me

with your orders, or you trample my daisies?''

''Aye, you can yell so loudly that the gulls will come in from the sea to see what is happening. That has nothing to do with the core of us. What is between us will grow, Hastings, and become more powerful as time passes. Do you believe that?''

''Aye, I must for I love you more than I love life. When Marjorie visits Oxborough in five years, you swear you will not stare at her and whisper about her silvery hair?''

''I will spit at her feet.''

She laughed, lifting her hips just a bit. He bit her chin. ''Obey me, Hastings, and hold yourself still, else it won't go well for you.''

She laughed. ''Even if I were to enrage you in the future,'' she said, giving him that siren's sloe-eyed look, ''I now know exactly what to do to make you forget every shred of your anger. Aye, I know exactly how to make you as blissfully happy as Gilbert the goat with a new boot to chew.''

''I know that you do.''

She stared up at him, forgetting for a moment that he was beginning to move slowly within her. ''What do you know?''

''My mother loves me. Her loyalty is to me. Dame Agnes and Alice are very fond of my mother. They also believe she has sound advice. They don't believe my advice is so bad either. Indeed, there was a good deal of laughter.'

''What does that mean?''

He moved more deeply now, and she felt him touching her as only he could. She didn't think again for some time. When at last she was breathing more easily, feeling the heat of him against the length of her, knowing that a woman couldn't be happier or more content than she was at this moment, she said again, ''What do you mean that you mother loves you? Naturally she loves you. You are he son. What do you know? What is this about Dame Agnes and Alice? What about laughter?''

''My mother told me you were always in your best humor when you were working in your herb garden. She said it was there that I had my best chance of having you decide to work your skills on me.''

She was frowning ferociously up at him. He leaned down and kissed her open mouth. ''Do you not remember, Hastings? I came upon you twice in your garden. That first time you gave me a provocative look and talked me into taking you into the forest to punish you. The next day, I was no sooner a shadow on your mugwort than you were hurling yourself against me and begging me to take you back again.''

''Aye, I know all about that, but why do you bring it up and in such detail? You sound as if you know more than you should about the entire matter.''

''Ah, now I have your attention.'' He gently came out of her and went down onto his back. He drew her against his side, but she reared up over him, staring down at him. ''My mother told me what Dame Agnes and Alice had advised you to do. She was laughing when she said that you had wondered if this would always be their only advice. When I saw them, I agreed that it was the best advice they could ever serve you. They told me everything, Hastings.''

She closed her hands about his throat and tried to squeeze, but her hands just weren't big enough. ''I should be furious with all of you. I should yell and stamp and throw the laver at all of you.'' Then she leaned down and kissed him, shrugging those lovely white shoulders of hers. She whispered against his mouth, ''Alice said that men were simple. Dame Agnes said that the second time more skill was required but she believed I could do it. I too believed it was wonderful advice.''

He squeezed her against him. ''All of us decided that it would calm your humors and make you realize that your husband wanted you more than he wanted Oxborough itself or a string of titles. Did I not prove myself to you those two afternoons in the forest, Hastings? I let you do just as you pleased to my man's body. Did I not compliment you on your skill?''

''No, all you did was moan and groan and thrash about.''

She fell silent. She was still furious at the women who had advised her with such seriousness. She had trusted them, yet they had discussed everything with him and Lady Moraine. "I cannot believe that they told you, that they asked you what you thought of their advice to me."

"I made only one or two corrections in their advice." He shrugged, knowing she wanted to hit him since she couldn't manage to strangle him. "Do you want me to tell you exactly what they were?"

"I know what they were," she said, and stroked her hand down his belly to find him. "Aye, I know exactly what they were."

She moved against him and he smiled against her hair, then he groaned. He wanted to talk to her, not make love to her again. He sought to distract her and himself, particularly himself, since her hand was caressing him. "I can feel that small curve now. Thank you."

There was a muffled mewling sound. Hastings released him. He sighed. They sat up and pulled up the covers. A ruffled Trist slipped from beneath a sheet and came up to Severin's chest. They lay down, taking turns stroking his thick fur.

"You didn't ask Trist to advise you, did you, Severin?"

"Trist always knows what I'm about."

The marten mewled loudly and stretched himself out over the both of them.

"He has also disrupted our play." Trist batted Severin's chin with his paw.

"You are well, are you not, Hastings?" She felt his hand lightly rest on her belly.

"Aye, but I believe I will not fly off any more cliffs until after our babe is born. No, don't stiffen up, it annoys Trist. It was a jest, Severin, just a jest. I am very well. You are not to worry. Now, should we move Trist and continue with our play?"

Severin's hand was quiet on her belly. She heard his breathing even. Trist was stretched his full length atop both